THE LAST TUDOR

PHILIPPA GREGORY

SIMON &
SCHUSTER

London · New York · Sydney · Toronto · New Delhi

A CBS COMPANY

First published in Great Britain by Simon & Schuster UK Ltd, 2017
A CBS COMPANY

1 3 5 7 9 10 8 6 4 2

Simon & Schuster UK Ltd
1st Floor
222 Gray's Inn Road
London WC1X 8HB

Simon & Schuster Australia, Sydney
Simon & Schuster India, New Delhi

www.simonandschuster.co.uk
www.simonandschuster.com.au
www.simonandschuster.co.in

A CIP catalogue record for this book
is available from the British Library

Hardback ISBN: 978-1-4711-3305-3
Trade Paperback ISBN: 978-1-4711-3306-0
eBook ISBN: 978-1-4711-3308-4
Audio ISBN: 978-1-4711-6781-2

Typeset in Plantin by M Rules
Printed and bound by CPI Group (UK) Ltd, Croydon, CR0 4YY

Simon & Schuster UK Ltd are committed to sourcing paper
that is made from wood grown in sustainable forests and support the Forest
Stewardship Council, the leading international forest certification organisation.
Our books displaying the FSC logo are printed on FSC certified paper.

For my sister

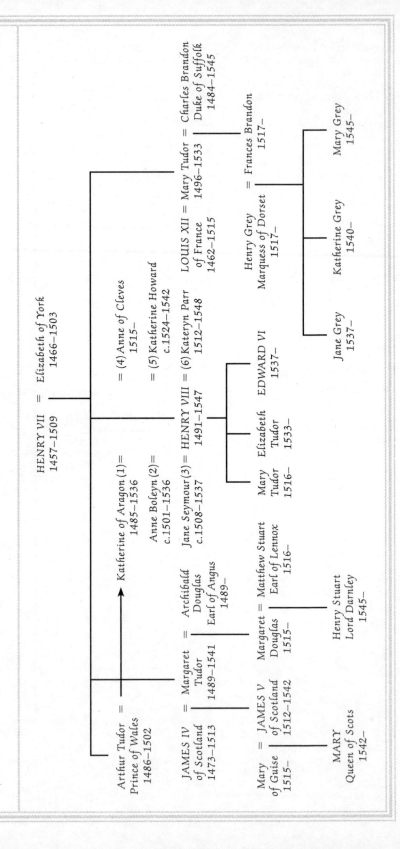

THE TUDOR AND STUART HOUSES IN 1550

HENRY VII = Elizabeth of York
1457–1509   1466–1503

Arthur Tudor = Katherine of Aragon (1) =
Prince of Wales   1485–1536
1486–1502

= (4) Anne of Cleves
1515–

JAMES IV = Margaret = Archibald
of Scotland   Tudor   Douglas
1473–1513   1489–1541   Earl of Angus
1489–

Anne Boleyn (2) =
c.1501–1536

= (5) Katherine Howard
c.1524–1542

LOUIS XII = Mary Tudor = Charles Brandon
of France   1496–1533   Duke of Suffolk
1462–1515   1484–1545

Jane Seymour (3) = HENRY VIII = (6) Kateryn Parr
c.1508–1537   1491–1547   1512–1548

Mary = JAMES V   Margaret = Matthew Stuart
of Guise   of Scotland   Douglas   Earl of Lennox
1515–   1512–1542   1515–   1516–

Mary   Elizabeth   EDWARD VI
Tudor   Tudor   1537–
1516–   1533–

Henry Grey = Frances Brandon
Marquess of Dorset   1517–
1517–

MARY   Henry Stuart
Queen of Scots   Lord Darnley
1542–   1545–

Jane Grey   Katherine Grey   Mary Grey
1537–   1540–   1545–

THE SEYMOUR FAMILY IN 1550

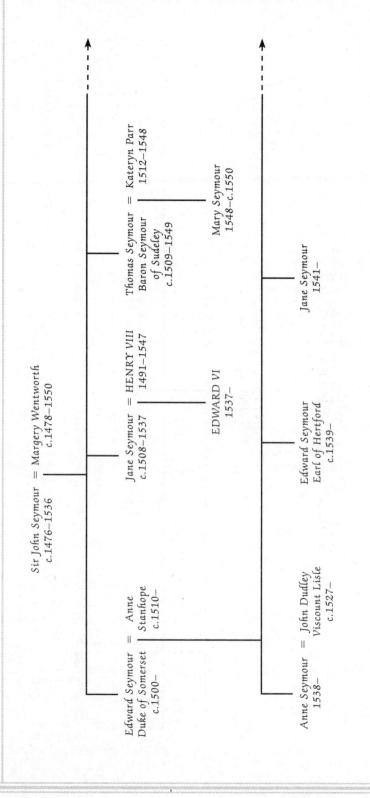

THE DUDLEY FAMILY IN 1550

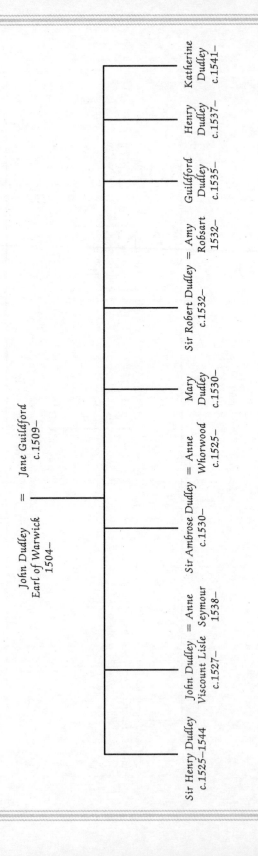

John Dudley = Jane Guildford
Earl of Warwick   c.1509–
1504–

Sir Henry Dudley
c.1525–1544

John Dudley = Anne
Viscount Lisle   Seymour
c.1527–   1538–

Sir Ambrose Dudley = Anne
c.1530–   Whorwood
c.1525–

Mary
Dudley
c.1530–

Sir Robert Dudley = Amy
c.1532–   Robsart
1532–

Guildford
Dudley
c.1535–

Henry
Dudley
c.1537–

Katherine
Dudley
c.1541–

BOOK I

JANE

BRADGATE HOUSE, GROBY, LEICESTERSHIRE, SPRING 1550

I love my father because I know that he will never die. Neither will I. We are chosen by God and we walk in His ways, and we never swerve from them. We don't have to earn our place in heaven by bribing God with acts or Masses. We don't have to eat bread and pretend it is flesh, drink wine and call it blood. We know that is folly for the ignorant and a trap for papist fools. This knowledge is our pride and glory. We understand, as more and more do in these days: we have been saved once and for all. We have no fear, for we will never die.

True, my father is worldly: sinfully worldly. I wish he would let me wrestle with his soul, but he laughs and says, 'Go away, Jane, and write to our friends the Swiss reformers. I owe them a letter – you can write for me.'

It is wrong of him to avoid holy discourse, but this is only the sin of inattention – I know he is heart and soul for the true religion. Also, I must remember that he is my father and I owe obedience to my father and mother – whatever my private opinion of them. God, who sees all, will be the judge of them. And God has seen my father and forgiven him already; my father is saved through faith.

I fear my mother will not be saved from the fires of hell, and my sister Katherine, who is three years younger than me, a child of nine years old, is almost certainly going to die and never rise again. She is unbelievably silly. If I were a superstitious fool I would really think she is possessed; she is quite beyond hope. My baby sister, Mary, was born into original sin and cannot grow out of it. She is quite tiny. She is as pretty as a little miniature version of our sister, Katherine, tiny as a doll. My lady mother would have sent her away as a baby to be raised far from us, and spare us the shame, but my father had too much compassion for his last stunted child, and so she lives with us. She is not an idiot – she does her lessons well, she is a clever little girl – but she has no sense of the grace of God; she is not one of the elect like Father and me. One like her – whose growth has been blighted by Satan – should be particularly fervent for salvation. I suppose a five-year-old is a little young to renounce the world – but I was studying Latin when I was four, and Our Lord was the same age as I am now when He went to the Temple and preached to the wise men. If you do not learn the ways of the Lord when you are in the cradle, when will you make a start?

I have studied since I was a child. I am most probably the most learned young person in the whole country, raised in the reformed religion, the favourite of the great scholar and queen Kateryn Parr. I am probably the greatest young scholar in Europe, certainly the most educated girl. I don't consider my cousin Princess Elizabeth a true student, for many are called but few are chosen. Poor Elizabeth shows no signs of being chosen, and her studies are very worldly. She wants to be seen as clever, she wants to please her tutors and exhibit herself. Even I have to take care that I do not fall into the sin of pride, though my mother says, rudely, that my principal care should be that I do not fall into being completely ridiculous. But when I explain to her that she is in a state of sin she takes me by the ear and threatens to beat me. I would gladly take a beating for my faith, just as the saint Anne Askew did, but I think it more pleasing to God to apologise, curtsey and sit down at the dinner table. Besides, there is a pie of pears with burnt cream for dinner, which is my favourite.

It really is not easy to be a shining light in Bradgate. It is a

4

worldly house and we are a big household. It is a great building, a brick-built house as red as Hampton Court, with a gatehouse that looms as large as that palace and set among the huge forest of Charnwood. We have every right to royal magnificence. My mother is the daughter of Princess Mary, who was Queen of France, the favourite sister of King Henry VIII, so my mother is heir to the throne of England after the late king's children, my cousins the princesses, Mary and Elizabeth, who are heirs to their younger brother, King Edward. This makes us the most important family in England, and we never forget it. We keep a houseful of retainers, more than three hundred, to serve the five of us, we own a stable filled with beautiful horses and the parkland all around the house, and farms and villages, rivers and lakes at the very heart of England. We have our own bear for baiting, kept caged in the stables, our own bear pit, our own cock-fighting ring. Our house is one of the biggest in the Middle Lands, we have a great hall with a musicians' gallery one end and a royal dais at the other. The most beautiful countryside in England is ours. I have been brought up to know that all this land belongs to me, just as we belong to England.

Of course, between my lady mother and the throne are the three royal children: Edward, the king, who is only twelve like me, and so he rules with a lord president, and then his older sisters Princess Mary and Princess Elizabeth. Sometimes people don't count the two princesses as heirs, since they were both named bastards and denied by their own father. They would not even be included in the royal family but for the Christian kindness of my teacher Kateryn Parr, who brought them to court and had them acknowledged. Even worse, Princess Mary (God forgive her) is a declared and open papist and heretic, and though I am bound to love her as a cousin, it is a horror to me to be in her house, where she keeps the hours of the liturgy as if she is living in a convent and not in a reformed kingdom, for all England is Protestant now under King Edward.

I don't speak of Princess Elizabeth. I never do. I saw more than enough of her when we both lived with Queen Kateryn and her young husband, Thomas Seymour. All I will say is that Elizabeth should be ashamed of herself and she will have to answer to God for what she did. I saw it. I was there during the chasing and the tickling and the romping with her own stepmother's husband. She led Thomas Seymour – a great man – on to imprudence and then to his death. She was guilty of lust and adultery – in her heart if not in his bed. She is as guilty of his death as if she named him as a treasonous plotter and led him to the scaffold. She willed him to think of himself as her lover and her husband, and the two of them as heirs to the throne. She may not have said so much: she did not have to say so much. I saw how she was with him and I know what she made him do.

But – no – I do not judge. I will not judge. I never judge. That is for God. I have to retain a modest thought, an averted gaze, and compassion as from one sinner to another. And I am certain that God won't think of her either, when she is in the fires of hell, praying too late for her unchastity, disloyalty and ambition. God and I will pity her, and leave her to her infinite punishment.

At any rate, since Princess Mary and Elizabeth were both declared illegitimate, and are both clearly unsuited for the throne, these half-sisters to King Edward have less of a legal claim than the daughter of King Henry's favourite sister, Queen Mary, which is to say: my mother.

And this is the very reason, the very reason, why it is so important that she study the reformed faith and put aside brilliant adornment. She should avoid feasts and drinking, she should dance only with the most chaste ladies of her household and not ride around the country on that great horse of hers all day, hunting whatever is in season as if she were some sort of hungry beast of the field. The great woods around our house echo with her hunting horns, the meadows are flushed for game. Dogs die in the bear pit, heifers are slaughtered outside the flesh kitchen. I am so afraid that she is lustful (the Tudors are terribly lustful), I know that she is proud (all the Tudors are born tyrants), and anyone can see that she is extravagant and loves worldly show.

I should reprimand her, but when I say to my tutor that I am nerving myself to tell my mother that she is guilty at the very least of pride, wrath, gluttony, lust, and greed, he says nervously to me, 'Lady Jane, truly: better not,' and I know that he is afraid of her, as is everyone – even my father. This only goes to show that she is guilty of unwomanly ambition, as well as everything else.

I would be as fearful as all the weakly others, but I am borne up by my faith. I really am. This is not easy if you follow the reformed faith. Courage is easy for papists – each fool has a dozen objects to instruct and encourage him: the icons in the church, the glass in the windows, the nuns, the priest, the choir, the incense, the heady taste of wine, which they convince themselves tastes salty of blood. But all these are vanity and emptiness. I know that I am borne up by faith because I go down on my knees in a cool white chapel in silence, and then I hear the voice of God speaking to me alone, gently like a loving father. I read my Bible for myself, nobody reads it to me, and then I hear the Word of God. I pray for wisdom and when I speak I know it is in the words of the Bible. I am His handmaiden and His mouthpiece – and that is why it is so very wrong for my mother to shout, 'For the love of God, take that long face out of here, and go hunting before I chase you out of the library myself!'

Very wrong. I pray that God will forgive her, as I do. But I know He will not forget the insult to me, His handmaiden; and neither will I. I take a horse from the stables but I do not go hunting. Instead I ride with my sister Katherine, a groom following behind us. We can ride all day in any direction and never leave our lands. We canter through meadows and skirt fields where the oats are growing, green and thick, we splash through fords and let the horses drink the clear water. We are children of the royal family of England, happiest in the English countryside, blessed in our inheritance.

Today, for some reason, my mother is all smiles and I have been told to wear my new dress, a gown of deep red velvet, which came from London last week, with a rich black hood and sleeves, as we have honoured guests for dinner. I ask our lord chamberlain who is coming, and he says it is the former Lord Protector, Edward Seymour the Duke of Somerset. He was in the Tower for treason and now he is released, and returning to the Privy Council. These are the dangerous times that we live in.

'And he's bringing his son,' says the chamberlain, and he dares to wink at me, as if I am some light-hearted girl who would be foolishly excited by the news.

'Oh, how exciting!' says my light-hearted sister, Katherine.

I give a patient sigh and say that I will be reading in my bedroom until it is time for me to dress for dinner. If I close the door between my bedroom and our privy chamber it may be that Katherine takes the hint and stays out.

Not so.

Within a moment there is a tap on the linenfold-panel door, and she puts her fair head into my private room and says: 'Oh! Are you studying?' As if I ever do anything else.

'Certainly, that was my intention when I closed my door.'

She is deaf to irony. 'What do you think the Duke of Somerset is coming here for?' she asks, tripping into the room without any invitation. Mary trails in behind her, as if my rooms are a royal presence chamber and anyone can get past the sergeant porter if they have good enough clothes.

'Are you bringing that disgusting monkey in here?' I cut across her as I see him riding on her shoulder.

She looks shocked. 'Of course I am. Mr Nozzle goes with me everywhere. Except when I visit the poor bear. He is afraid of the poor bear.'

'Well, he can't come in here and spoil my papers.'

'He will not. He will sit on my lap. He is a very good Mr Nozzle.'

'Take him out.'

'I won't.'

'Take him out, I command it.'

'You can't make me.'

'I am the oldest and these are my rooms ...'

'I am the prettiest and I am visiting you from politeness ...'

We scowl at each other. She shows me his silver chain that goes around his scrawny black neck. 'Jane, please! I will hold him tight,' she promises me.

'I shall hold him for you!' Mary offers, so now I have the two of them clamouring to hold the monkey, who should not be in my rooms anyway.

'Oh, just go!' I say irritably. 'Both of you.'

But instead Katherine turns and hauls Mary up into a chair where the child sits, no bigger than a doll, smiling at me with all the charm in the world.

'Sit straight,' Katherine reminds her, and Mary puts back her shoulders and sits up tall.

'No! Just go!'

'I will, as soon as I have asked you this question.' Katherine is happy because she is getting her own way as usual. She is ridiculously pretty, and about as sensible as Mr Nozzle.

'Very well,' I say sternly. 'Ask your question, and then go.'

She takes a breath. 'Why do you think the Duke of Somerset is coming here?'

'I have no idea.'

'Because I know. So why don't you? I thought you were supposed to be so very, very clever?'

'I don't want to know,' I say simply.

'I can tell you. All you know is stuff in books.'

'Stuff in books,' I repeat the words of an ignorant child. 'Indeed. I do know "stuff in books" but if I wanted to know worldly news I would ask my father, who would tell me the truth. I would not go round eavesdropping on my parents and listening to servants' gossip.'

She jumps up on my big wooden bed as if she is planning to stay until dinner time, and then props herself up against the pillow as if she is going to sleep here. The monkey makes himself comfortable beside her, and runs his skinny little fingers through his own silky fur.

'Does he have fleas?'

'Oh, yes,' she says indifferently. 'But not lice.'

'Then get him off my bed!'

In reply, she gathers him into her lap. 'Don't fuss, because it is so exciting. They're coming for your betrothal!' she announces. 'There! I thought that would make you jump.'

I am jumping so little that I keep one steady finger in the book to mark my place. 'And where d'you get that from?'

'Everyone knows,' she says, which means that it is servants' gossip, as I predicted. 'Oh, you're so lucky! I think Ned Seymour is the most handsome young man in the world.'

'Yes, but you like anything in hose.'

'He has such kind eyes.'

'Certainly he has eyes, but they do not have the power of emotion, only of sight.'

'And a lovely smile.'

'I imagine that he smiles like anyone else, but I have not bothered to look.'

'And he rides beautifully and he has beautiful clothes and he is the son of the most powerful man in England. There is no greater family than the Seymours. No-one richer. They are wealthier than us. They are even closer to the throne than us.'

I think, but I don't say, that the greatness of the family was no protection for Thomas Seymour, who was beheaded just a year ago because of Elizabeth, and not even his older brother could save him. Then the brother, the Lord Protector himself, was disgraced, and is now trying to scrabble back into power.

'The handsome son of the Lord Protector,' she breathes.

As usual, she is in a muddle. 'He's not Lord Protector any more, his post has been abolished,' I correct her. 'The council is run by the Lord President, John Dudley. If you want an alliance with the coming men it's the Dudleys.'

'Well, he's still the king's uncle, and Ned is still Earl of Hertford.'

'Edward Seymour,' I correct her.

'Edward or Ned! Who cares?'

'And does everyone say that I am to be betrothed to him?' I ask.

'Yes,' she says simply. 'And when you're married, you'll have to go away again. I shall miss you. Although all you ever do is complain that I am stupid, it's much nicer when you're here. I missed you when you lived with Queen Kateryn. Honestly, I was quite glad when she died – though very sorry for her, of course – because I hoped you'd come home to stay.'

'Don't go, Jane,' Mary suddenly wails, following hardly any of this.

Despite knowing that the Bible says that a disciple must leave his house, or brethren, or sisters, or father, or mother, for the sake of the gospel, I am rather touched by this. 'If I am called to a great place in the world I will have to go,' I tell her. 'Our cousin King Edward has a godly court, and I should be happy to live there, and if God calls me to a great place in the world then I will be a model for those who look up to me. And when your turn comes I will show you how to behave if you will do exactly as I tell you. Actually, I'll miss you too, and little Mary, if I have to go.'

'Will you miss Mr Nozzle?' Katherine asks hopefully, crawling down the bed and lifting him towards me so his sad little face is close to mine.

Gently, I push her hands away. 'No.'

'Well, when my turn comes to be married, I hope he's as handsome as Ned Seymour,' she says. 'And I shouldn't mind being the Countess of Hertford, either.'

I realise that this will be my new name and title, and when Ned's father dies, Ned will become Duke of Somerset and I shall be a duchess. 'God's will be done,' I say, thinking of the strawberry leaves of a duchess's coronet, and the heavy softness of ermine on my collar. 'For you as well as me.'

'Amen,' she says dreamily, as if she is still thinking of Ned Seymour's smile. 'Oh, Amen.'

'I very much doubt that God will make you a duchess,' I point out.

She looks at me, her blue eyes wide, her skin, pale like mine, now flushed rosy. 'Oh, pray it for me,' she says trustingly. 'You can get me a duke if you pray for me, Jane. You know you're so godly, you can surely get God to give me a duke. Ask Him for a handsome one.'

To give Katherine her due, I have to admit that Ned Seymour is as charming as all the Seymours. He reminds me of his uncle Thomas, who was the kindest man I have ever known, husband to my tutor Queen Kateryn before Elizabeth destroyed their happiness. Ned is brown-haired with hazel eyes. I have never noticed before that they are kind eyes, but my sister is right, he has a pleasing warmth, and a quite irresistible smile. I hope he does not have sinful thoughts behind that knowing gleam. He was brought up at court, companion to my cousin the king, so we know each other, we have ridden together and learned dancing together, and even studied together. He thinks as I do – as we all do – all the clever young people are Protestants. I would call him a friend, in so far as anyone is ever a friend in the bear pit that is a royal court. He is a great one for the reformed faith, so we share that too, and behind his light-heartedness he has a serious thoughtful mind. My cousin King Edward is scholarly and grave like me, so we love to read together. But Ned Seymour makes us both laugh. He is never bawdy – my cousin the king will have no fools around him – but he is witty, and he has charm; he has that intense Seymour charm that makes friends wherever he goes. He is a boy that makes you smile to see him, a boy like that.

I sit with my mother's ladies at dinner, he sits with his father's men. Our parents are seated at the head table on the dais above all of us, and survey the room, looking down on us. When I see the tilt of my mother's overly proud chin I remember that the last be first, and the first last, for many are called, but few chosen. She, in particular, I am certain can never be chosen; and when I become a duchess I will outrank her, and she will never be allowed to shout oaths at me again.

When the tables are cleared away, the musicians play, and I am commanded to dance with my mother's ladies and with my sister Katherine. Of course, Katherine flirts her skirt around and lifts it too high, so that she can show off her pretty shoes and her twinkling feet. She smiles all the time towards the top table where Ned is standing behind his father's chair. I am sorry to say that once he winks at us. I think it is for the two of us, and not directed at Katherine. I am pleased that he is watching us dancing – but I think less of him that he should wink.

Then there is general dancing and my mother orders me to partner him. Everyone remarks how well we look together even though he is a full head taller than I am. I am very small and pale; none of us Grey girls are big-boned; but I am glad to be dainty, and not a stout thing like Princess Elizabeth.

'You dance beautifully,' Ned says to me, as we come together and wait for another couple to finish their part. 'Do you know why my father and I are here?'

The movement of the dance separates us and gives me time to think of a dignified reply.

'No, do you?' is all I manage.

He takes my hands as we progress down the line of other dancers. We stand and make an arch with our hands and he smiles at me as the others duck their heads and wind their way through. 'They want us to marry,' he says cheerfully. 'It's agreed. We are to be husband and wife.'

We have to stand opposite each other while another pair of dancers makes their way down the set, so he can see my response to this news from him. I feel my cheeks grow warm, and I try not to beam like an eager idiot. 'It is my father who should tell me, not you,' I say stiffly.

'Shall you be pleased when he does?'

I look down so he can't see what I am thinking. I don't want my brown eyes to shine like his. 'I am bound by the Word of God to obey my father,' I say.

'Shall you be pleased to obey him and marry me?'

'Quite.'

My parents obviously believe that I should be the last person to be consulted, for I am not summoned to my mother's rooms until the next day, when Edward and his father are preparing to leave and the horses are actually standing at the open front door, the scent of the English spring blowing into the house with the ecstatic singing of courting birds.

I can hear the servants taking out the saddlebags in the hall below as I kneel to my parents, and my mother nods to the servant to shut the door.

'You're to marry Edward Seymour,' my mother says briskly. 'Promised; but not betrothed in writing. First, we need to see if his father can get himself back on the council and work with John Dudley. Dudley is the man now. We have to see that Seymour will work with him and rise again.'

'Unless there is any chance of the other matter . . .' my father says, looking at my mother with meaning.

'No, he's certain to marry a princess from abroad,' my mother says.

I know at once that they are talking of Edward the king, who has said publicly that he will marry a foreign princess with a queenly dowry. I, myself, have never thought anything different, though some people say that I would make a wonderful queen, and I would be a light and a beacon of the new reformed religion and speed religious reform in a country that is painfully half-hearted, even now. I make sure that I keep my head bowed and I don't say a word.

'But they're so suited,' my father pleads. 'Both so scholarly, both so devout. And our Jane would be such a rightful heir to Kateryn Parr. We raised her for this; Queen Kateryn trained her for this.'

I can feel my mother's eyes scrutinising me, but I don't look up. 'She would make the court into a convent!' she says, laughing.

'A light in the world,' my father replies seriously.

'I doubt it will ever happen. At any rate, Lady Jane, you can consider yourself promised in marriage to Edward Seymour until we tell you different.'

My father puts his hand under my elbow and raises me up from my knees. 'You'll be a duchess, or something better,' he promises me. 'Don't you want to know what might be better? What about the throne of England?'

I shake my head. 'I have my eyes on a heavenly crown,' I tell him, and I ignore my mother's vulgar snort of laughter.

SUFFOLK PLACE, LONDON, SPRING 1553

It is as well that I don't set my heart on handsome Ned Seymour as a husband. His father's return to power is short-lived and ends in his death. He was caught conspiring against John Dudley, and arrested, charged and then executed for treason. The head of the family is dead, and the family ruined again. His famously proud wife, Anne Stanhope, who once had the criminal pride to push my tutor Dowager Queen Kateryn to one side so that she might go first in to dinner, is widowed and imprisoned in the Tower. Ned does not come to court at all. I was lucky to escape marriage with a young man who – however kind his eyes – is now the disgraced son of a traitor.

It is as well that I never let my father's ambition enter my prayers either, though I cannot help but know that all the reforming churchmen, all the Protestant believers, every living saint in England, wants me to marry the king and to lead a kingdom of pilgrims to our heavenly home. Not that my cousin King Edward says this – he insists that he will marry a royal from somewhere abroad; but clearly he cannot tolerate a papist princess. Of all the Protestant girls, I am the most suitable, devoted to the religion that he and I share, childhood friends and the daughter of a princess of the blood.

Significantly, my father has ordered that I am taught rhetoric – a royal skill – and I choose to study Arabic and Hebrew as well as Latin and Greek. If the call ever comes for me to take the crown, I will be ready. I lived with Queen Kateryn Parr: I know that a woman can be a scholar and a queen. Actually, I am better prepared than she was. But I will not fall into the sin of coveting the crown.

The king's half-sisters do not follow my example in either study or religious devotion. I wish that they did. They do all they can to maintain their positions at court and their places in the eyes of the world but not in the sight of the Lord. None of the royal cousins walks in the light as I do. Princess Mary is a determined papist and only God knows what Elizabeth believes. The other direct heir, Mary of Scotland, is a papist, being raised in sinful luxury at the court of France, and Margaret Douglas, daughter of my great-aunt Margaret who married a Scotsman, tucked away in Yorkshire is said to be a papist too.

But Princess Mary is the closest heir to the throne and we have to show her every respect, whatever we think of her religious beliefs. My own mother and John Dudley's wife ride in Princess Mary's train as she enters London with a great show of force, as if to remind everyone that she is the king's heir and that they are all the best of friends.

Alone, of our family, I refuse to wear ornate clothes and ride in Mary's train. I will not peacock about in a richly embroidered hood. But she sends me gowns as if she hopes to buy my cousinly love and I tell her lady-in-waiting Anne Wharton that I cannot endure to hear that a vain thing like Princess Elizabeth is praised for dressing more modestly than me. I shall wear nothing but the most sober garb. There shall be only one royal theologian in England, one heir to the reformer Queen Kateryn Parr, one maid to lead the reformed Church, and it shall be me. I won't be seen to dress more gaily than Elizabeth, and I won't riot along in a papist train.

That was the end of cousinly love. I don't believe that Princess Mary had any great affection for me anyway, since I once insulted the enormous crystal monstrance that holds the wafer for Mass on her chapel altar by asking her lady-in-waiting why she curtseyed to it. I intended to wrestle with her soul – engage her in a holy discourse where she could explain that she, as a papist, believes that the bread is the very body of Jesus Christ. Then I would have shown her that it was nothing but bread – that Jesus himself meant the disciples to understand that He was giving them bread at the Last Supper, real bread, and inviting them to pray for Him at the same time. He was not saying that it was His body. He was not speaking literally. Surely, any fool can see this?

I thought it would be an extremely interesting discussion and one that would have led her to true understanding. But unfortunately, although I knew exactly what I intended to say, she did not reply as I expected. She did not speak at all as I thought she would, she only said that she was curtseying to Him that made us all – a completely nonsensical answer.

'How?' I asked, a little flustered. 'How can He be there that made us all, and the baker made Him?'

It didn't come out right at all, and God must forgive me that I did not build up to the argument, repeating my point three times, as in my rhetoric lessons. I did it much better in my bedchamber than I did in the papist chapel at Beaulieu, and this can only be because the devil protects his own, and Anne Wharton is under his hairy hoof.

I went back to my room to do the speech again in the looking glass. I saw my pale face, my bronze hair, my little features and the tiny speckle of freckles over my nose that I fear spoils my dainty prettiness. My pale skin is like the finest porcelain except for this dusting that comes in the English summer like seeds from the willows. I was hugely convincing when I played both sides of the argument on my own: I shone like an angel when I wrestled with the soul of the imaginary Anne Wharton. But the real Anne Wharton was impossible to persuade.

I do find people are very difficult to convert; they are so very stupid. It is hard to raise sinners to grace. I practised a few lines to myself and I sounded as powerful as a preacher; but while I was rehearsing my argument Anne Wharton went to Princess Mary and told her what I said, and so the princess knew me as a committed enemy to her faith, which is a pity, for she was always kind and petted me before. Now she despises me for my belief, which she sees as error. My outstanding faith as error! I shall have to forgive that, too.

I know that she will not have forgiven this, nor forgotten it, so I am not comfortable following my mother and riding in Princess Mary's train, but at least Princess Elizabeth is in a worse position. She cannot even come to court since her disgrace over Thomas Seymour. If I were her I would think myself in a hell of shame. Everyone knows that she was all but his lover, and after his wife's death he admitted that he planned to marry Elizabeth and steal the crown. God save England from an intemperate woman like Elizabeth! God save England from a papist queen like Mary! God help England if Edward dies without a boy heir and the country has the choice of the papist, the flirt, the French princess or my mother!

Princess Mary does not stay for long. Her brother's palace is not a happy court. My cousin King Edward has a cough that he cannot clear. I can hear it rattle when I sit beside him and read to him from Plato – a philosopher that we both love – but he gets weary quickly, and has to rest. I see my father's hidden smile as he observes that I have been reading Greek to the King of England, but everyone else is only worried that he looks so ill.

Edward manages to attend the opening of parliament but then he takes to his bed. The councillors and the lawyers go in and out of his bedroom and the rumour is that he is planning the succession and writing his will. I find this hard to believe. He is only fifteen – we are the same age – I cannot believe that he is making a will. He is too young to prepare to die. Surely the summer will come and he will go on progress and in the warm weather he will lose his cough and be well again? I think if he would just come to Bradgate and sit in the gardens and walk by the river and take a boat out on our wide, beautiful lakes he would be certain to get well again. His will can be stored with all the great papers of the council and forgotten about. He will marry and have a son and all the calculations of which heir might attract whose support will be forgotten. He will marry a great princess from Europe with a mighty fortune, and I will become her friend and a great lady at court, probably a duchess. I might marry Ned Seymour despite his father's disgrace. He might regain the title; I might still be a famously learned duchess and a light before the unworthy.

GREENWICH PALACE, SPRING 1553

The court travels to Greenwich, everyone's favourite palace, downriver from the noise and smells of London, its golden quayside washed by the tide twice a day, shining like a heavenly shore. It would be a mirror of the kingdom of heaven, except for the almost total absence of the godly. Father and I are rowed with the king in the royal barge, but Edward lies back on the cushions, wrapped in furs as if he is shivering, and when the guns roar from the Tower and the ships at anchor fire their cannon, he flinches at the noise and turns his pale face away.

'He will get better, won't he?' I ask my father quietly. 'He looks terribly ill; but he will get better in summer?'

He shakes his head, his face dark. 'He has made a will,' he says. I can hear the excitement tremble in his voice. 'He has chosen his heir.'

'Doesn't the throne have to go to the eldest kin?'

'Of course. It should be Princess Mary. But how can she be queen when she has sworn obedience to the Bishop of Rome? How can she be queen when she is certain to marry a papist foreigner and set him over us? No, the king has done the right thing, he has obeyed God's will and excluded her from the succession – just as his father did.'

'Can the king name his heir?' I question. 'Is it even the law?'

'If the throne is his property then of course he can name his heir,' my father says. His voice is quiet so that the boy shivering in the furs cannot hear, but there is an edge to his tone that shows that he will not tolerate contradiction. These are arguments that are being carefully rehearsed in every corner of the court. 'The crown is property: just as we all own property. A man must be free to dispose of his property, every man can choose his heir; Henry VIII chose his heirs. And – most importantly – a young man like Edward, raised in the reformed religion, with never a papist thought in his head, is not going to leave his throne to a servant of Rome. He would not tolerate it – and John Dudley will make sure that he does not.'

'Then who?' I ask, thinking that I probably know the answer to this.

'The king – and his advisors – would prefer the nearest in line, of the reformed religion, someone who is likely to have a son to take the throne.'

'There has to be a Tudor boy?'

My father nods. It is like a curse that has been laid on this family. The Tudors have to have sons to take the throne, and they are extraordinarily hard to come by. From King Henry's six wives he got only one son: Edward. His older sister, Margaret, had only one son, James, who had a girl: Queen Mary of Scotland, who lives in France and is betrothed to the dauphin. Margaret's daughter was from a Scots lord and is both papist and probably illegitimate: Cousin Margaret Douglas; so her son, Henry Stuart, hardly counts. King Henry's favourite sister, Queen Mary, was my grandmother, and the king named her line to inherit; and her daughter, my mother, is still alive. Mother has just us three girls, and surely will never have another baby. Princess Elizabeth has no betrothal planned for her – who would take a royal bastard with uncertain parentage and so little dowry? Princess Mary has been promised and denied to almost every king in Europe. Clearly, not only is there no Tudor boy among all of us, there's no prospect of one.

'But none of us is with child,' I say, thinking of all us royal cousins. 'If they want the throne to go to a Tudor boy, there is none. None of us five heirs is even betrothed. None of us is married.'

'And that's why you're going to be,' he says briskly.

'Married?'

'At once.'

'I am?'

'All of you.'

'The Princess Mary, and Elizabeth?'

'Not them. You and Katherine and Mary.'

GREENWICH PALACE,
SPRING 1553

Katherine is no help at all in defending us against this sudden plan. My lady mother commands her to come to court on a flying visit, and Katherine is thrilled by the rooms and the servants, the foods and her gowns. She dresses Mr Nozzle in a coat of Tudor green and buys a pure white kitten with her ribbon allowance. She calls him 'Ribbon', of course, and takes him everywhere in the pocket of her cape. Her only regret is that she has been taken away from the horses at Bradgate, and the bear. She was hoping to tame the bear with kindness so that he could be a dancing bear instead of a killing one. She is not horrified, as a virgin maid should be, at the sudden prospect of wedlock; she is completely delighted.

'I'm to be married? Oh, God be praised! Thank God! At last! To who? To who?'

'Whom,' I say coldly.

'Oh, who cares? Whom should care? Whom am I marrying? Tell me!'

'Henry Lord Herbert,' I say shortly. 'The Earl of Pembroke's son.'

She blushes red as a rose. 'Oh! So handsome!' she breathes. 'And he's young, our age, not some old heap of bones.' She has a pretty small bird clinging to her finger, and she lifts it to her face and kisses its beak. 'I am to be married!' she tells it. 'And to a handsome young lord!' The bird cheeps as if it understands her, and she puts it on her shoulder where it spreads its tail for balance and puts its head on one side to look at me, as bright-eyed as my sister.

'Yes,' I say levelly. 'He's perfectly pleasing.'

'And he's godly,' she says to cheer me. 'He's Kateryn Parr's nephew. Surely, you must like him.'

'Actually, I do.'

'How happy we shall be!' She gives a little twirl on the spot as if her feet have to dance for joy. The little bird flaps and clings on. 'And I shall be a countess!'

'Yes,' I say drily. 'And his father will be locked down hard into an alliance with our father and with John Dudley Duke of Northumberland.'

She doesn't think about this, the three most powerful men in the country, the three leaders of the reformed faith, coming together and marrying their children to each other to provide against betrayal. Trusting each other so little, so faithless in their shared faith that they barter their children to confirm their agreement, like Abraham taking Isaac up the mountain with wood and a knife to burn him for God.

'Oh, but who are you to marry?' She pauses in her self-absorbed jig. 'Who do they have for you? Are they staying with Seymour?' She gasps. 'Oh! Not the king? Tell me! Tell me you're not going to marry the king and be Queen Jane?'

I shake my head, glancing towards the door. 'Hush. This is all because the king is so ill. Their greatest hope is that they can show him that one of us has a son, so that he can make that boy his heir. They want us both to marry at once, get with child, and show him the boy as his heir.'

'I could be the mother of the King of England?' she yelps. 'Me? Not you? If I get a boy before you do?'

'Perhaps.'

She clasps her hands and laughs with delight. 'So who are you to marry?'

'Guildford Dudley,' I say shortly.

My sister skids to a standstill. 'Not Ned Seymour after all? They're switching horses? You're to have the young Dudley boy?'

'Yes.'

'The tall fair one?'

'Yes, of course.'

'The mummy's boy?'

'Yes, Guildford.'

'Well, that's a comedown,' she crows. 'You won't like that! The second to youngest son of a new-made duke? You won't get your ducal strawberry leaves off him!'

My hand itches to slap her silly face. 'It's not a question of like or dislike,' I say steadily. 'It is my father's wish to ally with the Lord President of the council. It is Father's determination that we shall be wedded and bedded so he can show the king his heirs to bring up in the reformed religion. Even little Mary is to be betrothed – to Arthur Grey, the son of the Baron of Wilton.'

She gives a scream. 'The baron with the scarred face? The ugly one?'

'Yes.'

'But Mary's only eight! And Arthur must be twenty!'

'He's seventeen,' I say grimly. 'But in any case, Mary is far too young to be married, and she's too small. If she does not grow, how could she give birth? She has that twist in her spine; I don't think she could birth a child. It's all completely wrong. She is too small, and you are too young, and I am promised before God to Ned Seymour. Our parents gave our word. I don't see how any of these weddings can go ahead. I don't believe it can be God's will. You must join with me and speak against them.'

'Not me!' she says smartly. 'I'm not defying our lady mother. If I can have Mr Nozzle with me I'll stand behind you as you argue; but I can't face up to her on my own.'

'So that they don't marry you to a stranger! So they don't marry you while you're still a child,' I exclaim.

'Oh, I can marry Herbert,' she assures me. 'I'm not too young. That can go ahead. I don't object to it. The rest of you can refuse if you want, but I want to be married.'

'None of us can marry anyone,' I rule.

There is a silence; she pouts at me. 'Oh, Jane, don't spoil everything! Oh, please don't!' She clasps my hands, and the bird cheeps encouragingly.

'I'm going to pray on it. I have to listen to God.'

'But what if God agrees with you?' she wails. 'When does He ever want anything nice for us?'

'Then I will have to tell Father that I have doubts.'

He does not see me alone: that in itself warns me that I will not get a hearing. He fears my eloquence: 'Oh, for pity's sake don't let her go on and on,' my mother always says.

I go into the royal presence chamber like a Daniel going in to the lions. Edward the king is not in his court. He is behind the closed doors of the privy chamber, or he may even have retreated to the room behind that – his study and his bedroom. Out here, the court goes about its business as if there is nothing wrong. The Marquess of Northampton, William Parr, and his wife, Elizabeth, nod at me with a peculiar smile, as if they know all about everything – which they probably do. I sketch a little curtsey and feel even more uneasy.

My mother and my father are playing cards with Sir William Cavendish and his wife, Elizabeth, my mother's good friend our aunt Bess. The table is in the window bay so they have some privacy in the bustling room. My parents look up as I come through the crowd of people. I notice that people make way for me. The news of my betrothal to the son of the Lord President must have spread already and my importance has grown with the news. Everyone shows respect to the Dudleys. They may be a new family, but clearly they have the knack of taking power and holding it.

'Deuce,' my mother says, putting down a card, and makes an absent-minded gesture of blessing over my head with her free hand as I curtsey to her.

Aunt Bess gives me a warm smile. I am a favourite of hers and she understands that a young woman has to find her own way in the world by her own lights.

'I have a queen,' my father says, showing his hand.

My mother laughs. 'And perhaps queens count, after all!' She turns to me, pleasantly enough. 'What is it, Jane? Come to take a hand? Are you staking your necklace?'

'Don't tease her,' my father intervenes hastily, as I open my mouth to abjure the sin of gambling. 'What is it, child, what do you want?'

'I would speak with you,' I look at my mother. 'Privately.'

'You can speak here,' she rules. 'Come closer.'

Tactfully Sir William and his lady rise up and stand a little to one side, her ladyship still holding her cards so that she can return to the sinful game without a moment's delay. My father signs to the musicians to play and half a dozen ladies form up to dance. At once the men bow and join them, and in the noise of the dance nobody can hear me when I say: 'My lord father, lady mother, I believe that I cannot be betrothed to Guildford Dudley. I have prayed on it, and I am certain.'

'Why ever not?' my mother asks. She is so little distracted from her game that she looks at her cards and slides a few crowns across the table to the pile in the middle with only half her mind on me.

Lady Bess shakes her head, as if she thinks that my mother should attend to me.

'I am precontracted,' I say firmly.

My father glances up at my pale face. 'No, you're not.'

'I believe I am,' I say. 'We all said that I should marry Ned Seymour. We made a verbal promise.'

'Nothing in writing,' my mother remarks. To my father she says: 'I raise you another crown. I told you she would be like this.'

'A word is as binding as a letter.' I speak to my father, whose word, as a reformed Christian, must be his oath. 'We made an agreement. You made an agreement. Ned spoke to me, as his father said he should: I assented.'

'Did you promise?' my mother enquires, suddenly interested. 'Did you give your word to him? Did you say "I will"?'

'I said "quite".'

She laughs out loud and my father gets up from the table, takes my hand and tucks it in the crook of his elbow, leads me away from my mother and from the dancers. 'Now listen here,' he says gently. 'There was talk of a betrothal and we agreed that it might take place. But everyone knew it depended on Seymour's return to power. None of my girls will be married except to the advantage of the family.

'And now everything has changed. Seymour is dead, his wife still imprisoned for treason, and his son has lost his inheritance. There is no value in any connection with them. You can see for yourself, a clever girl like you, this place is run by John Dudley.

The king is not going to make old bones. It's sad but we have to face it. He's going to leave his throne to whichever cousin of the reformed religion has a son to take his place. One of you will get a son, and she will be queen regent until her boy is of age, and then the boy will take the throne. D'you see?'

'What about Elizabeth?' I ask, although it goes against the grain with me to put her forward. 'She's of the reformed religion. She's next of kin.'

'Not her. There are no plans for her to marry, and certainly, she wouldn't be allowed to choose a husband for herself, not after that business with Thomas Seymour. I think she has shown us all that she is very far from being a wise virgin.' My father allows himself a little chuckle. 'It's a Tudor boy we want; a girl is no good for us. The king – God bless him – hopes to live long enough to see his heir christened in a reformed church. We didn't expect this, we didn't prepare for this, but he isn't well, and he wants this settled now. You can do that for him. It would be godly work to ease his troubled con-science. You marry Guildford Dudley, take to childbed, and the king knows that he is getting two young people, raised in the reformed Church, with two experienced fathers to advise them, and a boy in the cradle to come after him on the throne. D'you see?'

'He is so ill?' I cannot believe it.

'At any rate, he wants to know who will come after him, if he dies before he can marry and get his own son.'

'The baby would be his heir?'

'If he doesn't have a son of his own.'

This seems like a distant prospect. 'But I gave my word,' I say. 'You gave yours. To Ned Seymour.'

'Forget it,' he advises me briefly. 'Edward Seymour is dead and his boy Ned is with a guardian who will dispose of him as he thinks fit. Not another word about it. You have to be an obedient daughter, Jane, or you will be made to obey.'

My mother, bored of waiting, strides to his side.

I screw up my courage. 'Please forgive me,' I say to them both.

'But I have prayed on this, and I believe that I cannot marry anyone without being released from my promise to the former Earl of Hertford. I gave my word to you and you gave yours to the Seymours. There were no vows, but God sees and hears all. I cannot simply pretend that I never said it.' Near to tears at my own defiance, I look from my hesitant beloved father to my flint-faced mother.

'You can't refuse us,' my mother says flatly, 'because we are your parents, and we will make you.'

DURHAM HOUSE, LONDON, MAY 1553

She is right, of course. And as if to emphasise the importance of the Dudley family, I am to stay at their great London palace, Durham House, and my wedding is to be held here. It is to be a joint wedding, there will be three brides: me, my sister Katherine, and the Dudley girl, Katherine, who is marrying Henry Hastings, the eighteen-year-old son of the Earl of Huntingdon. My little sister Mary is to be publicly betrothed, but her wedding and bedding will wait until she is older. Everyone seems very pleased about this, though they must see, as I do, that these are the great men of England signing an alliance in the blood of their children. I wonder if I am the only person who prays to God to tell me why these three men should need to be so sure of one another. What danger do they think they will face if they don't lock each other into marriage? Why do we all six have to be married at once in the same ceremony? My sister Katherine thinks it will be to her advantage as she is undoubtedly the prettiest of us three brides. That is her only concern.

Clothes from the royal wardrobe arrive daily, jewels from the royal treasury are loaned to us, precious stones are given. My cousin the king is too sick to attend the wedding, but he sends us bolts of cloth: black silver cloth of tissue embossed with roses, purple and white tissue, cloth of gold and cloth of silver, a trimming for my hood of thirteen table diamonds, seventeen great pearls, a girdle of gold. The tiltyard is painted and hung with flags: there is to be a tournament. Everyone in London who has so much as a knighthood will come to the great dinner that the cooks prepare days in advance. There will be dozens of courses, the fountain in the central courtyard will flow with wine, hundreds will sit down to dinner in their finest clothes and eat scores of dishes, thousands will watch them. I will be at the centre of attention, a Tudor heir, dressed as richly as a princess, marrying a Dudley boy.

'This is heaven,' Katherine says, holding a scarf of violet silk against her flushed face.

'No, it is not,' I tell her. 'And it is heresy to say so.'

'It's as good as Easter,' Mary says, her speech muffled by the pastry that she is cramming into her mouth.

'It's nothing to do with you,' I say. 'You are to be betrothed, but not to marry. There's no excuse for gluttony, and stand up straight.'

Obediently, she straightens her back as Katherine twirls around, draped in cloth of silver as we wait for the dressmakers. The groom of the royal wardrobe has sent more great bolts of velvet and silk and Katherine already has some priceless lace draped over her head like a veil. 'There's no excuse for vanity either,' I say sourly.

'I am half in love with him already,' Katherine bubbles. 'He came to give me a gold chain yesterday, and he pressed my hand when he left. What d'you think he meant?'

'My mother pressed my hand too,' I say, showing her the bruises on my wrists. 'She tells me that is love, as well.'

'It is motherly love,' Katherine asserts.

Mary looks solemnly at the marks. Our mother, our nurses,

our governesses and our father have all beaten each of us, at one time or another. Only my tutor John Aylmer has had authority over me but never used a rod. I tell him that is why I love learning.

'It's the best thing that could happen to us.' Mary parrots what she has been told. 'It puts us in line for the throne.'

'It's hardly the best thing for you,' I tell her. 'You can't give birth to the King of England.'

She flushes a little. 'I am a girl like any other,' she says. 'My heart is as big as yours, and I don't doubt I will grow tall.'

Mary's staunch courage always makes me melt. I hold out my arms to her and we hug. 'Anyway, we can't disobey them,' I say over her fair head.

'Don't you love him? Even a little?' Katherine breathes.

'I will love him when we are married,' I say coldly. 'I will have to love him then, for I will have promised before God to do so.'

My sisters are disappointed in the wedding service: they hoped it would be in Latin and filled with ceremonial and incomprehensible oaths, noisy with music and trumpets, drowned in regalia, drenched with holy water, and choking with incense. Instead it has the simple honesty of my religion and I am deeply glad that the Dudleys are a godly family who turned to the reformed religion as soon as the king gave his people the Bible and the preachers spread the word. The purity of our wedding is a living reproach to the papist Princess Mary, who pointedly does not attend – neither the ceremony nor the two days of lavish celebrations that follow. Our cousin Margaret Douglas is not invited either. She is in Scotland, visiting the Nobody that she calls her father. Since John Dudley himself gave her a licence to leave the kingdom I imagine that he wanted her out of the way.

I am not dressed plainly, as a Protestant should dress, despite my declared wishes. I wear royal purple with an overgown of gold brocade embroidered with diamonds and pearls. They spread my chestnut hair over my shoulders and it hangs down below my waist. It is the last time I will wear it loose as a maiden. I am by far the grandest bride and Katherine, with her golden hair and her gown of cloth of silver, is by far the most beautiful. But I don't begrudge her joy in her dress and her looks. If she had any sense she would know it is just worldly show.

There is dancing and jousting; two companies of masquers: one of men and one of women; there are players and musicians. The Dudleys invite all of their household to attend, and throw open the gates of their great house so that everyone in London can come and see our magnificence. The whole thing goes on forever and is only spoiled by a disaster with the food. Some dish was bad and it left many guests vomiting with sickness and others voiding themselves. Many who overate and drank too much on the first day have to send their excuses and not come on the second. Lady Dudley, my new mother-in-law, is completely mortified that she had to spend half the day groaning in her chamber over her churning bowels. I do not think that it was a sign, for God speaks through His Holy Word – and not through stars or sweats or gales. But I do think that it is a powerful reproach to my mother and father that my wedding should turn the guests' stomachs – just as it sickens me.

We are a mismatched band. My stunted sister Mary's promised husband, Arthur Grey of Wilton, towers above her. He is a young man already and thinks himself his father's companion and fellow. He is far too old to be a playmate to Mary; she is far too young to be a wife to him. Of course she is too small to be wedded and bedded, and I think she will never be able to lie with a man and bear a child with her spine that was twisted at birth. Of course, Arthur Grey must secretly despise her. I thank God that they will live apart for some years and that she is to stay at home with our mother. I imagine they will get the marriage dissolved before she has to go to her husband.

My new sister-in-law, Katherine Dudley, is a plain vain thing. They have given her to Henry Hastings, a highly educated scholar and courtier. He looks at his little bride bobbing up and down with a patient smile that will soon wear thin. My sister Katherine's husband, Henry Lord Herbert, the young son of the Earl of Pembroke, never says one word to anyone throughout the whole two days. He is as white as a corpse and so sick that he can hardly stand. They say that they dragged him from his deathbed though he swore he could not walk to the altar. He is only fifteen years old. I hope that he does not make my sister a widow before she is a wife. Certainly, they cannot consummate the marriage while she is so young and he is so ill, so she is spared the ordeal that they force on me. These three unions that cannot be consummated only make me feel worse. I am the only girl who has to be both a bride and a wife, in deed as well as in name.

'I don't see why you have such a long face,' Katherine my foolish sister says. 'You knew that if you were married you'd have to be fully married. It would be just the same for me if he were not ill.'

'And me,' Mary says.

'It wouldn't be the same for you,' I say to Mary.

'I don't see why not,' she says stubbornly.

I am too exhausted to argue with her. 'And you're too young,' I say to Katherine.

'No I'm not,' she says. 'And anyway, you certainly aren't.' She gives a little tweak to the kerchief I wear over my hair to indicate that I am now a married woman. 'Come on, you're to be first to go to your wedding chamber. Lucky you.'

I feel unfairly forced, as my mother and new mother-in-law and all their ladies appear at the door and then come with me to the bridal chamber, watch as my ladies undress me, and then abruptly leave me with my new husband.

It is not that he is unpleasant, not in any way. He is a handsome young man, fair and with a pleasing open face and bright blue eyes. He is far taller than I am. The top of my head does not even reach to his shoulder and I have to crane my neck to look up at him, but for all his height he is light on his feet – a good dancer, they say – and he rides, hunts, jousts, just as he should. He has been raised in a godly household and is well read. If we were not married, I could say nothing against him but that he looks to his mother for every single thing. The big baby looks at her before he even opens his mouth, before he sits or stands.

He is not my choice, he would not be my choice, and I am afraid that I am not free in the sight of God to marry him. But since we are married I can say nothing against him at all. A godly wife is obedient. He has been put over me as Adam was put over Eve. I shall have to be obedient to him, whatever I think of his judgement.

Our wedding night is as awkward and as painful as I expected. I don't even think it would have been any better if I had married Edward Seymour, though he might have been more confident than Guildford and perhaps would not have made me feel quite such a fool for not knowing what has to be done. The difficulty is that none of my books tells me anything about love, except in the most abstract sense. None of my books says anything about the pain, except the pain of sin. None of them warns me that the worst of it is the misery of having a total stranger struggling to do something to me – neither of us knowing exactly how it should be done, and when it goes all wrong, blaming me. I didn't even know that anything was wrong except that at first it hurt and then it was disgusting. He is not inspired by desire or affection, and neither am I. I wait till he falls asleep and then I get up and pray for strength to bear this, as I have to bear everything else in this vale of misery, in the place which He hath set.

Finally, the guests say their farewells, Katherine goes to her new family home at Baynard's Castle to put her pale husband back in his sickbed, and nurse him like a mother, since his own mother is dead. My father and mother go home to Suffolk Place with little Mary; but I am left in a strange house, with the servants clearing up the mess of a two-day feast, with my mother-in-law locked in her chamber, and my new husband sulky and silent now that she is not here to tell him what to say or do.

◆◆◆

In the morning I am allowed to go home to my family but only to Suffolk Place. I am pining for the summer fields of Bradgate, but I have to stay in London.

'My lady mother says you can go home if you want to,' my young husband says ungraciously. 'But she says I have to dine with you the day after tomorrow and spend the night at your house.'

'All my books are there,' I say, trying to excuse myself. 'I need to go home to study.'

'My lady mother says that you may.'

I don't ask him if they expect me to return soon. I think it better not to know. Perhaps I will be able to spin out a visit to our London house till the summer, and then if the king goes on progress John Dudley and his sons may attend without their wives, and I may be able to go to Bradgate. The thought that I might get there, to ride in the woods and to see the harvest come in, to walk under a strawberry moon and take a boat out on the lake, is the only thing that keeps me at peace through the first days of my marriage. That, and my books, of course. I can always open a book and hide myself in that inner, private world.

The idea that I would want to go to Bradgate, that I would seek my mother as a refuge from a home even less kindly than hers, makes me understand for the first time what God said to Eve: *I will increase thy sorrow, when thou art with child: with pain shalt thou bear thy children, and thy lust shall pertain unto your husband, and he shall rule thee.* Truly, it is a sorrow to be a woman; and Eve shows us that to be a wife is even worse.

It is agreed between Lady Dudley and my mother that I can live with my parents at Suffolk Place, as long as I visit the Dudleys regularly and dine with them often. The first weeks of my marriage are spent like this. But Lady Dudley breaks this arrangement by coming into the privy chamber before dinner, as Guildford and I are sitting in awkward silence, and saying: 'Now you must send for your clothes and all your things, Jane. You are to stay tonight and you must stay after. You will live here now.'

I rise and curtsey to her. 'I thought I was to go home,' I say. 'My mother is expecting me home tonight.'

She shakes her head. 'It is all to be changed. My lord has written to me that you must be here. You have to stay here with us. We have to be ready.'

Guildford, on his feet at the first sight of his mother, kneels to her, and she rests her hand in blessing on his curly head. 'We have to be ready? He's worse?' he asks eagerly.

I look from the woman to her kneeling son. 'Who's worse?'

She gives an irritated little tut at my ignorance. 'Leave us,' she says to the ladies who have come in with her. 'Sit down, Jane. Guildford, sweet son, you come here to me.'

He stands behind her, like Mr Nozzle clinging to Katherine, watching my face as his mother tells me: 'The king, God bless him, is worse. You knew at least that he was ill?'

'Of course I knew that. I often sit with him.'

'Now he is worse. His doctors say that he will not survive the summer.'

'The summer?' This is impossibly soon. I thought that he might live long enough to marry and have a child. I had no idea that they were saying that we might lose him within the year. 'God save His Grace,' I whisper, shocked. 'I did not know. But how can it be? I thought he was only—'

'That's not important,' she cuts me off. 'What matters most is his will.'

Actually, what matters most is his eternal soul. But I cannot tell her that now.

'He has changed it,' she says. There is a ring of triumph in her voice. 'Changed it, and all of the council have sworn to the changes.' She glances up at Guildford as he smiles down at her. 'Your father has seen to it,' she says. 'He is prepared for everything.' She turns back to me. 'The king has excluded his half-sisters from the succession,' she says briskly, ignoring my gasp of surprise.

I get to my feet, as if I must stand to find the courage to argue with her. 'That cannot be,' I say slowly. I know that Princess

Mary is the next in line; whatever I may think of her religion there is no denying her right. Heirs cannot be named at random. The throne is not to be given away. My cousin the king knows this, the country knows this. Whatever my father says it cannot be that the king could choose his heir. There is no Tudor boy. He cannot prefer one cousin over another.

'It will be,' Lady Dudley says. 'And she will know it for a fact when he dies.'

I am suddenly afraid that this is treason. Surely, it is treason to speak of the death of the king, surely it is treason to speak against the princesses?

'I think I had better go home,' I say.

'You'll stay here,' she raps out. 'This is no time for you to run to your mother.'

Scornfully I look at her son, who clearly never has to run to his mother for he is always under her wing.

'You have to be here so that my husband can fetch you to the Tower,' she explains.

I gasp. The last man fetched to the Tower by her husband ended with his head on the block: Edward Seymour.

'No, you fool,' she says irritably. 'You will have to go to the Tower on the death of the king. You will have to be seen at the Tower. My husband will want to keep you safe.'

It is simply too incredible, and too ridiculous for me to consider. I know that my father and my mother will never allow me to be taken to the Tower by John Dudley.

'I'm going home,' I say firmly, and I walk to the door. I will not be part of this. My barge is waiting for me at the pier, my ladies are waiting for me in the gallery. Nobody can stop me going home to my mother with the news that the Dudleys have run mad, that they think that they can change the succession, and they want to take me to the Tower.

'Stop her,' Guildford's mother orders him.

He steps forward and takes hold of my wrist. I round on him. 'You let me go!' I spit, and he flinches back as if Katherine's kitten had suddenly turned on him and scratched his face.

I don't wait for a second chance. I dive out of the room and take to my heels. I run through the palace, I clatter across the gangplank. 'Cast off!' I say breathlessly, and then I laugh because I am free.

SUFFOLK PLACE, LONDON,
JUNE 1553

I see that my mother is in a state of fury before I have even entered the room or have a chance to tell her that I am mistreated by Lady Dudley. She is striding up and down her privy chamber, my father sitting at the table, silently watching her, his fingers steepled together, his expression guarded. She whirls around as I come in and then she sees my white face.

'They've told you, then.'

'Lady Dudley told me,' I say quietly. 'But I don't understand. I came away at once, Father.'

'Tell her!' my mother commands him. 'Tell her what John Dudley has done and you have all agreed!'

'It became clear to the king and to us all that he will not live to have children of his own,' my father says heavily. 'His doctors doubt that he will even live to see your son born.'

'And with Princess Mary and Elizabeth set aside, then I am the next heir,' my mother asserts loudly.

'The doctors say weeks, not even months.'

'Blessed God! So soon?' I murmur.

'I should inherit in weeks, not even months!' my mother squawks.

'But the king was determined to get to a male heir, as soon as possible,' my father continues, overriding her grunt of protest. 'And so he wanted to pass over your mother – for the good of the country – to the next generation, to you and your sisters – and to the generation after that: your son, Jane.'

'But you said—'

'So he has named you as queen, and any son that you have will be king after you. He can't name a boy as yet unborn, so he names you.'

'And the whole council, including your father, have signed to this!' my mother exclaims. 'Excluding me! Casting me aside! And they expect me to agree! They go to the king and sign away my right!'

'I don't see what else we could do,' my father says patiently. 'I put your case very strongly, but it was the solution of the king's own devising to get us to a king within a generation.'

'It puts John Dudley's grandson on the throne!' my mother explodes with anger. 'That is why he has brought the council round to the king's wishes! John Dudley planned this from the very beginning: Jane crowned queen in my place, and Guildford Dudley beside her, and that tribe of Dudley brothers become royal dukes! Whereas I – the daughter of the Queen of France, the niece of the King of England – am passed over. And you tell me I must agree to it!'

Quietly my father regards her. 'Nobody is denying your royal blood,' he says. 'It is that which brought the king to Jane in the first place. Your right passes to her, and you become My Lady the Queen's Mother, the greatest woman at court after her.'

'I shall have to pray on this,' I tell him. 'It cannot be right. The king has sisters.'

'The king prayed on it, we all did,' he says. 'God told him that it was the only way to get a Tudor boy on the throne.'

'And I am to have him?' I ask, thinking of Guildford's painful fumblings. 'I am to conceive a Tudor heir, and give birth to a Tudor boy where five wives could not?'

'If it is God's will,' my father reminds me. 'And you will be Head of the Church of England. Think of that, Jane. Think of that.'

I go to pray. My little sister Mary finds me in the chapel, on my knees, gazing blankly at the white wall behind the bare table of the altar. All around us like ghosts are the shadowy outlines of the paintings of the saints showing through the limewashed walls, frescoes that were bright and inspiring when the chapel was first built and people needed such toys because they had no Bible and were not allowed to pray directly to God. I must do anything to save my country from slipping back into those times, enslaved to a distant pope, with a papist queen preaching lies to an ignorant people.

'The Duchess of Northumberland, your mother-in-law, has sent for you,' Mary whispers. She stands beside me as I kneel and her head is the same height as mine. 'Sent one of her ladies-in-waiting to tell our lady mother that you have to go home to them at once. She said that you were disobedient and that it would be the undoing of all of us if you are not to hand when they need you.'

I look up but, stubbornly, I don't move. 'I won't go.'

'Our mother said that you would not go, she said that you could stay here, and Lady Dudley said in that case she would keep Guildford at her home, and you would be known for a disobedient and estranged wife.'

I look blankly at my little sister. 'I have to obey my husband. I swore to be his wife,' I say miserably.

Mary's eyes are huge in her pale face. 'That's what Mother said.'

'She insists I go back?'

'You have to go,' Mary nods. 'Mother says it is her wish.'

I rise to my feet. I feel as weary as my cousin the king, fighting for his life while everyone quarrels about his legacy. 'I'll go then,' I say. 'God knows what is going to happen next.'

My stomach churns as the barge carries me back to the Dudleys' house. I can see my tall husband waiting on the pier, and as the barge comes up alongside and rocks gently, he gives a little bow. When the gangplank is run ashore and the rowers hold the boat fast to the ropes he gives me his hand to help me step down to the quayside. I glance up at the blank windows of the house, which seem to overlook the gardens and the river as if they were watching for me and are not best pleased.

'Yes, my father sent me to meet you,' he says. 'He's watching us from his windows. He wants to see you in his rooms at once.'

'I'm not well,' I say. 'I am sick.'

'That won't get you out of it,' he says unsympathetically. 'He came home from Westminster the moment that he learned you had gone to Suffolk Place. Against his wishes, against my mother's request, against my orders.'

'I really am sick,' I say to him. 'I will have to go to my room. I can see no-one. Ask your father to excuse me, tell him that I have to lie down.'

'I'll tell my lady mother,' he says, 'but she'll probably just come into your room and make you.' He hesitates, like one unhappy child warning another. 'You can't lock your door, you know. There's no key. If you go to bed she'll just come and pull you out.'

'She can't beat me,' I say with grim humour.

'Actually, she can.'

He turns from me, and leaves me there, in the garden, standing alone but for my ladies, until one of them comes up and takes my arm and helps me to my room.

Within moments, just as her son predicted, Lady Dudley opens the door, enters without knocking and looms over me, her face avid. 'Are you sick in the morning before chapel?' she asks.

'Yes,' I say. I try to sit up but to my surprise she presses me back down on the pillow.

'No, lie down, rest. And do you have a faintness in your head?'

'Yes.'

'Are your breasts tender?'

I find this so intimate from a woman to a daughter-in-law in whom she has shown no previous interest, that I flush and do not answer.

'When are you due to have your course?'

I never have any idea – sometimes it comes late, sometimes it does not come at all. 'I think it is this week, or perhaps it was last week.'

Her cross face does a strange convulsion, I understand she is moved. She takes my hand. 'You shall rest,' she says with sudden gentleness. 'Rest, my dear.'

There is a clatter from the courtyard outside my window as the Dudley horsemen all come into the yard and shout for grooms and for the men-at-arms. The noise pounds into my head and I turn my face from the bright window.

'You can go to the manor at Chelsea and rest,' she offers. 'You like it there, don't you?'

I lived there with Queen Kateryn when she was newly widowed and writing her book. It is my favourite place in all the world. 'I love it there,' I say. 'But I thought your husband said that I have to be here?'

'Oh, no, no, no. You can go there, while we wait for news,' she says. 'Guildford can visit you, and my husband can send you news. Your ladies can go with you.' She is smiling as she pats my cold hand. She has never been so gentle with me before. 'You can be quiet there, and eat well. I have had thirteen babies,' she confides. 'I know all about it.'

Does this mad woman think I am with child? Bearing her grandson? Well, whatever she means, I am not going to argue with her, not if she is sending me to Chelsea without Guildford.

'I'll tell them to prepare your rooms at the old manor,' she says. 'You can go by our barge as soon as they are ready for you. See how well I look after you! But rest for now.'

I close my eyes and when I open them, she has gone.

THE OLD MANOR, CHELSEA,
JULY 1553

I can hardly believe that my friend, my teacher, my almost-mother Queen Kateryn is not here with me at Chelsea. Every time I raise my eyes from the page I expect to see her, at her table, reading and taking notes.

This was her house, and I was her favourite ward, a little girl she was making in her own image, as beloved as a daughter. We walked together in the gardens, we played in the orchard, we sat beside the river and every day, without fail, we studied in the beautiful rooms that look down on the gardens and out to the river. If she missed the crowds and the excitement of the royal court, she never gave any sign of it. On the contrary, she lived as she had always wanted: as a scholarly lady, remote from a sinful world, happy with the man she loved, free at last to devote herself to study and to prayer. It was from this library that she sent her book to the printers. Here, she invited the greatest scholars of the day to preach. Now I feel as if she has just stepped into the garden, or walked along the gallery, and that I may see her at any moment, and it comforts me. The life that she made for herself here is the life I want for myself: this scholarly peace.

In this period of quietness, I choose to read all that I can about dwarfs, as I think that my sister Mary is not just bird-boned, or underweight, or slow to grow – my father has used all these excuses to keep her at home. I fear that she may never grow any bigger; and I wonder why such a thing should be. I learn almost nothing from the Greek philosophers, but in ancient Egypt there were dwarf gods, and some high-born courtier-dwarfs. I write to tell Mary all about this but I don't mention the behaviour of dwarfs at the Roman courts. None of that is suitable information for a young woman who is the daughter of an heir to the throne. Indeed, I am surprised to find it in Kateryn Parr's library at all.

I live here almost alone except for my ladies. Every other day Guildford rides out to see me, gives me what news he knows – which is never much – and then returns to the court where they are keeping a selfish vigil over my poor cousin the dying king. Sometimes Guildford dines with us but usually he eats his dinner with his parents and sleeps at their house. My ladies ask me if I miss him – a husband so handsome and so newly wed – and I show them a thin smile and say 'not particularly'. I never say that it is a great relief to be without his heavy presence in my bed, sweating under my thick covers, weighing down his side of the bed. He has to attend me, just as I have to endure him; we are bound to lie together by the law of the Church and the command of our parents; but why a woman would do it for pleasure, or even seek it, I cannot imagine.

But I do remember that Queen Kateryn was happiest in the mornings when Thomas Seymour came barelegged out of her rooms. I know that my mother relishes her time with my father, and Lady Dudley is obviously ludicrously devoted to my father-in-law. Perhaps it is something I will grow into when I am taller and stronger. Perhaps, as a pleasure of the flesh, you have to have a lot of flesh to feel the pleasure. If I did not feel so sick in my belly and so feverish it would perhaps be better. But I cannot imagine being so fat and so healthy that I would long for Guildford's clumsy thrusting, or giggle when he slapped my bottom.

This is the only time I have ever found that my books fail me. There are some Greek papers about the conception of children but they are all about the phases of the moon. There are some terrifying pictures of a baby being cut from a dead mother, and a lot of theology about Our Lord being conceived by the Holy Ghost on a virgin – and there are some thoughtful writers who question how this could be. But nobody seems to have written anything about a real woman. It is as if I, and those of my sex, exist only as a symbol. The books say nothing about the strange mixture of pain and shame that Guildford and I suffer wordlessly and awkwardly together. They say nothing about how a baby is made from this painful coupling. I don't think anyone exactly knows, and, of course, I cannot ask.

Guildford talks to me in the morning, he tells me that the king's illness has been announced to the parliament and the churches are praying for his recovery. Princess Mary and Princess Elizabeth have been invited to court and they are both waiting in their country houses for news.

'Will they come?' I ask.

'I don't know,' he says. 'My father will know.'

'What is going to happen?' I ask him.

'I don't know. My father will know.'

'Can't you ask him?'

He gives a funny little scowl. 'No. Do you ask your father what his plans are?'

I shake my head.

'He talks to John and Ambrose or Robert.' Guildford names his older brothers. 'They all talk together, they know what's happening. But they're much older than I, they have been at court and they've been in battles. They can advise him, he listens to them. I am just . . .' He trails off.

'What are you?'

'Bait to catch you,' he says, his voice hard as if he is insulting us both. 'A fat fly for a stupid trout.'

I hesitate, ignoring his rudeness and the hurt in his voice. 'But how will we know what we are to do?'

'Someone will tell us,' he says. 'When they want us, they will send for us. Dead fly and trout together.'

It is the first time that I have had a sense of him as a young man, not yet twenty, who has to obey his family, as I have to obey mine. It is the first time that I have seen he is anxious about what is planned for us. It is the first time that I have thought: we are in the same situation, together. Our future will be together, we will grow up together, we have to face whatever is going to happen together. I give him a shy little smile. 'We just have to wait?'

Surprisingly, he touches my fingers with his, as if he shares my sense of being caged, like the bear at Bradgate, waiting for the dogs to come. 'We have to wait,' he agrees.

It is Mary Sidney, Guildford's older sister, who comes one afternoon, cloaked and hooded as if she were a heroine of one of the poems that she loves so much, her dark blue eyes bright with excitement, her slim frame trembling.

'You have to come!' she says, whispering though we are alone in my private chamber, except for my ladies, seated in the window, catching the last light of the setting sun on the books they are reading.

'Did your father send you for me?'

'Yes!' she says excitedly. 'You are to come at once.'

'I am not well,' I tell her. 'I am sick all the time as if I am being poisoned.'

'Of course you're not being poisoned. You have to come now.'

I hesitate. 'My things, my books . . .'

'Come, it's just for a visit. You won't need anything. Come now.'

'As I am? Without anything?'

'Yes! Yes!'

My ladies bring my cloak, and my hat. There is no time to change my gown. I take a fur to wrap around me on the barge for the wind is cold on the darkening water.

'Come on!' Mary Sidney says. 'Hurry up.'

The Dudley barge is waiting for us, but the ducal pennants and the standard are furled and tied. We go on board without a word and they cast off in silence and start to row, swiftly and smoothly. At once, I think that they have made a mistake and are going the wrong way – upriver, away from the city, westward. I cannot understand this. If my poor cousin is worse, we should be going to him at Greenwich Palace, downriver. But the flowing inward tide is with us and the boat springs forward with each splash of the oars in the water, so that Mary and I, sitting side by side on the seat under the awning, rock forward and back with every movement. I put my hand to my belly where I feel a grip of fear or nausea, or both.

'Where are we going?' I ask.

'Syon House,' she says.

I give a little gasp. Syon House is where Katherine Howard was held before she was taken to the Tower and beheaded.

'It's my father's house now,' Mary says impatiently, as if she guesses that I am afraid. 'He just wants to meet us there.'

'What for?'

She shakes her head. 'I don't know.' She settles back, folds her hands inside her cape and stares over the heads of the labouring rowers, over the darkening river as the wooded banks and fields slide by. We pass water meads where heron flap slowly up out of the flooded fields, and fold themselves into high trees, we pass wet pasture where the cattle squelching in the mud look at us reproachfully as if we are to blame for spoiling their cloudy drinking water, and not their own heavy hooves. We pass thick woodland where the trees bend down to their own reflection and all I can see is branch meeting reflected branch, and green leaves to greener weed. The last glow of the sun turns grey, Mary straightens the fur around my shoulders and a thin waning moon rises behind us, throwing a pale yellowish light on the glassy waters like a will-o'-the-wisp urging us onward to our destruction.

'Do you really not know why they have sent for me?' I ask Mary, very quietly, as if the darkening sky must not hear.

She shakes her head as if she too does not dare to break the silence, and an owl hoots and then I see it, white as a ghost, thick wings spread, as it weaves from one tree to another, and then we hear again that mournful call.

It is hours before she says: 'There!' and I can see the lights. It is Syon House.

SYON HOUSE, ISLEWORTH, JULY 1553

They berth the barge precisely at the pier, make it fast, run out the gangplank, and bow to us as we disembark. There are servants with torches, and they light the long allée up to the great house. My lord father-in-law has rebuilt the old abbey into a private house, but he has left whole walls and the stone tracery of beautiful windows standing bleak and pale in the moonlight so I can almost hear the whisper of plainsong and the chant of the nuns weaving around the skeleton of their home.

We go past the stones as if they were nothing: the teeth of a skull on an old battlefield. We ignore fallen statues, a gold arrow in the grass, a piece of stone carved like an ivy branch, the top of a sarcophagus. Mary Sidney looks to neither right nor left, and nor do I as we walk through the rubble of the old faith, up a small flight of steps, through the big doors and inward and inward until we are in a long gallery, gloomy with dark wooden panelling, perhaps the old room of the abbess when she sat among her devout ladies. Now it is echoey and empty, there are cold embers in the huge stone grate and the only light comes from a wrought candelabra with bobbing candle flames placed beside a heavy chair. There are bleached panels on the wooden walls where the pictures of holy scenes have been taken away, rightly so, for *Cursed be he, that maketh any carved idol or molten image, an abomination of the Lord;* but it makes a gloomy room look wretched.

I look at Mary and say: 'Where is everyone? Why have we come here?'

'I don't know,' she says; but now I am certain she is lying.

She goes to the door and opens it to listen. From the distant kitchen we can hear the clatter of pans and the sound of voices, but the great rooms that open off the huge hall are silent. Mary closes the door and looks at me, as if wondering what she should do with me. I wrap my cloak tighter round my thin frame and look back at her.

'Your eyes are huge,' she says irrelevantly. 'Don't be so frightened. You have to be brave.'

'I'm not frightened,' I lie.

'You look like a doe at bay.'

My faith should support me as strongly now as it does when I am safe in my bed at Bradgate. I know that God is with me. *'O Lord my God, I cried unto thee, and thou hast healed me,'* I say quietly.

'Oh, for heaven's sake,' Mary says impatiently. 'You've just come for dinner with your father-in-law!' She drags a stool to the massive fireplace. After a moment's hesitation I copy her and we sit like a pair of old gossips on either side, and she throws on some kindling and a little log. It gives out no heat but a flickering light that drives the dark shadows to the corners.

'Is it about the king?' I whisper.

'Yes,' she says.

'Has he named me as queen?'

She compresses her lips as if to keep the words in her mouth.

'Will it be ... soon?'

She nods, as if it is too terrible to say, and we sit in silence after that and then the door is opened and a manservant comes in, wearing the Dudley livery. 'His Grace wishes to see you in the great hall,' he says.

Mary and I follow him down the stairs, he throws open the double doors and we go into the brightly lit room. At once I am dazzled by candles and firelight, the room is crowded with the great men of the kingdom and their unending trains of hangers-on. There is a blaze of wealth from jewels on the hats, and the thick gold chains sprawling over a dozen broad chests,

fat as pouter pigeons. I recognise half a dozen of them. My sister
Katherine's sickly husband is missing, but his father, William
Herbert, is here, his brother-in-law, William Parr Marquess of
Northampton, is standing beside him. Francis Hastings and
Henry FitzAlan are talking together in a huddle but fall silent
when they see us. We walk into the sudden hush of the room
and my father-in-law, John Dudley, nods at Mary as if to thank
her for a service, and then, one after another, they all pull their
hats from their heads and stand in silence. I look around, half-
expecting that the king has come in behind me, or perhaps
Princess Mary. But then John Dudley himself, the Duke of
Northumberland, greatest man in the council, sweeps off his
pearl-encrusted hat and bows very low to me. 'The king is dead,'
he says. 'God save his immortal soul. He named you as his heir.
You are queen, God bless and keep Your Majesty.'

I look at him blank-faced, and I think, stupidly, that this must
all be a dream: the evening sail on the river, the silent house at
the end of the long journey, the cold hearth, and now these great
men looking at me as if I should know what to do, while they pin
a treasonous title on me.

'What?' is all I say. 'What?'

'You are queen,' John Dudley repeats. He looks around the
room. 'God save the queen!'

'God save the queen!' they all bellow, their mouths wide open,
their faces suddenly flushed, as if shouting all together can make
a thing true.

'What?' I say again. I think I will wake up in a moment and
this will seem ridiculous. I will be in my bed at Chelsea. Perhaps
I will tell Guildford of my terrible dream and he will laugh.

'Fetch my wife,' John Dudley says quietly to the man at the door,
and we wait in awkward silence. Nobody meets my gaze but everyone is looking at me. I keep thinking: what do they want me to do? I
say a little prayer: 'Holy Father, tell me what to do. Send me a sign.'
Then my mother-in-law, Lady Dudley, comes in and my mother
is with her. This should comfort me but seeing those two rivalrous
enemies united in a sudden determination frightens me worse than

before. Elizabeth Parr comes in too and stands beside her husband the Marquess of Northampton, and her face is bright and hard.

My mother takes my cold hands in an unkind grip. 'Jane, the king my cousin is dead,' she says loudly, as if announcing her royal blood to the room.

'Edward dead?'

'Yes, and he named you as the new queen.' She can't stop herself from adding: 'Through my right.'

'Poor Edward! Oh! Edward!' I say. 'Was it peaceful for him at the end? Was it his illness? Did he have a preacher with him?'

'Doesn't matter,' my mother-in-law says, wasting no time on the soul of my cousin. 'He named you as queen.'

I look into her determined face. 'I can't be,' I say simply.

'You are,' my mother repeats. 'At the end, he named our line. You inherit through me.'

'But what about Princess Mary?'

'She was named as a bastard by her own father in his will, and besides, we will never accept a papist queen,' Lady Dudley interrupts. 'Never.'

'Princess Elizabeth?' I whisper.

This time, neither of them troubles to reply. I don't even name Mary Queen of Scots, though her claim is as good as ours.

'I can't do it,' I whisper to Lady Dudley, and I look askance at the room filled with men. 'I really can't.'

'You have to.'

One by one the councillors drop to their knees till they are all at the height of my shoulders and I feel as if I am besieged by determined gnomes, no taller than my little sister.

'Don't!' I say miserably. 'My lords, I beg you, don't.' I can feel the tears running down my face, for my poor cousin, dead so young, and for me, alone in this terrible room with these terrifying men on their knees, and these women who will not help me. 'Don't, I can't do it.'

As if I have said nothing, as if they are deaf to a refusal, they crowd closer on their knees. It is nightmarish. They rise; they come one after another to bow low and kiss my hand. I would pull my hands away but my mother supports me with an arm around my back, and a grip on my armpit. Lady Dudley holds my hand outstretched so that these great strange men can press their fleshy lips on my clenched fist. I am choking on my sobs, the tears pouring down my face, but no-one remarks on it. 'I can't,' I wail. 'It is Princess Mary who must inherit. Not me.'

I twist in their hold. I think they will drag me to the scaffold. I defied my cousin Mary once when I insulted her faith. I dare not do it again. To claim the throne is an act of treason, punishable by death. I dare not do it. I will not do it.

The doors of the great hall open and my father and Guildford come in together. 'Father!' I cry out as if to my saviour. 'Tell them that I cannot be queen!'

He comes to my side and I feel the intense relief of a rescued child. I think that he will save me from this misery, and tell them all that it cannot be. But he too bows low to me, as he has never done before, and then he says in his sternest voice: 'Jane, you were named queen by our late beloved king. It was his right to name you, it is your duty to accept the inheritance he has given you. It is your God-given duty.'

I give a little scream, 'No! No! No, Father! No!'

My mother tightens her grip on my shoulders and gives me a little shake. 'Be quiet,' she snaps in an undertone. 'You were born for this. You should be glad.'

'How can I?' I choke on my sobs. 'I can't! I can't!'

Wildly, I look around the stern faces for anyone who might understand and take my part. Guildford comes close to me and takes my hand. 'Be brave,' he says. 'This is a great opportunity for us. This is wonderful. I am so proud of you.'

I look at him blankly, as if he were speaking Russian. What does he mean? What is he saying? He gives his pretty-child smile and then releases me and moves towards his mother. No-one cares that I refuse, nobody hears that I will not take the throne. They will crown me with or without my consent. I am like a trapped hare with one foot in a snare. I can twist and turn, I can scream, but nothing will save me.

THE TOWER, LONDON,
JULY 1553

I wear a new gown of gold-embroidered green velvet. They must have had it made in my size in secret, waiting for this day. When they lace the bodice round my waist I think it is as tight as a noose around my neck. That is when I know for sure that this is no surprise bequest from a dying cousin, the act of a moment; this is a plan that has been made for some time; the dressmaker was told the measure of my waist many months ago. My father-in-law, John Dudley, the leader of the council, will have directed this gowning, this crowning, my father agreed to it, and all the lords of the council swore to it, and then my poor weary cousin Edward made it his own and commanded them to turn against his half-sister Mary, the rightful heir.

My mother consented to be passed over in my favour. She will have wrestled with her pride for weeks. All of them have had months to still their consciences – if they ever had any. But I have to take my fears to God and wrestle with my God-given duty in just a few days, and now I have to put on my new gold-embroidered green gown, get into the royal barge, sit on the throne under the golden canopy, and be rowed with the royal pennants flying, to the Tower, to prepare for my coronation.

I have only ever been in the royal barge as a companion to my cousin, but now I sit on the central throne, and feel how the cold wind comes off the river to this exposed seat. When we come alongside the quay there are hundreds of people, all along the riverbank and inside the Tower, staring at me, and I feel ashamed to be stepping from the barge and going to the Lions' Gate under borrowed colours. I am surprised how glad I am to have Guildford at my side to accompany me in my lonely terror. He takes my hand to walk with me, and then steps back to let me go before him, as prettily as if we were dancing at our wedding. I am glad of the canopy over my head, as if it will shield me from the sight of God as I walk towards treason. My mother, walking behind me, holds my train, pulling at it left and right, like a ploughman steering a reluctant horse, slapping the reins to force it to harrow the heavy earth.

As we go into the shelter of the Tower I see that there are more crowds of people waiting to greet me. Crowded among the group of ladies is my sister Katherine. Her bewildered gaze meets mine.

'Oh, Jane,' she says.

'You call her "Your Majesty",' my mother snaps, and she flips the train of my gown as if she is throwing the reins.

Katherine bows her golden head in obedience but looks up at me, her blue eyes astounded, as I walk by. She falls into step behind me, her pale-faced husband tagging along with her. We go to the royal chambers, and I flush with embarrassment as we thrust ourselves rudely into Edward's private rooms, into the royal chapel, into the royal bedchamber. I can't see how I can be here, I certainly shall not sleep here – how could I sleep in the king's bed! Everything that belonged to him has been hastily stripped out and the floor swept, and fresh rushes put down, as if he had been dead for months and not for four days. But even so, I feel as if he might walk in at any moment and I will be shamed to be caught posing in his chair.

But these are no longer Edward's rooms, his private rooms; they have to be mine, and as we stand there, awkwardly displaced, the door bangs open and the grooms of the royal wardrobe heave in a cavalcade of great chests of gowns and jewels from the wardrobe and treasury. All the beautiful gowns worn by Kateryn Parr are here. I remember her in them. The capes that belonged to Anne of Cleves, the Seymour pearls, the French hoods of Anne Boleyn, the Spanish gold work of the very first queen, dead before I was born. The only gowns that fit me are the pretty little ones that belonged to Katherine Howard, beheaded for treason when she was only a few years older than me, forced into marriage like me, named as a queen before she had learned to be a woman grown.

'Beautiful shoes,' Guildford says, showing me the embroidery and the diamonds on the toes.

'I won't wear a dead girl's shoes,' I say with a shudder.

'Then cut the diamonds off and give them to me,' Guildford laughs. He is plunging into the chests like a puppy dragging out toys. His mother smiles indulgently as he balances a jewelled hat on his fair head and swings a velvet cape around his shoulders.

Katherine looks at me, her blue eyes wide. 'Are you all right?' she asks me.

'Leave them alone,' I say irritably to Guildford. 'I'm not going to wear old furs and jewels.'

'Why not?' he demands. 'They're the royal goods. Why wouldn't we look our best? Who has a better right than us?'

I turn to Katherine. 'I think I'm all right,' I say unsteadily. 'You?'

'They say I'm your heir,' she says feebly. 'They say I am the next queen after you.'

I can't help it, I let out a little scream of laughter. 'You are to take the throne if I am dead?' I demand.

Her face is like a doll's, frozen and pretty, blank without thought. 'I hope not,' she says feebly. 'For both of us.'

Her hand goes to the pocket of her cape.

'Have you got Ribbon the kitten in there?' I ask.

She shakes her head. 'I'm not allowed.'

William Paulet the ancient Marquess of Winchester steps forward with a leather box edged with gold at the corners and fastened with a gold hasp. I look at him as if he is bringing me an asp.

'I thought you should try the crown,' he says with a toothless grin. 'Try it!'

'I don't want it!' I exclaim with sudden revulsion. It is Edward's crown; there is not a doubt in my mind that it should be Princess Mary who wears it next. 'I don't want it!'

'I'll wear it,' Guildford says suddenly. 'Give it to me. I'll try it.'

'We'll get another size for you,' the marquess says, smiling at my husband. 'This is too small for you. This was worn by Anne Boleyn at her coronation.'

How can such a thing be other than cursed? The last queen to wear it was dead within three years of their slapping it on her head. I take Guildford by the arm and pull him away from the open box and the golden crown, heavy with jewels. 'You cannot be crowned king,' I say quietly to him. 'Only if parliament asks it, and I endow you with it. You are not named as Edward's heir. I am. If I am to be the queen you have to be my husband, not a king.'

'Guildford is king consort,' his mother interrupts me, coming behind us. 'He'll be crowned king at your side.'

'No.' I feel, wildly, that this is worse than my usurpation. I, at least, am Tudor. I, at least, am in line. My line at least was named in King Henry's will. But Guildford is the grandson of a tax collector executed for treason. He cannot take the throne, the idea is ridiculous. It is to insult the royal line. 'My cousin the king nominated me, through my mother. If you crown Guildford it is obvious that we are not acting as the royal line, but from sinful ambition. My cousin was ordained by God in his king-ship. I inherit from him. I am a Tudor and a queen. Guildford is nothing more than a Dudley.'

'You will find the Dudleys are the greatest family in the land! You will learn that my husband is the kingmaker!' his mother rounds on me fiercely. 'We have made you queen, and we will make our Guildford king.'

'Not so! I passed over my inheritance to Jane!' My mother raises her voice and comes swiftly to my side. 'It is Jane who is to take the throne. Not your son.'

'Now look what you've started!' Guildford whispers furiously to me. 'You're such a fool! I am your husband! Why wouldn't you crown me? I am your master, you have sworn to obey me, how can I be anything less than a king when you are queen? And now look! You have upset my mother.'

'I can't help that! I have prayed on this, Guildford. God has called me to this great place. I don't want it, but I can see that

He has called me to test my faith. But He has not called you. He did not call you. You are not the heir: I am.'

White with rage, he cannot find the words to answer me. 'Disobedient wife!' he spits at me. 'Unnatural! That is treason alone! Never mind the rest of it!'

'Don't say that word!' his mother hisses at him as he turns on his heel and flings himself from the room. She gives me a furious look and rushes after him. I am left trembling with temper and distress, the open box with Anne Boleyn's crown on the table before me and my sister, wide-eyed, staring at me.

The Marquess of Winchester, who started all this with his foolish promise of a crown for Guildford, turns to my uncle Henry FitzAlan the Earl of Arundel, and William Herbert, Katherine's father-in-law, raising his eyebrows as if to ask how the country is to be ruled by a warring family. 'I thought all this had been agreed?' he asks slyly.

'It is agreed,' Katherine's father-in-law says swiftly. He, for one, wants no difficulties, this is his plot too. His son, at his side, nods as if he knows anything about it.

'It was not agreed by me,' I say. I suddenly feel the hand of God spread over me, I suddenly know my own mind. I am not a fool and I know the right thing to do here. I am no longer drowning in fear; I can see my way. 'I will accept the crown, since it is God's will that I should, since I can do God's work. But there is no such destiny for Guildford. It is I who inherit the crown from King Edward, God bless him, and Guildford, my husband, takes the throne at my side.'

I sense, rather than see, that my sister Katherine has drawn a little closer, as if to say that she is here as my heir, that we are the girls of royal blood who are named to inherit. We are not fools or pawns. My husband will not be crowned king, her husband will not be crowned king.

'But he has to have a title,' Katherine's father-in-law remarks thoughtfully. 'A royal title. After all . . .'

He does not finish, but we all know that he might say – after all, the Duke of Northumberland would hardly do all this just to put Henry Grey's daughter on the throne. Who cares for me, after all? How would my accession benefit the Dudleys? Guildford must get a title from this day's work, at least; his family will want their fee. *Thou shalt not muzzle the mouth of the ox that treadeth out the corn*, and the Dudleys are greedy bullocks.

'I shall make him a duke,' I offer. That's a royal title. He shall be Duke of Clarence.'

The last Duke of Clarence was drowned in a vat of malmsey in this very place, for his overweening ambition. I don't care if they make the comparison.

I sleep with Katherine my sister in the royal bed, one of my ladies on a truckle bed on the floor beside us, the silky sheets warmed for me with a golden pan, the mattress stabbed in case of a hidden killer. Guildford does not come to me and in the morning my stomach pain is worse and I wake to find that my course has come and I am bleeding.

Katherine leaps out of bed and strips back the covers. 'How disgusting!' she says. 'Why would you do this? Didn't you know your course was coming?'

'No,' I say. 'It doesn't always come at the same time. How would I know it would come now?'

'You couldn't have chosen a worse time or place.'

'I hardly chose it!' Of course, this has never happened before in the king's rooms: there has never been a queen in these rooms, in this bed. All the queens live in the queen's apartments. Katherine and I have to bundle the soiled sheets out to the laundry, and the groom of the linen looks disgusted. I am so terribly shamed. We have to send for clean petticoats and a bowl for me to wash and they bring jugs of hot water and scented towels and I feel so disgraced that when I finally get to chapel I put my face in my hands and pray to God that I bleed to death and am released from this terrible duty.

As soon as I get to the presence chamber and seat myself on the throne I receive a message from my mother-in-law. One of her ladies comes in and curtseys low, a royal curtsey, rises up and tells me that Her Grace the Duchess of Northumberland will not be attending court this morning, and that she and her son Lord Guildford are retiring to their house at Syon.

'Because I will not make him king?' I ask bluntly.

The woman blinks at my frankness. 'My Lord Guildford says that it is not enough to be a duke, and if he is not a king then, clearly, he cannot be married to the queen.'

'He is leaving me?' I ask incredulously.

She blushes at the terrible snub. She drops into a curtsey again and stays down, her eyes on the floor.

I feel again the furious determination that I now recognise is God working through me. He gives me strength. He gives me clarity. I turn to my uncle Henry FitzAlan the Earl of Arundel, standing at my side. 'Please go to my lord husband and tell him that his queen commands that he stays at court,' I say through gritted teeth. 'And tell Her Grace his mother that I expect her here also. Neither of them may leave without permission. They know that.'

He bows to me and leaves the room. I look around at the other lords; some of them are hiding their smiles. I know that I will be shamed by my blood leaking out and staining my gown if I don't get away to the garderobe at once. I look at Katherine for help and she looks back at me blankly. She has no idea what to do. 'I am unwell,' I say. 'I am going to my privy rooms.'

They all drop to their knees and I walk past them, my ladies following. I can barely stand with the pain in my belly, and I walk with a stupid sort of sideways sidle, trying not to let the blood leak out; but I force myself to get to the royal chambers and I don't cry from pain and fury till the door is shut and I am alone.

I have never bled so heavily, I have never felt so sick. 'I am being poisoned,' I whisper to my maid as she takes away the bloody napkins and the rust-coloured water. 'There is something terribly wrong.'

She looks at me, her mouth agape. She does not know what to do. Overnight she finds herself in service to the Queen of England, and now I tell her that I am being murdered. Nobody knows what to do.

THE TOWER,
LONDON, JULY 1553

It gets worse rather than better. My brother-in-law the sinfully handsome Robert Dudley has failed to arrest Princess Mary – or Lady Mary, as we now all have to call her. He is riding around Norfolk on a string of handsome horses making sure that no-one goes to help her; but he has not taken her into his keeping.

Half the lords tell me that she is certain to flee to Spain and this must be prevented at all costs for she will bring a papist army down on us, to the destruction of ourselves and the damnation of all of England. The other half say that she must be allowed to leave, so that she is exiled forever and there is no-one to lead a rebellion against me. But instead of either of these, she does the one thing that is the very worst for us, the one thing that nobody predicted a woman could do: she raises her standard at her great house at Kenninghall, and writes to my council and tells them that she is the true queen and that they will be pardoned for their treason if they admit her to London and the throne at once.

This is the worst thing for the righteous cause of reform. I know that God does not want her to take the throne, and that all her promises of allowing all faiths, and not forcing her heresy on the good Christians of England who have so recently seen the light, are part of the devil's work to undo all that

Kateryn Parr believed, that Edward achieved, and that I have sworn to continue. Princess Mary cannot take the country back to Rome and destroy our chance of creating a kingdom of saints. I am bound by God to oppose her, and I insist that someone muster an army and go and capture her. If she has to be imprisoned in the Tower for treason, so be it. She has had every opportunity to get a better understanding of the Word of God, she studied with Kateryn Parr just as I did, but she persisted in error. If we capture her and the council insists that she has to die for treason against the throne, against me, then so be it. I will find the courage to send her, and all heretics, to the scaffold. I will not be a weak link in the mighty army of God. I am called, I am chosen, I will suffer affliction as a good soldier of Jesus Christ, I will not be called and found wanting.

I spend hours on my knees in my rooms and my sister Katherine kneels beside me as I pray for guidance, my sister Mary beside her. Katherine is not at one with the saints. I can see that she is dozing and I dig her in the ribs with my elbow and she starts and says 'Amen'. It does not matter. I must be staunch and true. Katherine is my companion and my sister. She can sleep, just like Saint Peter slept while Jesus was in an agony of spirit, even so I will take step after step towards a holy crown of sainthood.

In response to Princess Mary's claim to be the true heir, the council proclaims me as queen and all the lord lieutenants are sent to their counties to make sure that everyone knows that the king is dead and I am his named heir. Proclamations are pasted all over London, preachers make the announcement from their pulpits.

'Does anyone object?' I ask my father nervously.

'No, no, not a word,' he reassures me. 'Nobody wants the Spanish brought down on us, nobody wants to return to the rule of the Pope.'

'Princess Mary must surely have some supporters in the country,' I say anxiously.

'Lady Mary,' he corrects me. 'You would think so – but

no-one has stood up for her, whatever they think privately. Of course, the country must be riddled with papists, but they are not declaring for her. John Dudley has ruled the roost for so long, he prepared for this. As long as the Spanish don't try to meddle.'

'We must muster an army.' I have no idea how an army is mustered.

'We are doing so,' he says. 'I shall lead them.'

'No,' I say suddenly. 'Truly, Father, I can't do this without you. Don't leave me with the Dudleys, not with Guildford and his terrible mother and father. Don't leave me here with only Mother and the girls and no-one to speak for me in the council. Mother says nothing against Lady Dudley, and Katherine is worse than nobody, Mary is too little. I have to have someone here.'

He hesitates. 'I know that your mother would rather that I did not ride against her cousin Princess Mary. And I am not a military man ...'

'John Dudley must go!' I exclaim. 'It's all his idea. It's his plan. And besides, he put down the Kett rebellion only four years ago. He should be the one to go.'

'Don't get upset,' my father says, a wary eye on the flush of colour in my face, and my raised voice. He looks over towards my ladies and gives my mother a nod as if she must come and calm me.

'I am not upset,' I say quickly. I have to reassure everyone, all the time. 'I just need my family around me. Guildford has his: his brothers work for him, his mother is here, his father has done all this for him. Why should the court be filled with Dudleys, and you be sent away when I have only Katherine and Mary and Mother here?'

'I'll stay, don't fret. God is with us and you will be queen. John Dudley's force will take the princess, even if she gets to Framlingham Castle and raises her royal standard there.'

'Lady,' I remind him. 'Lady Mary. And it's not her royal standard. It's mine.'

John Dudley holds a great farewell dinner before he leaves London, a strange combination of sinful boasting and sinful fear. His speech is not heroic. I have read enough history to know that a man about to march out to defend his faith and his queen should sound martial. Instead of declaring the justness of his cause and the certainty of his victory, he warns everyone that he is risking his life and reputation, he conveys a real anxiety instead of false confidence.

Guildford and I are seated side by side, looking over the hall, the cloth of estate over my chair, not his, my seat raised higher than his, as his father threatens the council that he will betray them if they betray him. This is not the sort of speech that Caesar makes before he marches out to general acclaim, and so I tell Guildford.

'These are hardly loyal Roman tribunes,' he replies scathingly. 'Not a single one of them is trustworthy. Any one of them would turn their collar if they thought they were on the losing side.'

I am about to explain why he is wrong when his father suddenly turns towards us, makes one of his grand oratorical gestures and speaks of me. He tells them that I am queen of their enticement, forcibly placed on the throne rather than by my own request. Guildford and I blink at one another like a pair of owlets in a nest. What about my God-given destiny? What about my cousin's right to will his throne to me? What about my mother's legitimate claim enshrined in the will of Good King Henry, handed over to me? Guildford's father makes my coming to the throne sound like a plot, rather than an act of God; and if it is a plot then it is treason.

John Dudley marches north-east to Suffolk, and those of us left in London embark on the business of government, but it feels like masquing rather than ruling until we know that Lady Mary is captured. Guildford does not dispute his name or title but dines every day on his own, in state, enthroned like a king under a cloth of gold canopy, with fifty dishes coming out to him, to be distributed among the huge court he has invited to give the impression of greatness. Sometimes I feel, madly, that he is usurping my usurpation, a plot inside a plot, a sin upon a sin. He and his court of knaves drink to excess, and are rowdy. I can hear the yelling and the singing while I am dining with my ladies in my rooms. This would be bad enough, since gluttony is a hidden danger to salvation, but worse than this is that Guildford gets news of his father and his brother before the news is reported to me.

It is his brother Lord Robert who is raising troops against Lady Mary in Norfolk; it is his father, John Dudley, who is marching on her from London to Framlingham. Naturally enough Guildford's court is where the men go and ask for news, mine is a court of ladies and we are easily excluded. It is not that the messages do not come to me; they do come, everyone knows they must report to the monarch. But first they stop to tell the men. Of course, a queen's court is bound to be the resort of ladies, but how am I to be a ruling queen if I am not at the centre of the councils of men?

This is a puzzle for me that I had not foreseen. I thought that once I forced myself to accept the crown of the King of England then I would have the power of the King of England. Now I understand that taking power as a queen is a different thing. Men have sworn their fealty on their bended knees; but they do not enact manly loyalty to a woman, and – truth be told – I am very small and slight, and even with God at my back I am not imposing.

And these men are faithless. The very night after John Dudley marches out, I hear that William Paulet the Marquess of Winchester, who was so foolishly quick to offer Guildford the crown, has taken himself off to his own London home without permission, and Katherine's father-in-law William Herbert tries to leave as well. I will not accept this disloyalty against the will of God, and I send at once for the marquess and tell him to come back to his post.

I call the Privy Council together and I tell them that I am locking the gates of the Tower every evening at dusk and I expect every lord of the council to be inside. I expect all the ladies to attend me, my sisters too, my mother and my mother-in-law, my husband as well. They have put me on the throne in the Tower, and beside the throne and inside the Tower they will have to stay with me. Only if we stand together, with the saints in heaven, will we triumph, as John Dudley marches towards Lady Mary like the devil claiming his own.

William Herbert slinks back into my presence chamber, before midnight. I stay up late, my mother and my mother-in-law Lady Dudley with me. Even Guildford is with us, sober for once. Herbert's son, still pale and sickly, comes in the room behind him, Katherine my sister half a step behind her young husband.

'You have to stay here, my lord,' I say abruptly. 'We need you here in case there is news. We may need to call a council at any time.'

He bows to me but he says nothing. He has no defence.

'And I expect my sister's companionship,' I say. 'You may not take her away without my permission.'

I cannot stop myself glancing at my mother to see if she agrees with me. She nods; even Lady Dudley makes a little gesture of agreement. Everyone knows that we have to stick together.

'Nobody may leave,' Guildford says as if I have not already made that clear. 'It is my father's wish.'

We have to work together, we cannot appear disunited. We are the soldiers of God – we have to march in step – so the council meet, and we all agree that they shall write to Lord Richard Rich, who swore for me, but has now vanished, and remind him that he must stay loyal. The counties of Norfolk are wavering, the East is becoming uncertain. They are afraid that the sailors on ships in port will declare for Mary. They hold the meeting, they send the letter, but later in the morning Katherine comes to my rooms and pulls at my sleeve while I am writing, making me blot the paper.

'Look what you made me do! What is it?' I ask her.

'We're leaving,' she says in a tiny whisper. 'I have to go right now. My father-in-law says so.' She shows me her pet monkey in the crook of her arm. 'I have to put Mr Nozzle in his cage. He has to come, too.'

'You can't go. I told him, I told them all. You were there, you heard it. You all have to stay.'

'I know you told them,' she says. 'That is why I have come to you, now.'

I look at her. For the first time in our lives I look at her and see her not as a slightly irritating younger sister, part of the familiar landscape of Bradgate, like a pale rose in the garden that I pass every day, but a real girl, real as me, a young woman, suffering as I am suffering. I look at her white face and her dark emotional eyes and the strain that she is showing, and I feel no sympathy but much irritation.

'What's the matter with you? Why are you looking like a wet May Day?'

'They're all coming with us,' she says miserably. 'Lots of them, anyway. Your council – the Privy Council – they're coming with us to Baynard's Castle. They have agreed with my father-in-law, William Herbert, to meet there. They are leaving you, and going with him. I am sorry, Jane. I can't stop them ...' She trails off with a little shrug. Obviously, she can't stop the lords of the land doing as they think fit. 'I did say that they should not ...' she begins feebly.

'But I commanded them to stay here! What do they think they are going to do at your house?'

'I am afraid that they're going to proclaim Lady Mary.'

I just look at her, aghast. 'What?'

She looks back at me. 'I have to go, too,' she says.

Obviously, she has to obey her young husband and his all-powerful father.

'You can't.'

'Can we ask someone?'

She is so ridiculous. 'Ask who? Ask them what?'

'What we should do? Could we send a message and ask Roger Ascham?'

'The scholar? What do you think he could do? Now that my Privy Council is running away with your father-in-law, and proclaiming a papist as queen?'

'I don't know,' she snivels.

Of course she doesn't. She never knows anything.

'Father has to tell them,' she says in a whisper. 'The Privy Council. Father must tell them not to come to Baynard's Castle and turn against you. I can't.'

'Well, tell him to tell them! Fetch him here now!'

'He won't. I already asked. Our lady mother won't.'

We are silent for a moment, more like sisters than we have ever been before, united in apprehension as it dawns on me that the right thing does not always happen, that the saints do not always march unstoppably to heaven, that the godly do not necessarily triumph, that the two of us have no more authority than little Mary. The monkey, Mr Nozzle, pulls her handkerchief from her pocket and presses it into her hand.

'What about me?' I ask.

I see for the first time that there are tears in her eyes. 'I don't suppose you could come, too?' she says. 'Come to Baynard's Castle with everybody?' She gives a gulp. 'Say you're sorry to Lady Mary? That it was a mistake? Come with me?'

'Don't be stupid,' I say harshly.

'If you and I were to say it was all a mistake? If I were to back you up and say you didn't mean it? That they made you?'

I see her tighten her hold on the jacket of her pet monkey as if he might give witness, too.

'Impossible.'

She shakes her head. 'I didn't think you could,' she says, and hands me her damp handkerchief and goes without another word from the room.

I look around me. Now I see that some of my ladies are missing and now I realise they have been absent since prayers this morning. My rooms are thinning out; people are deserting me.

'You are none of you to leave here,' I say harshly, and the heads bob up, as if they are all planning to run away from the Tower as soon as I am out of the room. This is infidelity, this is false faith. I think that women are especially inclined to dishonour. I hate them for it, but I can do nothing against them now. I cannot imagine how they can live with themselves, how they can pray. God will repay them for infidelity to me, His daughter. The mills of God grind slow; but they grind exceeding fine, as these great ladies and their dishonest husbands will learn.

We process to dinner as usual. Guildford sits beside me on a lower chair, the golden cloth of estate extending over me. I look around the hall – there is no buzz of conversation, nobody seems to have any appetite. I could almost shrug. They all wanted this – why would they regret their own actions? Surely they know that this world is a vale of tears and we are all miserable sinners?

The great door at the end of the hall opens, and my father comes in, walking stiffly as if his knees are sore. I look up but he does not smile at me. He moves towards me, the conversations die away and the room falls silent as he comes on.

He stands before me, his mouth working, but still he says nothing. I have never seen him like this before, I have a cold sense of dread that something terrible is about to happen. 'Father?' I ask. Then suddenly, he reaches up and gets hold of a corner of the cloth of estate and tugs so hard at it that the posts that hold it steady over my chair fall sideways like cut timber, with a clatter, and the awning rips.

'Father!' I exclaim, and he rounds on me.

'This place does not belong to you. You must submit to fortune,' he says suddenly.

'What?'

'You must put off your royal robes and be content to live a private life.'

'What?' I say again, but I am playing for time now. I guess that we have lost, and he has chosen this strange behaviour – more like a masque than a father speaking to his beloved daughter – so that it can be reported that he took down the cloth of estate with his own hands. Or perhaps words fail him; they don't fail me; they never fail me. 'I much more willingly put them off than I put them on,' I say. 'Out of obedience to you and my mother I have grievously sinned.'

He looks stunned. As if the flapping awning had spoken, or that block Guildford, who gawps at my side.

'You must relinquish the crown,' my father says again, as if I am arguing for keeping it, and he goes from the room before I can reply. He does not bow.

I rise from the throne and walk away from the tattered canopy. I go to my private rooms and my ladies follow. I see that one of them pauses to speak to my father's servant.

'We will pray,' I say as soon as the door is closed.

'I beg your pardon,' the woman says from the back. 'But your father sent a message to say that we can leave now. May I pack my things and go to my home?'

In the quietness of the deserted rooms I can hear the cheering from outside the Tower gates. The fathers of the city have commanded that there shall be red wine flowing in the fountains and every fool and knave is getting drunk and shouting, 'God save the queen.' I go and look for my father. He will know what I should do. Perhaps he will take me home to Bradgate.

At first I cannot find him. He is not in the throne room, nor in the royal rooms behind the throne room. Not in the presence chamber, nor in the private rooms. He is not in Guildford's quarters, which are quiet for once. Even Guildford is subdued, playing cards with only half a dozen cronies. They rise to their feet when they see me and I ask Guildford if he has seen my father and he says 'no'.

I don't stop to ask why he is so pale and strained, why his rowdy companions are so unusually quiet. I want to find my father. He is not in the White Tower, and so I go outside and run across the green to the chapel of Saint Peter in case he is praying alone before the small silent altar; but he is not there either. It takes me a long time to walk to the stables and just as I enter I hear the bells of St Paul's pealing over and over again, a jangle of noise, not the hour, not the chimes of the hour, just a full peal over and over, and then all the other bells join in, a cacophony as if all the bells of London are ringing at once. Beyond the walls of the Tower I can hear people shouting and cheering. The ravens burst from the trees of the Tower gardens and from their hidden perches all over the Tower and swirl up at the noise like a dark cloud, a foreboding thundercloud, and I clap my hands over my ears to block out the noise of the cease-less shouting bells and my sudden fear of the cawing birds. I hear myself say irritably: 'I have no idea what this noise is for!' But I do know.

I run into the stable yard like a poor girl, my hands to my head, my skirts muddy, and find my father is on the mounting block, hauling himself into the saddle. I go to the horse and put my hand on his rein.

'What is happening, Father?' I have to yell over the noise of the bells. The gate to the stable bangs open as half a dozen lads abruptly run out, leaving it unfastened. 'What in the name of God is happening now?'

'We've lost,' he says, leaning low down from the saddle to put his hand on my head, as if he is blessing me in farewell. 'Poor child. It was a great venture; but we've lost.'

Still, I don't understand him. I think that I don't understand anything. I can't hear. That is the trouble: that I can't hear what he is saying. The bells are so loud, the ravens so noisy, I must have misheard him.

'What have we lost? I knew we were withdrawing. I knew she was defending Framlingham. Has there been a battle? Was John Dudley's troop defeated?'

'No battle. She won without a sword unsheathed. London has proclaimed Mary,' he says. 'Despite everything I have done for you. That's why they're ringing the bells.'

I drop my hand from the rein and stagger back from the big horse and my father immediately takes it as his signal to go. Without another word he spurs his horse towards the open stable-yard gate. I run after him.

'But what are you doing?' I shriek up at him. 'Father! Where are you going?'

'I'm only one man,' he says, as if that explains everything.

'Where are you going?'

'I'm going to proclaim Mary as queen, and then I will go and beg her pardon.'

I am running beside his horse as he rides to the gateway, but I can't keep up. I am falling behind. The gate is thrown open and I can see, outside, people dancing in the street and embracing each other, throwing coins in the air, people hanging out of the windows to shout the news down to those in the street, and all the time the terrible racket of the bells of hundreds of churches all clanging and clattering all over London at once.

'Father, stop! Wait for me! What am I to do?'

'I will save you,' he promises me, and then he spurs his horse on and canters through the open gate and gets through the crowd before anyone can recognise him as the father of the girl who was queen for less than two weeks.

I stand like a fool looking after him. He will save me: that must comfort me. He has ridden out to save me. We have suffered a great reverse but my father has gone to make it right again. I must wait here and he will come back and tell me what I must do now. Whatever we were doing here – and now it seems to me like a dream when you wake and almost laugh, and take the nightmare to God in prayer for it was so strange and wild – whatever we were doing here, it is over. Or at any rate, I suppose it is over. Unless it is a temporary reverse and we will be restored.

My father will save me as he has promised to do. John Dudley will have a plan. I had better get back to my rooms and make sure that no-one else leaves. We don't want to look disorderly. We don't want to be Laodiceans, a people condemned for indifference as neither hot nor cold; we don't want to shame Our Lord in the sight of His enemies. I had better look as if I am as sure of my father on earth as I am of my Father in heaven.

I begin to think that it is as if they made me queen for a day like a Lord of Misrule, a fool in a paper crown, while I really thought that I was the true queen, and my tinsel sceptre was heavy and my duties great. I begin to think that I have been capering. I am afraid that people have been laughing at me.

I will die of embarrassment if this is the case, I can bear to be anything but ridiculous, and so I must stay in my rooms and order my ladies to stay with me, and Guildford's court to stay with him. The cloth of estate was thrown down by my own father and I don't tell anyone to put it up again. The throne is taken away without a word being spoken, the great seal of office is missing somewhere, the keys of the Tower are gone from the hook, and my rooms are empty.

And now I find I was far too slow to keep my ladies with me. It is like the end of summer when one moment at Bradgate I notice that the swallows are circling the turrets faster and faster, and then suddenly there are none, and I don't even know the day when they left. Just like the swallows, my ladies are vanished from my rooms. I did not know that they would go; I did not see them leave. Even my mother is missing, disappeared like a dark-backed swift. She went without telling me, taking Mary with her. I think worse of her than I do of Katherine, for at least that bruised reed came to me to say that she would have to leave. The only women left in the Tower are some lowly wives, the servants, the wife of the constable of the Tower who lives here, and my mother-in-law, Lady Dudley. Abandoned here, she looks ghastly, like a whale marooned on a cold beach, accidentally aground. She sits on her stool, her hands empty, no Bible to read, no shirts to sew, an idle woman with her plans in wreckage around her.

'Have you heard from your husband?' I demand.

'He has surrendered,' she chokes, her voice thick with grief. 'At Cambridge. Surrendered to those who were proud to call him their lord only the day before.'

I nod rapidly, as if this makes any sense to me, as if I am hearing her, but this is far beyond my understanding. I have never read anything to prepare me for a reverse like this. I don't think there has ever been a reverse like this, not in any history that I have studied. A complete defeat without a battle? No defence at all? A great army mustered and marched out, but then turned around to go quietly away? It is more like a fairy tale than a history.

'Well, I shall go home,' I decide. I sound determined, but secretly I am hoping she will order me to her house in London, or command me to wait here for my father to rescue me.

She shakes her head. 'You can't. They've closed the gates on the Tower,' she says. 'D'you think I would be here with you if I could leave? You were a queen; but now you are a prisoner. You bolted the gates to keep your people in; now they are bolted to keep you in. You will never see your home again. God grant that I do.'

'I shall be the judge of that!' I snap; and I turn and go out of the room to Guildford's great chamber.

It is all but empty. I pause in the doorway as a wave of nausea overcomes me at the smell of old roast meats. A few men gather at the fireplace at the far end. A few servants collect goblets and some dirty plates. Guildford is alone, sitting on his great chair, the posts for his vainglorious cloth of estate leaning drunkenly to one side and another. He is like a jester playing at being a king, but with no court.

'Everyone's gone,' I tell him as he stands and bows to me.

'Are we to go?' he asks. 'Does my mother say we can go home now?'

'She says they have bolted the gates to keep us in, and they have arrested your father.'

He looks aghast. 'I should have warned him,' he says. 'I should have gone with him. If only I had ridden with him, at his side, as his son!'

'You're drunk,' I say viciously. 'And you know nothing.'

He nods, as if this is interesting information. 'You're right,' he tells me. 'Right on both points. I *am* drunk. And I know nothing.' He gives a little giggle. 'You can be very sure that half of London will be drunk tonight, and they will all know nothing. Especially, they will know nothing of us: us Dudleys.'

Guildford remains drunk for days, in his new rooms in the Beauchamp Tower where he is confined, without his court, without his friends, with only two servants to pull him out of bed in the morning and push him back into it at night. He is not allowed beyond his rooms, so I suppose he is a prisoner until Lady Mary pardons us. His mother keeps a silent vigil in my rooms. She is very poor company.

I study my books. Strangely, there is nothing for me to do. I am not allowed to leave the Tower, the gates are closed, but inside the high walls I can go where I like – across the green to the chapel, to the muniments rooms, to the gardens, to the stables. I like to walk on the ramparts between the towers overlooking the river in the evening. The cooler air settles my churning belly. I am still bleeding, I am still sick. Something is poisoning me. I don't think I will be well till my father takes me back to Bradgate. I have started to dream that I am in my bedroom at home, over-looking the lake, but then I wake and hear the noise of the city and the flat light of the morning skies and realise that I am still far from my home.

I hear a clatter from the Byward Tower gate and peer over the wall to see who is entering. They are prisoners, there is a guard around them, and there are half a dozen men. I can hear the jeers of the crowd outside the gate, silenced when the gate slams shut and the bolts are drawn. I can just see the face of the leading prisoner. Lord, it is my father-in-law, John Dudley, walking proudly with his head up and his hat in his hand, and now I recognise his sons among the disgraced party. I thank God for His grace that my father is not among them. The Dudleys have been arrested and my father is free. He will be meeting our cousin Princess Mary and explaining how it came about, apply-ing for my release. I thank God that it is the Dudleys who will be blamed for all this. It was their plan, and everyone knows it. They have been vaultingly ambitious for years, now they will be brought low, and serve them right.

The party is divided. My father-in-law goes to St Thomas's Tower over the watergate, and his sons are taken to the Beauchamp Tower to share their brother Guildford's rooms. I watch them go down the steps, bowing their heads to enter the low doorway, and I feel nothing – neither sympathy nor fear for them. There is a little struggle as John Dudley tries to force his way down the steps to be with his sons. I can see the youngest, Henry, is crying. I suppose that Guildford will be glad to be with his brothers, but he will find that being drunk and knowing nothing will not save him now that his father is arrested.

I think I had better go back to my rooms, but when I get there I find that my clothes and my books have been moved, and I am now to live in the house of Mr Nathaniel Partridge, the gentleman-gaoler of the Tower. It is a pretty house, facing inwards over the gardens, looking towards the White Tower. My rooms are a good size and comfortable. I still have three ladies-in-waiting and a manservant. It makes no difference to me, I tell Mrs Partridge, the wife of the gaoler: 'Outward show means nothing to me. While I have my books and my studies and I can pray, I need nothing else.'

She bobs a little curtsey, not the deep obeisance that she used before the Dudleys came in, under arrest. I find this very irritating, but then I remember that it is outward show, and I care nothing for it.

'Leave me,' I say quietly. 'I am going to write.'

I think I shall write my account of these days, and send it to my cousin Princess Mary. I think I should explain to her how all that has happened was not of my doing, and, if the deathbed wishes of my cousin the king are to be ignored, then I am content to become a subject once more, and for her to be the heir once more; indeed, to be crowned queen. As Tudors we have seen, God knows, enough changes. Her own mother was set aside and accused of a sham marriage, her title taken away. She herself has been Princess and then Lady Mary twice in her lifetime. Princess Mary of all people will understand that my title can be taken away as readily as it was forced on me and that my conscience is clear.

The next day, I hear a bustle under my bedroom window. By pressing my face against the cold windowpane I can just see that it is young Henry Lord Hastings, Katherine Dudley's feeble husband, and it looks as if he is leaving the Beauchamp Tower where the Dudley boys are kept. He is laughing, shaking the hand of another man who has clearly come with the warrant for his release. The constable of the Tower, Sir John Gage, stands to one side, his hat in his hand. Clearly, young Henry is once again an important man, no longer an accused traitor like his new brothers-in-law. Of course, Princess Mary is bound to be merciful to her friends, and Henry is related to her governess, Margaret Pole, who died at the very spot where they now so light-heartedly exchange compliments. Henry must be pleased to be out of the Tower, which has been such an unlucky place for his family. As I watch him leave, striding along to the main gate, I see another man is coming in.

They pass without even the smallest gesture of recognition, so I think it must be a stranger, and then I realise that of course Henry Hastings will make no gesture of recognition to anyone coming inwards. Like my husband, who said he was drunk and knows nothing, everyone will know nothing and recognise nobody in these days. Everyone who associated with the Dudleys will want to show that they know nothing and recognise nobody. Henry Hastings will be a stranger to anyone walking into the Tower: his own father is left in here, completely ignored. It is not safe to know anyone. And so it is done – Henry goes past this new arrival without another glance, just a little gesture of drawing himself away, a little turn of his head so their eyes do not meet.

Smiling at this bitter masque, I watch him go, and then I turn my attention to the newcomer. At first I don't recognise him. His head is bowed, his steps are slow, he looks like all the men who come in now: as if the breath has been knocked out of them, cut down to the height of gnomes, as they were when they all kneeled to me.

So who is this new man, shuffling into prison? Which of my many self-appointed advisors is this, forced to face the wrong that he has done? I can see only the top and the back of his head but I feel certain that I know him – something about the set of his bowed shoulders, something about the dawdling feet. I cry out. Suddenly I hammer on the thick glass of the window, hurting my palms as I slap them against the leaded panes. I scream but he cannot hear me. This broken man is the only one I can trust: 'Father! Father! My father!'

I request permission for my father to be housed in my rooms. This is foolish of me: he is not a guest in the royal palace; I am no longer a queen to allocate the rooms. I am under house arrest and he is a prisoner in the cells. I realise that everything has changed: everything. Not only can he not live with me, I am not allowed even to see him. I demand to see my mother.

'She is not even in London,' the gentleman-gaoler of the Tower, Mr Partridge, says awkwardly. 'I regret to tell you, Your ...' he stammers over my title. 'At any rate, she has gone.'

'Where is she?' I ask. 'Is she at home?'

'She is not at your home,' he says. He speaks slowly, choosing his words with care. 'She has gone to the queen to sue for pardon.'

I am so relieved I could almost weep. Of course! She will speak to her cousin to get a pardon for my father. God be praised! 'She will send for me, and for Father. We will go home to Bradgate.'

'Indeed, I hope so.'

'Where is the queen?'

He looks shifty, as if he thinks it better that I don't know. 'She is coming,' he says. 'She is on her way to London, by easy stages. Going slowly.'

'I want to see her too,' I say bravely. After all, she is my cousin. Once I was her little favourite. She knew that I was not of her faith and yet she still offered me pretty gowns. I wish now that I had been more gracious in my opposition to her wrong-thinking. But none the less, we are still kinswomen. I should speak to her. It would be better for me to explain to her directly.

I am composing a justification, but I should perhaps apologise to her in person.

He looks at the floor, at the toes of his boots; he does not raise his eyes. 'I will tell them that you request an audience with Her Majesty the Queen,' he says. 'But I am told that you are not to be released.'

'Until the queen sends for me,' I say.

'Until then.' But he does not sound as confident as I did; and I was pretending.

THE TOWER, LONDON, AUGUST 1553

I keep watch from the window, like a bereft child, but I never see my father again, though I see more men from my short-lived council coming in under arrest. Then, as the days go on, I see them, one by one, going out again. They are all released. Of course the queen is merciful. Why should she not be? She has defeated this ill-considered rebellion and won by public acclaim what she could never, as a heretic, deserve. She should thank her enemies rather than punish them, for they united the country for her. She makes them all pay huge fines – each one of them will pay her a fortune.

I think, wryly, that she has little choice but mercy – if she executed every one of her Privy Council that bent his knee to me, she would have no Privy Council at all. Every nobleman in England called for me to be queen; she has no choice but to release them. Instead of beheading them, she will raise funds, just as her father and grandfather used to do: fine them and swear them to her service with terrible penalties on their estates.

'Your father has been released,' my lady-in-waiting remarks to me after morning prayers.

'What? How do you know?'

'He left in the night, the Partridges' little maid told me.'

'He has escaped?' I stammer. I cannot understand what has happened.

'No. He was released. But he chose to go out quietly before the gates opened at dawn. The little girl thought you would want to know that he is safe. She is of the reformed religion like you. She was proud to take him his ale from the alehouse and his dinner from the pie shop. She thought it was an honour to serve a man that risked his life for the reformed faith.'

I nod like a little doll with a head that rocks when it is tapped. Nod, nod, nod. I go to the corner that I have reserved for prayer and reading my Bible. I kneel and I thank God for my father's safety, for the mercy of the queen and for the persuasiveness of that great woman my mother. She must have promised the world and hereafter to get a royal pardon for her husband. I should be very glad that she is persuasive and that she has worked for my father. My father is safe. That is the most important thing. I should be very glad. I don't let myself wonder that he did not come to see me before he left, nor why I am not released with him. I know that my parents, who have always commanded my obedience, will order me to their side as soon as they want me. I know that we will be together again. I know that we will be at my home, at Bradgate. No-one will take that from us, no-one will ban me from my little bedroom, the ornate garden, the fields, the woods, the library with the hundreds of books. Only God knows, in His mercy, how glad I shall be to get there.

The summer weather gets hotter. My room is cold and damp in the night, and stifling at two in the afternoon. I am allowed to walk in the enclosed garden before the Partridges' house or sometimes Mrs Partridge and I walk on the walls that overlook the river. At twilight there is a fresh wind from the sea. When I smell the salt on the cool air I feel suddenly uplifted as if I might soar on it like the crying seagulls. I feel as if I might spread my wings and fly with them. The city seems quiet. I am surprised. I would have thought that the godly could not have borne a papist queen, I would have thought they would have risen against her; but it seems that the combination of Princess Mary, the concealed power of Spain, and the hideous power of the Antichrist have done what my advisors swore could not be done – put a papist woman on the reformed throne of England and not a word said against her.

I spend my afternoons in study and my evenings in writing. I have no objection to the little house, to the garden below it, with the gate to the green and the White Tower dominating the site. I can live in my own world, like a monk in his cell. I am working on a new translation of the psalms, and also on my letter proclaiming my innocence to the queen. I think I must explain to her that if she has released all but my senior advisors – John Dudley and his sons – then she can release me. She has forgiven my mother, whose lineage put me on the throne, who is actually closer than I am to the Crown, she has released Lady Dudley my mother-in-law, who insisted that I should try the crown. She can release me. It is nonsensical if she does not.

'Your mother-in-law went to Queen Mary,' Katherine my sister whispers to me on one of her rare visits to bring me clean linen and physic as I still have spasms in my belly and I am still bleeding a little. Mr Nozzle the monkey balances on her shoulder, and puts his dark little face into his hands. 'Lady Dudley the duchess went to Queen Mary; but the queen would not even admit her.'

'No!' I am as diverted as a bawd on a fish quay offered a sprat of gossip. I recognise an ignoble gleam of family pride. 'No! Really! Did she know that the queen had seen our lady mother?'

'Yes, but of course our lady mother is of the royal family and a favourite of our cousin the queen. Are the Dudleys of royal blood?' she smiles.

'No, of course not; but he is a duke.'

Katherine shakes her head. 'Not for long. I think they will take his fortune and his title.'

'But why? Since the queen has forgiven so many others?'

'He did a terrible thing,' Katherine points out. 'You know what I mean . . .'

She trails off and looks at me, widening her eyes, as if I, so much better read and better educated than she, must know the words she will not say. She puts up her finger to Mr Nozzle on her shoulder, and he holds it as if for comfort.

I look at her with a face of stone and then see the easy tears well up in her blue eyes.

'Jane! You do know!'

'I promise you I don't know what you mean, and goggling your eyes at me does not tell me anything.'

'Because he was a traitor,' she whispers. 'He tried to put a false queen on the throne. It is a sin against the Crown, the country and God. Everyone says he must die. Because he was a traitor. It is not that he sent out papers, or wrote letters, like our father did. It was not words; it was deeds. He took a proper army against the queen, and his sons proclaimed a false queen at the point of a sword. They're all going to be executed. They have to be.'

Still, I look at her blankly. 'Die? The Dudley boys?'

I don't think it's possible that these five handsome young men should die. It's not possible that their father – such a calculating, cunning man – should negotiate his way to the scaffold. The boys are too vital, their father is too clever. None of them can die.

'And you too, Jane,' she says, speaking slowly as if she is spelling something out for our little sister, Mary. 'You do know, don't you know? Since you were the false queen that they raised up. The Dudleys have to die for proclaiming a false queen, and you were her. So they are saying that you will have to die, too.'

I look at my pretty sister, the only one who has dared to speak this terrible lie. 'Oh, no, they can't kill me,' I am shocked that she should even say it.

'I know!' She is in complete agreement with me. Mr Nozzle nods his grave head. 'I really think they can't. Surely, they can't? But the thing is, Jane, they say that they will.'

Katherine is a fool and I have known this forever. I don't even argue with her; for what is the point of citing authorities and giving her pages that she simply can't read? I might as well speak to her monkey or her kitten. I know that I have done nothing but obey my father and mother, and then obey my husband and his father and mother. This is not treason. It is no crime at all. It is a God-given duty: *Honour thy father and thy mother, that thou mayest live long in the land which the Lord thy God shall give thee.*

Queen Mary – who studied as I did, with Queen Kateryn Parr, all four of us, Kateryn, Mary, Elizabeth and I bent over our books together – will know this as well as I do. I will 'live long' upon the land because I have honoured my father and mother. It would be completely contradictory if I were to be executed for obeying my parents. It would be to deny the truth of the Bible and nothing can do that.

I complete my explanation for the queen, and when I am completely satisfied with it for rhetoric and grammar and the cleanliness of the pages, I send it to her. I expect she will read it and follow my reasoning and order my release. I make it clear to her that I had no idea why Mary Sidney took me to Syon House, and that she herself probably did not know, either. I had no desire for the crown myself, and I still do not. Once they had persuaded me of the legality and the rightness of the act, I did the best that I could. I don't see what else anyone can ask of me. I had to obey my parents and follow the logic of an argument. As it happens, I thought it was the right thing to do – but I cannot be blamed for thinking that God's work would be best done by a queen who studies His Word and follows His laws and is not in thrall to Rome. I don't explain that to the queen, because I know that she would not agree, and a righteous word is not always pleasing, even though the argument is incontrovertible.

I write at length, telling the new queen that I was advised – indeed, ordered – to take the crown by those who were set over me as older and wiser. 'The error imputed to me has not been altogether caused by myself,' I say – which is as tactful as I can be, given that all of her court and all of her present advisors were once mine. I don't hesitate to blame John Dudley or his wife or son, indeed I point out that I have been ill ever since I was forced to live with them, probably poisoned.

While I am waiting for her reply I continue with my studies and with my work of translation. I send for more books. I need to consult the authorities as I work and it is hugely irritating that some of these books are not available to me now, because the Pope has ruled that they are forbidden books and nobody can bring them to me. Banned! They are banning books written about the Bible by thoughtful commentators on the Word of God. This is how the Antichrist makes his way into the minds of men and women. This is how political tyranny is supported by religion. It comes as no surprise to me when I cannot get hold of the studies that I need, and so I have to quote from memory and make a note in the margins to check them when I am released to my own library at Bradgate where I can read everything I want.

I try not to be distracted by a tremendous noise from the city, cheering and trumpeting and church bells ringing. I sharpen my quill and turn the page of the Greek grammar that I am studying. Now I can hear the yelling of the apprentices and women shrieking with joy. I don't go up on the walls to look down; I can imagine what all the fuss is about. I don't really want to see my cousin entering London through Tower Gate in triumph and releasing her favourites from prison. I just hope that she sends for me soon.

I understand that first the guilty must be tried and executed before the queen pardons me. But I wish that I had been spared the sight of the false priests and even that old Antichrist himself, Stephen Gardiner, the enemy of reform, the persecutor of Queen Kateryn Parr, going into the chapel at the Tower to celebrate Mass for the turncoat traitors. I take my cushion to serve as a kneeler and I set my back to the window and lean my forehead against the cold stone wall to pray for my immortal soul, as the wicked old man preaches a sermon and raises the Host and generally makes magic and paganism in the chapel where I have so recently prayed directly to God without the need of anyone swishing about here and there in robes before the hidden altar, waving incense or spraying water.

Not everyone thinks as I do. My father-in-law, John Dudley, recants his faith, makes his confession and abases himself before bakers' bread and vintners' wine, pretending that they are body and blood in the hope of pleasing the queen and gaining a few years of miserable life in exchange for losing the full glory of heaven. Bread from the baker, wine from the cellar – the poor heretic swears that it is the real body and real blood of God. This is not faith as we have faith. This is superstition and magic. He has lost his immortal soul for this pathetic attempt to buy his life.

They take him out, and Sir John Gates, who served him, and Sir Thomas Palmer, who did nothing more than a hundred others, they take the three of them out to Tower Hill and behead them like common criminals.

I am deeply shocked. I can't mourn John Dudley, I have no reason to grieve for him. My father-in-law at his last hour turned into a papist and so he died an awful death betraying the true reformed faith of my cousin the king and me, a far worse betrayal than the treason he confessed. At the end he thought to barter a few days of sinful life for the certainty of eternity and he took the wrong choice then, as he did with me.

'I am only young,' I tell my sister Katherine, who comes to visit me without invitation, 'but I would not forsake my faith for love of life! But his life was sweet, he longed to keep it, you may say—'

'No, I wouldn't say that—'

'So he might have thought the sacrifice of his soul was worth the while, you will say—'

'Honestly, I wouldn't—'

'He did not care what it cost him. Indeed, the reason is good; for he that would have lived in chains to have had life—'

She is breathless with trying to interrupt me. 'I wouldn't say any of that!' she protests. 'But I can understand why a husband and a father of such handsome boys would not want to leave them, would swear to anything to keep his life.'

'God says whoever denies Him before men, He will also deny them in His Father's kingdom,' I say flatly.

'But when the queen forgives you, you will have to pray with her,' Katherine reminds me. 'I do it already. I sit behind her and I copy everything she does. Honestly, Jane, it makes no difference to me. Up and down and bowing and crossing oneself. Why does it matter? You would not declare against the Mass, surely? You would do all that they ask of you, you would bow when they raise the Host—'

'It is pigswill. The Host, as you now call it, is pigswill,' I say flatly, and she claps her palms over her face and looks at me earnestly, through her fingers.

'Jane . . .' she whispers.

'What?'

'You will talk yourself to the scaffold.'

'I will never deny the Lord my God,' I say grandly.

'Jane . . .' she says again.

'What?'

'I don't want to lose you.'

I am diverted by the moving bulge in the pocket of her cape. 'What have you got there?'

'Ribbon the kitten. I brought him. I thought you might want him for company.'

She hauls out of her pocket the white kitten with blue eyes. He opens his mouth in a tiny pink yawn and lolls a miniature rosy tongue. He has sharp little teeth and his paws are limp with sleep.

'I don't want a kitten,' I say.

She looks ridiculously disappointed. 'Wouldn't he be company for you? I am sure he is not at all heretical.'

'Don't be stupid.'

THE TOWER, LONDON, NOVEMBER 1553

It is the command of this so-called gracious queen that us prisoners who denied her heresies and follow the risen Lord shall walk just like He did before the people. I know that it is she who is shamed by this masque, not me. I don't fear being tried for treason, I am glad of it. I can give testament from the dock, I can be a Daniel coming to judgement. I am ready. I am to be tried with the handful of other remaining prisoners at London's Guildhall, as public a disgrace as she can contrive. She does not realise that, for me, this is holy. I am honoured to walk from the Tower to Guildhall to my trial. I am no more shamed than Jesus was carrying His cross. She thinks she will expose me to abuse from the crowd; but this will be my martyrdom. I am glad to do it.

The streets from the Tower to Guildhall are lined with guards, our procession of prisoners is led by the executioner's axe, followed by Archbishop Thomas Cranmer, the godly priest who gave us the English prayer book, and who translated the psalms with my dear Queen Kateryn. He has been in the Tower since he opposed the queen introducing the papist Mass. He was my tutor with Queen Kateryn, I know him well; I have every faith that if he is following the axe, the Lord is going before it. I am proud to come behind such a good man. I would follow him to the gates of heaven.

But unfortunately, I am not walking in his footsteps, for immediately behind him comes my husband, Guildford, pale and clearly frightened, and only then me, escorted by two of my ladies-in-waiting. Behind us come two other Dudleys: Ambrose and Henry. At least they look dignified and even defiant.

I wear a black gown, a black hood trimmed with jet and a black furred cape. I carry an open prayer book in my hands and I read it as I walk, though the small print jiggles before my eyes and, to tell the truth, I can see nothing. It doesn't matter; I know the prayers off by heart. The point is that I am carrying it, that I appear to be reading it, anyone looking at me can see that I depend on the Word of God, as spoken by His Son, as written in His testament, as translated by Queen Kateryn and me. I do not depend on the mumblings of a priest or the long service in Latin that greets me at Guildhall. I am redeemed by my faith in the Word, not by the crossings and the dip- pings and the fancy robes and the censing that goes on before the judges come in and cross themselves and whisper 'Amen' and do everything they can to show that this is papist against reformer, lies against truth, heresy against God, sheep against goats, them against me.

The trial is nothing but a recital of nonsense from men who know perfectly well what happened, but dare not say it now, to those who know it just as well but whose future depends on denying it. Everyone lies. I am not invited to speak, only to make a con- fession. There is no chance for me to explain the power of the Word of God.

The judges, who are as guilty as the accused, condemn all

the men to die by being dragged to their place of execution and there hanged, and then being cut down, their bellies opened and their entrails drawn out, and then their arms and legs cut off. This is hanging, drawing and quartering, and it is exactly like a crucifixion. It will take place on Tower Hill, which they should rename Calvary. I listen to the verdict and I don't even tremble because I simply cannot believe it. Queen Kateryn's dearest friend and mentor to be eviscerated for heresy? It was Thomas Cranmer who gave extreme unction to the dying King Henry. He wrote the *Book of Common Prayer*. How can he be a heretic? How can his friend's daughter disembowel him?

As for me, my position is worse and equally contradictory. They sentence me to death by either the axe, like a traitor, or fire, like a heretic, on Tower Green. I listen to the lies they say and the deaths they threaten, and I am stony-faced. Anne Askew, a common woman, was burnt to death at the stake at Smithfield for our faith. Do they think that Our Redeemer, who supported her, will fail me? Do they think I don't dare martyrdom as she did? I dare it – will they?

I have faith. I think they will pass sentence but delay and delay, and when everyone is quiet and has forgotten all about us they will release us all to our homes: Thomas Cranmer, the Dudley boys, me. The death sentence is a threat to frighten others into silence and submission. It is not my doom. I will wait, I will study, I will not fear. The time will pass, and I will be released to my home at Bradgate and I will sit at my desk beneath the open window and hear the birds in the trees and smell the scent of hay on the summer winds, and Katherine and Mary and I will play hide-and-seek in the woods.

'I am not afraid,' I explain to Katherine.

'Then you're mad!'

I take her hands, which pluck at her gown, at the basket that she has perched on her knees, filled with fruit, jiggling it as if it were a baby, the nephew that she will never have from me.

'I am not afraid, because I know that this life is just a vale of tears through which we pass,' I tell her impressively. '*Blessed are ye men whose strength is in ye, in whose heart are your ways. Which going through the vale of misery, use it for a well and the pools are filled with water.*'

'What?' she asks wildly. 'What are you talking about now?'

I draw her to sit beside me on the window seat. 'I am ready,' I tell her. 'I will not fail.'

'Beg the queen's pardon!' she suddenly says at random. 'Everyone else has done. You don't need to renounce your religion, you just have to say you are sorry for the rebellion. She's read your letter. She knows it wasn't your fault. Write to her again and tell her that you know you were wrong, you will annul your marriage, you will attend Mass, and then you can live quietly at Bradgate, and I will live with you, and we can be happy.'

> '*Do never think it strange,*
> *Though now I have misfortune.*
> *For if that fortune change,*
> *The same to thee may happen.*'

My sister gives a little scream. 'What are you saying? What are you saying now?'

'It is a poem I have written.'

She is wringing her hands in distress. I try to take hold of her but she jumps to her feet and goes to the door. 'I think you are mad!' she exclaims. 'Mad not to try to live!'

'My mind is on heaven,' I say steadily.

'No it isn't,' she says with a sister's sharp wit. 'You think that she is going to forgive you without you apologising. You think that you are going to win where John Dudley failed. You think that you are going to proclaim your faith and everyone is going to admire you for it, just like Roger Ascham the tutor does, and that ridiculous man in Switzerland.'

She catches me on the raw. I am furious at the insult to my spiritual teacher Henry Bullinger. 'You're jealous!' I spit at her. 'You name great men, but you have never understood their teaching.'

'Jealous of what?' she raises her voice. 'Of this?' Her gesture takes in the low-ceilinged interconnecting rooms, the view over the enclosed gardens, the Tower walls beyond them. 'You're in prison, condemned to death, your husband a prisoner condemned to death. There is nothing here that I would be jealous of! I want to live. I want to be married and have children. I want to wear beautiful gowns and dance! I want life. And I know you do, too. Nobody could want to die for their faith at sixteen. In England! When it is your own cousin on the throne? She will forgive you! She has forgiven Father. Just ask her forgiveness and come home to Bradgate and let us be happy! Think of your bedroom there, of your books. Think of the river path where we ride!'

I turn from her as if she were tempting me. It is easier if I think of her as a worldly temptation, a little gargoyle-faced thing, not my pretty blonde sister with her simple appetites and her foolish hopes. 'No,' I say. *'For whosoever will save his life, shall lose it: but whoso loseth his life for My sake shall find it.'*

I hear her little whimper as she faces the door and raps on it to be released. She has not been taught to argue as I have been taught from babyhood; she has education but no scholarship. It is very unlikely that she could ever persuade me of anything, my silly little sister. But I am moved by her tears. I would comfort her if I could, but I am called. I don't turn to her but I remind her: *'For I am come to set a man at variance against his father, and the daughter against her mother-in-law.'*

'Mother,' she says, muffled from behind her sleeve. She is mopping her streaming tears.

I am so surprised that I take her by the shoulder and turn her round to face me. 'What?'

'Mother,' she says again. 'It's supposed to be son against the father and the daughter against the mother, not mother-in-law. You got it wrong because you hate Lady Dudley. And that just shows you, Jane. This is not the Word of God. This is you trying to get your own back on the Dudleys. You hope that the queen will forgive you without you changing your faith, and then John Dudley, who died renouncing his faith, will look like a coward and a heretic and you will look braver than him.'

I flare with rage at her simplicity. 'I am a martyr to your stupidity! You understand nothing. I am amazed that you know the scripture, but you use it wrongly, to shake my confidence. Go now; and don't come back.'

She turns to me and her blue eyes blaze with the Tudor temper. She has pride, just like me. 'You don't deserve my love for you,' she says, with her own silly logic. 'But you have it anyway, when you least deserve it. Because I see the trouble you are in even if you are too clever to know.'

THE TOWER, LONDON, FEBRUARY 1554

I had thought that the queen would release me for Christmas, but the twelve nights come and go and while the rest of the country is forced to celebrate the Lord's birth with a Latin Mass, I praise Our Lord as a good Christian should, with prayers and reflections and no pagan bringing in of the green, no masquing or idolatry, no excess of drink or food. Indeed, I don't think I have ever kept a Christmas so well before – my day was entirely devoted to prayer and meditating on the birth of my Saviour, and reading my Bible. There were no presents and no feasting, and that is how I have always wanted to spend Christmas, and I have never been allowed this isolated purity before. I am so glad to be alone and fasting.

'But how completely miserable!' Katherine wails. She comes

from our London house, with gifts from my mother and father, and a new hood from her own wardrobe. 'Jane, couldn't you get a bough of holly? Not even a Yule log in the fireplace?'

She releases a little tame robin that has come with her, and it perches on the empty stone lintel and trills, as if to complain that there is no greenery and no music.

I don't even answer her, I just stare her down, until I see her lip tremble and she says feebly: 'Surely, you must be so lonely?'

'I am not,' I say, though the truth is that I am.

'You must miss us, your sisters, even if you don't miss our lady mother.'

'I have my studies.' But they don't take the place of conversation, even the frivolous foolish conversation of ignorant girls.

'Well, I miss you,' she says boldly, and she comes into my arms and puts her wet face into my neck and sobs loudly into my ear. I don't repulse her, I hold her tighter. I don't say, 'I miss you too,' for what would be the point in both of us crying? And besides, I am living my life as a disciple of the Lord. I should miss nothing. If I have my Bible I need nothing else. But I hold her tightly, as if I am holding a puppy: it is comforting though meaningless.

'I have a secret to tell you,' she says, her damp cheek against my ear.

'Go on.' We are not alone but my lady-in-waiting is seated at a little distance, beside the window for the light on her sewing. Katherine can whisper into my ear and the woman will think that we are crying together.

'Father is raising an army.' It comes to me like a thread of sound.

I can hardly hear her. I make sure that I keep my face hidden. 'To rescue me?'

I look as if I am weeping on Katherine's rounded shoulder though I have to control myself not to jump and scream with delight. I always knew that my father would not leave me here. I always knew that if my lady mother could not persuade Queen Mary to release me, then my father would fetch me by force. I always knew that they would, neither of them, just leave me here. I am their eldest daughter, and the heir to the Queen of England. It's not as if I am a nobody who could be easily forgotten.

'Is it not terribly dangerous?' I ask.

'Oh, I don't think so,' my sister whispers back. 'Nobody wants Queen Mary any more. Not now that she's marrying the Spanish prince.'

My mind is whirling. I didn't know any of this.

'She's marrying?'

'Philip of Spain.'

'There will be an uprising against him? They will put me on the throne in her place!'

'I think so,' Katherine says vaguely. 'I think that is the plan.'

'It's not an uprising for Elizabeth, is it?' I ask, suddenly suspicious.

'Oh, no,' she says. 'Elizabeth has become a papist. She has asked the queen to send her crucifixes and chalices for her own chapel and she has put her chaplain in a surplice and cope.'

Not even a feather-head like Katherine could misunderstand signs like this. 'Are you, at any rate, sure that Father is coming for me?'

She nods. She has grasped this fact at least. 'I am certain.'

We pull apart and her eyes are shining and her cheeks are flushed.

'Take the bird when you go,' I warn her. 'You know I don't like them.'

To wait for rescue, knowing that your heavenly and earthly fathers have not forgotten their faithful daughter, is to be on the brink of adventure. It illuminates my days and makes my prayers passionate and hopeful rather than apologetic, waiting for a pardon. I knew, I always knew for a certainty, that the people of England, having been free to read, free to think, and free to pray directly to their Saviour, would never return to the slavery of the mind and soul of the papist Church. I always knew that they would rise up against the Antichrist as soon as it was clear to them that their faith was being betrayed. It was a matter of time, it was a matter of faith. I must wait and be patient, as He is patient.

And more than this: I could have warned Queen Mary that any husband would want to take the crown – for this is just what happened to me. This is just what Guildford did as soon as they proclaimed me queen. Our cousin the eleven-year-old Mary Queen of Scots in France will find that her promised husband will usurp her power, too, as soon as he is old enough. God has placed husbands over their wives. They will claim their place even though the wife is a queen and should be set over them. Queen Mary may be old enough to be my mother but I feel that I could tell her: this is what men do. They marry a woman who is their superior and at once they envy her position, and at once they usurp her. This is why there have never been ruling queens in this country, only regents when the king is away. This is why there are no duchesses on the Privy Council. If a man wins an honour it is his; if a woman wins it then it belongs to her husband. This is why the queen executed John Dudley, but spared me. She read what I wrote, she saw that the throne was inherited by me but claimed by him for his son. She knew at once that I might be true but Guildford covetous. I could have warned her that any husband would steal her power and that the English people will never accept a Spanish king. She is not eight months into her reign and already she has destroyed herself. I am sorry for her, but I have no regret that my father is arming against her.

So must it be; so may die all heretics.

I wait for the hour of my rescue but it does not come. I wait for Katherine to come and tell me what is happening, but she does not visit me either. Suddenly I am not allowed to walk in the garden or on the flat roofs of the Tower buildings, but nobody will tell me why. The days are dark, with mist off the river and lowering clouds. I don't want to walk in the garden anyway, I tell Mrs Partridge. There is nothing growing at this time of year, the trees are bare of leaves, the green itself is a patch of mud. There is no need for anyone to forbid me. I am imprisoned by wintry weather, not by the will of the queen. Mrs Partridge compresses her lips and says nothing.

From somewhere in the city I can hear the noise of men shouting and the rattle of handguns going off. Without doubt it is my father, coming for me at the head of his army. My books are tidy on my table, my papers tied together, I am ready to go.

'What is happening?' I ask Mrs Partridge quietly.

She crosses herself, as if it were a natural gesture to ward off ill luck.

'God forgive you!' I say at once at the terrible gesture. 'What ridiculous waving about are you doing? What good do you think that would do anybody? Why not clap your hands to scare away Satan while you're at it?'

She looks me directly in the eye. 'I pray for you,' is all she replies, and she goes from my rooms.

'What is happening?' I shout. But she closes the door behind her.

THE TOWER, LONDON, THURSDAY 8 FEBRUARY 1554

I have a visitor, John Feckenham, whose idolatry is proclaimed by his long cream-coloured woollen robe, tied at the waist with a leather thong, and a white hood that he pushes back from his square flushed face. A Benedictine monk, come to visit me, poor fool.

He catches his breath from the climb up the stairs to my rooms. 'Steep,' he manages, gasping, and then ducks his head in a bow. 'Lady Dudley, I've come to talk with you, if you'll have me.' He has a strong accent, like a butcher or a dairyman, nothing like the refined accent of my Cambridge-educated tutors. It makes me smile, as if the cowman was preaching.

'I have no need of guidance from a blind man in darkness,' I say quietly.

'I have weighty news for you.' Indeed, he looks quite bowed down with whatever he has to tell me. I think of my father, on his way to me now, at the head of his army, and I know a clutch of fear in my tender belly. I hope that nothing has gone wrong. But surely, if something had gone wrong they would not send a strange heretical priest to tell me? A fat heretical priest with a round face and an uncouth accent? It is to insult me.

'Who has told you to give me this news?' I ask. 'Who burdened you, a heavy man, with such weighty news?'

He sighs again, as if he is sad as well as blown. 'I'm not here to chop logic with you,' he says. 'The council commanded me to give you the news and the queen herself has ordered me to free you from the superstition in which you have grown up.'

'To free me from the superstition in which I have grown up?' I repeat coldly.

'Yes.'

'How long do you have?' I force a laugh.

'Not long,' he says very quietly. 'They have confirmed your sentence of death. I am so sorry. You are to be beheaded tomorrow. We don't have long at all, Lady Dudley.'

I feel as if I am struck dead by the very words. I can't breathe; my belly, always quivering with flux, goes suddenly still. I dare say that my heart ceases to beat. 'What? What did you say?'

'I am truly sorry, my child,' he says gently.

I look into his broad flushed face. 'What?'

'You and your husband, Guildford Dudley, are to be executed. Tomorrow.'

I see that he has tears in his eyes. The tears, and his awkwardness, his flushed face, his stertorous breathing, convince me more than his words.

'When did you say? When?'

'Tomorrow,' he says quietly. 'May I talk with you about your immortal soul?'

'Oh, it's too late for that,' I say. I cannot think straight, there is a noise in my ears and I realise it is the rapid thudding of my heart. 'Oh, there's not enough time to attend to so many things. I did not think ... I did not think ...' In truth, I did not think that the queen my cousin would turn vulture; but I see that her false religion has driven her mad, as it does so many.

'I could ask them to give me more time to wrestle with your soul,' he says hopefully. 'If I could tell them that we were talking. If I could assure them that you might repent.'

'Yes,' I say. 'All right.' Even a day may give my father time to get to me. I must stay alive so that he can rescue me. Every day he comes closer, I know it. He will not fail me; I must not fail him. Even now he may be fighting a battle south of the river. I must be here when he crosses the bridge.

THE TOWER, LONDON, FRIDAY 9 FEBRUARY 1554

John Feckenham comes at dawn, as he promised, carrying with him his box of tricks of bread and wine and goblet and stole, candles and incense and all the furniture and toys that he can bring out to confuse the unwary like a village mountebank making merry for silly children. I look at his wooden box and I look at his honest face.

'I am not going to change my religion to save my neck,' I say. 'I am thinking about my soul.'

'I, too,' he says gently. 'And the queen has given us three days to talk of holy things.'

'I always liked to study and debate.'

'Then talk to me now,' he says. 'Explain to me what you understand by these sacred words ... *Take ye, and eat ye, this is my body, which is broken for you. This do in the remembrance of me.*'

I nearly laugh. 'Do you not think I have been disputing the meaning of this almost all my life?'

'I know it,' he says steadily. 'I know you were raised in error, my poor sister.'

'I am not your sister,' I correct him. 'I have two sisters only. If there was a brother, I would not be here now.'

I can hear the clatter of a guard at the Lions' Gate and the noise of many men coming into the Tower. I hear the shout to stand, and the noise of men allocating cells. I know that I look startled. 'I'd like to see . . .'

He doesn't move from his seat so I suppose that he knows who they are bringing into the Tower under arrest. I go hastily to the window and look across the garden. I recognise my father, my poor father, and a ragtag of men, arms gone, standards down, horses gone, clearly defeated.

I turn back to Feckenham. 'My father is arrested again?' I ask him. 'You came here with words of advice but you didn't tell me this, the one thing that I didn't know, that I need to know!'

'He was treasonous again,' he says bluntly. 'He and Sir Thomas Wyatt tried to enter London at the head of their army.'

'To save me!' I say with sudden anger. 'Who could blame him for trying to save me when I am under sentence of death and he has loved me for all my life? I have been his favourite daughter, devout like him, a scholar like him. How could a man like that leave his daughter to die without lifting a finger to save her? Nobody could ask it of him.'

We are quiet for a moment. I am facing him, flushed and with tears in my eyes, and he looks resentful, like a pork butcher, cheated in the market over the price of sausages. He drops his head and his ready colour spreads over his broad cheeks.

'He didn't rise up for you,' he says gently, and his words are like a bell tolling the death knell. 'Not for you, my dear. He rose up to put Princess Elizabeth on the throne. But it is because he rose for her, that they are going to execute you. I am sorry, my child.'

'He raised an army for Elizabeth?' I can't believe it. I have told my father what sort of girl Elizabeth is. Why would he rise for her, so malleable in her faith and so unreliable as a house guest?

'He did.'

'But why kill me, if my father rose for Elizabeth?' I whisper. And then, scholar that I am: 'It makes no sense. There is no logic.'

His wry smile tells me that he agrees. 'The queen's Spanish advisors want to show that no-one can survive rebellion against them,' he corrects himself, 'against Her Majesty.'

I hardly care. All I care about is my father. 'He was not coming for me? He was never intending to save me? It was all for Elizabeth, and not for me?'

Feckenham knows that this is the worst thing. 'You would have been released, I am sure.' He sees the downturn of my mouth, and the angry tears in my eyes. 'We cannot know what the conspiracy planned until they confess. Shall we pray to your Father in heaven who loves you? You always have Him.'

'Yes,' I say brokenly, and we kneel together to pray the Pater Noster in English, the prayer that Jesus taught us Himself, where we all are told that God is 'Our Father'. I have a Father in heaven even if I don't have one on earth. Brother Feckenham prays in Latin, I speak the words in English. I don't doubt that I am heard. I don't doubt that he is heard, too.

THE TOWER, LONDON,
SATURDAY 10 FEBRUARY 1554

They charge my father and he will stand trial for his part in the plot. It was a big, treasonous conspiracy, and it might well have succeeded. They were going to put Elizabeth on the throne and marry her to Edward Courtenay, our Plantagenet cousin, one of our family and one of our faith. Elizabeth denies all knowledge of this, of course. For a girl so well educated she manages to be impressively ignorant when it suits her. But this conspiracy means that our cousin Queen Mary must regard all her kins-women as a threat. Elizabeth, me, Katherine, even little Mary, Margaret Douglas and Mary of Scots in France – any one of us could be named as Queen of England in preference to her. We all have an equally good claim; we are all suspect.

I am so anguished that it is a relief when there is a tap on the door and John Feckenham comes in, his big red face creased in a tentative smile, his fair eyebrows upraised as if he is afraid that he is not welcome.

'You can come in,' I say ungraciously. I take a breath and give my prepared speech: 'Since I have been granted these days of life to talk with you, though I do so little lament my heavy case that I account it a more manifest declaration of God's favour towards me than ever He showed me at any time before.'

'You have prepared,' he says, recognising at once the opening words for a debate, and he puts his books down on the table, and seats himself, as if he knows that wrestling with my soul will be hard work for a misguided heretic like him.

THE TOWER, LONDON,
SUNDAY 11 FEBRUARY 1554

My lady mother and Katherine are allowed to visit Father; and Katherine leaves our father and mother to be alone together – as they always want to be – and comes to my room.

She does not know what to say to me, and I have nothing to say to her. We sit in awkward silence. She cries a little, stifling her sobs in the sleeve of her gown. While she is sitting so close, gazing at me with her tear-filled eyes, I cannot study, write or pray. I cannot even hear my own thoughts. I am just gripped in a whirl of her regrets and fear and grief. It is like being churned in a butter-tub; I feel myself going rancid. I don't want to spend my last day like this. I want to write an account of John Feckenham's discussion with me, of my triumph over his wrong-thinking. I want to prepare my speech for the scaffold. I want to think; I don't want to feel.

We can hear the noise of the carts bringing the wood to build the scaffold and the workers shouting for their tools, and guiding the carts to the green. At every rumble of the wood being tipped on the paving stones, at every rasp of the saws and tapping of a hammer, Katherine flinches, her pretty face white as skimmed milk, her eyes the colour of ink.

'I will die for my faith,' I say to her suddenly.

'You will die because Father joined a rebellion against the crowned queen,' she bursts out. 'It wasn't even for you!'

'That may be what they say,' I reply steadily. 'But the queen has turned her back on those who believe in the true way to God, broken her promise that people might worship according to their conscience, and is throwing the country under the command of the Bishop of Rome and the hidalgos of Spain. So she has turned against me because of my faith and that is why I shall die.'

Katherine claps her hands over her ears. 'I won't listen to treason.'

'You never listen to anything.'

'Father has lost us everything,' she says. 'We are all destroyed.'

'Worldly goods,' I say. 'They mean nothing to me.'

'Bradgate! Bradgate doesn't mean nothing to you! So why say so? Our home!'

'You should turn your mind to Our Father's house in heaven.'

'Jane,' she implores me, 'tell me one kind word, one sisterly word before I say goodbye!'

'I can't,' I say simply. 'I have to keep my mind on my journey and my joyful destination.'

'Will you see Guildford before he dies? He's asked to see you. Your husband? Will you be together for one last time? He wants to say goodbye.'

Impatiently, I shake my head at her morbid sentiment. 'I can't! I can't! I will see no-one but Brother Feckenham.'

'A Benedictine monk!' she squeaks. 'Why would you see him and not Guildford?'

'Because Brother Feckenham knows I am a martyr,' I flash. 'Of all of you, only he and the queen understand that I am dying for my faith. That is why I will only see him. That is why he will come with me to the scaffold.'

'If you would just admit that this is not about your faith, this is nothing to do with your faith – it's only about Father's rebellion for Elizabeth – then you wouldn't have to die at all!'

'That is why I won't talk with you, or Guildford,' I say in a sudden storm of unsaintly temper. 'I won't listen to anyone who wants me to see this as a muddle by a fool, which leads to the death of his daughter, a pawn. Yes! Father should have rescued me; but instead he rode out for another pawn and his failure has condemned me to death!' I am swept with rage and sorrow. I have raised my voice, I am shouting at her, panting. I feel that I have to claw myself back to peace, to calmness. This is why I cannot argue about worldly things with worldly people. This is why I cannot bear to see her, to see any of them. This is why I have to think and not feel.

She looks at me with her mouth open and her eyes wide. 'He has ruined us,' she whispers.

'I'm not going to die thinking about that,' I hiss at her. 'I am a martyr for my faith, not for a foolish accident. I will never die, and my father will never die either. We will meet in heaven.'

I write to my father. I always knew he would never die and now I am setting off on a journey, and I don't doubt that I will see him at journey's end.

The Lord comfort Your Grace ... and though it has pleased God to take away two of your children, my husband and myself, yet think not, I most humbly beseech Your Grace, that you have lost them, but trust that we, by leaving this mortal life, have won an immortal life. And I for my part, as I have honoured Your Grace in this life, will pray for you in another life.

THE TOWER, LONDON, MONDAY 12 FEBRUARY 1554

Two of my ladies, Mrs Ellen and Elizabeth Tylney, stand with me at the window, waiting for the news that my husband of eight and a half months is dead. They pull me away from the window, laying hold of my arms, my shoulders, as if I am a child, as if I should not see the truth. The lieutenant of the Tower, John Brydges, stands at the door, his face stern, trying to feel nothing.

'I can watch,' I shrug them off. 'I have no fear of death.' I want them to know that even in the valley of the shadow of death I am quite without fear. I want them to note it.

God supports me, but I am still horribly shocked when the cart goes by my window, rattling back from the scaffold at Tower Hill. I knew he had been beheaded but I had not thought that the body would be a head shorter than I remembered him. His actual head has been tumbled into a basket beside the blood-stained body. It is pitiful, it is like a butcher's shambles where the animals are beautiful beasts no longer but only sliced skinned parts. There is the only man I ever had in my bed, and who was to me such a threat, such a potency. There he is, cut up, like a banned book with chapters ripped out. His body is headless, it looks so odd. They have dropped his handsome face into a basket and tossed his corpse into bloodstained straw. This is a horror I was not prepared for. I always thought of death as the shining shore, never as a butchered beast, the stiffening of a familiar body, pieces of a boy in a dirty cart.

'Guildford,' I whisper, almost to remind myself that it is him and not some trick of play-actors.

The executioner, robed in black, with a high black hood making his faceless head grotesquely tall, walks heavy-footed, behind the tailgate. The cart goes to the chapel, the executioner goes to stand beside the newly built scaffold on the green, his hands folded over his axe, his head bowed. With a start, I real-ise that he is here, not as part of Guildford's procession, but for another purpose altogether. He has come to behead me. Although I thought I was prepared, this gives me a heart-stopping jolt. My time has come. However unjust – really, however illogical and contradictory – I, too, will be diminished, reduced, beheaded.

I pause to write in the prayer book for John Brydges. I write at length, lost in this last moment. I am myself. Words never die. I think: *In the beginning was the Word, and the Word was with*

God, and God was the Word. I think that I understand this: my body will die but my words will live. The bloody wreckage of Guildford's body has shaken me – but I still cling to the words that never die. My teacher and mentor Kateryn Parr understood this. She faced death without fear. I will do so, too.

'*Forasmuch as you have desired so simple a woman to write in so worthy a book, good Master Lieutenant,*' I begin.

I do so like 'Forasmuch'. I think it has genuine dignity. I write a paragraph, and then another, and then I sign my name, and Brother Feckenham looks at me and says gently: 'You can write no more. It is time.'

I am ready. I have to be ready. There is nothing more to write. I have written a description of my discussions with Brother Feckenham, I have written to the queen, to my father, to Katherine. Now, finally, I write a farewell and I have finished my work. I am in my black gown and I have my prayer book in my hands, open.

'I am ready,' I say, and I note the pitiful cringing that makes me want to say: 'Wait! Just wait a moment! Something else I must do! One moment, one second, one heartbeat more . . .'

John Feckenham leads the way and I hold my prayer book – my English prayer book – before me, and I try to read from it as we go down the narrow stairs, through the little garden, out of the garden gate and slowly towards the scaffold on the green. Of course, I can't really see the words as we walk down the stairs, or down the garden path: nobody could. But once again it shows everyone that I am walking to the scaffold with a prayer book before me. Kateryn Parr the queen wrote these prayers, translated them from the Latin. Here I am, going to the scaffold with this evidence of my righteousness in my hand. This is our work. I am prepared to die for it. I will die with it in my hands.

The ladies behind me sob and sob in strangled gulping weeping. I hope that everyone can see that I am not crying like them. I hope that everyone can see that I am praying as I walk, my book before me, my whole presence deeply devout, showing that I am certain of resurrection. We all climb the ladder to the scaffold and assemble on the platform. There are very few people come to watch me be martyred. I am surprised how few. I speak to them.

I was afraid my voice would tremble but I do not tremble. I pray for mercy and I tell everyone, clearly, that I will be saved by the mercy of God – not by prayers from a priest, not by paid Masses in a chantry. I ask people to pray for me while I am alive, I mean them to understand that I don't need prayers after my death for I will go directly to heaven. 'No purgatory,' I want to add, but everyone knows that is what I mean.

I read the Miserere in English, for God can understand English and it is superstition to think that He has to be addressed in Latin. John Feckenham follows me, speaking the words in Latin, and I think how beautiful the language is, and how sweet it sounds today, chiming and interweaving with the English words in the damp misty air with the seagulls calling over the river. I remember that I am only sixteen and I will never see the river again. I can't believe I will never see the hills of Bradgate again, or the paths where Katherine and I used to walk under the trees, or my old pony in the field, or the caged old bear in the pit. The prayer lasts an oddly long time, a timeless time, and I am surprised when it ends and I have to give things: my gloves and my handkerchief, my prayer book. The ladies have to prepare me for this, my final royal appearance. They take off my hood, my black hood trimmed with jet, and my collar. Suddenly the time is racing past when there were things that I wanted to say, that I wanted to make sure that I saw before this moment. I am sure there are last words that I should say, memories that I should recall. It's all happening too fast now.

I kneel. I can hear Brother Feckenham's steady voice. They put on the blindfold before I have had my last glimpse of the seagulls. I meant to look at the clouds, I meant to be sure of my last glance of the sky. Suddenly I know fear and I am in the white blankness of a daylight blindfold.

'What shall I do? Where is it?' I scream in a panic, and then someone guides my hands to the block and its solid square roughness tells me that my destiny is inexorable. This is the material world indeed, this is the most material thing I will ever touch. I realise it is the last thing I will ever touch. I grip the block, I even feel the grain of the wood. I have to put my head down on it. I note that the blindfold is wet with my tears, soft and hot against my closed eyelids. I must be crying and crying. But at least no-one can see, and whatever happens next, I know that it is not death for I will never die.

BOOK II

KATHERINE

BAYNARD'S CASTLE, LONDON, SPRING 1554

I have sent you, good sister Katherine, a book, which although it be not outwardly trimmed with gold, yet inwardly it is more worth than precious stones. It is the book, dear sister, of the laws of the Lord: It is His Testament and Last Will, which He bequeathed unto us wretches, which shall lead you to the path of eternal joy, and if you, with a good mind, read it, and with an earnest desire follow it, it shall bring you to an immortal and everlasting life.

It will teach you to live and learn you to die . . . win you more than you should have gained by the possession of your woeful father's lands . . . such riches as neither the covetous shall withdraw from you, neither the thief shall steal, neither let the moth corrupt . . .

And as touching my death, rejoice as I do and consider that I shall be delivered of this corruption and put on incorruption, for as I am assured that I shall for losing of a mortal life, find an immortal felicity.

Farewell good sister, put only your trust in God, who only must uphold you,

Your loving sister,

Jane Duddley

I read, with growing disbelief, this sermon – the only goodbye from my older sister that I will ever get. I read it again, only
this time I am furious. I really don't know what she thinks I am
going to do with this miserable letter. I don't know what good
she thinks it will do me. I have to say that if it was me about to
die, I wouldn't write such a letter to little Mary. What a thing
to write! How would it ever comfort her? I read and reread it
though my eyes are so sore from crying that I can't see her careful clerkly hand. Nothing is crossed out, nothing is blotted. She
did not cry over writing as I am crying over reading it. She did
not desperately scrawl it in a passion to say goodbye to me, her
little sister who looks up to her and loves her so much. She wasn't
anxious to tell me that she loves me, that she is thinking of me,
that she is heartbroken that we won't grow up together. We will
never now be ladies at court giggling over our admirers, we will
never be learned old ladies reading to our children. She thought
through these elegant paragraphs and wrote them as they came
to her, with refined scholarship, without hesitation. And all about
God. God! As usual.

Of course, as soon as I have read it and reread it, I know
exactly what I am going to do with it. Not ball it up and hurl
it into the fire, in a rage of grief, which was my first impulse.
I am going to do what she wanted me to do. She didn't even
have to tell me; she knew that I would know. She didn't have to
spoil her holy detachment with a practical instruction. I know
what she wants without her saying. I am to send this letter, this
cold-hearted unsisterly letter, to her so-called important friends
in Switzerland and they will print it and get it published and
send it out to everyone. And everyone will read it and say what
a wonderful letter of piety, what a saint the girl was, what wise
advice to her little sister, how certain it is that her faith has taken
her to heaven. How lucky we all are to have been blessed with
her presence.

Then everyone will admire Jane and quote this damned
letter forever. They will print it in England and Germany and
Switzerland as part of the wonderful scholarship of Jane Grey,

proof that she was an exceptional young woman whose memory will go on and on, whose life will be a sermon to the young. And if anyone thinks of me at all, they will think that I am a very stupid frivolous girl to be the recipient of the last letter of a martyr. If Mary Magdalene had arrived at the empty tomb on Easter morning and failed to notice the gardener who was the risen Christ, and so ruined the miracle of Easter for everyone forever, I would be her: the secondary player in the greatest scene, who completely fails in her part. If Mary Magdalene tripped over a rock and hopped about clutching her toe – that would be me. Everyone is going to remember Jane the saint. Nobody is going to think twice about me – the stupid sister who received her last great letter. Nobody will think that I wanted and deserved a last letter, a proper letter, a personal letter. And no-one will give a second thought to our little sister Mary, who doesn't even get a miserable sermon.

If Jane were not dead I would be really furious with her about this. 'Learn you to die'! What a thing to write to a sister who has always loved her! If she were alive I would go to the Tower right now and knock off her black hood and pull her hair for writing such a heartless letter to her little sister, for writing to me – to me! – that I should be glad that we have lost all our money, that I should be glad that we have lost our home, that I should be glad to have a Bible rather than jewels. As if I would ever rather have an old Bible than my lovely home, a Bible instead of Bradgate! As if anyone would! As if I don't love jewels and pretty things and prize them above everything else in the world! As if she doesn't know this, as if she hasn't laughed at me for my silly vanity a hundred times!

And then I remember, with a gulp of horror like ice in my belly, that her hood is off her head already, and her head is off her body, and if I pulled her plait then her head would swing like a ball on a rope in my hand, and I find I am screaming and I put my hands over my panting mouth until I choke down my retching sobs.

I sleep out of sheer weariness in my bed in the quiet house. My husband, Henry, does not come to lie with me. I suppose that he never will. I think he is probably forbidden even to see me. Certainly we have not been left alone together since Queen Mary returned in her triumph to London. I imagine the Herberts are desperate to get the marriage set aside, and free him from the terrible disadvantage of a wife whose sister was beheaded for treason. They will be writing out confessions and swearing that they hardly knew us Greys at all. It was such a brilliant marriage only nine months ago: then I was a catch, now I am an embarrassment. I stay in my rooms and when I go to dinner I sit at the ladies' table and I keep my head down and hope that no-one speaks to me, for I don't even know what my name is: am I Katherine Herbert still? Or am I Katherine Grey again? I don't know who I am supposed to be, I don't know what I am supposed to say. I think it safer to say nothing.

I would pray for my father but I don't know what prayers are allowed. I know we're not to pray in English any more, and absolutely forbidden from doing anything that is not part of the old Mass. I understand the Latin well enough – I'm not completely ignorant – it just seems odd to me to be praying in a language that most people can't understand. The priest turns his back on his congregation and celebrates the Mass as if it were a secret, between him and God, and this is so odd to me who has been brought up with the communion table on the chancel steps and everyone coming up for bread and wine. The people mumble the responses, uncertain of the strange words. Nobody knows what is holy, nobody knows what is right, and nobody knows who I am – not even me.

They take my father to trial and they find him guilty again. I think that since the queen pardoned him once before, surely she is certain to repeat the pardon? Since it is the same offence? Why would she not? If treason was not too bad the first time, is it that much worse for being done again? I can't see my mother to ask her if she hopes to save her husband as she did last time, because I don't go anywhere. I don't leave Baynard's Castle. I don't know if I am allowed out. I think not.

Nobody is going to ask me if I would like to go on a visit;

nobody takes me anywhere in the barge or even invites me to come out with them. Nobody ever asks me if I want to ride out. Nobody speaks to me at all but the servants. I don't even know if the guards on the outer gate would open the great doors for me if I walked towards them. For all I know I am a prisoner in my husband's house. For all I know I am under house arrest, facing a charge of treason myself. Nobody tells me anything.

Actually, nobody goes anywhere. Nobody goes out at all except my father-in-law, who huddles on his best jacket and hurries to court to sit in public judgement on the very many men who were his allies only weeks ago. Now they are charged with treason and hanged one after another at every crossroads in the city. Elizabeth herself, the half-sister, the heir, and for all I know, the best-hidden plotter, is suspected of treason, and I can't say I care very much if they behead her too. Since they could behead Jane, who never wanted the throne in the first place, I don't see why they should hesitate over Elizabeth, who has always wanted it so very badly and is a very nasty girl, so vain and such a centre of gossip.

I can't even see my little sister Mary, who is with my mother in our London house, Suffolk Place. I don't see anybody except my father-in-law and my so-called husband at dinner and at chapel, where we pray four times a day, whispering strange words over and over again in the candlelit dusk. They don't speak to me then, but my father-in-law looks at me as if he is surprised I am still there, and he can't quite remember why.

I give him no cause for complaint. I am as devout as if I were an enclosed nun – a very reluctant enclosed nun. It's not my fault! I was born and bred into the reformed religion and I learned Latin for my studies, not to mutter with a priest. I know grammar, but I never learned the prayers by rote. So the psalms and the blessings are as meaningless to me as if they were in Hebrew. I keep my head down and I mutter pious-sounding noises. I bob up and down and cross myself when everyone else does. If I were not so terribly sad, I would be bored to death. When they tell me quietly, just before Matins, that my father has been beheaded with the other traitors, I feel more exhausted than unhappy, and I don't know what prayers should be said for him. I think that since Queen Mary is on the throne, he must have gone to purgatory and we should buy Masses for his soul, but I don't know where you would buy Masses while the abbeys are still closed, and if they would do him any good, when Jane said there was no such place as purgatory anyway.

I feel only how very, very tiring this all is, and all I really care about is when can I go out, and if I will ever be happy again? I think this must mean that I am, as Jane said, totally without the gift of the Holy Spirit, and for a moment I think I shall tell her that she is right and I am a very worldly ninny, but inexplicably sad; and then I remember that I shall never tell her anything, ever again, and I remember that is why I am sad.

Unbelievably, my mother – the most unlikely angel in the world – delivers a true miracle. She has been constantly attending court, begging the queen that we, the innocent victims of my father's ambition, his surviving little family of three, be forgiven his treason. My lady mother pursues the queen's goodwill as if it were a plump deer, and in the end brings it to bay and cuts its furry throat. Once Jane is gone and can no longer be the unwilling centre of any rebellion, once my father is dead and buried, the queen gives us back one of our houses, Beaumanor, near Bradgate Park, and the whole beautiful park of Loughborough stocked with our game, and we are allowed to live richly once more.

'What about the bear?' I ask Mother when she tells me of this extraordinary reprieve.

'What bear?'

'The Bradgate bear. I was taming him. Will we move him to Beaumanor?'

'For God's sake, we have been an inch from the scaffold and

you are talking to me about a bear? We've lost him with Bradgate, and the hounds and the horses. They'll all go to someone in the queen's favour. My life is ruined, I am a heartbroken widow, and you talk to me about a bear?'

Jane would have stood up to her and insisted that the bear should come with us to Beaumanor. I can't. I don't have the words and I cannot tell her that I feel that the bear, like Mr Nozzle, like every living thing, deserves to be seen and considered, is fit for love. I should like to tell her that I am heartbroken too; but I can't find the words for this and she is, anyway, not interested.

'Go to the Herberts,' she snaps. 'Fetch your things from them.'

BEAUMANOR, LEICESTERSHIRE, SPRING 1554

I feel that we have got home safe, ducked our heads as the scythe passed over us. Mary and Mother and I, Mr Nozzle and Ribbon the kitten, the horses and hounds (but not the bear) are home but not home, close to the park, near enough to see the tall chimneys of our old house, missing our old house – but at any rate alive, and living together in a state of constant mild bickering that tells us that we can speak, that we can hear, that we are safe.

And we are lucky – far luckier than the others. My father never comes home, I will never see my sister again. They bury her in pieces in the chapel, and Elizabeth our cousin enters the Tower as a prisoner suspected of treason in the rebellion led by Thomas Wyatt and my father. Only the queen can say if Elizabeth will come out or if more Tudor blood will water the green, and she is not telling. For sure, I will never go there if I can help it. Never. Never.

I am glad to be safely far from London but I wish we could have gone back to Bradgate House. I miss Jane's room and her library of books, and Mr Nozzle misses my bedroom and his little bed on the window seat. I miss the poor bear. It is a relief to be away from the chilly silence of the Herberts' house and I learn that my marriage has been put aside and can be forgotten as if it never happened. Mary and my mother and I live together, as the three survivors of a great family of five, and Adrian Stokes, our master of horse, comes with us to Beaumanor, carves the meat at dinner and is attentive to my mother and kindly to Mary and me.

At least I can sit beneath the tree where Jane and I used to sit and read, and listen to the nightingale high in the branches at dusk, and my mother can gallop around and hunt as if none of this had ever happened, as if she had not lost a husband and a daughter, as if I never had an older sister.

So much for the loss 'of your woeful father's lands' – I think of Jane's letter and think how I will tease her that we have got most of the lands back, woeful or not. I shall ask her what is worth the most now – an old book or hundreds of acres? – and then I remember, just as I remember with a jolt every day, that I can't tell her that she was wrong, that land is bound to be worth more than an old Bible. That I will never tell her anything again.

Mary has grown hardly at all in the months that we have been in London. She is still a tiny thing, a pretty child. She has learned to stand straight, denying the little twist in her spine, so at least her shoulders are level and she walks and dances with miniature grace. I think that perhaps she has simply stopped growing from unhappiness and will never be older, just as Jane will never grow old either. It's as if my two sisters are frozen in time, one a bride and one a child. But I don't say anything to Mary about this, as she is only nine years old, and I don't say anything to my mother, who has drowned the runt of every litter that her hounds have ever had.

BEAUMANOR, LEICESTERSHIRE, SUMMER 1554

By midsummer my mother has achieved even more: she gets Mary and I appointed to court and we are all three to be the constant companions of the queen who executed my sister and my father. We go back to court as welcome cousins, and none of us, not even little Mary, betrays for a moment any doubts we might have about this. I put it out of my mind completely. If I thought about it I would go mad. My lady mother demonstrates every day her fidelity and kinship with her beloved cousin the queen, it is 'my dearest cousin' all the time, to make sure that nobody ever forgets that we are related; royal but not claiming inheritance.

No-one ever forgets the other cousins either: Elizabeth the bastard, now under house arrest at Woodstock, Mary Stuart, the foreigner in France, betrothed to the French dauphin, and Margaret Douglas, married to an earl and favoured by the queen more highly than any of the rest of us, because of her loudly proclaimed papist faith.

It is as good as a masque to see the anxiety when we cousins prepare to process in for dinner. Elizabeth should be here, walking behind her half-sister. She is the nominated heir in the will of King Henry, and Queen Mary cannot change that. She has taken advice to disinherit Elizabeth, but they told her that parliament would never stand for it. Why parliament would stand for killing Jane but not disinheriting Elizabeth only they, in their fearful conferences, can tell. But anyway, Elizabeth is still under arrest and perhaps will never come back to court again.

So the queen takes her place, alone at the head of all her ladies, a small stocky figure richly dressed, with a kind square face crunched up with worry. And wait! Here is my mother, dripping with jewels, always in a brocade gown of green (which declares 'À Tudor' to the deafest of loyalists). She is next in line for the throne after Elizabeth – and since Elizabeth is not here, she should be hard on the queen's heels. But wait! – and nobody dares to form a procession until these first places are organised – last in, at an ungainly gallop, comes Lady Margaret Douglas, formerly known as the bastard of Margaret Queen of Scots and her bigamous husband. But only formerly known, because she is now legitimate – Queen Mary has ruled it, the Pope has ruled it. The facts do not matter; what matters is what everyone says. And if she is legitimate, and the daughter of Margaret Queen of Scots (the older sister of Henry VIII) then she goes before my mother, who is legitimate and the daughter of Mary Queen of France (the younger sister). But in his will he names our line, and so did the will of King Edward . . . so who knows who should be the next heir? Who knows who should walk on the queen's heels? Not me, for sure. Not anyone waiting to go in to dinner.

It turns into a hushed wrestle. Lady Margaret the Legitimate pushes rudely in front of me and I step back with false deference and assumed good manners. She is Queen Mary's favourite, faithful to Rome, loudly faithful to her cousin now she is queen. She is a big woman with thick greying hair packed under an old-fashioned hood. She spent her life in and out of favour of the old king, in and out of the Tower, too, and she is used to elbowing for her place. Beside her, I am like an exquisite daughter, perhaps granddaughter. I am fair, I am dainty, I am thirteen years old, the true and legitimate granddaughter of the famously beautiful Tudor Queen of France. I step back with a little patient sigh, looking a hundred times more royal than she does, pushing in with a grunt.

She and my mother go elbow to elbow, almost fist to fist. It is as good as a wrestling match on the village green, every night. Queen Mary glances back and throws a smile, a word to one or to the other of them and the order is settled. We can process to dinner.

Mary, the smallest maid-in-waiting in the world, moves with me as if we were dancing partners. We look so pretty together that nobody remarks that she is tiny compared with everyone else. They laugh at her and pet her, and they tell my mother that she must feed her game and roast meats to make her grow. Nobody thinks that there might be anything wrong with her, and my mother says nothing. With her finest daughter lost to her, she's not going to undervalue the two that she has left. I see Mary eyeing the court dwarf, Thomasina, sometimes, as a bad-tempered kitten will challenge a small cat. Thomasina, who is fully grown at less than four foot, and excessively proud, ignores Mary completely.

When I first meet the Herberts, father and son, it is as if we are strangers. My marriage is annulled as if it had never been and neither of them says one word to me. The Earl of Pembroke bows as if he cannot quite recall me; his son Henry inclines his head with faint regret. I ignore them both.

I don't care for them, I don't care for anything at court. I have become a young lady of the royal house again. I am restored. I can hardly believe that I ever had a sister Jane at all, for no-one ever mentions her. I had no father, I had no sister Jane. Little Mary and I are Queen Mary's loyal maids-in-waiting and my mother accompanies her everywhere as her favoured cousin and senior lady at court. I have my own rooms in the queen's apartments, while Mary sleeps in the maids' rooms with the other girls. We are acknowledged as the queen's cousins and we make new friends and companions.

I meet Janey Seymour, who is sister to Ned Seymour, the handsome boy who came to be betrothed to Jane all that long time ago. I like Janey at once. She is a clever girl, a scholar like Jane, she even writes poetry that rhymes and yet she is playful and funny. She strikes me at once as an ideal friend: she is pretty like me and learned like Jane. She hoped to be Jane's sister-in-law, she is the only person at court that speaks of her. We have shared a loss, and now we can be friends.

The two of us agree on everything, silently disapproving when the queen accepts a proposal of marriage from a man eleven years her junior and a thousand times better-looking, the dazzlingly handsome Prince Philip of Spain, who comes to England with a court of darkly delicious friends and proceeds to make all us girls quite giddy with desire, frantic to be admired.

They are all so rich, they are unspeakably, unimaginably rich! A girl cannot be blamed for quietly learning a few words of Spanish and praying for one of the dons, almost any one of them, to notice her. Their dark capes are all embroidered with gold or silver thread – real gold, real silver. They wear ropes of gold, chains of gold at their shoulders, flung around their necks as if they were scarves. Their hats are embossed with pearls, they wear rubies as lightly as garnets, and every single one of them has an enormous ungodly crucifix worn under his linen or clasped proudly visible at his throat. I can't help but smile to think how Jane would have shuddered at the display of both wealth and heresy in the one vain act. I miss her all over again when I remember her widened hazel eyes, her scandalised face, the purse of her disapproving lips.

The girls of Queen Mary's rooms whisper to themselves whether they should like to marry one of the handsome hidalgos and go away to Spain forever, and I think – yes, I would. God knows I would. I wouldn't trouble myself over heresy and righteousness; I want to dance and wear a small fortune on my fingers. I want someone to love me, I want to feel alive, I want to feel madly alive every moment of every day, since I have seen how easily and quickly a girl can die. 'Learn you to die!' I have learned; and I only want to live. Janey Seymour says that my heart rushes just like hers does, that we are both girls who have to live life at a gallop. We are young and we have to have everything all at once. She says this is what it is to be young and beautiful – not like the queen, who is nearly forty and slow as a fat old mare who has been left out in the pasture for too long.

The queen marries Prince Philip of Spain at Winchester and she makes a poor showing. She is pale with nerves, and her square little face takes on the folded scowl of her bad-tempered father when she is anxious. She stands like he did in his horrible portraits, her feet spread apart under her thick gown, pugnacious as a hen. Heavens! What a determined old lady she is! I know it's not her fault – I am not such a fool as to think that a woman should be blamed for not being young and beautiful – though of course I prefer the young and the beautiful, being one of them myself. But at least she looks as well as she can on her wedding day, she dresses as she should, she wears a gown of gold for her wedding, her sleeves are embroidered with diamonds – and then we start the breathless wait to see if she can bear him a son.

HAMPTON COURT PALACE, SUMMER 1555

While she is enduring a tiring pregnancy in hot weather, Queen Mary finds it in her heart to forgive her difficult half-sister and succumbs to the persuasion of her husband, Prince Philip, to release Elizabeth from Woodstock Palace. Our kinswoman comes to court dressed very modestly with a small hood over her ginger hair, wearing Protestant black and white, as charming and enthusiastic as any spinster aunt-to-be.

Her presence only adds another runner in the gallop to be first behind the queen when she walks anywhere. But surely, though Elizabeth may compete for precedence, she cannot truly think that she has any chance of being named as the queen's heir? Her mere presence reminds everyone of the religious divide, for everyone knows that Elizabeth is the Protestant heir just as my sister was.

When the court moves to Oatlands, my mother goes home to Beaumanor and, without a word of warning to me or Mary, puts off black and marries her master of horse, Adrian Stokes, who has served us and cared for the horses and hounds for as long as I can remember. Mary says that our lady mother could not afford his wages and could not bear to lose his care of her horses, but I think that she is glad to be rid of the name of Grey, which is blazoned over every illegal reformist pamphlet, and famous throughout Christendom. With Adrian Stokes she can bury her treasonous name with her traitorous husband and reformist daughter, and pretend, like everyone else, that they never existed.

It's all very well for her. She becomes Mrs Stokes (though I know she will always demand to be called Lady Frances, and receive a deep royal bow), but I am still Lady Katherine Grey. Mary is still Lady Mary, and there is no way for us to change our names unless someone marries us too. There is no hiding that we, along with Elizabeth, Mary of Scots and Margaret Douglas, are the last remaining Tudors, all of us with a claim to the queen's throne, all of us hanging around court and waiting for the outcome of this speedy conception. One of us certain to inherit, unless she has a healthy baby – a thing her mother did only once.

OATLANDS PALACE, SURREY, SUMMER 1555

God knows, not I, why nothing ever goes right for us Tudors. Queen Mary does not get the son she longs for. She goes into confinement with a good belly on her and all us ladies of honour are very charming when we sit with her and sew baby clothes, and when we come out we toss our heads and say that we really cannot discuss intimate female matters with the handsome Spanish courtiers. I make much of saying that a maiden like myself (never an abandoned wife, a girl whose marriage was annulled within weeks) cannot remark on how well the queen is doing today, such things are a mystery to a virgin like me. We keep this up – it is absolutely delightful – from the seventh month to the full nine, and then (with less conviction) for the tenth. Now it appears that it really is a mystery to all of us – maids and midwives alike. We conceal our growing anxiety as best we can and we say that she has mistaken her dates, and the birth will be any day now, but even I think this is a bit far-fetched.

In this time of waiting Elizabeth is a complete lickspigot, charming to all the ladies, thoughtful and attentive to the lords, breathlessly concerned as to the health of her beloved half-sister and seductive as an expelled nun to her sister's own husband, Philip of Spain, who clearly sees her as the guarantor of his safety if his old wife dies in childbirth.

I ask my lady mother what is happening with the queen and why she does not labour and bear her child like a normal woman – and she snaps at me and tells me that of all the stupid girls in the world I should be the last one to ask where the heir to the throne is, since every day that there is no birth, she is the first legitimate heir and so my position gets better and better. I whisper 'Elizabeth?' and my lady mother says sharply, 'Declared a bastard by her own father?' and raps me on the knuckles with her riding whip. I take it I am going to get no helpful maternal advice from her, and I ask her nothing more.

Another month goes by and the queen's belly simply goes down, as if it were nothing but pasture bloat in a greedy old sheep that broke into clover, and now we all say nothing at all as she comes out of confinement and rejoins the court as if nothing had ever happened.

It's agony for her, of course, because she is madly in love with King Philip and he is as polite and as patient as a man can be with an older wife who imagined herself pregnant and made them both look like fools; but actually it's very embarrassing for all of us: all the English courtiers who made so much of our queen's fertility, all of us maids who bustled around making ourselves important. Worst of all is Elizabeth, dripping with sympathy but walking in to dinner behind the queen, right on her heels, as if Philip's attention to her proves that she is heir, and everyone quite forgets about my mother's claims, and about me.

In these circumstances – ridiculous and unpredictable, and just typical of the stupidity of everyone – I find that I have had the misfortune to inherit my mother's ambition. Really, I would have expected to despise it, seeing where it has got us so far. But I can't help myself, I resent anyone suggesting that I am not the heir and I am starting to struggle in the nightly squabble for precedence.

It's not so much that I think I should be queen – I wouldn't want to displace Queen Mary – but I do want to be her heir. I just can't see that anyone else is fit for the crown. I can't be happy at the thought of Elizabeth being queen; I can't imagine her in Jane's place; nobody could. She's so unworthy! In every way, from her terrible yellow hair – it's not golden at all like mine – to her skin, as sallow as a Spaniard's, she is unfit to be Queen of England. I would have stepped back willingly for a little prince who was the heir to Spain and to England, born in wedlock to two ruling monarchs. But I will never step back for my great-uncle's bastard – especially as nobody knows if Elizabeth is even that. Her mother was taken in adultery with five men! Elizabeth could well be the daughter of the king's lute player – who knows?

But during this dull time of embarrassed regret, with no Prince of Wales in the cradle and little prospect of another pregnancy, I am not the only one who is thinking of my rights. I seem to have become of great interest to two people – two men, actually. One is my former husband, Henry Lord Herbert, who always turns his head and gives me a little hidden smile when we maids walk past him. I don't smile back exactly, I give him a look a little like Jane used to put on when she read something that she thought unlikely: a sort of sceptical raised eyebrow, a sort of looking down my nose. I think it's rather charming, and I cuff Mary my sister when she remarks that I am gurning at Henry Herbert as if I wished we were still married.

I say it hardly befits her, whose head comes only to the top of my bodice, to comment on my appearance. 'You're no taller than the queen's dwarf,' I say crushingly. 'Don't tell me that I'm gurning.'

'I am no dwarf,' she says firmly. 'I was born small but royal. I am quite different from Thomasina. Everyone says so.'

I can't challenge her petite dignity. 'Oh, and who are all these people who say so?'

'I do,' she says with huge dignity. 'And it is me who matters.'

She has always been quite untroubled that she is so short and not growing any more. Jane once told her that dwarfs in some heathen country were worshipped as gods, and it filled her with pride. She thinks very highly of herself for one who stands so low. I think it very odd that I should have had one sister who despised the world of the flesh, and one too tiny to desire it, and here am I, born between the two of them, tall and pretty, the most eager girl for worldly pleasures in all of the court.

'I suppose you want to marry him again,' Mary says sagely. 'I would have thought that the way they treated you would have put you off the Herberts forever.'

I tell her, not at all! Not at all! We were never married, not at all! Just as she was never betrothed either. The marriage is denied and forgotten and I have no idea why he smiles so charmingly at me. He should have kept me as his wife if he likes me so much, if he had the sense to go against his family's orders and follow his heart. But he made the mistake of letting me go and now he sees that I am a centre of attention at court, I am pleased to think he regrets it.

But the other gentleman – actually nobleman – who is taking an interest in me is even more surprising: the Spanish ambassador, Count de Feria.

I'm not a fool. I don't think that he has fallen in love with my fair prettiness, though he is kind enough to tell me that I am like a little alabaster statue, my skin so clear and my hair as fair as an angel's. He tells me they would kneel to my beauty in Spain, that I look like a painting of an angel in stained glass, luminously beautiful. I enjoy all this, of course, but I know very well that it is not my looks – even if they are the very best at court – that interest him. Of course it is my royal kinship, my proximity to the throne. And if the Spanish ambassador takes an interest in me, does that mean the heir of Spain – the King Consort of England himself – is also taking an interest in me? Concealing his attraction to me by an empty flirtation with Elizabeth? Am I, in fact, being groomed for the throne by the papists, just as Jane was pushed there by the reformers? Do the Spanish hope that when the queen dies they can declare me as their heir, and Philip will marry me, and rule through me?

I don't ask the Spanish ambassador this directly; I am too clever for that. Of course I understand how these games of power are to be played. And he says nothing directly, except that I am admired by King Philip, and do I have a kindness for Spain? Am I a determined reformer like my poor sister or do I incline to the true Church?

I look down modestly, and I smile at my feet and say that no-one could help but admire King Philip. I say nothing in the least heretical or even argumentative but I swear to myself that I will be no-one's puppet. Nobody will ever order me again. If anyone is thinking of pushing me onto the throne, just as they pushed my sister, they will find that I am queenly in my own right; they will find that if they put the crown on my head, I will keep it, and my head as well. No-one is going to tempt me into a usurpation that cannot be maintained. Nobody is going to tempt me to insist on my inheritance. I will be a careful wise servant of my own interests. I will not risk anything for my faith. If God wants me on the throne of England then He will have to make the effort Himself.

But I listen carefully when the Spanish ambassador goes beyond flattery to plotting. If the Spanish persuade Queen

Mary to name me as heir, and then support me, I am certain to succeed.

'And, despite your sister's faith, do you incline naturally to the old religion?' Count de Feria asks me, sweet as the marmalade that he spoons onto my plate.

I look up at him from under my eyelashes as he invites me to deny my dead sister and everything she believed in. 'Of course I follow the queen's religion,' I say easily. 'I have had to learn it all from the very beginning, and learn the Latin Mass too, since I was brought up in a household filled with reformers praying in English. But I have been glad to study and learn the truth.' I hesitate. 'I am no heretic.'

Of course I am not. The queen my cousin who came to the throne so kindly, assuring us all that everyone should find God in their own way, executed my sister for her faith, and now brings in the Holy Inquisition to torture everyone else and burn Jane's fellow believers. Not me! I am not going to be imprisoned for a form of words. I am not going to be beheaded for failing to curtsey to the Host, or forgetting to dip my fingers in the stoup, or any other thing that is life and death today, but did not even exist yesterday. Now the altars are hidden behind the rood screen so the priest's work is all a mystery. Now there are statues in every niche, and a candle before every one of them. Now there are saints' days when nobody works, and fast days when we are supposed to eat nothing but fish. There are all sorts of practices that I have had to learn in order not to look like a reformer and the sister of a dangerous reformer martyr. I bob and genuflect and sniff the incense with the most faithful. Nobody is going to name me as a heretic because I turn my back on the hidden altar and don't pop up or down at the right moment.

I am determined on this. I am going to do whatever anyone asks of me. I am going to win a fortune from this most devout queen, and then she is going to choose a handsome man for me to marry and have beautiful sons. Then I will be the papist heir to the throne with one of the faithful in the cradle and I don't doubt she will name me as the next queen. This is my destiny.

I will help it on its way but I won't take any risks. So I smile at her husband's ambassador, who is all but asking me if I want to be queen, and I make sure that he knows that there is no-one in England more suitable.

Except for Margaret Douglas, of course, who thinks it should be her, except for little Mary Queen of Scots in her palaces in France who thinks it should be her with a French army to press her claims. Except for Elizabeth, the least likely heir to her half-sister, disqualified by the law, by religion, by temperament and by birth.

Elizabeth the Unhappy comes to court and sighs in the corners as if her heart is breaking for the imprisoned clergy and the martyrs burning at Smithfield. Elizabeth dresses very plainly, the liar, as if she does not love beautiful clothes and rich jewels. She is a peacock hidden in black. Elizabeth comes to Mass and holds her hand to her side as if she is in too much pain to bow to the Host, and sometimes she manages to faint and be carried out so that the waiting crowds outside can see her dying for her reformist faith, and think the queen is cruel to her half-sister. Elizabeth the minx recovers with remarkable speed and can later be seen walking in the gardens with King Philip, his eyes on her downturned face as he leans towards her to hear what she is whispering.

I think that Elizabeth is playing a long game and planning that the queen, who is sicker and quieter every day, will die, and then King Philip will marry her and make her his wife and Queen of England in Mary's place. As the Spanish ambassador courts me, his master the king courts Elizabeth, and I see her maidenly reserve is as sincere as mine, and we both have our eyes on the throne.

She and I meet every day in attendance on the queen – and we bow to each other with careful politeness and we kiss as cousins, and I swear we both think: why, you are further from the throne than I am! What are they promising you? And I swear we both think: and if I am ever queen you will know it!

WHITEHALL PALACE, LONDON, WINTER 1558

And that is why it is such a terrible shock when, with every reason to name me, with the veiled support of the Spanish, with every demonstration I could give her of my papist piety, as soon as Queen Mary's sickness and sorrow become fatal she names Elizabeth – Elizabeth! – names her at the last possible moment, on her deathbed, and half the country goes mad for the Protestant princess, who now rides into London and takes her throne as if she were the legitimate heir of royal blood and not a lucky bastard.

After all I have done to prove myself a good papist Queen Mary fails me, fails her loudly proclaimed faith that so many have died for. She does not even mention the true papist and heir, her other cousin Mary Queen of Scots, who is now married to Francis of France and has the gall to proclaim herself Queen of England, as if my branch of the family were not named to come before hers. Queen Mary does not even mention Margaret Douglas though she promised to make her heir. She plays us all false and names Elizabeth. Elizabeth, her enemy!

'Why did Queen Mary not name you?' I demand of my mother, forced into honesty with her for once, driven by resentment into frankness. 'Why did she not name me?'

My mother's face is darkened with impotent fury. She will now have to serve as loving cousin and lady-in-waiting in Elizabeth's rooms and she does not expect a girl young enough to be her daughter, and with every reason to dislike her, to be a particularly generous mistress. My mother, who married her master of horse in order to reassure Queen Mary that she had no plans to marry a man with a claim to the throne, and no royal-blooded son on the way, now finds herself with no great name and no heir either, for Adrian Stokes is a nobody and all her babies from him have died. She made herself unimportant to please Queen Mary, but finds that all she has done is step back for Queen Elizabeth.

'Will you put that damned rat out of here?' she shouts.

I have a new puppy, a pretty pug called Jo, who comes with me everywhere. I bend down and quietly put her out of the room. She whines and scrabbles at the door and then sits sorrowfully on the wooden floorboards outside, to wait for me.

'Queen Mary always had strong family feeling,' my mother says through her teeth. 'Despite it all. She came to the throne by her father's will and she did not think it should be overturned. He recognised Elizabeth as his child and in his will he named her to come after her sister, Queen Mary. He named my line to follow Elizabeth only if she has no heirs, and so that is what the queen willed.' She takes a breath and I can see her fighting to master her temper, a struggle so vigorous that I think she may give herself a fit. 'In accordance with tradition. In accordance with King Henry's will, God bless him.'

'But what about me?' I demand. I think I have been saying this for all my life. 'What about me?'

'You have to wait,' my mother says, as if I am not eighteen and desperate to get on with my life, to eat at the feast, to dance at all the celebrations, to wear the beautiful gowns from the wardrobe, to flirt with all the reformist young men who suddenly appear at this exciting new court, which gives up Latin in a hurry, and reads the Bible in English and has to pray only twice a day.

'I can't wait,' I wail. 'I have been waiting every day since Father named Jane as queen. All I ever do is wait for something to happen to me, and hope that this time it's nice. Janey Seymour says—'

'I've heard more than enough of Jane Seymour,' my mother says brusquely. 'Are you staying with them again this month? Aren't they tired of your company?'

'No, they're not, and yes I am staying at Hanworth unless you order me to be with you at court,' I say, defying her to forbid me the company of my best friend. 'It's not as if we will be drowning in favours from Elizabeth and should be there early to catch the bounty. I don't see why I should be there as all Elizabeth's friends come out of wherever they have been hiding. I don't see that I should have to stand and watch all day as Elizabeth orders new gowns from the wardrobe that should have been mine.'

'It's not about gowns; gowns are not important,' my mother says, wrong again.

HANWORTH PALACE, MIDDLESEX, SPRING 1559

Instead of watching Elizabeth glorying in the treasures and the throne that once belonged to my sister and should have come to me, I go to stay with Janey and her mother, Lady Anne Seymour, at their lovely house in the country. I take Mr Nozzle the monkey and the little cat Ribbon and the new puppy Jo, and everyone loves them at Hanworth, and nobody tells me to put them in their cages. I am sure that nobody at court misses me at all, except perhaps Henry Herbert, whose lingering glances tell me that now he thinks he made a big mistake when he let them part him from the queen's cousin. My other former admirer, the Spanish ambassador, is very subdued, waiting to see how his royal master – safely far away on his own lands – manages the new queen and if she will have him in marriage as she promised.

I doubt that she even notices that I am absent. Of course it is exciting that suddenly all the serious Spanish have vanished and the sorrowful Queen Mary is dead, and everyone is young and reformist and flirtatious. Elizabeth, in the plumb centre of it all with her head turned by her sudden safety and importance, goes everywhere with Robert Dudley, my sister Jane's brother-in-law, as if they were sweethearts, suddenly given the keys to their own palace. They are practically hand in hand; they must be dizzy with relief. It is a miraculous transition from the prison rooms of the Tower to the royal apartments overnight. They both must have thought that they would put their heads down on the block and now they rest their cheeks on the finest of linen embroidered with coronets. Her mother was beheaded, so was his father. Both of them have carved their names on the walls of a Tower cell and counted the days till their likely trial. It must be heaven to come through that darkened gateway and find yourself on the road to court. My sister, of course, took the opposite journey – from royal rooms to the scaffold – and it was Robert's father who was the cause of her imprisonment. The plot for Elizabeth was the final straw and reason for Jane's execution. I don't forget this when I see their triumph: beggars' triumph. I wonder that they are not ashamed.

But nobody thinks of it but me, and I try not to think of it at all. Elizabeth's new court is crowded with people dashing back from Switzerland or Germany, or wherever they have been hiding from the Inquisition. The horses must be foundering on the roads all the way from Zurich. Our great friend Lady Bess Cavendish, widowed, married to another rich man, and a convinced Lutheran, turns up at court and is best of friends with us again, and a great adherent of Elizabeth. The Duchess of Suffolk, our young and beautiful step-grandmother Catherine Brandon, reappears from exile with her commoner husband and two adorable little children. The whole world wants places and fees and favours, all of them suddenly the best friend of the loneliest girl in England. Elizabeth's lady governess, Kat Ashley, is back at her side after a spell in the Fleet Prison for treason. No longer is Elizabeth the despised half-bred sister: she is the Protestant princess who has restored the reformed faith to England; she is the heroine of all reformers, as if my sister Jane had never been, as if I – a born reformer, born royal – did not exist.

I get no credit for having been sister to a queen, a queen of only nine days but proclaimed by everyone who is now crowding into the Protestant court. Elizabeth has no sense of family feeling: she was terrified of her father, nervous around her half-brother, King Edward, who loved Jane so dearly, and the declared enemy to her half-sister, Queen Mary. While I was raised by a mother who spoke every day of our royal kinship, Elizabeth was raised alone, her mother dead, her father marrying other women. So I am not surprised that she doesn't greet me with any pleasure, and I allow myself to raise my chin, to raise my eyebrows and speak to her as a near-equal. To outshine her in grace and beauty every day in these hours of her loudly acclaimed triumph is my only revenge. She is ridiculously vain, quite desperate to be thought the most beautiful girl at court, in England, in the world – but here am I: slim where she is dropsical, bright-eyed where she is tired, light-hearted where she has every day new responsibilities and learns of new things to fear, a survivor just as she is, but fair-skinned and blonde where she is – to tell the truth – swarthy and ginger. I can drive her mad just by walking across the room, and so I do.

It's as well for me that she is surely too busy worrying about supporting the Protestants in Scotland, settling the religion of the English, struggling to get herself named as Supreme Governor of the Church of England – as if a woman could be such a thing! – to object to my little acts of defiance. It's as well for me that I have Hanworth to run to, for my mother rails at me and calls me a fool to torment an anxious young woman newcome to her throne, but I think of it as Jane's throne, and mine, and I think of Elizabeth as the vain scramblingly ambitious daughter of a lute player and a whore.

She promises that she will name her heir, but she does not. She should name me, but she avoids my name. Until she behaves as a queen should do – marries and gets an heir or names one – she will win no respect from me, and for sure, she returns me none.

'You're so right,' Janey Seymour says emphatically. She turns her head to cough into her sleeve and her whole body shakes with the strength of the spasm. But she is smiling when she turns back to me, her eyes feverishly bright. 'You're right, everyone knows that she is not the true heir, everyone knows that she is illegitimate, but there is nobody to take your side. All the reformers believe that Elizabeth is the best that they can get, and not even the papists dare to suggest Mary Queen of Scots, half French as she is.'

I have Mr Nozzle on my lap and I am tickling his fat little tummy. His eyes are closed with pleasure. Every now and then he gives a little yawn or perhaps it is a silent laugh. 'If I had been married . . .' I think of the Dudleys planning, campaigning and fighting for Jane. Where might I be now, if I had a powerful family to conspire for me, if my father were still alive? If I had a husband and his father saw what we could be?

'Oh, yes, but the Herberts aren't going to risk anything against Elizabeth.'

'I never think of Henry Herbert,' I lie, and Janey catches my eye and goes off into a peal of laughter that ends in a coughing fit.

'Of course you don't. But you're still heir to the throne, and his father doesn't forget that! He's always so polite to you now!'

'I don't care!' I toss my head, and sit Mr Nozzle up on his little bottom so he watches us with his serious eyes.

'But you have to marry,' Janey says, when she has her breath back. 'Elizabeth isn't going to find you a good match. She wants nobody courting but her. She'd make us all into nuns if she could. Does your mother plan nothing for you now that Queen Mary did not name you as heir after Elizabeth, now that Elizabeth does not promise you?'

'She's hoping that Elizabeth will come to favour us,' I say. 'I'd get a better match if Elizabeth would only recognise us, her family. But obviously, she thinks only of herself. I have been quite forgotten. I don't even have my rightful place in the privy chamber. I'm not in the inner circle. You would think I am a complete stranger, waiting about outside in the presence chamber like some unknown petitioner, when my place is inside like a kinswoman. Queen Mary would never have treated us so.'

Janey shakes her head. 'It's just jealousy,' she says as the door to her privy chamber opens and her handsome brother Ned puts his head into the room, and, seeing that Janey and I are alone, comes in.

'What webs are you spinning, little spiders?' he asks, and throws himself down on a stool at the fireside between our two seats.

I can feel myself sit up a little in my chair, and lift my face to the light and tilt it to the best angle. I have adored Edward Seymour ever since he was betrothed to my sister Jane and I told her then that he was the most handsome young man in the world, with the kindest eyes; but she would have none of it. Now I see him almost every day, and he teases me with the familiarity of an old friend, but I still think he is the most handsome young man in the world.

'We're speaking of marriage,' says Janey, daring me to disagree.

'Not of our marriages,' I say hastily. 'I have no interest in marriage.'

'Oh, how cruel!' Ned says with a wink. 'There will be many broken hearts at court if you live and die a virgin.'

I giggle and blush and can think of nothing to say.

'Of course she must marry,' Janey says. 'And someone of the best family. But who? What d'you think, Ned?'

'A Spanish prince?' he asks. 'Isn't the Spanish ambassador your great admirer? A French milord? Surely a girl like Lady Katherine Grey, so close to the throne, so beautiful, can look as high as she likes?'

'Really!' I say, trying to look modest but completely thrilled by this improper conversation. 'It is for my friends and family to decide.'

'Oh, not a Spaniard! She doesn't want to go away to Spain,' Janey says airily. 'I can't let her go. She must have a handsome Englishman, of course.'

'I don't know even one,' Ned asserts. 'No-one handsome enough. I wouldn't know where to begin. All my friends are plain as bullocks, and I—' He breaks off and looks directly at me. 'You wouldn't consider me? I am wonderfully well connected.'

I can feel the colour rising in my cheeks. 'I . . . I . . .'

'What a question!' Janey clears the little catch in her throat. 'Are you proposing marriage, Ned? Beware, for I am a witness!'

'In the absence of anyone worthy . . .' His eyes are on my burning cheeks, on my mouth. I almost think that he might lean forward and kiss me, he is so close and his gaze is so intimate.

'You speak in jest,' I manage to whisper.

'Only if you like the jest,' he replies.

'Of course she likes it!' Janey says. 'What girl does not like a joke about love?'

'Shall I write you a poem?' he asks me.

He is a wonderful poet; if he were to write a poem about me I would be famous just for that. I really think that I will faint from the heat in my face and the pounding in my ears. I can't look away from his warm smiling eyes and he goes on staring at my mouth as if he would lean forward, closer and closer to a kiss.

'Have you been hunting?' I ask at random. 'How is the horse?'

How is the horse? I was embarrassed before; now I wish I could simply die. It is as if I can think of nothing to say but nonsense, as if my lips want to betray me to him, to assure him that I can think of nothing when he is so close. Janey looks at me with a mystified gaze and Ned laughs shortly, as if he understands completely the whirl of foolishness that I am in. Lazily, he gets to his feet.

'The horse was very helpful,' he says, smiling down on me. 'You know: trotting about here and there, galloping when needed. He is a very good horse. He stops when he is bidden, which is pleasant too.'

'I know,' I swallow, while Janey watches both of us with a sudden attentive interest.

'I'll come back to take you both in to dinner,' Ned offers. Standing at his full height he is magnificently handsome, tall, brown-haired, brown-eyed, he looks lean and strong in his riding breeches and high boots. He pulls down his jacket so it fits around his slim waist and bows to me and to his sister and goes from the room.

'Oh my God! You love him!' Janey crows and makes herself cough again. Mr Nozzle jumps from my lap and goes to the door as if he would follow Ned. 'You sly little thing! All this time I was thinking of Herbert and yet you love my brother, and kept it secret all this time! "How is the horse?" Oh Lord! "How is the horse?"'

I am near to tears with laughter and shame. 'Oh, don't say anything! Don't say another word.'

'What were you thinking?'

'I wasn't thinking at all!' I confess. 'I was just looking at him. I couldn't think of anything while he was looking at me.'

She puts a hand to her heart. 'Well,' she says, snatching at a breath, 'I think that answers our question. You shall marry Ned and I will be your sister-in-law. We Seymours are the equal of any family in England, your own father picked out Ned for your sister Jane. Now you can marry him and how happy we will be! And I will be aunt to a little heir to the throne. Nobody can deny your importance when you have a Tudor-Seymour boy in the cradle! I expect Elizabeth will be his godmother and name him as her heir until she gets her own boy.'

'Elizabeth would run mad if we married,' I say with pleasure.

'Completely. But then she'd have to take you into her privy chamber, as one of her senior ladies. You would be her cousin twice over, like it or not. She'd have to make your son her heir; everyone would insist on it. Just think! My nephew for King of England!'

'My Lady Hertford,' I say, trying the title on as I might drape a bolt of fabric against my face to see the colour against my fair skin.

'It suits you,' Janey says.

It starts as little more than a joke. Janey and I must have proposed half a dozen suitors for each other in the years that we have been friends, but as Ned rides with us, and walks in the garden, takes us in to dinner and bets on the cards that we play in the evenings, he continues his warm flirtatious intimate tone with me and I blush and giggle and slowly, slowly, find a reply. Gradually, carefully, it turns from a joke into a real courtship, and I know that I am, for the first and last time, really truly in love.

Everyone can see it. It is not just Janey who remarks that we are a beautiful couple, matched in height and looks and breeding. The whole household conspires to leave us together, or direct us to one another.

'His lordship is in the stable yard,' one of the grooms says to me as I come from the front door to go riding.

'Lady Katherine is in the garden walking her pug,' they tell him when he rides in after an errand for his mother.

'The ladies are in the library . . . the young ladies are sewing in the privy chamber . . . his lordship is at prayer, his lordship is coming home at midday . . .' Everyone directs Ned to me, and me to him, until we spend all day every day together, and every time I see him I feel a thrill as if it were the very first time I have ever seen him, and every time he leaves me I wish he would never go.

'Do you love him truly?' Janey whispers longingly when we are supposed to be going to sleep, bedded down together in her big wooden bed with the curtains drawn around us, my pug and kitten and Mr Nozzle the monkey all tucked up with us.

'I can't say,' I reply cautiously.

'You do then,' she says with satisfaction. 'For anyone can say "no".'

'I shouldn't say,' I amend.

'So you do.'

Of course Ned and Janey's mother, Lady Anne Seymour, sees this as well as anyone else, and she calls her two children into her private chapel one morning. I am not invited. I am certain that she is going to ban them both from seeing me any more. We will be separated, I know it. I shall be sent home. I shall be disgraced. She will say that a sister of Jane Grey cannot be seen to be flirting with Jane Grey's former betrothed. She is a redoubtable woman who thinks very highly of herself. She may have married beneath her in her second marriage, but her first husband was the greatest man in England after the king and she insisted on her position as wife of the Lord Protector. She will tell her son and heir that she has already planned his marriage with someone very important, and that he may not court me.

'She did,' Janey confirms, dashing back from the chapel to the bedroom that we share. She gasps and puts a hand to her heart. 'I came as quick as I could. I knew you would be desperate to know what she said.'

I snatch Ribbon the cat off her chair so she can sit, but I have to wait as her colour comes and goes, and she gets her breath. As soon as she can speak, she says: 'She told Ned that he must not single you out, that he was not a suitable companion for you, nor you for him.'

'Oh my God!' I say. I drop down onto the bed and clasp Janey's hands. 'I knew it! She hates me! What did he say? Is he going to give me up?'

'He was wonderful!' Janey exclaims. 'So calm. He sounded so grown-up. Not at all worried. I never thought he would stand up to our mother like that. He said that young people may well accompany each other, and that there was no reason that he should avoid you, either here or at court. My lady mother said that he should not single you out as he does, and he said that it was obvious that the queen had no objection to a friendship between the two of you, as she had never said anything against it, and she knows that you are here together.'

'He said that?' I am stunned at his confidence.

'He did. Very coolly too.'

'And what did your mother say?' I ask faintly.

'She looked surprised and she said that she had nothing against you, and nothing against our friendship, but that no doubt the queen has plans for both of you, and they will not be for you to marry Ned. She said that the queen would not want to bring a cousin like you even closer to the throne by making you a Seymour.'

'Oh, Elizabeth doesn't care!' I say. 'She has no plans for me. She delights in having no plans for me. She doesn't think twice about me.'

'Well, that's just what Ned said!' Janey says triumphantly. 'And he said that while both of you were free there was no reason that you should not be in each other's company, and he bowed and left, just like that.'

'Just like that?' I repeat.

'You know how he bows and walks away.'

He moves like a dancer, light on his feet yet with his shoulders set, like a man to be reckoned with. I know just how he bows and walks away.

GREENWICH PALACE,
SUMMER 1559

At the end of my visit, I pack up my pets, Mr Nozzle the monkey, Ribbon the cat and Jo the puppy, into their little travelling baskets, and go back to court to attend on the queen and to live with my mother and Mary in smaller rooms than we had under Queen Mary, furnished with the second-best goods that the groom of the chambers has picked out for us, since we are no longer favourites. My mother makes Mr Nozzle live in a cage and complains if Ribbon tears at the colourless tapestries. I say nothing about Ned and he does not come to court as he promised he would. There is not a doubt in my mind that his mother is keeping him at Hanworth. If I were recognised by Elizabeth as I should be – as her cousin and her heir – his mother would be quick enough to encourage our love. But as it is, she is fearful of the future with my cousin on the throne. Elizabeth has no family feeling, and she is doing her best to reassure the papists, she has no need for a Protestant heir.

My mother is ill and sometimes withdraws from court altogether. Mary goes with her to Richmond. There are no struggles for precedence behind Elizabeth; my mother has lost all heart for the fight.

The only person who singles me out at all is the Spanish ambassador, Count de Feria, and he is still so charming and so admiring and so warm that I cannot resist confiding in him and I tell him that I think I will never be happy in England while Elizabeth is queen and he says – so invitingly! – that I should go to Spain with him and the countess where they will introduce me to the families of all the handsome noblemen who have gone home with Philip. He tells me that there is a new treaty between England and France and the young Mary Queen of Scots has been cheated by her royal French family in order to get peace. She will never be allowed to press her claim to the English throne again. She is discounted. I am the only heir to England.

I laugh – for how could I ever go to Spain? But I promise him that I will always take his advice, that he is my only friend, and that I shall marry no-one without confirming my choice with him. But I am not so indiscreet as to tell him that I have already chosen.

NONSUCH PALACE,
SURREY, SUMMER 1559

The absence of Ned from court goes on and on, and now I hear that he is said to be unwell and has to stay with his mother to be nursed. They are a very sickly family. I don't think Janey has been well since the day I met her, but she has never let it stop her attendance at court before. I would have thought that nothing could have been better for them both than travelling with the court on progress – riding every day and in clean air. I am sure that would be the best thing for them. I am afraid that his mother is trying to keep Ned from me, and this is so terribly unfair on me as I have done nothing to displease her or him. It is all the fault of Elizabeth, whose bad treatment of me makes everyone avoid me.

She persecutes me in a dozen small ways. I get poorer rooms than I should, I take precedence in processions but she does not favour me in private. I am not invited to draw pretty gowns from the royal wardrobe – she never gives me anything. Ladies-in-waiting are paid a small fee and make their fortunes from gifts and favours; but I never get anything from Elizabeth and nobody is ever going to pay me for an introduction as it is well known that she never talks with me.

I take a small satisfaction that when the court goes on progress, Elizabeth has to order the royal wardrobe to issue gowns to all her ladies, and of course, I wear them better than anybody. Her great flirt, the master of horse Robert Dudley, may try to forget that I was once his sister-in-law, but he still sees that I am mounted well on a strong hunter. Elizabeth may not favour me, but she cannot conceal that I am the most beautiful girl at court, exquisite when I am dancing, striking when I am riding. My step-grandmother, who was a famous beauty in her day when she was the young wife of my grandfather Charles Brandon, kisses me on my forehead and says that I am far and away the prettiest girl at court, just like she was at my age. We travel for some weeks and then we go to Nonsuch Palace, which is a fairy-tale place set in beautiful grounds beside the river. The widower Henry FitzAlan the Earl of Arundel owns the palace and remembers his duty to the family of his first wife, my aunt, and brings me forward in all the entertainments he has laid on for the court. When Ned Seymour and Janey finally join the court they find me dancing in the masques and leading the hunt on my new horse, at the very centre of the summertime entertainments.

The daily rhythm of court life brings Ned to my side at chapel and breakfast, hunting and dinner, dancing and playing cards. Every day the court plans and performs a new event. My uncle Arundel has organised plays and masques, dances and picnics, races, tournaments. Robert Dudley is everywhere, with little touches of pretty ceremonies, extra celebrations. He is at the centre of everything and nobody can take their eyes off him. He is a man restored to wealth and favour and he has the golden sheen of success on him. Elizabeth the queen is openly, obviously, shamelessly besotted with him. She cannot stop herself looking for him; her face lights up when she sees him. She is drawn across the room to him. I can see them look for each other, and see no-one else. I think only I fully understand this. I know what she is feeling, because it is the same for me.

In the council room of the palace the senior lords, especially the old ones, call Privy Council meetings while the court is at play. There are constant emergencies, and messengers from parliament come every day urging her to marry Philip of Spain's cousin, or the French prince; someone – anyone! – to give her a powerful ally and the chance of a son and heir. But Elizabeth rides all day neck and neck with Robert Dudley and dances with him all night, and any woman at court could tell the council that she does not even hear them. Helpfully, she agrees that she must be married, that the safety of the kingdom requires a great foreign consort, and the future of the kingdom must be secured by an heir, but her dark eyes follow Robert Dudley round the room as he goes from one beautiful girl to another but always ends up at her side.

Everyone is watching this courtship, and in the heady atmosphere of a court where the queen is openly, madly in love with a married man, everyone is free to flirt and even steal away and kiss. The older men and advisors who are so bad-tempered and grave, the older women who are so insistent on modesty and always hark back to how things used to be, are simply ignored when the Queen of England rides out with her horse shoulder to shoulder with the man they are beginning to whisper is her lover, their hands hidden, entwined, as they ride home.

Certainly no-one is watching me, no-one is watching Ned. We meet in Janey's bedroom when she is too ill to get up from her bed. I am there to care for her; he is a good brother, visiting his sister. As she lies on her pillows and smiles sleepily on the two of us, we sit in the window and hold hands and whisper. We meet in every corner and doorway around the court for an exchange of half a dozen words and a brush of his kiss on my hand, on my neck, on the sleeve of my gown. When he passes me in the gallery he catches at my fingers, when he plays a lute and sings a love song he glances first at me, as if to say: these words are for you. We play cards together with Janey and my aunt Bess, now Lady St Loe, in the evening and we dance together when they call for partners. Everyone knows that Ned Seymour always partners Lady Katherine. Nobody else even asks me to dance, none of the girls flutter at Ned. Even the old ladies at court – his mother, my mother, and their sharp-eyed friends – have to observe what a pretty couple we make, so tall and so fair with royal connections on both sides.

What nobody sees is that when the dancing is over, we go to the corner of the great hall and his hand comes around my waist and he turns me towards him as if we are still dancing and he might hold me close.

'Katherine, you are my sweetheart,' he whispers. 'I am mad for you.'

His touch makes me dizzy. I think I will faint but he holds me up. I let him put his hand under my chin; I allow him to turn my face up to his for a kiss. His lips are warm and urgent, and he smells deliciously of clean linen and orange water. He buries his face in my neck and I feel him nibble the lobe of my ear. I cling to him, so that I feel him down the length of my body, his strong arms, his broad chest, his hard lean thigh against me.

'We have to marry,' he says. 'It is a jest no longer.'

I can't nod for his mouth is on mine. He releases me for a moment and I put my hand on the back of his neck to pull him back into the kiss.

'Marry me?' he says as his mouth comes down again.

HAMPTON COURT PALACE, SUMMER 1559

Álvaro de la Quadra, the new Spanish ambassador, comes striding down the garden path in his sweeping bishop's robes to bring me the news, as if we are friends and conspirators.

'Thank God I found you! The King of France is dead!' he says.

'My lord,' I say quietly. I am not as confident with him as I was with Count de Feria. He seems to think that we have an agreement, as if he has inherited me from the previous ambassador, an alliance rather than a liking.

'God bless him,' I say. 'But I thought he was just injured

jousting?' I am walking down the gravel path towards the allée of yew trees, with Janey leaning on my arm. Ned is going to meet us here, as if by accident.

'No! No! Dead! Dead!' says Ambassador de la Quadra, completely ignoring Janey and taking both my hands. 'They have kept vigil beside his bed in vain. They have done everything they could, but nothing could save him. He is gone, God preserve and keep him. His son little Francis is king and your cousin Mary will be queen.' He lowers his voice. 'Think what this means to you!'

I am thinking. I had no idea that the French king was so seriously injured. Men are hurt all the time in the joust, but what jouster kills his king? The French court will be in uproar and he will be succeeded by his son, Francis II. This makes my cousin Mary Stuart queen twice over. She was already Queen of Scots, now she will be Queen of France. Her importance has doubled, trebled, exploded. Now she is queen of a huge country that is determined to grow greater. Now the French king himself will support the claim of his wife to the throne of England, with the French army behind him. Every papist in this country will prefer Catholic Queen Mary to Protestant Queen Elizabeth. Many more would say that she has been the true heir all along. She is the granddaughter of Margaret, the Scots queen who was Henry VIII's sister, and her first husband the Scots king. Unlike Elizabeth, she is undeniably legitimate, royal on both sides, and more than anything else, she will have the great might of France behind her.

'Queen of France and Scotland,' I say thoughtfully. 'There she is, a girl no better born than I, not named in Henry VIII's will like me; but she is queen of two countries before she is twenty-one.

'And so everything changes again,' the ambassador says to me quietly, taking my arm and leading me from Janey, who turns back for the palace, waving me away with my grand friend.

'I don't see why,' I say. 'And I should go back inside with Janey Seymour.'

'Because the new French queen's Guise kinsmen will be eager for her to take her throne in Scotland and push back the reformed religion. Because they will encourage her to make her claim for the English throne. They won't care about peace with England like the old French king; they want to rule Scotland and invade England from the south and the north.'

Really, he is too much for me and I am afraid of his quiet voice, which weaves an argument thread by thread like a snare. 'But this is nothing to do with me, Your Excellency. I don't see why you come running to tell me.'

He smiles as if this is news that will make me happy. 'I will send you word,' he whispers. 'And we will come for you. An entourage will come for you.'

'What?' I ask, for this is completely unexpected. 'What entourage?'

He smiles at me as if we have some long-standing secret agreement, and he says that my moment will come. 'We will release you,' he says, 'from the burden of your life here.'

Thank God that Ned steps quickly from a side path and then nearly jumps back again when he sees the ambassador. I say loudly: 'Here is my friend Janey Seymour's brother come to fetch me to her. Your Excellency must excuse me,' and I dash to Ned, who openly clutches at my hand. He waits only for the ambassador to bow and leave us before taking me in his arms and kissing me.

'Ned, what are they thinking of?' I demand wildly. 'He says they are going to release me from the burden of my life? Are they going to kill me?'

'They're planning to kidnap you and marry you to a Spanish heir,' Ned says tightly. 'When I saw him with you then, I thought he might be persuading you to go with him. I heard it from someone just back from Madrid. It's talked about all over Europe. They want a Spanish ally on the throne of England again. Someone they can trust. The old French king is dead and the Spanish won't tolerate the new French queen as the heir to England. They won't allow France to stretch her borders any more. They will back you against Queen Mary of Scots as the heir of England, and force Elizabeth to name you.'

'I can't do anything about that.' I give a frightened little moan. 'Elizabeth has to choose me of her own will. I can't make her. And I can't be the enemy of France! They can't call me that. I can't be the Spanish-favoured heir for England against my cousin the Queen of France. Why don't they see that I can't do anything?'

He shakes his head, looking grim. 'No. It's worse than that. They don't think that they can persuade Elizabeth to name you as heir, and they don't think she can hold the country against a French invasion for Mary. They won't allow a French queen on the throne of England. The plan is that they'll take you, and declare you as the true heir, and invade to put you on the throne.'

I give a little scream. 'Ned! They can't make me do that!'

'If only your mother would speak to Elizabeth! If only Elizabeth would declare you as her heir, if only we could marry I would make you safe.'

'I won't marry a Spaniard,' I gabble. 'I won't! I won't! I'll only marry you.' I cling to him and I am distracted at once by his arms around me, his kisses on my face, the warmth of his mouth going down my neck. 'Oh, Ned,' I whisper. 'We can't wait any longer. This changes everything. Don't let the Spanish take me. I will be your wife. I won't be forced to the throne like Jane. I won't die like her without ever being loved.'

'Never,' he says. 'They're all as bad as each other, queen and Spanish ambassador, your mother and mine. All they think about is the throne. They don't think about us at all. We were born for each other, we have to be together.'

I melt against him; I cannot care for the consequences. I want to live, I want to be loved, I want to be his wife. Ned gives a little groan and pulls me down to sit in an arbour. I press forward on him, he fumbles with his breeches, I lift my skirts like a whore in Southwark. I don't care. I don't want to think. I don't want to die young without love. I don't want to go another moment without him. He pulls me towards him and I gasp with the sudden pain that is such a joy, and then I gasp again for the flood of pleasure, and then I sigh, my face buried in his shoulder, and I am overwhelmed with the sensation and I am blind and deaf to anything but our own hushed panting and then a long deep sigh and silence.

We can be together for only a moment. As soon as I realise where I am, what I am doing, I have to scramble off him, take a snatched kiss, and dash back to my room. I change my dress as fast as possible, hurrying my women with the laces on my sleeves, the slow tying of my bodice, snapping at my maid as she pins my hood on my rumpled golden hair, and I get to Elizabeth's rooms at a half-run and join her court at the back, hoping that no-one has seen that I am late.

Her dark gaze sweeps the rooms, like a peregrine falcon looking for prey, halts at my blushing face, comes back to me. 'Ah, Lady Katherine,' she says, though she has not singled me out for months. I bob a shallow curtsey, swallowing down my fear. I am beloved of a great man, I am a Tudor. We are betrothed. This is more than she can say for sure.

'I see you do not trouble yourself to be on time,' she remarks. 'I did not see you in chapel either.'

All of her ladies shrink back from the royal bad temper, making an avenue of gowns between me and the queen, and everyone looks towards me. I see Sir William Cecil's tired face, irritable with impatience at the distraction. He is Elizabeth's great advisor, and it tries his exhausted patience when she squabbles with her ladies when there is so much for her to do in the kingdom. I see Robert Dudley, who looks at me as if we are strangers. I see my aunt Bess St Loe. She glares at me, as if she wishes I would behave better, and I see Mary's little face half-hidden among the maids-in-waiting, and her grimace at my discomfort.

I think how faithless they all are. My sister was a queen, and I am five minutes late to Elizabeth's presence chamber because I have been meeting with a man who loves me, a good man, who will defend me from the enemies of the kingdom, and they behave as if I am a naughty schoolchild and this bastard claimant can scold me.

I curtsey again, biting my tongue. 'I am sorry, Your Majesty,' I say as sweetly as I can.

'Were you meeting the Spanish ambassador in a hidden place?' she asks.

William Cecil raises his eyebrows at her indiscretion. De la Quadra, the Spanish ambassador, at the back of the room, bows blandly, as if to say – not at all.

'Not at all,' I say steadily.

'The French ambassador?' she suggests. 'For I hear on all sides that you are discontented at court, and I must say, I do not know how I might please you. Nor,' she says, savouring her spiteful joke, 'why I *should* please you, given that it was your sister who took my throne.'

It is her speaking of Jane that makes me forget myself. I feel a flare of rage, as hot and as passionate as my earlier rush of desire. I will not have this red-headed usurper insulting my sister. 'You need not strive to please me,' I spit. 'And I am only a little late.'

She could leave it at that; she has bigger things to worry about than my pertness. But her plucked brows arch high in surprise at my reply. 'You are quite right for once, I have no obligation to be good to you,' she says nastily. 'For sure, you are no good lady to me. What do you bring to my service? You are late and rude, your mother is ill and always absent, and your sister half-size. I don't have full measure of a lady-in-waiting from any of the three of you. Or should I say two and a half?'

My anger flares out of control at her joking about my little sister. 'You need do nothing for me. Nothing could compare with what you do for the Dudleys! For sure, you bend over backwards for him,' I say loudly and slowly, straight into her pale face, her rouged cheeks, her eyes widened with horror.

There is a little scream from Bess St Loe, and I see Robert Dudley scowl. Mary's hands are clapped over her mouth, her eyes wide above them. Elizabeth herself says nothing, but the hand that grips her fan is shaking as she fights to get herself under control. She does not look at Robert Dudley, at this insult to the two of them; but she glances up at William Cecil, who inclines his head as if he would whisper in her ear. He need say nothing: she knows that if she responds to me with anger she might as well pin my words on the door of St Paul's: everyone will hear what I have said. Cecil mutters urgently, telling her to ignore me, pass off my outburst as a joke.

She opens her rouged lips and she laughs loudly, like a cawing crow. 'You are merry, Lady Katherine,' she says, and rises up from her throne, and walks the length of the presence chamber and speaks to someone else, someone of no importance, as if she would run away from me and my righteous disdain.

I sense Ned at my side, even before I turn my face and see him. His eyes are bright with pride. '*Vivat!*' he says. '*Vivat regina!*'

I am in terrible disgrace for insulting Elizabeth. No lady-in-waiting dares to be seen with me, and the Spanish ambassador bows to me in public but avoids me in private. I think that no-one pays any attention to me at all but Ned, my beloved Ned. But if he loves me, I don't care that I am neglected by everyone.

Elizabeth is in the darkest of bad tempers, hag-ridden by thoughts of our cousin Mary Queen of Scots inheriting the great throne of France with her powerful kinsmen to back her claim on England. Nobody dares to speak to approach her, only Robert Dudley can distract her from her fears.

'You take care,' my little sister Mary says, affecting the wisdom of a woman two feet taller than she is. 'You can't afford to offend the queen. There's only one woman at court that can speak honestly to her. There's only one woman at court who can reprimand her.'

I laugh. 'D'you mean Kat Ashley's great remonstrance?'

Mary's ready smile beams at me. 'Lord, I wish you had seen it,' she says. 'It was as good as a masque. Mrs Ashley on her knees begging the queen not to favour Robert Dudley so openly, swearing that she would lose her reputation, reminding her that he is married and that she should not be constantly in his company, and Elizabeth, saying that if she loved Sir Robert she didn't know who could stop her.'

'But what did you all say?' I demand. 'You ladies.' This scene took place in Elizabeth's bedroom when she was dressing. Kat Ashley, her former governess, is the only woman brave enough to tell Elizabeth that the country thinks she is a complete whore and Robert Dudley an ambitious adulterer. My sister was lucky enough to be spectator to this scene. She was holding Elizabeth's gold-tipped laces, waiting to lace her shoes, when Kat went down on her knees to beg the queen not to behave like a whore.

'We all said nothing, because we're not brave fools like Kat Ashley,' Mary says stoutly. 'I'm not reckless with a temper like you. You think I'm going to tell the Queen of England not to chase after the man she loves? You think I'm going to stand up to her like you did?'

'He's not free to love,' I say primly. 'And neither is she. There's the difference between them and me and Ned. She is a queen who should marry for her country, and he is a man already married – and there is me and Ned, young and free and both noble.'

'You're never talking of marriage with Ned?' Mary demands.

I go down on my knees to her, so that our faces are level. 'Oh, Mary, I am,' I whisper. 'I am! I promise you that I am.'

HAMPTON COURT PALACE, OCTOBER 1559

Ned is high above me, mounted on his handsome horse, dressed in dark blue velvet, his jacket embroidered with darker blue thread, his bonnet of velvet trimmed with navy ribbon. I stand at his horse's head, Mr Nozzle balancing on my shoulder, and look up at him.

'How is the horse?' I say, and we both laugh at the thought of my awkwardness with him, only months ago, and now our confident joy.

He is going to the Charterhouse at Sheen, to ask my mother for permission for us to marry. 'Don't forget to remind her that Elizabeth can have no objection,' I say to him. 'Don't forget to tell her that I am old enough to know my own mind.'

'I'll tell her,' he assures me. 'There can be no reason for your mother to refuse. It is what she and your father wanted for your sister. If I was good enough for Jane I must be good enough for you. Both our families have risen high and been brought low, and now you have no great dowry and are not favoured by the queen. But anyway, it does not matter to me.'

'I should not be brought low,' I say irritably. 'I am not brought low in the eyes of others. The Spanish ambassador said that there is no heir to Elizabeth but me. And anyway, I am on the rise again. She is so furious with our cousin Margaret Douglas for sending her son Henry to the coronation in France, that she is ready to forgive me for being rude to her.'

Ned gives me a smile and my heart turns over. 'It doesn't matter who Elizabeth likes and dislikes. We are royal kin and so she should give her permission. You are her cousin and a Tudor, I am a Seymour. She cannot refuse our wedding.'

It will take him an hour to get to Sheen. I fuss over his saddle, the girth, the stirrup leathers, like a wife. 'Be careful on the way!' I say, though I know he has men in his livery riding with him. There is no danger for him. There are many threats against the life of Elizabeth, but the rest of us, the royal family, are beloved. Everyone remembers that Queen Jane, who died so tragically giving birth to King Edward, was a good English Seymour. And my family, the Greys, are loved for our Queen Jane. The ordinary people speak of her as a saint. It is only Elizabeth who likes to pretend that Jane was never crowned queen. It is only Elizabeth who wants to pretend that she is the last Tudor.

'I'll be back the day after tomorrow,' he says. 'And I shall call you my wife within the month.'

I wave goodbye and I don't care who sees me standing, watching him go. I don't doubt him, I don't doubt that my mother will give permission in a moment. She has always liked him, and the Seymours are a great family. His mother has reluctantly allowed our marriage on the condition that my mother speaks to Elizabeth. There should be nothing to stand in our way.

CHARTERHOUSE, SHEEN, OCTOBER 1559

My mother is ill – she is much troubled by her spleen (I have to say, this is not surprising in a woman with such an evil temper). But as soon as she has heard Ned's mission she orders me and Mary to join her and her husband, Mr Stokes, and Ned at Sheen. She says I must tell her myself if I want Ned as my husband. She receives me in her presence chamber like the daughter of a queen that she is. Mary walks behind me like a miniature lady-in-waiting.

It is as formal as a betrothal. I tell my mother: 'I am very willing to love my lord of Hertford,' and she rises from her chair, comes to me, smiles, puts my hand in his, and says that she would be glad to see me settled and well married.

Adrian Stokes, standing deferentially behind her, is no nobleman but a good sensible man, and he advises us, too. We all agree that Elizabeth the queen will have to be handled carefully. This summer she has been besotted with Robert Dudley and had no time for anyone else, but if I am asking to marry the cousin of the late king she will turn her attention to me and observe me with more care. She is as prickly over her prestige as any bastard, and as fearful for her title as any usurper. We must never, never indicate that we know that we are better bred and more entitled to the throne than she. We have to hope that she overlooks the fact that I, a Tudor heir, want to marry Ned, a Seymour, a royal relation.

Everyone agrees that my mother must write to Elizabeth the queen and ask for permission and then go to court to persuade Elizabeth in person. Jointly, the five of us compose a courtly letter. We write:

The Earl of Hertford doth bear goodwill to my daughter the
Lady Katherine and I do humbly beseech the Queen's Highness
to be a good and gracious lady unto her and that it may please
Her Majesty to assent to her marriage to the said Earl.

I say – but what if she says 'no'? She is spiteful enough to say 'no'. And Ned takes my hand and promises me: 'If she says "no", we will marry in secret and she can say "no" to the wind.'

So the letter is drafted with Mary acting as clerk, and my mother is to copy it out fair in her best hand, but before she can do so, she takes to her bed and says she cannot go to court while she is so bloated and so sick, she certainly cannot bear to see Elizabeth when she is not in her best looks, we will have to wait until she is better.

'So what happens now?' I demand of Ned.

'I'll go back to court myself and prepare for the letter,' he promises me. 'I have friends; we are a family with influence. I can ask people to speak for us to the queen. We have my mother's permission and yours. We don't need anything more.'

WINDSOR CASTLE,
AUTUMN 1559

Ned and I return to court separately, so that no-one knows we have been conspiring together, and then we hesitate. It feels impossible to break into Elizabeth's whispered conversations with Robert Dudley and make her attend to our affairs. There is a queue of people before us: foreign ambassadors proposing marriage, William Cecil with handfuls of bills for her to sign, trying to persuade her to support the Protestant Scots lords who are arming against their French regent. Now Elizabeth is to be named as Supreme Governor of the Church, even though she is a woman. I think of what my sister Jane would have done with that chance to save the soul of the country, and save the Scots from papistry, and it is a bitter thought. At any rate, the queen has no time for Ned and me, and we cannot find a chance to interrupt.

The court is a place of nervous gossip. Elizabeth is so anxious about the French and the Scots that she cannot let Robert Dudley out of her sight; but still she entertains Sir William Pickering as a suitor, and speaks every day of the archduke Ferdinand as if she intends to marry him. It feels as if everyone, from the blackbirds in the apple-heavy orchards to the queen in her chamber, is with their mate. Ned and I are only one of very many couples kissing in shaded doorways.

The Scots Protestant lords rise up against the regent Mary of Guise and defeat her. They call on Elizabeth for help and of course she dares to do nothing. If Jane were Queen of England she would have sent a righteous army. But though William Cecil argues till he is exhausted in the Privy Council and the queen's rooms, Elizabeth does not dare to send more than a secret fleet of ships to supply the Scots lords.

While everyone is arguing whether this is enough, or if the queen should send an army, Ned and I slip away and pursue our secret love affair, safely hidden from the queen and from her advisors, and known only to his sister Janey and my little sister, Mary. The two of them conspire for us: Janey invites me to her rooms when Ned is there; Mary stands watch when we meet on the pier at the river or in the autumn woods of Hampton Court. We ride together, following behind the queen and her lover, as the leaves whirl down in gold and bronze all around us. We walk behind them, a careful pace apart from one another, the pug Jo trotting along behind us, while they walk whispering, arm in arm. Elizabeth clings to Robert Dudley during this new crisis. Clearly, she does not dare to do her duty by the people of her faith. Clearly, only Robert Dudley can give her confidence to defy William Cecil's advice. I simply don't care about it. I am in love, all I want is the rare alignment of the early stars on the autumn nights which will tell me that the queen is in a good mood and my mother is well enough to come to court to ask for permission for me to marry.

Perhaps only William Cecil, the queen's long-standing advisor, sees our secret courtship, and I imagine that he approves. He is a quiet man who misses nothing. Now and then he gives me a little smile or has a polite word with me as we pass in the gallery, or our horses happen to be alongside one another, when the court is riding out. He is a staunch believer in the reformed religion, and he knows that I was raised in the same faith as my sister Jane and I would never choose any other. His scholarly Protestant wife, Mildred, loved Jane, and I think he looks for my sister in me. His strong faith inspires him to urge the Privy Council and the queen to support the Protestant lords of Scotland and free that kingdom from the Pope as well. I know he favours me as the Protestant heir, and he speaks for me to the queen's advisors, if not to her. He would never accept my cousin Margaret Douglas, who is half papist and in disgrace anyway, and never, ever Mary Queen of France, where her mother's family, the Guises, are persecuting those of our faith with the utmost cruelty.

WHITEHALL PALACE, LONDON, NOVEMBER 1559

It is Janey who is with me when the messenger comes from my stepfather, Adrian Stokes, to tell me that my mother is terribly ill, and not likely to last many more days, and Mary and I must come at once, and it is Janey who holds my hands tightly while I blink a few reluctant tears from my eyes and think that now I will have to go into mourning and wear black, and go to the dreary Charterhouse and stay there, when everyone else is in the finery of the Christmas feast.

'You'll have to tell your sister,' Janey says.

Mary sleeps in the maids' dormitory, and I go to find her. They get up as late as they can and I can hear the noise of them romping even through the thick wooden door. The mistress of maids should really keep them closer: the maids are supposed to learn how to behave at court, not to racket about like urchins and flick each other with their bed linen as they are doing now, to judge from the shrieks and screams of laughter.

I tap on the panelled door and walk in. Mary is jumping on the bed, splashing nearby girls with her washing jug clutched in her hand. One of the girls is threatening to throw a bowl of cold slops, and they are all chasing each other on and off the beds, pulling at the bed curtains and screaming for mercy. It looks tremendous fun. If I were not so old, so grown up, almost betrothed, I would be tempted to join in. But anyway, I am here to deliver sad news.

'Mary!' I shout over the noise and I beckon her to the door.

She bounces down from the bed and comes over, her cheeks rosy, her dark eyes bright. She is such a tiny little thing, no taller than a child, I cannot believe she is fourteen years old. She should have been betrothed long before now. Soon, she will have no mother to make arrangements for her. But anyway, I don't know who would marry her. She is of royal descent, but in the court of Elizabeth that is only a disadvantage.

I put my hand on her thin shoulder and bend down to speak in her ear. 'Come out, Mary. I have bad news for you.'

She throws a cloak over her nightgown and follows me to the gallery outside the maids' room. Their screams of laughter are muffled when Janey closes the door and stands a little away from us.

I realise I don't know what I should say. This is a girl who has lost her family before she is a woman grown: her sister and her father to the axe, and now her mother is dying. 'Mary, I am very sorry. I am come to tell you that our mother is dying. Adrian Stokes has written to me. We have to go to Sheen at once.'

She does not respond. I bend down lower to look into her pretty little face.

'Mary, you knew that she was ill?'

'Yes, of course I knew. I am short, I am not an idiot.'

'I will be a good sister to you,' I say awkwardly. 'We two are all that are left now.'

'And I will be a good sister to you,' she promises grandly, as if her little influence could ever be of any benefit to me. 'We must never be parted.'

She is so sweet that I bend down and kiss her. 'I am going to marry soon,' I tell her. 'And when I have a house of my own you shall live with me, Mary.'

She smiles at that. 'Until I marry, of course,' she says, the funny little thing.

CHARTERHOUSE, SHEEN,
WINTER 1559–60

At last Elizabeth pays my family the recognition that we deserve. She celebrates my mother in death in a way that she never would do in life. She gives my mother a grand funeral, a royal funeral at Westminster Abbey, with dozens of mourners and the court in black, and shields inscribed with my mother's name and royal titles. Mary and I, in black velvet, are chief mourners. As her coffin lies in state, the Clarenceux Herald bellows that it has pleased God to summon: 'the most noble and excellent prince the Lady Frances, late Duchess of Suffolk.' If she had not been dead already, my mother would have died of joy at being named officially royal, and by Elizabeth's herald.

John Jewel, who is friends with all of my sister Jane's old spiritual mentors, preaches the funeral sermon in reformist style, and I think that Jane might have been pleased to see that her mother was buried in the religion that she died for. It is odd and painful to think of Jane, a queen, her head in a basket, tumbled into the traitors' vaults in the chapel at the Tower, and here is my mother laid to rest in the greatest of ceremonies, drowned in honours, with banners of arms over her hearse.

The ladies of the court draped in black, their black leather gloves paid for by the queen, follow my mother's coffin, which is shrouded in black and cloth of gold, to show her importance.

Bess St Loe takes my hand. 'I loved your mother very much,' she says to me. 'I will miss her. She was a great lady. You can call on me as your friend, Katherine. I will never able to take her place, but I will love you for her.' For a moment, seeing her emotion, I could almost cry for the loss of a mother; but if you are a

Tudor you don't really have parents. Your mother is your patron, your child is your heir, you fear the failure of them both. I don't need Aunt Bess to tell me that my mother was a great lady, and nobody could say that she was a good mother; but it is consoling to see that the court finally recognises her royalty and thus ours.

But there is more.

Elizabeth chooses this moment to restore our title as Princesses of the Blood. In death, my mother has achieved the ambition of her life: to have us recognised by Elizabeth, named as her cousins, defined as royal, titled as 'Princess', and so the first of all the possible heirs. My mother, God forgive her, would have thought it cheaply bought by her death, well worth the sacrifice. Jane died for claiming our mother's rights; now they are given to us, her sisters, at her mother's funeral.

Mary and I are immensely dignified mourners, our heads held as stiffly as if we are wearing coronets already. I glance behind to make sure that she is upholding our new honours, and I give her a little smile. Her head is up, her shoulders straight, she looks like a miniature queen. We retire after the ceremony to the Charterhouse at Sheen, and I burn with impatience to get back to court to see if at last Elizabeth pays me true cousinly respect, grants me my proper place in the privy chamber, and precedence among the ladies. I should follow her, one pace behind her for the rest of her life, and at her death I should step up to the throne. Now, at last, I can speak to her as a cousin about my marriage.

'I shall marry as soon as I am out of mourning,' I exult to Mr Stokes, my stepfather. 'We should ask for permission now, while the court is still in black and Elizabeth is in such a generous mood.'

He looks exhausted. He is genuinely grieved at the loss of his wife. Unlike us, her two surviving children, he truly loved her. 'I am sorry,' he says stiffly. 'I spoke to Lord Hertford after the funeral. It must be he who speaks to the queen, now that your mother has gone.'

'Oh, very well. What did Ned say?' I demand confidently. I

have Jo the pug on my lap, entwined with Ribbon the little cat, and I gently pull her silky ears. 'Does he want to wait till I go back to court after mourning? Or is he going to speak to her now, while we are still away?'

Adrian Stokes shakes his head, his eyes on my face. 'I am sorry,' he says awkwardly. 'I am very sorry, Katherine. I know your mother would have been sorry, too. But I don't think he will undertake it. He said as much to me, actually. Without your mother here to argue your case to the queen, his mother has changed her mind and does not want the match to go ahead. Lady Seymour does not want to speak to the queen without your mother to support her, and neither does he. Put it bluntly: neither of them dares.'

I can hardly believe what he is saying. 'But she has just made me a princess of the blood!' I exclaim. 'She recognises me as a member of the royal family! I have never been so high in her favour!'

'That's the very thing,' he replies. 'Now you are named a princess she will be all the more determined to command your marriage, and she won't want you to marry someone with a claim to the throne himself.'

'To Hertford!' I raise my voice to my stepfather. 'She should command my marriage to Hertford! And you should insist on it for me!'

He shakes his head. 'You know that I have no influence, Lady Katherine. I am a commoner without great wealth. But I know that the queen won't want to marry you to a lord who has his own claim to the throne. And she won't let you marry while she is unmarried herself, and risk you having a son who would have a stronger claim than she does. I can see what the Seymours are thinking: obviously the queen won't want a Tudor-Seymour boy at court until she has a husband and son of her own. The Seymours don't want to take the risk of offending her.'

'None of you understand her!' I exclaim. 'She doesn't think like that, she doesn't plan ahead like that! All she thinks of is being at the centre of attention and holding Robert Dudley at her side.'

'I think she does think very carefully,' he cautions me. 'I think she is having you watched, and I think she will take no risks that might create an heir with a strong claim to her throne.'

'Elizabeth doesn't watch me!'

'William Cecil does.' He sees the shock on my face and gives a helpless little shrug. 'He watches everyone.'

'Are you saying that she will not let me marry, till she has married and given birth to her own son and heir?'

He nods. 'Almost certainly,' he says. 'It would be to set up an heir with a stronger claim than her own.'

'That could be years.'

'I know. But I think she will not endure a rival.'

'She will be the ruin of me,' I say flatly.

His sandy eyebrows come together in a frown as he wonders what I mean by 'ruin'. 'I hope not,' he says. 'I hope that you have been careful both with your reputation and with the queen.'

I think of the arbour, I think of the moment of fierce pain and joy, I think of sobbing against his shoulder and whispering, 'I am all yours.'

'We are betrothed to marry!' I say.

'It is traditional to have the queen's permission,' he reminds me gently. 'It was the law. The queen could restore the law. But anyway, the Seymours say they won't ask for it.'

'What about my mother's letter, asking the queen for permission for Ned and me to marry? I can give it to Elizabeth if no-one else has the courage to present it. We can say we found it in her papers, that it was her dying wish?'

His tired face darkens. 'That letter,' he says. 'That's how I know that you're being watched. Your mother's letter has gone from her private closet. Your mother was spied on, and someone has stolen her letter. For your own safety, Katherine, you have to forget all about this.'

'They can't just steal a letter to the queen! They can't just go through our papers and take what they want. Who would do such a thing?'

'I don't know. I don't know why. But at any rate it's gone, and we can't get it back. I think you can do nothing but put him out of your thoughts and out of your heart.'

'I can't forget!' I exclaim. 'I love him. I have given him my word! We are betrothed!'

'I am sorry,' is all he says. And then he says something even worse: 'He is sorry, too, I know. I could tell. He was very sorry that he will never see you again.'

'Not see me again?' I whisper. 'He said that?'

'He said that.'

We are very quiet and dull at Sheen. Mr Nozzle shivers in the cold draughts from the ill-fitting doors and Ribbon the cat will not go out for his business and get his paws wet so I am always clearing up after him. Jo the pug whimpers the moment that I leave the room, as if to say she is lonely, too.

At least I have not missed a merry Christmas at court. Janey writes to me and says that the place is as miserable as when Queen Mary was on the throne, for Elizabeth is sick with fright as to whether she dares to send English troops to support the Scots Protestant lords. Of course she should do so. This would be a courageous thunderclap, bringing the gospel to people who will never hear it unless she acts. But Elizabeth will not follow the path of righteousness and she is afraid of the Regent of Scotland, Mary of Guise, the mother of Mary Queen of Scots, the new French queen. The French will invade to support their kins-woman against the rebellion of the Scots Protestant lords, and once they are in Scotland what is to stop them marching south on Elizabeth? My sister Jane would have sent an army of saints to support the godly lords against a papist regent in a moment. So too would any strong monarch of England. But Elizabeth believes nothing in her heart, and will not fight a war of religion. Worst of all for her is that William Cecil, a reformer as fierce as anyone in my family, has said that if she will not accept his advice to support our faith in Scotland, he will not offer it, and he has left court and gone home to his wife, Mildred.

'Elizabeth will be hopeless without him,' I say to Mary, reading this to her, the two of us in our mother's privy chamber with icy rain pouring down the leaded glass windows. 'I dare say she will lose the throne if the French march against her.'

'They are certain to invade, aren't they? If she declares war against them in Scotland? They will invade across the Narrow Seas in the south and come down from Scotland at the same time.'

I nod, deciphering Janey's urgent scribble. 'And she doesn't have an army,' I say. 'Or any money to raise one. As long as she doesn't send Ned to Edinburgh!' I say. 'Does this say Hertford?'

'No,' Mary says. 'Howard. It says Elizabeth is sending her cousin Thomas Howard to Edinburgh. Ned is safe.'

I clasp my hands together as if I would fall into prayer on the window seat. 'Oh God, if I could only go back to court and be with him! If I could just see him!'

'If the French invade England it will be to put Mary Queen of Scots on the throne, not you,' Mary observes.

'I don't want the throne!' I say irritably. 'Why does nobody ever understand that? I just want Ned.'

WHITEHALL PALACE, LONDON, SPRING 1560

I say that I don't want the throne, but I cannot prevent a flare of ambition when I return to Whitehall to find myself an honoured member of the court, as I should always have been. The queen's principal advisor, William Cecil, has won the argument about supporting the Scots Protestants, and is back in his place, pressing for an English army to go to Scotland, urging the rights of the Protestants – well aware that I am the Protestant heir. He always bows and exchanges a brief word of greeting with me, as if I am of interest to him now, as if he thinks that the time might come when he is my advisor, and Elizabeth is gone.

I am the favourite of the whole palace. I am a beloved royal princess, no longer a despised visitor. I am not a neglected poor relation but the recognised heir to the kingdom. I have the strange sensation of being in a place that I know well and yet everything is different. There is a new reality behind the costumed smiles, as if it is Act Two of a masque and the actors have changed their faces behind their shields and the same people must now be taken as completely different.

My cousin Margaret Douglas has offended the queen deeply. A servant of her husband, Matthew Stuart, has been caught reminding the French ambassador that Margaret is next of kin to our cousin Mary Queen of France and Scotland, and her husband, as Earl of Lennox, is heir to the throne of Scotland. This is obviously true, but anyone could have warned her that such a message would be reported at once, and Elizabeth would be frightened and furious. Margaret should have played on her main strength of being extremely plain, and old, and then perhaps Elizabeth would have forgiven her royal blood. Anyway, the court is hugely amused that William Cecil is ordered to rifle through old documents, stored away in the muniments room, to prove that Margaret Douglas, the daughter of Henry VIII's sister, Queen of Scotland, is, in fact, illegitimate, and so neither she nor her pretty son Henry Stuart can have any claim to the throne of England. As though her reputation could be worse than Elizabeth's, whose mother was beheaded for adultery with five named men!

I thank God that nobody can question my paternity. I descend in a straight and legitimate line from King Henry's favourite sister, Queen Mary, married to his best friend, Charles Brandon, through my mother, the unimpeachably virtuous and bad-tempered Frances Brandon, and now that I am in favour again, my resemblance to my beautiful royal grandmother is suddenly apparent. Many people remark to each other that I am as pretty as the Tudor princess, and admire my fair York colouring.

Robert Dudley, who is in and out of the privy chamber, and openly admitted to the royal bedroom, declared as the queen's most trusted friend, is courteous to me as a kinsman. Our families overlap so often – he was the brother-in-law of my sister Jane, and so a brother-in-law to me – he is the most favoured suitor to my cousin the queen, and is now happy to remember our kinship. Suddenly, I have friends, where before I was living among strangers. I could almost think myself widely liked and generally admired. I start to say 'my cousin the queen' just as my mother did, and Mary laughs at me behind her little hand.

But my triumphant return to court, my discovery of so many new friends, even the favour of the queen, does not compensate me for the loss of Ned. The young man who claimed me freely, of his own will, as his lover, who sought the blessing of his mother and the permission of mine, now walks past me as if he does not see me, and when we are accidentally face to face, he bows to me as if we are nothing more than polite acquaintances.

The first time that his cool gaze goes over me and beyond, I think that I will faint with unhappiness. It is only Mary at my elbow, her head not reaching my shoulder, who keeps me upright. She pinches my arm so hard that she leaves a bruise and she mutters at me: 'Head up! Chin up!'

I glance at her, completely bewildered, and she beams up at me and adds: 'Heels down! Hold tight,' like our father when he was teaching us to ride, and that recalls me to myself. I walk with my hand on her shoulder and I can barely make my feet take one step after another. We go to chapel together, she supports me as if I am sick, and when I kneel behind the queen I bow my head and ask God to release me from this pain.

I am so bitterly unhappy to think that Ned has given me up to avoid the displeasure of a queen who would never sacrifice her own pleasures. Elizabeth allows herself joy in her lover, but I may not even speak to the man that I love. I watch her as she beckons

Robert Dudley to lift her down from her horse, or dance with her in the evening, when she walks with her head practically resting on his shoulder, and summons him to her privy chamber where they are left alone together, and I find I hate her for her selfishness, for thinking only of her own pleasure and never thinking of me. I blame her bitterly that I am parted from the man I love, and I will die a lonely spinster, while she indulges herself in a shameful adulterous public love affair.

Now, she publicly swears that she will marry the Habsburg Archduke Ferdinand as soon as he comes to England – she promises that she will make a Spanish alliance to keep England safe – but it is obvious to everyone that she is lying, and that any husband of hers would be cuckolded before his ship had even docked at Greenwich.

The Spanish have learned this now. The new ambassador is offended, his household sulky. William Cecil is quite distracted, trying to maintain our friendship with the great power of Spain to balance the great threat from France. The Spanish ambassador, Álvaro de la Quadra, finds himself beside me as we walk by the river towards a lighted arbour where we are going to listen to some poetry one evening, and he mentions that the archduke has heard of my beauty and would far rather marry me than go through the long-drawn-out and discredited process of courting Elizabeth. One day I might be a great Queen of England with the archduke at my side and Spanish power behind me. In the meantime I could be a treasured archduchess with an envied place at the English court, the centre of papist ambitions.

'Oh, I couldn't say,' I whisper. I am horrified that he should dare to say this so clearly to me. Thank God no-one is in hearing and no-one has seen us but one of William Cecil's men who happens to pass by. 'Your Excellency, you do me too much honour. I cannot hear such things without the permission of my cousin the queen.'

'No need to mention it to her,' he replies swiftly. 'I spoke to you in confidence, so you understand what might be. If you wished it.'

'Really, I don't wish for anything,' I assure him.

It's true. I don't wish for the throne any more. I want to be a wife, not a furiously bad-tempered spinster queen. I want a husband, and none but Ned. I could not bear the touch of another man's hand. If I live until I am ancient, if I live until I am as old as fifty, I will never want anyone but him. We pass each other in the gallery, at dinner, on the way to chapel, in miserable silence. I know that he loves me still. I see him look across at me when he is at chapel and I have my face covered in my hands so he cannot see me peeping through my fingers at him. He looks as if he is ill with longing, and I am not allowed to comfort him.

'I swear to you, he loves you as much as ever,' Janey says mournfully. 'He's pining away, Katherine. But my mother has forbidden him to speak to you and warned him of the queen's displeasure if she knew. I can't bear it that you're not together. I tell him that he has a worse illness than I do. And his cure is just here! You are the cure for his illness.'

'If only your mother would speak to Elizabeth!' I say.

Janey shakes her head. 'She doesn't dare. She told me that the Privy Council has told Elizabeth that she must find a safe husband for you at once. With English troops mustered to fight against the French in Scotland they are terrified that you will come out against her, or even leave the country. They are frightened that the Spanish will take you. They want you safely buried in marriage to a low-born Englishman who will keep you home and diminish your claim.'

'I wouldn't go to Spain!' I say desperately. 'Why would I? Where would I go? The only man in the world that I would marry is here. I have no interest in the archduke or anyone else! And why should I marry a low-born Englishman? Why should I be insulted?'

I am horrified by Janey's gossip that they want to marry me to some nonentity and forget about me, but I feel even more afraid when I am told that the Scots lords have proposed that I should be married to my cousin the Earl of Arran, one of Elizabeth's cast-off flirts with a claim in Scotland, so that England can offer a rival Protestant queen to the rebellious Scots, and they can mass behind Arran and me, and defeat the French. They will marry me to Arran and make me Queen of Scots.

'What am I to do?' I say to Janey. 'Are they all mad? Will they never stop trying to marry me to one dreadful man after another? Did she acknowledge me as princess just to sell me in an alliance? You must tell Ned that someone is going to kidnap me, if he does not save me.'

Ned does not rescue me; he cannot. His mother has forbidden it, and she is not a woman to be disobeyed. He does no more than look longingly at me, and walk away. Robert Dudley does nothing for me. He thinks only of himself and of Elizabeth. He is at her side every day in these dangerous times, and I think if she could not cling to him she would lose her wits. Of course, it is William Cecil, who knows all about everything, who speaks to me. He bows very low as he comes out of the Privy Council meeting, and offers me his arm to walk along the gallery to the queen's rooms. I flutter my fingers a little as if I would be released but he keeps a warm gentle grip on my hand, and so we enter together, and I see from the determined upturn of Elizabeth's painted lips that the two of them have agreed that I must be kept close, and they have choreographed a little dance for me to perform.

'Oh! Cousin Katherine,' she says, turning away from Robert Dudley as if she is more interested in me than in him. 'Dear Cousin.'

My curtsey is as shallow as I dare to make it. 'Cousin Elizabeth, Your Majesty,' I say, since we seem to be closely related today.

'Come and sit with me,' she says, indicating the stool beside her chair. 'I have hardly seen you all day.'

There have been many days when she has managed to endure my absence, and never before have I been invited to sit with her.

I glance to one side where Ned is watching this mumming, and his expression freezes and he looks down to the ground, as if he dare not even smile at me. He is so afraid of Elizabeth's displeasure, and I am like a mouse under the paw of a fat ginger cat.

'What a darling little dog!' Elizabeth exclaims.

I look down at Jo, who presses against my feet as if she is afraid that I will follow court protocol and offer her to the queen, who looks at her with no warmth in her face.

'I love Katherine like a daughter,' the queen says to the air over my head. Even she, great liar that she is, lacks the bravado to meet my eyes. Everyone takes in this surprising announcement with blank faces. I see the bright interested stare of the Spanish ambassador. 'She is like a daughter to me,' she repeats loudly. Then, as the meaning of her words dawns on her, she softens her voice to speak to me: 'You must miss your mother very much,' she says.

I bow my head. 'I do, Your Majesty,' I confirm dutifully. 'She was most devoted to me and to my little sister, Mary.'

'Oh, yes, Mary,' says the queen absently. Mary steps forward from the maids at the mention of her name and the queen nods towards her as she curtseys. Clearly, Mary is not to be bathed in affection, only me.

Elizabeth leans forward. 'You must always tell me if you feel lonely or unhappy,' she says quietly. 'I know what it is to be a girl without a mother. I know what it is to be friendless at a great court.'

I would play my part in this masque better if I knew what on earth I am supposed to do. The queen puts her heavily ringed hand on my shoulder; her fingers are cold. I wonder who is supposed to benefit from this performance. Certainly, not I.

'I am not friendless at court, if I have your favour,' I say tentatively, looking up into her expressionless face.

She presses her hand on my shoulder. 'You do. You are very dear to me. After all, you are my closest kin.'

That's it then! She has named me as her closest kin. I am her heir. I am next to the throne. She has done it, and she cannot take it back. I glance up and see William Cecil is watching me. He has heard this. Indeed, he will have written the script and plotted every move.

'And may I come to you with a request?' I gaze into her beady black eyes. There is not a flicker of true tenderness: she is making a deal with me as if we were fishwives on the quay weighing a salted cod.

'Ask me!' she says with her false smile. 'Ask me anything, and see what I will do for a loyal and loving cousin!'

'I will,' I promise her, I promise myself, and I promise Ned in my heart.

Robert Dudley kisses my hand with a hidden smile, as one favourite to another. William Cecil walks with me in the gallery and tells me how the war is progressing in Scotland, as if I need to know. I realise that he is teaching me the statecraft that he has studied under four reigns. He wants me to know that I must play my part as the Protestant heir to a Protestant queen. It is important that I understand that the throne is advised by the lords, that the lords share the thoughts of the parliament. I must understand that Elizabeth's place on the throne is unsteady – half the country is yet to be convinced by our religion, the great European powers are natural enemies to us and the Pope calls for a holy war against us. As her heir I will attract temptation, con-spiracies, promises. I must report to him. I must never endanger Elizabeth. I must play my part in making a Protestant succession in a Protestant country.

People curtsey low as I walk by, and Mary and I are allocated more ladies to wait on us. Suddenly, I need someone to carry my gloves. Mary moves out of the informal camaraderie of the maids' rooms, and together we live in grander rooms with our own ladies-in-waiting, and we make a small court within the court, the two of us served as princesses. I dress Mr Nozzle in a livery of Tudor green and Jo and Ribbon have plaited collars of green silk. Ribbon wears a little bell of hammered silver and sleeps on a cushion of green velvet.

I go everywhere in the centre of a hushed storm of deferential curiosity. The wardrobe supplies me with wonderful gowns of velvets and cloth of gold. My rise to prominence brings so many questions, but there is no-one that I can safely consult. Can it be that Elizabeth has decided to wait for Robert Dudley to be free to marry, and is naming me as her heir to buy herself time? His wife may die of some illness, or old age, and Elizabeth might marry him at last. Or since she is Supreme Governor of the Church, will she use her power to declare her lover's marriage annulled, and marry him herself? Nobody can complain of her behaviour if she has given England a legitimate Protestant heir – me.

And if so, would it not be wise to let me marry the man of my choice, an English nobleman, close to the throne, loyally reformist? Do Ned and I suddenly represent an irresistible boon to Elizabeth: royal family, Protestant convictions, and surely fertile? If I were to put a legitimate Tudor boy in the royal cradle, does that free Elizabeth to please herself? Will she end all debate by adopting my baby and giving England that rarity: a healthy Tudor boy? Do I dare to ask for Ned as the favour that she has promised me? Do I dare to summon Ned to my new rooms and speak to him in front of everyone?

Elizabeth continues to single me out for her affections. I sit at the head of the ladies' table at dinner, while Mary is raised on a cushion at the other end. Only I am to carry the queen's fan in the evening, only I hold her gloves as we walk together to the stables. I have a new horse; when we go hawking I have a falcon on my fist. I play cards with her, and at chapel I kneel behind her to pray. Undoubtedly I am being groomed to inherit. The Spanish ambassador steps back from our secret conversations, but his bow is very deferential. Robert Dudley gives me his hidden seductive smile. Ned meets my eyes across the presence chamber and I know that he wants me. Surely, if I can ask my cousin the queen for any favour I can tell her that I want to marry a loyal English nobleman and we can both serve her for life?

◆◆◆

Janey says: 'I have a surprise for you. Come to my room.'

It is an hour before dinner and the other ladies of the bed-chamber are with the queen, watching the maids lace her gown, each standing with an item: her golden hood, her jewel box, her fan. Each of them is waiting her turn to step forward in the ritual of dressing the goddess so that she can go to her dinner and flirt with any man who has the good luck to catch her volatile fancy tonight. Every third night it is my turn to serve her, every fourth night my little sister, Mary, stands holding the jewels. Now and then Janey is well enough to offer the golden hood, but tonight we are both free.

Like little girls playing truant from a despised stepmother, we slip past the maids' chamber and Janey opens the door to her bedroom, we go in . . . and there is Ned.

I stop on the threshold; I know I gape at him as if I cannot believe that it is him, waiting for me, as if he has stepped out of my dreams.

'Ned?' I say wonderingly.

He crosses the room in one stride and takes me into his arms. 'My love,' he says. 'My love, forgive me. I could not be without you for another moment.'

I don't hesitate, I don't pause for pride or anger, my arms are around his neck, pulling his head down, his mouth to mine, we fumble and then we kiss. The taste of him, the familiar scent of him, makes me tremble. I want to cry and laugh at once. 'Ned,' is all I can say.

The kiss goes on forever. I hear, in the back of my mind, the quiet click of the door as Janey goes out and closes it behind her. It occurs to me that really I should be coldly furious with Ned and make him beg my pardon, but my hold on him tightens. I cannot bear to release him, I don't think I can ever bear to let him go. I cannot think, I have no thoughts, all I know is desire.

When he slackens his grip just a little, I am dizzy and I let myself go deliciously limp in his arms. I feel I have spent so long trying to be strong and trying to be brave and now I can lean on the man that I love. He helps me to the window seat. I want to lie along it, to feel his weight come down on me and his thigh press against me; but we sit side by side, his arm around my waist as if I am so precious to him that he cannot bear to let me go.

'You came back to me,' is all I say. Then: 'You have come back to me? This is not just . . . You have come back to me?'

'Of course,' he says. 'You are the love of my life, my only love.'

'I couldn't bear seeing you every day and not touching . . .'

'Nor I! I used to watch you in chapel.'

'I know you did,' I interrupt. 'I used to peep at you and see you were looking at me. I hoped so much . . . I prayed . . .'

'Prayed for what?'

'Prayed for this.'

He takes my hand and presses it to his lips. 'You have this. You have me. We shall never be parted again.'

'Your mother . . .'

'I shall explain it to her. She shall not stop me.'

'But the queen . . .'

'We shall marry,' he says decisively. I feel my heart leap just to see the firmness of his mouth. I want him to kiss me again.

'I will ask her . . .'

'She favours you, she's made that clear to everyone. And it's not just her, it's not just her whim. Cecil has advised her that she has to keep you close. That's why she's being so kindly. She is terrified that you will be married by the Scots or by the Spanish, and taken away.'

'Oh God,' I whisper. 'Don't let them part us.'

'Never. So we won't ask anyone, for fear that they refuse. We will marry and tell her when it is done. We'll tell them all when it is done, and then what can she or anyone do?'

'She can be furious,' I point out. The court has grown wary of Tudor rage. Where Queen Mary would sink into despair, Elizabeth will scream and throw things. The only man who can soothe her then is Robert Dudley. The only man who can advise her is William Cecil. She shouts down everyone else.

Ned, my lover, my husband-to-be, shrugs his shoulders as if

she does not frighten him. 'She will be furious but it will blow over. We have seen her furious with Kat Ashley, we have seen her rage at Cecil until he left court. But he came back, and she did as he advised. It will be the same for us. She will rage, we will leave, she will forgive us and restore us to our places within a month. Besides, it is in her interest that we are married so that you are safe. Cecil will advise her of that. Dudley will tell her to smile on lovers.'

'I want to be safe.' I nestle a little closer. 'I want to be safe with you. Oh, Ned, I have dreamed of this.'

'I have dreamed of you, too,' he whispers. 'I have written a poem to you.'

'You have?'

He feels in the inside pocket of his jacket. 'I carry it with me,' he says. 'I wrote it when you were in your mourning black and I used to see you, with your hair so golden and your skin so creamy pale. You were like a portrait, like a marble statue wrapped in velvet, and I thought that I would never touch you again. I thought we were like Troilus and Criseyde, parted like them.'

'Read it!' I whisper. Really, this is as good as a Romance.

'She stood in black said Troilus he,
That with her look hath wounded me.
She stood in black say I also
That with her eye, hath bred my woe.'

I give a shuddering breath of delight. 'May I have it?' Nobody has ever written a poem to me before, nobody ever wrote one for Jane for all that she was such a great scholar and a queen. People wrote sermons for Jane but this is a real thing, a poem, a love poem from a man. Better than that: a love poem from a poet, a famous poet. A sermon simply doesn't compare. He presses it into my hand and I hold it to my heart.

GREENWICH PALACE,
SUMMER 1560

This is living, I think feverishly. This is what it is to be young and
beautiful and alive, and not absorbed by some miserable creed
that makes you learn to die and not delight in life. This is what I
hoped when I came out of the Tower and left my sister behind,
to be beheaded and buried in pieces in the chapel. This is how
I believed my life should be and now it is: vivid and passionate
and far more wonderful than I ever dreamed.

Ned and I still go past each other in silence, with our eyes
averted, but he winks at me in chapel and he holds me deliciously
close when he lifts me down from my horse. Now, when the
movement of the dance brings us together, his hand is warm
and he presses my fingers. When the dance takes us face to face
he comes so close that I can feel his warm breath at my ear, his
hand at my waist is confident, drawing me against him. We are
secret lovers as we were once secretly estranged, and when I turn
away and pretend not to see him I want to giggle. I quite forget
that I used to want to cry.

The court is at play in the summer weather and nothing seems
to matter at all. It is as if all the stern rules of courtly behaviour
are suspended, all the grim restrictions of belief are lifted. There
is no 'learn you to die' any more, there is no death. There is no
fear of the future, nor who will be heir, nor will the queen conceive, or will there be war. There is nothing but sunny weather
and pretty clothes and beautiful days. All of the dour misery of
Queen Mary's court is swept away like old strewing herbs, all
the fearful suspicion of King Edward's years is gone. All the men
who plotted and planned and schemed against the throne and

against each other are dead, and we their children are sworn to live for the joy of living. We have learned to live.

William Cecil has gone to Edinburgh to make peace between the Scots lords and their French-born regent. Elizabeth's reluctant army has done enough to win us peace and Elizabeth is reckless without Cecil's supervision, as if she thinks that if he is not watching, no-one can see her. She and Robert Dudley live openly as lovers. He comes to her room as if he were her husband, he laughs at her, he takes her in his arms, he is obeyed as if he were king consort.

Every day we ride out, the hounds running before us. Robert Dudley brings his mistress a string of horses, each one more spirited and beautiful than the last, and the two of them ride neck and neck as if they were invulnerable. Every day they outrun the court and then disappear into the woods, only emerging when it is time to dine in the beautiful tents that the servants have put up in the clearing, and the tables are laid and the wine and water poured. Openly, they ride off together, shamelessly they return, their faces bright with unspoken joy. Everyone else rides behind the hounds for a little while and then takes their horses to the river and lets them drink, or dismounts to idle in the shadows, or goes away to somewhere quiet and hidden to kiss and whisper.

The sun is hot but the clearing is shaded by the fresh green leaves of the oak and beech trees, and the birds sing incessantly as if they are a choir in harmony with the musicians who are hidden in the branches. The smell of woodsmoke and roasted meat mingles with the lush scent of crushed grass and herbs where the servants have spread carpets and rugs and cushions, so that we can sprawl at our leisure, and drink wine and tell stories and poems. Sometimes we sing together, old country songs, and sometimes Ned reads his poetry, but never 'She stood in black', which is for me, and is mine alone.

We are a court of young, beautiful people. The older wiser ones have no patience with all-day picnics when we do not get home until dusk, riding side by side, whispering promises. They are full of warnings about the careful work that William Cecil is doing in Edinburgh, and how it will all come to nothing if Elizabeth does not give England an heir to inherit the peace. But Elizabeth's relief at the end of war with Scotland makes her giddy with joy. She is triumphant: she thinks winning the war makes her invulnerable. She is indiscreet; she thinks that the world is well lost for love. Even when the Privy Council warns that they have to slit the tongues of men and women up and down the country to stop them saying that she is Robert Dudley's whore, she still leans from her bedroom window in the morning, half naked, and calls to Robert Dudley to come to her at once.

Everyone at court knows that they have adjoining bedrooms with only a door between them. They may go to their own rooms at night, but everyone believes that Robert Dudley's valet stands outside his door all the night, because the Queen of England has crept through the hidden door and is inside. Even the country people who should know nothing of the court say that Elizabeth is besotted with her handsome master of horse, and many people think that they are married in secret already and that his poor wife, whatever-her-name-is, will be put aside by order of the queen, just as her father, King Henry, put his wives aside to marry another.

Then the news comes that the Regent of Scotland, Mary of Guise, is dead and the power of the French in Scotland collapses without her to uphold it. Cecil is coming home to London. He has made a triumphant peace treaty; but now Robert Dudley swears that he has gained nothing for all his hard riding: Newcastle to Edinburgh and back again. Elizabeth now wants more than Cecil's treaty: she demands thousands of pounds of compensation, the return of Calais, and Mary the Queen of France to be banned from using the royal crest on her dinner plates – everything from the most grave to the most trivial. She and Robert, like a queen and her husband, stand side by side before the whole court and greet William Cecil with a tirade of complaints.

The defeat of French rule in Scotland should have been hailed as a victory, but William Cecil, whose skill brought it about, is crushed by Elizabeth's ingratitude to him, unable to hide his fury that she is taking advice from Robert Dudley. The court divides in rivalry between those who see Dudley as the unstoppable star – husband and king consort-to-be – and those that say William Cecil must be respected along with the old lords, and that Dudley is an upstart from treasonous stock.

Elizabeth, having lovingly declared me as dear to her as a daughter, promising me that she will be a mother to me, that she will legally adopt me, that she will name me as heir, forgets all about me in this new crisis: as the man who has been a father to her and the man who has been a husband to her will not speak to each other for fury. All the court is certain that Cecil will abandon her, that Dudley will ruin her. There are whispers of plots to assassinate him; she has opposition on every side. She dare not agree that a country may choose its own heir. If the Scots are allowed to reject their Queen Mary, why do the English have to accept Elizabeth? In her anxiety for her lover, for her future, for the very nature of queenship, she has no time for me, no time for any woman.

'But I like being forgotten,' Mary my sister remarks. 'I suppose I am used to it, being so often below the eyeline. But it does mean that you can do what you want.'

'And what do you want to do, you funny little thing?' I ask indulgently, bending down so I can see her exquisite face. 'Are you getting up to mischief like half the court? Are you in love, Mary?'

Janey laughs unkindly, as if no-one would ever love Mary. 'You can have my suitor,' she says. Janey is being pursued by our old uncle, Henry FitzAlan Earl of Arundel. He is a great survivor of wives, his first was my aunt Katherine Grey, now he is free again and wealthy and desperate to put some royal blood into his golden cradle, into his rich nursery, into his family line.

'I don't need your cast-offs,' Mary dismisses the wealthy nobleman with a wave of her tiny hand. 'I have an admirer.'

I am not surprised. Mary has the Tudor charm, and a kind

nature that many a man would be glad to find in a wife. She would make a better wife than Janey Seymour, with her fragile health and her feverish energy. Mary is a little joy in miniature: when she stands before a knight in armour she can see her pretty face and her perfectly formed neck and shoulders reflected in his breastplate. If she were seated on a cushion behind a high table, and a man saw only our heads and shoulders, he would be hard-pressed to choose the greater beauty. It is only when she stands up that it is suddenly revealed that she is tiny, half-size. High in the saddle, on horseback, I believe she is prettier even than I am. She stands straight enough, she has her monthly courses – perhaps she could have a suitor, perhaps she could even be married.

'Every other lady in court is flirting. I am no different,' Mary says. 'Why should I be different?'

'Oh, who is flirting with you?' scoffs Janey.

'Never you mind,' says my redoubtable sister. 'For I have my business just as Katherine has hers. And I wouldn't let you meddle with me as you do with her.'

'I don't meddle, I advise her,' Janey says, stung. 'I am her great friend.'

'Well, don't advise me!' Mary says. 'I have a great friend of my own, greater than both of you together.'

WINDSOR CASTLE,
AUTUMN 1560

I love Windsor Castle, the rides down to the water meadows by the river, the great park with the herds of deer moving quietly in a ripple among the trees, and the castle perched high above the little village. We are to celebrate Elizabeth's birthday as if it were a feast as great as Christmas. Robert Dudley, as master of horse, appoints a master of ceremonies and orders him to hire players and choirs, dancers, and entertainers – jugglers and magicians. There are to be poets to hymn Elizabeth's beauty, there are to be bishops to pray for her long and happy reign. It is to go on for days to celebrate the birth of a girl whose mother died on the scaffold accused of adultery and whose father did not recognise her as his own for most of her life. I could almost laugh aloud to see Elizabeth order the court to celebrate her birth, when the older people remember what a bitter disappointment the girl baby was at the time and how indifferent everyone was to her for so long.

Robert Dudley is everywhere – the king of the court, the master builder of Elizabeth's happiness. William Cecil is self-contained inside a bleak silent fury. His hard-won treaty with France is to go ahead, but he gets no thanks for it. It is not celebrated as a diplomatic triumph, and he blames Elizabeth's poor judgement on her infatuation with Robert Dudley.

The master of ceremonies designs a beautiful dance that all the young ladies of the court must learn. We are all to represent different virtues: I am to be 'Duty', Janey is to be 'Honour'. She is well enough to dance, the flush in her cheeks has cooled and her eyes are not blazing with fever for once. Mary is to be 'Victory' and stand at the top of a tall tower that hides her tiny feet and shows her as a beauty. The queen's sergeant porter, the officer in charge of the safety of the whole court, is a tall broad man, bigger than any other, and they call him in to lift Mary into the top of the tower. Gallantly, he bows to her; she looks like a fairy under the feet of a giant. It is as good as a play. She puts out her little hand and he takes it to his lips, and then he puts his hands around her tiny waist and lifts her up. Everyone applauds, it is so pretty, and someone says that Mr Thomas Keyes, the sergeant porter, must put his deputy on the gate and come in to play his part in the masque. Mr Keyes bows, smiling, handsome in his Tudor livery, and Mary, her little hand buried in his huge paw, laughs and curtseys, her face bright.

Ned plays the part of 'Trust' and is paired to dance with

Frances Mewtas, who is a female trust – whatever that is – 'Gullibility' perhaps. I wish that she would swap with me, but I cannot ask her without revealing that I want to dance with Ned, and he does not think to hint to her that she might prefer to be 'Duty'. He even seems to enjoy her company. After their dance is finished they stand together, and when we all go outside to enjoy the sunset and take a glass of small ale, he goes with her hand on his arm and he pours a glass for her.

The dance goes off step-perfect. Elizabeth, enthroned, smiles as we dance before her, though I dare say she would rather be in Robert Dudley's arms herself. I know that I would rather be dancing with Ned than watching him. Frances Mewtas has painted her face, I am sure of it. She looks ridiculous and she sticks to Ned's side like a snail on a wall. I frown at him to show that I am displeased and he looks blankly back at me as if he cannot imagine that the sight of another girl, her hand on his arm, looking up into his handsome face, might displease me. He is such a taking young man, his smile so charming and his eyes so bright, I cannot bear to see him partnered with a little plain thing like Frances. I would have thought that she would have had the sense to know that he was longing to be with me. Surely she can see that it would be a prettier dance if Ned and I were together?

I have to stand beside Elizabeth's throne when the Spanish ambassador de la Quadra and the other ambassadors arrive to give her birthday gifts. I am to demonstrate that we are the best of friends, on the warmest of terms. I am publicly known as Elizabeth's heir, and Cecil's treaty proves that Mary Queen of Scots has surrendered her claim to the throne of England. Elizabeth remembers to turn her head and smile at me, and waves her hand to my little sister. My friendly intimacy with Elizabeth is choreographed, just like the dances. I am here to indicate that Mary Queen of Scots has no claim to the English throne, I am the heir-to-be and Elizabeth will nominate me at the next parliament.

De la Quadra bows very low and steps up to speak to the queen, but I am not attending to royal business, I am watching Ned, who is walking with Frances Mewtas through the people to the back of the hall where the candles throw intimate shadows and courting couples dawdle in the alcoves. I cannot see him, and I am not allowed to go to find him. This is an ordeal for me, and then I hear, almost in the distance, Elizabeth telling the Spanish ambassador that Robert Dudley's wife is dead of a canker.

I am so shocked as the words penetrate my anxious surveillance of the back of the hall that I stop looking for Ned and I stare at Elizabeth. Did she really say that Lady Dudley is dead? 'Or nearly so,' she corrects herself. 'Poor woman.'

De la Quadra looks as stunned as I am. Only good manners prevent him yelping: '*Qué? Qué?*'

Why would Elizabeth say such an extraordinary thing? What woman is dead one moment and 'nearly so' the next? Is Elizabeth blind and deaf to simple good manners? Does she not realise that it is not very charming of a mistress to release the news of an abandoned wife's death as if it were a matter of mild interest? And then muddle whether she is dead or not? And if the woman is dead, why is Robert Dudley not at his home, ordering mourning clothes, arranging her funeral? Or if she is on her deathbed, why is Robert Dudley dancing at Elizabeth's birthday feast and not at his dying wife's side?

I long to find Ned and tell him this extraordinary conversation, but when the presentation of gifts is over there is general dancing and I am still nailed to the dais behind Elizabeth, who is now whispering with Robert Dudley. Whatever she is saying, while he smiles down at her with his eyes on her mouth, they are not talking about cankers and deathbeds.

Ned is not among the couples on the floor. He is not among the men watching the women dancing. He is not cautiously working his way to the top of the room so that he can be near me. I can't see him anywhere, and I cannot see Frances Mewtas either.

I am trapped on the dais with Elizabeth, and Ned does not come near me. I don't see him again all night, though the court retires late as Elizabeth dances and dances, drinks her own health, and finally leads us from the room. Ned is nowhere to be seen among the men bowing as we withdraw. Frances Mewtas scuttles from one of the galleries at the last minute, all flushed, and joins the procession of ladies leaving the room.

I go to bed in tears, I am so furious and so pained. I did not think I could feel like this again. It is so much worse than the last time that I lost Ned. This time I have given him my promise, I believed us to be all but married.

I toss and turn in the hot sheets and my lady-bedfellow mutters sleepily: 'Are you ill, your ladyship? Shall I fetch you something?'

I make myself lie like a bolster but I can hear my hurt heart thudding in my ears. I hear the clock strike the hour, every hour from midnight till five in the morning, and only then, as it starts to get light and the servants start to clatter about and put fresh wood on the dying fires, do I fall asleep.

Elizabeth at chapel looks as if she has slept as badly as I have. I don't know what is wrong with her. There can be nothing wrong for her. She has everything to hope for. Her rival is dying or dead, her birthday is celebrated throughout the kingdom as if she were a beloved queen, Robert Dudley is at her side, as smiling and relaxed as a confident bridegroom. But Elizabeth shrinks from him. She asks for Cecil to be sent for. She walks with him, her head bent towards him in low-voiced consultation. He is urging her to stand fast, as she trembles and leans on him. Something serious is happening, but I am so absorbed in looking for Ned that I cannot be troubled with Elizabeth and her sudden changes of mood.

The court walks behind Cecil and Elizabeth, who are clearly not to be disturbed, until Cecil bows and steps back and someone else leaps forward to be presented to the queen and ask her for some favour. William Cecil finds himself alongside the Spanish ambassador, Mary and I walk behind them, their slow pace suiting Mary's short stride. I take her hand.

'I can manage,' she says, shrugging me off.

'I know you can. I just wanted some comfort. I am very unhappy.'

'Hush!' she says, unfeelingly. She is openly eavesdropping on the conversation going on ahead of us. I can hear snatches of Cecil's talk, over the lapping noise of the water on the riverbank. He is complaining of Elizabeth – a thing that he never, never does – telling the Spanish ambassador that he is going to leave court, that he cannot tolerate another day of it. I pinch Mary's arm. 'Hark at Cecil!' I say, shocked. 'What is he saying? He can't be leaving court again?'

Mary drops my hand and walks a little closer to the two men, while I hang back. Nobody ever notices Mary: she should be one of Cecil's many spies. She can weave her way around men as if she were a beggar child, and they never see her. She follows on their heels for a little while, quite unnoticed, and then she slows up and waits for me to catch up, her eyes shocked and wide, as if she has stared at horrors.

'He said that the queen and Sir Robert are planning to murder Amy Dudley, and Robert will marry the queen,' she whispers urgently, almost choking on her words. 'Cecil said it himself! I heard him. He says that they are giving out that she has a canker and the queen will marry Robert, but that the country will never stand for it.'

'He never said that to de la Quadra?' I see my own disbelief in my sister's face. 'The Spanish ambassador? When every word he hears goes straight back to Spain! Why would Cecil tell him such a thing?'

'He did. I could not mistake it.'

I shake my head. 'It makes no sense.'

'I heard it!'

'My God, are they really going to kill Amy Dudley? Shouldn't we stop them?'

I see my shock on Mary's face. 'Who could we tell? How could we stop them? If Cecil himself knows and is not stopping them.'

'But the queen can't just murder someone, not even a rival. It can't happen.'

'Cecil says it will be her undoing. He says the country will rise against her rather than have a murderer on the throne. He says he is going to his home.'

I can't understand any of this. Would Cecil really desert Elizabeth? The queen he has made? Would he leave her to commit a terrible crime that would cost her her soul and her kingdom? And if he did – I think, if he *does* – then will he come to me and offer to make me queen in her place?

'He said he couldn't bear to advise her with Robert Dudley whispering in her other ear; he said that the country would never tolerate a Dudley as king consort.'

'Well, that's true enough,' I say begrudgingly, thinking of my sister Jane refusing to crown this man's brother, her husband, Guildford, because of the treachery of his grandfather. 'No-one would accept a Dudley near the throne ever again.'

'But to say it to the Spanish ambassador?' Mary is aghast. 'He told the ambassador that she has no credit, that the country is bankrupted. I swear he said that she and Robert are going to murder Lady Dudley. He said it. He said it, Katherine!' She shakes her head in an odd gesture, as if she is tapping water from her ears. 'I couldn't believe what I was hearing. Cecil, denouncing the queen – to the Spanish?'

'It makes no sense,' I say. But then my misery for Ned overwhelms me. 'Nothing makes any sense,' I say bitterly, 'and this court is a world of lies.'

Mary must have heard rightly, for there is no mistaking Elizabeth's anxiety. She is avoiding Robert Dudley, and she spends as much time in her rooms as possible with the door closed to everyone but the ladies of her bedchamber. He used to stroll in and out without invitation, now the guards are before the door and nobody is allowed in. Publicly, she announces that she is unwell, but she prowls around her rooms like a woman more troubled in her mind than in her body. All of Sunday she is like a restless cat, stalking one way and then another. She goes to bed early, complaining of a headache, but I think it is her conscience that is paining her. If even half that William Cecil said is half true, then she has commissioned the murder of an innocent woman. This, I think, must be impossible; but then I remember her mother was Anne Boleyn and they said that she used poison against her rivals. Can it be that Elizabeth is poisoning a rival? Can Elizabeth bring herself to kill a rival?

The next day is my day of duty so I have to wait on her again. She looks pale and sleepless and so do I. I cannot go looking for Ned as I am not allowed to leave the queen's rooms without her permission. Frances Mewtas is not in attendance today, and for all I know, she and Ned are enjoying their leisure together. Together and unwatched. The thought of this is such a pain to me that I can hardly bear to stand against the wall, my hands clasped together, my eyes down, as Elizabeth paces up and down her privy chamber, twenty paces to one window, twenty paces to another. Robert Dudley comes in, and she tells him that she does not want to ride; she does not want to ride out this morning nor this afternoon, the horses can be unsaddled and turned out in the field, the court is not going out today.

He does not ask her why. That he does not challenge her tells me that he knows what is wrong with Elizabeth, that he shares her guilt. He merely bows and sends a message to the stables. As he turns his head to tell his groom, I see his glance go past the groom and past me to a man who stands waiting in the doorway. It is one of Robert Dudley's servants and he comes forward, his face very grave, and kneels before Dudley.

I am trembling as I stand behind the queen as if I too am expecting bad news. The queen and Sir Robert face the man together. Their hands are close and I think she would like to cling to him. The man hands over a letter and tells Robert Dudley, so quietly that no-one but Dudley and the queen and I can hear, that he is sorry to bring bad news: Lady Dudley is dead.

The queen goes so pale that she is almost yellow. I think she is going to faint. She stands as stiff as the giant sergeant porter at the palace gates. She is speechless. I find myself reeling too – I did not think that she could do such a thing. I would never have thought it of Robert Dudley.

She staggers as if her knees have gone from under her. I step forward and take her arm. 'Your Majesty?' I whisper. 'Shall I get you a glass of small ale?'

She looks at me unseeing and I flinch from the blankness of her suspicious glare. I think perhaps this is the face of a murderer. God spare me from her black look. I glance across the room and notice that Ned, who came in behind Dudley's servant, is watching the two of them as well. He smiles tentatively at me, his handsome face a little puzzled, and I look away. I cannot tell him what I know. At this, of all moments, he has failed me.

Robert puts his mouth to the queen's ear and whispers to her. She nods, and turns stiffly, goes out to the presence chamber and stands, one hand on her throne for support. I wait for Robert to bow to her and then turn to the court and announce the death of his wife, but he says nothing. The queen says nothing either. They look at each other, a long gaze of terrible complicity as William Cecil watches quietly from the back of the room. I have a horrible sense that there is a script to this play, but I don't know it.

I hardly know how we get through the day. Still the death of Lady Dudley is not announced. They serve breakfast and dinner, the court plays games and listens to music. In the evening there is some clowning and everyone who does not know the terrible secret laughs heartily and applauds. Elizabeth walks through it all like a little doll driven only by will. Her face is expressionless; she says nothing. I follow behind her. I feel as if the world is ending all around me and I have lost the only man I could trust.

It is not until the next day, three full days since Elizabeth first told the Spanish ambassador that Amy Dudley was dead of a canker, that the news is released. Elizabeth sits on her throne in the chapel posed in that sacred space with the honoured banners of the knights of the garter hanging from the walls, and announces, loud enough for everyone to hear, that sadly,

Amy Dudley has died. Those few people who had heard only that she was heartbroken at being abandoned by her husband, or complaining of ill health, gasp at the news of her death. Only Mary and I, and presumably William Cecil and the Spanish ambassador, must wonder why it has taken them so long to make the announcement.

Elizabeth exchanges a glance with Cecil that shows, in their carefully expressionless faces, that they are fully prepared for this. She inclines her head to listen to her lover. Her face is like stone. Dudley finishes speaking, bows and steps backwards, away from the queen, his head down, as if he is grieving for his abandoned wife.

'We are very sorry for your loss,' Elizabeth says regally. 'The court will go into mourning for Lady Dudley.'

A little gesture of her ringed hand tells everyone that they may talk, and there is a buzz of chatter, far more excitement than sorrow. Few people knew Amy Dudley: Robert, like other favoured husbands, always made sure that his wife was kept from court. Now he is free, suddenly, amazingly free. People approach Robert, offering their condolences but really congratulating him on his extraordinary good luck. That an unloved wife should die at such a moment! No-one doubts that he is the new king con- sort. Everyone assumes that they will marry at once. Ned comes towards me. Behind him, I see Cecil and Dudley and Elizabeth, heads together, like plotters. Robert Dudley looks sick, the other two blankly determined.

'What luck for Dudley!' Ned says. 'They are certain to marry now.'

'*They* are,' I say, but he does not hear the emphasis.

'How strange that the queen said that she was dead before Robert announced it to the court,' Janey says, joining us. 'You heard her, didn't you, Katherine? She said that she was sick of a canker, but then the poor woman goes and falls downstairs.'

'Did she?' Ned asks.

'I heard Cecil say something very different.' Mary joins us and speaks so quietly that we all have to bend to hear her.

'What did Cecil say?' Janey asks Ned.

'Ned didn't hear, for he was walking with Frances Mewtas and not with us. He had eyes only for her,' I say sharply. 'I was walking with Mary. Ned did not choose to be with me.'

Janey looks from my pale face to his. 'Katherine, we have been friends with the Mewtas family for ages. Frances' mother served our kinswoman Queen Jane Seymour. She's a good friend to us both.'

I hunch my shoulder. 'Oh, I am sure. But why would Ned dance with her, and walk with her and disappear all evening with her when I needed him? When I needed him so badly.'

'I did not!' he says indignantly. 'I danced with her as the dance master commanded me to do. You did the same with your partner.'

'I didn't walk with him after, and give him small ale, and spend the next evening hidden away somewhere with him. I didn't run after him and make a fool of myself, and of me,' I say, getting confused in my indignation. 'God knows what is happening here. I think the court has gone mad, and you were nowhere to be found. I didn't forget all the promises I made. I was not dishonourable.'

The colour drains from his face and his eyes go dark with rage. 'Neither was I. You do me wrong, madam.'

It is him calling me 'madam' as if we were old and heartless that makes me turn on him. 'How could you, Ned? After all you have said to me! After all you have promised. And I was trapped on the dais beside the queen, and I looked and looked for you . . . I couldn't see you, and I couldn't find you and I was stuck there and I didn't even see you before we had to withdraw.' To my own embarrassment I can hear my voice quavering and then I openly cry, in the middle of the court, where anyone can see me.

Mary comes to my side at once, puts her hand around my waist, and the two of us face the Seymours as if they are our enemies.

'Accuse me!' He is white and furious. 'Accuse me as you will. I have done nothing, and you should trust a man who is ready to risk everything for you.'

'You risk nothing!' I cry at him. 'It is I who have turned down the Spanish, and turned down the Scots, so I am trapped here with the queen, swearing that I will marry no-one! God knows what she can do, what she is capable of, God knows what she has done to a rival. And I've done all this for you; you've done nothing for me. You're such a liar!'

'He's not a liar,' Janey says quickly. 'Unsay it, Katherine.'

'He is, if she says so!' Mary says with instant loyalty.

'Ask Frances what he has said to her!' I spit at Janey. 'Frances Mewtas, your great friend. Ask her what lies he tells her – if she is to be your sister-in-law! For I will never be.'

I fling myself away from the two of them and run to the ladies' rooms, dropping a curtsey to the throne as I go. I will have to say I am ill and that is why I left without permission. I will have to go to bed. I long to go to my bed and cry all day.

My little sister, Mary, tells everyone that I am sick from eating undercooked apples and that the best thing for me is to be left alone. She comes to me in my private room off the ladies' chambers and behind her comes a servant with a plate of meat from the kitchen and some bread from the bakery.

'I can't eat,' I say, raising my head from the pillow.

'I know,' she says. 'This is all for me. But you can have a little if you want.'

She hauls herself up into a chair beside the bed, and passes me a glass of wine and water. 'Have you broken with Ned?' she asks. 'He's going round court with a face like a pig's bottom.'

'Don't be so vulgar.' I take a sip. 'Mother would have smacked you.'

'And our sister, Jane, would have closed her eyes and prayed for patience,' Mary chuckles. 'But it's how he looks. I cannot lie.' She breaks off a little piece of manchet bread and passes it to me. I nibble on it.

'He is courting Frances Mewtas,' I say. 'I know he is. I think my heart is broken.'

Mary raises her perfectly arched eyebrows. 'You couldn't have married him anyway,' she says. 'You'd never have got permission. And there's terrible news from Oxford. It turns out that Lady Dudley was not sick at all. She fell down the stairs and broke her neck. And worse than that, there's to be an inquest!'

'She's not sick? But everyone said . . . And the queen said . . .'

'Fell downstairs and broke her neck,' Mary repeats.

'My God! But what can an inquest do?'

'It can discover what happened. Because people are saying that she did not fall down the stairs but someone pushed her!' Mary says through a mouthful of bread and meat. 'And so Sir Robert has to withdraw from court, and go into mourning on his own. He's going to his house at Kew, and Elizabeth is prowling round her rooms like a hungry wolf. She can't go to see him, she can't even write to him. He's suspected of murder; she can't be connected. She doesn't go out and has almost imprisoned herself in her rooms. The court dines without her. Nobody knows what to do. And he – he is halfway to ruin. Everyone is saying that he murdered his wife to marry Elizabeth, and some people are saying that she knew.'

I am enormously cheered at the thought of Elizabeth losing Robert Dudley, just as I am parted from Ned. 'She did know! At any rate, she knew that Amy Dudley was going to die! But who is saying that it was Elizabeth?'

'The Spanish ambassador himself!' Mary reminds me. 'And he had it from Cecil. He has told everyone. She will never be able to see Dudley again. Everyone says she knew that he was going to kill his wife. And if they find him guilty of murder they will execute him, and serve him right.'

'They'll never behead Robert Dudley!' I say bitterly. 'She'll never let them. Not him. Not her favourite.'

'It doesn't matter who he is, if he killed his wife,' Mary declares. 'Not even Elizabeth is above the law of the land. If the Oxfordshire inquest names him as a murderer then she can't pardon him. And besides, he's hardly the first of that family to be beheaded.' She sees my face as I think of our sister who signed herself 'Jane Duddley'. She puts out her hand. 'I didn't mean her. I never think of Jane as a Dudley.'

I shake my head at the sudden vivid thought of my sister and the spoiled Dudley boy. 'They're none of them any good,' I say spitefully. 'But Robert was the best of them.'

Once again, Ned and I are estranged. I had thought he would come to me at once and beg my pardon, but he does not. I am miserable without him, but I cannot bring myself to apologise when I am not at fault. I see him walking with Frances Mewtas and dancing with her, and each time my jealousy and unhappiness are renewed. I am determined to punish him for his infidelity, but I think that no-one is in pain but me.

The court is subdued and uneasy. It seems as if nobody is happy as the days get shorter and the leaves turn colour, and the summer, which seemed as if it would last forever, drains away a little more every day. The blue fades from the sky and the clouds go grey and a cold wind gets up and blows down the Thames valley.

Elizabeth is lost without Robert Dudley, who is still away from court, skulking at his pretty house at Kew, wearing full black and shamed to the ground. He is waiting, as we all are, for the results from the Abingdon coroner and the judgement of the inquest jury. He may get back to court – he is a Dudley, after all: they bounce back after anything but beheading – but he can never marry the queen now. Even if the jury rules that his wife was killed by an accidental fall, everyone believes that he has packed the jury. It does not really matter if this is true or not. It is his reputation that is on trial and that is as dead as his poor wife. The struggle for the queen is over. Not even Robert Dudley can imagine that he will ever be accepted as a suitable advisor or courtier by the country, the Privy Council or even the queen herself. He has disqualified himself by the crime that he thought would advance his cause to the throne.

William Cecil is quietly victorious in the absence of his old rival. He manages to be at once regretful and dominant: the queen must marry a Protestant prince, Robert Dudley is infamed by the death of his wife. The queen, who was so besotted, is like a heartbroken widow without the man she loves. But her determination to survive as queen holds her tight as a vice. She says not one word of Robert, and her pinched little face is constantly turned towards Cecil, her head cocked for his discreet counsel, and she does exactly what he tells her. Nobody doubts that she will marry as he thinks best, since her attempt to marry for love has ended in death and disgrace.

I am back in favour, but I can't say it is a very merry place to be. Elizabeth is sick with silent longing for the man she loves; I, one pace behind her, am yearning for Ned. I almost want to tell her that I understand her pain, that I am feeling the same. But then I remember that it is her fault that Ned and I are parted. We are not doomed by sin, we were free to marry. It is her fault that I am so unhappy. One word from her would restore me to the only man I will ever love. But she will not say that word. She will never say it. She wants everyone to be as lonely and bereft as herself.

WINDSOR CASTLE, OCTOBER 1560

It gets colder and there is no more boating on the river for pleasure. The court is to return to London. Amy Dudley's death is named as an accident. Robert Dudley, his month of mourning concluded, his name as clear as it will ever be, is allowed back to court. Elizabeth, with the eyes of the world on her and on her lover, knowing that everyone believes him to be a murderer, greets him very quietly, and Robert Dudley joins the court with uncharacteristic gravity.

They have to be together, they cannot help themselves; everyone can see that. But there will be no talk of marriage ever again: William Cecil has seen to that. It was he who spread the rumours that Dudley would kill his wife, and it was he who told everyone that the country would never bear a Dudley as king. It doesn't really matter if either of these things is true or false: the whole of Christendom believes it, and Elizabeth and Dudley stoop under the shared burden of their shame.

My cousin Margaret Douglas, the poor woman – ugly, old and papist – is summoned to court during this gloomy time. She is not here to be honoured, but to be watched. Elizabeth, despairing of getting any truth from the long interrogations of Margaret's crazed advisors – a double spy, a soothsayer, a turncoat priest – has decided to keep a close eye on her at court. They know that Margaret has approached the French Queen of Scots, but they don't know what she has offered.

At once, all the issues of precedence begin all over again as the woman, a known papist, who should really be humbled by her disgrace, tries to push in front of me, the Protestant heir. I am so unhappy at the loss of Ned I really can't make myself care enough to push back. It is a relief when Margaret is allowed to return to her home in Yorkshire, still suspected, still papist, still old and ugly of course.

I decide that I will write to Ned and tell him that when the court returns to London and falls into the routine of city life, I don't wish to see him. I know this is meaningless: we cannot help but see each other, we are attending the same queen, we are serving at the same court. We will see each other every day.

'But I don't wish to dance with you, or have you lift me to my horse, or attend me to chapel or single me out in any way at all,' I write stiffly. I drop a tear on the page and I blot it with my sleeve so that he cannot see that I am crying over this. 'I wish you every happiness with Frances. I myself will never marry. I have been deeply disappointed in love.'

I think this is tremendously dignified. I enclose in the letter the precious poem that he wrote for me. I won't ever forget it. I know every line. I have carried it in a linen pouch next to my heart as if it were an amulet against despair. But now I think I will send it back to him and let him be sure that I am releasing him from all his promises of love, from our hopeful betrothal, from being Troilus and Criseyde. I send a messenger with the package to Ned's London house in Cannon Row and I tell him not to wait for a reply. There can be no reply.

The very next day we are walking back from chapel when Janey comes to my side with a letter sealed with the Hertford seal. 'I have this from Ned,' she says awkwardly. 'His messenger brought it at dawn. I think he was up all night writing to you. He commands me to give it to you at once. Please be my friend again. Please read this.'

'What's that?' asks my little sister Mary, from under my elbow, bright-eyed with interest.

'I don't know,' I say, but I can feel myself blushing with delight. It must be courtship. Courtship again. A man doesn't stay up all night writing a letter to accept his rejection and send the reply at dawn. He must love me. He must want me back. He must be trying to persuade me.

'Is it Ned?' Mary asks. She pulls my hand down so that she can see the seal. 'O-ho.'

'O-ho yourself,' I say. I step aside from the procession, which is following the queen to the great hall for breakfast.

'You can't be late,' Mary warns me. 'She's sour as crab apples this morning.'

'You go,' Janey says. 'If anyone asks, say that I am ill and Katherine has taken me to my room.'

Mary rolls her eyes impertinently, and follows the ladies. Janey and I step out of the garden door and into the cold deserted courtyard. I open the letter.

'What does he say?' Janey asks, her voice muffled through her sleeve that she holds to her mouth, trying not to cough in the damp air from the river.

I raise my blurred gaze from the letter, but I can't see her, my eyes are so filled with tears. 'He says he will marry me out of hand,' I whisper. 'As soon as the court returns to London. He says we are to wait no longer, that he will not listen to William Cecil's warnings nor to anyone else. He says Robert Dudley advised him to trust to time, but Robert Dudley did not trust to time and is ruined. Ned says that he will no longer trust and wait.' I burst into tears and grip her hands. 'Janey! He is going to marry me!'

WHITEHALL PALACE, LONDON, AUTUMN 1560

The Privy Council is meeting and the queen is attending with two of her ladies to stand behind her chair, but I am not required. Quietly, I drift from the presence chamber, up the stairs to the room for the maids of honour. Janey is waiting for me and we go to her private room off the main chamber.

She fusses over me, taking off my hood, combing my hair, and pinning the hood on again. 'This was a lovers' quarrel,' she says. 'Nothing more. Thank God that it is over and done with.'

I find I am smiling as if, suddenly, nothing mattered after all. 'He wrote such a wonderful letter.'

'He's a poet,' she replies. 'His heart is in his words. And Frances Mewtas is nothing to him.'

'He should never have taken her hand after they had finished dancing,' I say.

'He knows that,' Janey agrees.

'And the next evening, was he with her?'

'He did not even see her. He was playing cards with the squires. He promised me it was so, and I saw him myself. That was your jealousy.'

'I am not jealous!'

Janey regards me with her head on one side. 'You are not?'

I laugh but there is a catch in my throat. 'Janey, it is this place, full of lies. And being so uncertain, and having no permission to marry and never a good time to ask! And now with Elizabeth and Robert Dudley parted forever, and him back at court but not able to be with her, everyone despising him for being a wife murderer and Elizabeth too afraid to even speak to him ... how will she ever be happy again? We can never ask permission for our wedding! Elizabeth will never allow anyone happiness. Not when she has lost her own lover forever.'

In answer, Janey goes to the door, and makes a beckoning gesture. Ned slips in. I get to my feet. 'Ned,' I say uncertainly.

He does not scoop me into his arms this time, he does not sweep me off my feet. He bows very formally, then says, as if he has a prepared speech in his pocket, 'I have borne you goodwill of a long time, and because you should not think I intend to mock you, I am content, if you will, to marry you.'

He takes my hand. I can feel that I am trembling. From his pocket he takes a ring and he slides it on the third finger of my left hand, it is a betrothal ring. It is a diamond, cut to glitter, elegantly pointed along the length of my finger, as if it would join our two hearts with its bright fire.

'What d'you say?' he whispers. 'How d'you like me? How d'you like my offer?'

'I like both you and your offer, am content to marry with you,' I say solemnly.

'Will you witness our betrothal?' he asks Janey shortly.

'Oh, yes!' she gasps. She stands before us, looking from one to another.

'I, Edward Seymour, take thee, Katherine Grey, to be my wife *in futuro*,' he pledges. 'And in proof of this I give you this ring, and this purse of gold, and my sacred word.'

I have never attended a betrothal. I don't know what I am to do. I look up at the handsome face of my husband-to-be.

'You say the same,' he says.

'I, Katherine Grey, take thee, Edward Seymour, to be my husband *in futuro*,' I repeat his vow. 'And in proof of this, I accept this ring and this purse of gold and your sacred word.'

'And so I witness,' Janey volunteers.

Edward drops a little purse of coins into my hand, which symbolise that he is giving his fortune into my keeping, and then puts his hand under my chin, turns up my face, and kisses me on the lips. I think: I will never be alone or unhappy again.

'When shall we marry before a priest?' I whisper.

Again, it is Janey who has the plan. 'When the queen next goes hunting we could come to your house,' she suggests to Ned. 'I'll find a priest.'

'A preacher,' Ned specifies.

I think of how my sister Jane would never have let me be married by a priest of the old faith and I smile at him. 'Of course,' I say. 'But no-one who knows us.'

'A stranger,' Janey agrees, 'so that he tells no-one and does not know who you are. I will be one witness. Who shall be the other? Your sister?'

I shake my head. 'No, for when we tell the queen she will be furious and I don't want Mary to take the blame for me. I'll bring my maid.'

'Soon, then,' Ned says. 'As soon as the queen goes hunting. But we are as married now as we will be later. We are husband and wife. This betrothal is as binding as wedlock.'

Janey smiles. 'I'll sit in the maids' chamber,' she offers. 'No-one will come in.'

She goes out and the door closes behind her. Ned locks it and puts the key into my hand. 'I am your prisoner,' he says. 'You can do what you want with me.'

I hesitate. I can feel my own desire, I can hear it in the thudding in my ears.

'I am your promised husband,' he says with a smile. 'You really can do what you want with me.'

I take the ties of his linen shirt that fasten it at his throat and I tug at them. 'I want you to take this off,' I whisper.

'You want me naked?'

I am as hot as if I had a fever. I have to see his bare shoulders, his chest, the laces at his breeches. I long to see his thighs, his lean buttocks. I feel the heat in my face as he cups my cheek in his hand, and he says: 'Thank God that you want me as I do you.' He shucks off his shirt and I take a little breath at the sight of his lean torso, then I step forward and lean my flushed face against his warm bare chest.

He slides down his breeches, he is naked underneath. 'Command me,' he whispers.

'Lie down,' I say, and he stretches out, naked and shameless on his back, and I let myself creep up the length of his body and lie on him.

WHITEHALL PALACE, LONDON, NOVEMBER 1560

And then we have to wait, and it is delicious timeless pleasure and pain together. Every morning I hope that perhaps today Elizabeth will say that she is going to Hampton Court, or to Windsor for the hunting, or to New Hall or to Beaulieu or anywhere – I don't care where her ridiculous fancy takes her if she would just go! But day after day Ned is one side of the presence chamber and I am the other and we have to nod politely as if we were friends, and we dare not speak to each other until the evening dancing throws us together, and now, though we have so much more desire, we have more fear, and we dare not go to the corners of the room and whisper.

It is an exquisite joy to see him, to snatch a moment with him. It is agonisingly wonderful to wake in the morning and see that it is a good day for hunting: sharp and bright and cold, and surely Elizabeth will go today? And then, when she says nothing, it is a delightful torment to dance with Ned, and steal away with him for a kiss and dare to do no more. It is a passionate courtship and now I know the joy that his touch brings to me. It is lust deferred, it is love delayed, there is nothing in the world more delightful than being in his arms, unless it is knowing that I will be in his arms later . . . but not now.

William Cecil, the queen's advisor, comes over to sit beside me before dinner one evening, as we are waiting in the presence chamber for the queen to finish the lengthy process of dressing in her inner rooms.

'You are in your finest beauty,' he tells me. 'We shall have the Spanish proposing marriage to you again. I have never seen you look so well.'

I look down. I am no fool. I know that he is my friend, but I also know that he is first for his faith and then for England, and then for the queen, and everyone else comes after that. I have seen him triumph over the French in Edinburgh, and I have seen him triumph over Robert Dudley at court, and I swear I shall never make the mistake of underrating William Cecil. Only God and William Cecil know what he will do to keep a Protestant queen on the throne of England.

'Ah, my lord, you know I have no wish to go to Spain or anywhere,' I say. 'My heart is in England.'

'Is it safe in your keeping, though?' he teases me gently, as a favoured uncle will joke with a pretty niece.

'Certainly I would never throw it away,' I reply.

'Well, he's a handsome young man and you're very well suited,' he says with a knowing smile.

I stifle a gasp. The quiet advisor, who apparently goes around the court ignoring the foolish young people, thinking of nothing but statecraft, has spotted what no-one else but Janey and Mary know.

'I may be old but I'm not quite blind,' he says gently. 'But as her heir, you must have the queen's permission to marry, remember.'

Too late for that! I think gleefully. 'I know,' I say obediently. 'Will you speak up for me, Sir William? Should I ask her now?'

'All in good time,' he says, as if he has forgotten the urgency of young desire. 'Now, at last, she understands that she has to marry for the good of the country, now at last she sees that it has to be a marriage and an alliance – not a private matter. When she is betrothed she will be more tolerant of marriage for you, and for the other ladies of her court.'

'It is hard for us all to wait until she is ready, when she is so slow,' I remark.

He gives me a discreet smile. 'It is hard for us all to serve a queen who is slow to do her duty,' he says. 'But she will do her duty and marry the right man, and you will do yours.'

'She can never marry Robert Dudley now.'

I can tell nothing of what he is thinking by the gentle smile on his face. 'Indeed no,' he says almost regretfully. 'And now, thanks be to God, he knows it as well as all the rest of us. And so she will marry a prince of Spain or France or even Sweden or Germany, and you, and I, and all of England will sleep better at nights.'

'Is the court going hunting?' I ask, thinking of the nights.

'Oh, yes, to Eltham Palace, tomorrow.'

'I think I may ask to be excused,' I say. 'I have toothache.'

He nods. For all that he sees so much, he has forgotten that a young woman does not give up a day out for a toothache. He is too old to see that I am aching not with my tooth but with lust.

'I shall tell Her Majesty,' he says kindly. 'Keep out of cold draughts.'

CANNON ROW, LONDON,
DECEMBER 1560

Janey and I stumble along the riverbank, holding each other up in the slippery mud. We thought the easiest way to Ned's house in Cannon Row from the palace would be along the foreshore, as the tide is out and we are unobserved. But the path is blocked with rubbish – broken beams and wrecks of boats and some disgusting garbage, and my shoes are muddy and Janey is holding her side and panting by the time we reach the walls of Ned's garden and the steps to his watergate. We are alone, the two of us. We have never before walked out in London without guards and ladies-in-waiting and maids and companions. I feel thrilled by the adventure and Janey is beside herself with excitement. We did not even bring my maid as a witness. We sent my sister Mary out hunting with the court, not knowing what I am doing. We thought it safer to come quite alone.

Ned is at the watergate, peering through the portcullis, and he cranks it up himself and helps me up the steps, which are green with weed. 'My love,' is all he says. 'My wife!'

Janey comes up after us. 'Where's the minister?' Ned says. 'I thought you were bringing him with you?'

'I told him to meet us here. Is he not here?'

'No! I've been waiting from dawn. I would have heard if he had come early.'

'I have to be back at the palace by dinner,' I warn them. 'I'll be missed if I am not there.'

'You go in,' Janey says to the two of us. 'I'll go and find a minister.'

'But where will you find someone?' I ask her. Ned's hand is at my back urging me into the little house.

'I'll go to a church – or to St Paul's Cross if I have to,' she says with a breathless little laugh. 'I'll be back as soon as I can.'

Ned has prepared his room for a wedding feast. There are dishes and dishes of food on the sideboard waiting to be served, there are flagons of red wine and goblets made of Venetian glass, there is small ale and even water. The servants have all been sent out for the day. His bed is made, and I see the embroidered sheets invitingly turned back. He sees me glance and says, 'I suppose we do have to wait for Janey?'

'What if they were to come in?'

He laughs. 'Then will you take a glass of wine, Countess?'

I beam at my new title, remembering when I asked my sister Jane to pray for a duke for me. She must have done so, and God must have listened to her, for now I have a man who was the son of a duke and whose title might be restored by Elizabeth's good-will, if she ever has any. Then I will be a royal duchess. 'Thank you, my lord husband.'

He pours me a glass and one for himself. We sit in the window seat and look out over the muddy riverbank and the tide coming in, the seagulls soaring and bobbing down. He settles me with my back to his chest, leaning against him, his arms around me. I am embraced and held and I have never known such safety and comfort.

'I have never been happier,' he says. 'It is as if every moment I spend with you is a gift.'

'I know,' I say. 'I have loved you ever since I was a little girl and I thought that Jane my sister was going to marry you.'

'God bless her! I will make it all up to you,' he promises. 'You will never be alone and afraid again.'

'I will be your wife,' I say. 'I cannot be alone and afraid if we are one.'

He reaches into his pocket. 'I had this ring made for you. I sketched it out for the goldsmith as soon as we were betrothed.'

I give a little gasp of pleasure as he shows me his clenched hand then opens his fingers to show me his gift. It is exquisitely made. A hidden spring opens the broad ring and shows five golden links that form an inner ring.

'And I wrote you a poem,' he tells me.

I am entranced. I turn the ring over and over in my hand, admiring the little catch and how the entwined rings spring out and then hide again.

> *'As circles five, by art compact, show but one ring in sight,*
> *So trust unites faithful minds, with knot of secret might,*
> *Whose force to break (but greedy death) no wight possesseth*
> > *power,*
> *As time and sequels well shall prove; my ring can say no*
> > *more.'*

'A knot of secret might,' I repeat.

'I promise you,' he says. 'No wight possesseth the power to break us.'

'No-one,' I say, putting my hand in his.

The door bursts open without announcement and Janey comes in, feverish and flushed, with a rosy-faced red-headed man with a beard, dressed like one of the Swiss reformers in a black furred gown.

'Here,' says Janey, gesturing to both of us with a flourish.

He gives a short laugh at our clasped hands and the prepared bed, and bows to us both. Ned has the prayer book at the ready and he puts my wedding ring – my beautiful wedding ring with its secret might – onto the open page. The preacher recites the order of service and we repeat it after him. I am dazed: this is nothing like my first wedding at Durham House to a stranger, with my sister Jane going before me, marrying Guildford Dudley under protest, and two days of opulent feasting. I hardly hear the gabbled words in the strange accent; I hardly hear my own assent. It is over in moments and Janey sweeps the minister from the room and I hear the clink of a coin as money changes hands.

She is back in a moment. 'I'll drink to your health,' she says. 'My brother and his wife. God bless you!'

'God bless us all,' Ned says. He looks down at me, his eyes warm, watching me turn his ring round and round on my finger. 'Is it a good fit?' he asks.

'It's a perfect fit,' I say.

'And what children you will have!' Janey predicts. 'And so close to the throne! Tudor on one side, Seymour on the other. Say that you have a boy, and he is King of England?'

'Say we do?' Ned says meaningfully. 'How shall we do that?'

'Oh! No need to hint me out of the door, I'm away!' Janey says, laughing. 'I'll read a book or play the virginals or write a poem or something, don't worry about me. But we have to leave before dinner, remember. They will notice if Katherine is not in her place this evening.'

She flicks from the room, closing the door behind her. We are alone, my new husband and I. Gently, he takes the glass of wine from my hand. 'Shall we?' he asks courteously.

As if we are engaged in some strange and beautiful dance, I turn away from him and gently he unties the laces down the back on my stomacher, so I can slip the bodice off, and stand before him in my smock. He unties the laces on his jacket and we are matching in our white embroidered linen. I turn my back to him again and he unties the ribbons at the waist of my skirt and drops it to the floor. I step out of it, and the under gown, and leave them there.

With a little smile at me, he unties the laces on his breeches and strips so that he is naked but for his shirt; he takes the hem and draws it over his head so that I can see all of him, the whole lean length of him. He hears my little sigh of desire and he laughs, and takes the hem of my smock and draws it over my head, and though I turn away and put my arms across my breasts, suddenly shy, he takes my hand and draws me to the bed. He gets in first, pulling me in beside him, and I slip between the cool sheets and shiver, and then he is on top of me and kissing me and I forget embarrassment and cold sheets and even the wedding and the minister. All I can think is 'Ned' and all I can feel is my joy at the sensation, for the first time in my life, of his naked warm body against mine from his whispering mouth in my hair to our entwined feet.

We make love, and then we doze, and then we wake and are filled once again with desire as if we will never again sleep. I am dizzy with pleasure when I hear, as if from a long way away, a tap on the door and Janey's voice calling me: 'Katherine! We have to go! It's late.'

Shocked, Ned looks at me. 'It feels like minutes,' he says. 'What's the time?'

I look to the window. I came here in the cold bright light of a frosty winter dawn and now I can see the yellow of the setting sun. 'Ned! Ned! It's nearly sunset!'

'Fools that we are,' he says indulgently. 'Come up, my countess. I shall have to be your maid.'

'Hurry,' I say.

I pull on my clothes and he laces me, laughing at the intricacy of the fastenings. My hair is falling down and I want to wear my wife's kerchief over it, but he says I cannot; I must keep it with his two rings close to my heart until we are allowed to tell everyone that we are wedded and bedded.

'I shall wear my rings on a chain around my neck,' I promise him. 'I will put them on when I am alone in bed at night and dream that I am with you.'

He pulls on his breeches. 'It will be soon,' he promises me. 'I know Robert Dudley takes my side. He will speak for us.'

'William Cecil does, too,' I say. 'He told me so. And Elizabeth will forgive us. How can she not? How can anyone say it is a bad thing to do? Our own mothers gave their permission.'

'Ned!' Janey calls from behind the door.

I hand him the key and he opens it. Janey is bright-eyed,

laughing. 'I fell asleep!' she cries out. 'No need to ask what you two were doing. You look as if you had died and gone to heaven.'

'I did,' Ned says quietly. He puts my cape around my shoulders and we go out through the garden gate and down the little garden to the watergate. The incoming tide laps at the steps that were dry when we came, and Ned shouts for a wherry boat, which turns and comes to us. Ned himself opens the doors for the watergate and then hands me into the boat.

'Till tomorrow,' he says passionately. 'I will see you tomorrow and I won't sleep tonight for thinking about you and today.'

'Tomorrow,' I say. 'And then every tomorrow for the rest of our lives.'

I slip into the palace, hopping through the little wicket gate that is set into the enormous double doors, waving an apologetic hand to the queen's enormously tall sergeant porter, Mr Thomas Keyes, for not waiting for his ceremonial opening. 'I'm late!' I call to him and I see his indulgent smile. Janey trails behind me, her hand to her chest as she catches her breath. I am desperate to change my dress and be in the queen's rooms when we process to dinner but then I notice that something is wrong, and I pause and look around me.

People are not hurrying to dress; nobody is making their way to the queen's presence chamber. Instead it seems as if everyone is chattering on every corner, at every window bay.

For one terrible moment I think they are speaking of me, that everyone knows. I exchange one aghast look with Janey and then Mary breaks away from a knot of ladies and comes towards me.

'Where have you been?' she demands.

'What's happening?' I ask.

'It's the little King of France,' she says. 'He's been ill, terribly ill, and now he is dead.'

'No!' I say. This is so far from my guilty dash to get into the palace in time for dinner, so discordant with my pleasure-drenched day. I look at Mary and I realise that I simply have not understood what she is saying.

'What?'

She shakes my wrist. 'Wake up! The King of France has died. So our cousin Mary Queen of France is now dowager queen. It's not her throne any more. She doesn't have the French army behind her. She doesn't have a little dauphin in the cradle and she's not the most powerful woman in Christendom. Everything is changed again. She is not Queen of France, she is only Queen of Scotland.'

I glance at Janey, who is leaning back against a stone pillar, catching her breath.

'Then I am Elizabeth's heir without a rival,' I say slowly. 'Elizabeth has nothing to fear from Mary now she's only Queen of Scotland, and Cecil's treaty excludes her from the throne of England.'

I see the gleam of ambition in Janey's eyes and I smile at her.

'You're Elizabeth's heir,' Mary agrees. 'There is no other.'

WHITEHALL PALACE, LONDON, DECEMBER 1560

I live in a dream. The palace seems to me a wonderland of beauty as they bring in the great boughs of fir trees and pines for the winter season and they light the candles earlier every day. They raise the kissing bough – the woven willow stems twisted with green ribbons and the effigy of a little Baby Jesus at the heart of it. They tie it over the door to the presence chamber and Ned and I manage to meet, as if it is a surprise, under the bough at least twice every day and he takes my hands and kisses me on the lips for the good fellowship of the season. Only he and I know that we are drunk with the scent of each other, that our lips are soft and tender, that each touch is a promise of a later meeting.

The windowsills are lined with greenery and bright with candles, and the dried oranges give off a sharp perfume, which mingles with the smell of pine sap so I think myself in a winter wood. We practise dances every day and the dancing master scolds me and says that I must be in love, for my feet are all astray, and everyone laughs, and I laugh, too, for joy. I so want to tell all of them that it is true. I am in love, and I am beloved. Better than that: I am married, I am a wife. I have illuminated the terrible darkness that Jane's death laid on our family, and I am free from grief and guilt at last. My name is no longer Grey. I am Katherine Seymour, the Countess of Hertford. I am the wife of one of the most handsome and wealthy young men in England and when we tell everyone of our secret marriage we will become the leaders of the court, the proclaimed heirs, and everyone will admire us.

Ned steals me away to Janey's rooms and we snatch at moments for hurried lovemaking. I don't care if we have no longer than a minute. I am in such a fever to be held by him that I don't care if he has me like a girl of Southwark, up against a wall, or if he has no time for anything more than a swift kiss in a darkened corner.

One day he takes me to a quiet window bay out of the way of the noisy court and says: 'I have something for you.'

'Here?' I ask flirtatiously and am rewarded by a warm smile.

'Here,' he says lovingly. 'Take this.' Into my hands he puts a parchment document.

'What is it?' I unfold it and read. It is a deed of gift. I scan it quickly and see that he has given me a fortune in land.

'It is your dower lands,' he says. 'We had no parents or guardians to draw up our marriage contract so I am giving you this now. See your name?'

He has named me as his dearly beloved wife. I hold the

document to my heart. 'I shall love it for that alone,' I say. 'The land doesn't matter.'

'Nothing matters,' he agrees. 'Not land nor fortune nor titles. Nothing but us.'

The court has more news from France. The young dowager queen, my cousin Queen Mary, has gone into deep mourning for her young husband but it does not save her from being excluded from the royal family of France. She is not to marry the second son, she is not even to stay in France. Elizabeth has no sympathy for her at all, even though our beautiful cousin has lost her mother, and now her young husband is dead. All Elizabeth cares about – all I hear as I stand behind her chair during her low-voiced mutterings with William Cecil – is that if Mary decides to come to Scotland, how will that affect the Scots? Will they rise up against their new queen, as they rose against her mother, or will they take her to their hearts in a rush of sentiment like the savages they are?

Either way, I have become essential to the safety of England. It has never been clearer that Elizabeth must name me as her heir to parliament, to prevent her cousin Mary from claiming the position. Elizabeth turns to me with a sweeter smile than usual. She does not want to give anyone any reason to think that Mary Queen of Scots might some day become Mary Queen of England. 'A very distant cousin,' she calls her, as if she can rewrite the family tree that shows us as all equal cousins of each other. 'And England would never crown a papist queen.'

Cecil looks as if he is not so sure. 'A very good time to determine on your husband,' he points out. 'For no doubt Queen Mary will marry again, and you would be sorry to lose a suitor to her.'

Elizabeth widens her eyes. 'Are you saying that Erik of Sweden would prefer Mary to me?' she challenges him. 'Do you really think so?'

It is the most dangerous question in the world. Elizabeth has all the fears of the second-choice child; she has to know that she is everyone's preference.

'I am saying that we would not want Mary Queen of Scots to marry a strong power and have him on our doorstep,' Cecil says cleverly. 'Not if he was an ally that we wanted for ourselves. We have to make sure that if she comes to Scotland, it is not as a princess of France or Spain or even Sweden. If she does come to Scotland it would suit us best if it were as a widow without friends.'

'Is that possible?'

Cecil shakes his head. 'It's not likely. But you should at least have first choice of the greatest men of Christendom. She should not snap someone up before you, because she was quicker than you to choose.'

'Perhaps she will not marry again,' Elizabeth observes.

'Not her! She knows well enough that she has to have an heir for the throne of Scotland,' Cecil says steadily. 'She was raised up knowing that she has to do it, whatever her personal preference. She is eighteen, she is said to be healthy and beautiful so she is likely to be fertile. Every queen knows that she must give her country an heir. It is the duty of a monarch, a God-given duty.'

'I have an heir,' Elizabeth says, smiling over her shoulder at me. 'A young and beautiful heir to a young and beautiful queen.'

I curtsey and smile back.

'No-one can deny the rightful position of Lady Katherine,' Cecil says with his infinite patience. 'But the country would like a boy.'

WHITEHALL PALACE, LONDON, SPRING 1561

As the weather gets warmer I can meet my husband out of doors, and every day we walk together in the little patchwork gardens that are dotted around the palace. The birds are so tame here that they sit in the budding branches above our heads and sing as if they were as happy as we are. I put a bell on Ribbon the cat to safeguard the nestlings that will come soon in orchard and hedge and tree.

Sometimes Ned slips up to my rooms and my servants vanish, leaving us alone. Sometimes Janey walks with me to the little house in Cannon Row and dozes in the sunny presence room while Ned and I spend the whole afternoon in his bed. I cannot think beyond our next meeting; I dream of him when I am asleep. All the day I find I am feeling the silky texture of my linen, the exquisite delicacy of my lace, the shine of my brocade gown, as if the whole world is more intense because of my passion for Ned.

'It is the same for me,' he tells me as we walk by the river and smell the salt behind the cool wind from the sea. 'I am writing more than I have ever done, and with a greater fluency and understanding. It is as if everything is more vivid. The world is brighter, the light more golden.'

'How glad I am that we are married and don't have to be like them,' I say, nodding ahead to where the queen and Robert Dudley are dawdling, her hand on his arm as he whispers in her ear. 'I could not bear knowing that we would never be together.'

'I doubt that they are often parted. The whole country is gossiping about her, and now she has told the Earl of Arran that she will not marry him, and everyone knows that Dudley is the reason. I would never see you shamed, as she is. In Europe they say that she is a whore to her master of horse.'

I shake my head with wifely dismay. 'But how terrible if she has to marry without love!' I say. 'I would never have married anyone if I had been parted from you.'

'Nor I,' he whispers. Unseen by anyone he squeezes my hand. 'Are you waiting on the queen this evening? May I come to your room before dinner?'

'Yes,' I whisper. 'I dressed her yesterday. I don't have to attend her today. I'll leave my door unlocked.'

The season of Lent comes and is only slightly observed by Elizabeth's court, which seems to have thrown out the season of fasting with all papist observances. Correctly, we eat no meat, but the kitchen makes a feast out of every sort of fish, and it turns out that fowls and even game are not considered to be meat by the Protestant princess. I don't know what my sister Jane would have thought of this. I think Jane would have believed that the dietary laws should be strictly obeyed, and for sure she would have known every single one of them, including prohibitions of foods that no-one has ever heard of. I so wish that I could ask her.

Even now, seven years after her death, I find that I want to ask her, or tell her something almost every day. Oddly, I miss her far more than I miss my mother. I can bear the death of my mother because it was expected, because we had time to say goodbye, because – to tell truth – she was not a loving or a kind woman. But Jane's death was so sudden and unjust, and she was gone from me before I could ask her so many things, and even before I had become the woman I am today. And though she was right-eous and fierce in her scholarship and her religion, she was a real sister to me, we were playmates and girls together. I think that I would have become a different sister to her than the spoiled little girl she knew. I think she would have come to like me if we could have grown up together. I lost a sister that day on Tower Green, but I lost our future, too.

I don't know what she would think about a husband and wife lying together in Lent, and then it makes me giggle thinking of asking her. Just asking her would be shocking! If only she knew where love had brought me; if only she might have known love herself. 'Learn you to die!' makes my heart ache for her and I want to tell her: 'No! No! I have learned to love; and it is like a miracle from another world whereas dying is so earthly.' Without her advice, and easily persuaded by the urgency of desire and my lust for life, I decide to lie with my husband through fast days and holy days alike, Sundays included. I don't care! I will lie with him through the forty days of Lent and assume that, along with purgatory and with confessors, that sin has gone too.

'But do you not have your course?' Janey asks me when I tell her of my theological wrestlings with the old teaching of the Church and my own new reformist preference.

'No,' I say vaguely. 'I don't think I have had it since December.'

'You haven't?' She is suddenly attentive.

'No, I don't think so.'

'But now it is nearly March!' she exclaims.

'I know, but you haven't had yours either,' I say. 'I know because we had it at the same time, just before Christmas, do you remember?'

She flaps her hands dismissively. 'I am ill! You know I am ill, and I often miss my course. But it hardly matters with me! Obviously, it means nothing to me. But you are eating well and you are perfectly well and newly married, and now you have missed a course. Katherine! Don't you see? You might be with child!'

I look at her, quite aghast. 'With child?'

'How wonderful!' she says. 'If it's a boy he will be the next King of England! Think of it!'

'With child?' I repeat, amazed.

'I have prayed for it, and now I will see it!' she says. 'Please God I live long enough!'

'Why would you not live long enough?' Everything she says only confuses me more. 'Surely any baby would be born this year? Or will it be next year? How does one tell?'

'Oh, who cares? You must tell Ned.'

'I must,' I say. 'Whatever will he say?'

'He will be delighted,' she says with certainty. 'What man would not be delighted that his wife has the heir to the throne in her belly?'

I feel as if everything is going far too fast for me. 'I had not thought to have a child so soon, at any rate, not until everyone knew that we were married.'

'What did you think would happen, bedding him every

moment that you can?' She looks at me as if I am a fool, and I feel very foolish.

'But how does one know it has happened?'

'You knew what was happening well enough!' Janey's ribald laugh breaks out.

I flush. 'I knew that we were lovers, of course, but not that it would give me a child at once. My mother only had us three and she lay with my father every night for years.'

'Praise God that you are fertile then, and not stony ground like all the other Tudors.'

I am glad of this, but I would rather think of a Tudor heir as something very distant in the future. 'We'll have to tell everyone that we are married,' I say, feeling anxious now. 'Everyone will have to know. We'll have to tell them at once. Before I get fat. When does that happen?'

'They'll forgive the secret if you have a boy,' she predicts. 'If you can give Elizabeth a Tudor boy, heir to the throne, then you will be forgiven everything. My God, Cecil will be his godfather! What a relief for everyone! A son and heir for Elizabeth. You will be the saviour of England.'

'I must tell Ned,' I say.

'Tonight,' she says. 'Come to my room after dinner, before dancing. I'll tell him to visit me then. I'll say that I'm ill and miss dinner.'

Janey has made up her own bed for us, and the fire is lit in the grate and a little supper is laid out on the table before the fire for two people. Once again, she is our good angel. Ned comes in quietly, closing the door behind him, and looks from his sister to me, his wife.

'What's happening?' he asks. 'What's going on?'

There is silence. 'Katherine has something to tell you,' Janey prompts me.

I try to smile, but I am trembling. 'I think I may be with child,' I say. 'Ned, I hope you are happy? I think I may be with child.'

I cannot mistake the panic in his face. 'Are you sure?'

'Not at all! I'm not sure,' I say, as frightened as he is. 'Janey thought it so. I might be wrong.'

'Of course she's sure,' Janey says. 'She missed her course in January.'

'But sometimes I do miss one,' I say. 'And I forget to count. So I might miss one or two.'

'So you're not sure?' he repeats.

'Are you not pleased?' I can feel that my mouth is trembling. I so want him to be delighted, as Janey was delighted. For I am afraid of what this is going to mean for us, and I don't know what we are going to do.

He crosses the room in one stride and he takes my hand and kneels at my feet as if I were going to dub him a knight. 'Of course I am pleased,' he says, his face hidden from me. 'I am delighted. There is nothing that I want more than our child, and how wonderful that he should come so soon.'

'The heir to the throne,' Janey reminds him. 'The only Tudor boy of this generation. I don't count Margaret Douglas's boys.'

'If it's a boy. And if I'm not mistaken altogether,' I remind them.

'Boy or girl, I shall love this baby for his beautiful mother,' Ned says. He kisses my hand and then he rises up and kisses me on the mouth. Jane moves tactfully towards the door but he gestures that she shall stay.

'Wait, Janey, we need to talk. And besides, we can't use your bed now.'

He smiles at me and I realise that if I am with child, we cannot lie together until after I am churched after childbed. This is months and months away.

'I am not sure,' I say again. I cannot bear the thought that we will not make love when I feel the same urgent desire as always, when I am not even sure that I am with child. Surely this too is an outworn superstition that we need not observe?

'Of course,' Janey says delightedly. 'And we have to plan what we do.'

'We'll have to tell the queen,' Ned says.

'We have to tell her before I start to get fat,' I say. 'But not before then. There's no need for us to tell her before then, is there?'

'Perhaps we should. Then we could space it out, so it's not such a shock for her. First, we could tell her that we are married, and later tell her that you are with child.'

I say nothing. I feel quite sick with fear at the thought of telling Elizabeth that we are married.

'She should be pleased,' Janey says. 'It leaves her free to stay unmarried for all her life, if there is a boy baby in the royal cradle.'

'She *should* be pleased,' I say cautiously. 'But what if she isn't?'

'Oh, what's the worst she can do?' Janey demands boldly. 'Send you from court for a while? You'd be going into confinement anyway, and if she sends you into exile you can go to Hanworth for the birth, and Ned and I can come, too.'

'If she is furious . . .'

'Why would she be furious?' Ned asks me. 'All we have done is marry without her permission. That's not illegal since Queen Mary repealed the law. There can be no doubt that she would have given permission if we had asked her. She had no grounds for refusal and she has no reason for displeasure. People will blame us for being in a hurry, but nobody can blame us for honourable love. Our parents agreed! There can be no objection.'

I find my courage. 'We'll tell her,' I agree. There is a little silence. 'When will we tell her?'

'We'll have to choose our moment,' Ned says. 'Let's not say anything till the end of Lent. Perhaps at the Easter feasting when the court is merry again. There will be some music and dancing – there'll be a masque – she loves a masque and dancing. We'll tell her when she's enjoying herself.'

'Yes, that's a good idea,' Janey says. She gives a little cough. 'At Eastertide.'

If I had not been so absorbed in watching to see what Ned

truly thought of my news, trying to look past his well-acted joy to whether he is afraid as I am afraid, I would have seen that Janey is paler than ever. She coughs in her sleeve and there is a little spatter of red blood.

'Janey!' I say in dismay.

'It's nothing,' she says. 'A blister on my lip.'

Next day she takes to her bed and now Ned and I meet in her room without pretence. Every day after chapel we come to see how she is, and now for the first time I see she is very ill, and that her flushes and high spirits have been those of a girl beside herself with fever.

The physicians say that she will get better with the good weather, but I don't see why they are so hopeful as the sun rises earlier every day, and the birds start to sing outside her window, but Janey gets no better. One morning I go to her room straight after chapel but the door is closed and Janey's lady-in-waiting is sitting outside, her eyes red from crying.

'Is she sleeping?' I ask. 'What's the matter?'

Mrs Thrift shakes her head, her eyes filled with tears. 'Oh, my lady!'

'Janey! Is she sleeping?'

She swallowed. 'No, my lady. She's gone. In the night. I have sent for the physicians and her brother and he will have to tell the queen.'

I don't understand. I won't understand. 'What d'you mean?'

'She's gone, my lady. She's died.'

I take hold of the cold stone frame of the door. 'But she can't have died. I saw her just after dinner last night, I left her when she was going to sleep. She was feverish, she is always feverish; but not dying.'

The woman shakes her head. 'Alas, poor lady.'

'She's only nineteen!' I say as if that means she cannot die. I should know better: my own sister died at the age of sixteen and our cousin the king at fifteen – sick like Janey.

Mrs Thrift and I look at each other blankly, as if neither of us can believe she is gone.

'What am I going to do without her?' I say, and my voice is as plaintive as a lost child. 'How am I ever going to face all this without her?'

She looks alarmed. 'Face what, my lady?'

I lean my forehead against the wooden carved door as if my need for her will bring Janey back to me. I have lost my sister, I have lost my father, I have lost my mother and now my best friend. 'Nothing,' I whisper. 'Nothing.'

Ned is heartbroken at the loss of his sister. She was his greatest counsellor and his most enthusiastic admirer. She was the first audience for his poems; she used to read them to him and suggest changes. She told him that I was in love with him before I told her myself. She was his friend and confidante, as she was mine.

'She found the minister!' he says.

'She made me brave,' I say.

'She showed us that love is dauntless,' he agrees. 'Dauntless.'

'I don't know what I will do without her,' I say, thinking of this court, which is so filled with enemies and half-friends and pretend-friends; with Elizabeth, the great pretender, at the head of it all, turning her two-faced face this way and that.

'William Cecil says he thinks I should go to France,' Ned remarks. 'To attend the new king's coronation. It's a great honour for me, but I don't want to go now.'

'Don't leave me!' I say instantly. 'My love, you can't leave me! I can't be here without either of you.'

'Janey said I should go,' he says. 'She said that Cecil's favour is as good as a pension. His friendship will help us, Katherine. He will tell the queen of our marriage.'

'Yes, I suppose so,' I agree uncertainly. 'But I can't think of this now. I can't think like a courtier, with Janey just gone!'

'I shall have to make arrangements for her funeral,' Ned says sadly. 'I've sent a message to my mother and I'll speak again to my brother. And I'll tell William Cecil that I will go if I can; I'll tell him I'm not sure now.'

'I'll come to the funeral,' I decide. 'Everyone knows that I loved her like a sister.'

'You were her sister,' Ned says. 'In every way. And you are her sister by marriage. She was so happy about that.'

It is an impressive funeral. Elizabeth puts the court into mourning for Janey, acknowledging in death the kinship through King Edward that she mostly ignored in life. Bitterly, I think that Elizabeth does not want cousins, she does not want heirs, she wants all her relations to be as dead as her mother. But she does love a big funeral. She buries her kinswoman with all the honour that she withholds in life.

Ned's mother attends the burial of her daughter, although she leaves her low-born second husband at home. I think for a wild moment that I can talk to her, that this is a woman who married for love, without permission, as I have done. But she is rigid in her grief. She does not melt into tears, she does not turn to me as a daughter-in-law that she might have had, she does not even speak to her sons. She takes her place in the procession and she goes through the motions of mourning as if she wishes it were not happening, and she leaves court as soon as she can.

Ned has no time for anything but the planning of the funeral, the chariot for the coffin, the rehearsing of the choir at Westminster Abbey. Nearly three hundred mourners follow the coffin, me among them, and I see Ned's pale strained face illuminated by grief in the darkness of the great abbey. He looks towards me as if he feels my loving gaze on him and he gives me a small sad smile. Then the great anthem that he chose rings out from the choir, and Janey is laid to rest in her family vault next to ours. Janey and my mother's tombs are side by side, which is a comfort, though it makes it worse that my sister Jane is buried far away, in pieces in the Tower chapel.

Ned accompanies his mother to Hanworth for a few weeks after the funeral and although I write to him, he replies only once. He says that he is praying for Janey's soul and helping his mother box up her clothes and her few little things. I write at once and say that I will look after her linnets that she kept at Hanworth. But he does not even reply to that.

WHITEHALL PALACE, LONDON, SPRING 1561

While I wait for him to come back to court nobody is surprised by my quiet sorrow. Everyone knows that Janey and I were dearest friends, nobody suspects that I am missing Ned, too. The only event is news that my cousin Margaret Douglas has sent her pretty son to France to take their family condolences on the death of the French king. As though anybody cares what the Lennox family does! But the gossip is that she has ordered her son Henry Stuart to propose marriage to the widowed queen. If Mary Queen of Scots wants another pretty mother's boy to take the place of the one that she has lost, then she will have one conveniently to hand. But I imagine that she will want a man for a husband, and not a cat's paw. Certainly all her cousins prefer men they can respect: Margaret Douglas worships her husband, Matthew Stuart Earl of Lennox, Elizabeth's taste for adventurers is a disgrace, and I would never consider a man that I could not truly respect.

A few days after the funeral I find some blood on my linen nightgown and I suppose it is my course, come at last, come late. There is not much, and there is nobody that I can ask. I wish Janey were here. She would count the days with me and confirm that my course came late and there never was a baby. I feel such a fool to be uncertain and yet I don't have a wise woman or some old matron to tell me what to do. I have no friends with nurseries full of children, and I dare not consult anyone who might know, like the old ladies who keep the gowns in the royal wardrobe, because they are terrible gossips in a court that lives for gossip.

It is the first thing that Ned asks me when he comes back to court. He hands me the cage of linnets and I exclaim over them and take them to my room and hang them on a hook near the window, where they can have some sunshine on their pretty freckled wings.

'Katherine, my love, leave them,' he begs me. 'I have to talk to you.'

'We'll go into the gardens,' I say.

I walk a little ahead of him and we go to our favourite knot garden where the little gravel paths wind round and round the low hedges. But the walled garden is full of gardeners, raking the gravel and cutting the hedges.

'Not here!' Ned says in irritation. 'Let's go to the orchard.'

The blossom is pink and white, as thick on the boughs as if they were bowed down with rosy snow. Bees hurry like anxious dairymaids from one opening bud to another. I can hear a cuckoo calling and I look for her grey back. I love cuckoos. I hear them so often and see them so rarely.

'Listen,' Ned says urgently. 'I have my passport from Elizabeth to travel to France.' He shows me her signature, the affected 'E' and all the scrolling lines. 'But I will not go if you are with child. If there is any chance that you are carrying our baby I will stay, and we will tell the queen together.'

My dread of facing Elizabeth without Janey's support is almost worse than my dread of Ned going away. 'I don't know,' I say, distracted by the cuckoo that is calling so close that it must be almost overhead, hidden in the branches. 'I don't think so. I can't

be sure. I think I had a course, just after Janey's . . .' I can't say the word 'funeral'.

Ned squeezes my hand. 'I won't go unless you allow it,' he says.

'I suppose you want to go,' I say irritably. 'Paris and Rheims and everywhere.'

'Of course I'd like to see these cities, and attend the new French king's coronation. I want to learn about the world,' he says fairly. 'And it would do us no harm for Cecil to find me reliable. Of course it is a great opportunity for me. But I won't go if you are with child. I won't leave you. I promised. I am yours, Katherine, I am yours till death.'

I shake my head. I am so afraid of confessing to Elizabeth, and certain that Janey was wrong and there is no baby. I feel that I have lost everything in this sorrowful spring: my best friend, Janey, and the chance of her brother's baby, and now he is going away too. 'It's gone. I don't think it was ever there,' I tell him.

'Can a woman not tell such a thing?'

'I don't know what I am supposed to feel!' I exclaim. 'All I feel is frightened and terribly sad about Janey, and I don't dare to face Elizabeth. But I don't feel anything else. I am no fatter or anything.'

He looks at me as if I should know such mysteries, as if every girl in the world knows it by nature, and I am very silly that I do not.

'How am I supposed to know?' I demand. 'If everyone knew we were married I could ask your mother or some midwives. It's not my fault.'

'Of course it's not your fault,' he says quickly. 'Nor mine. It would just be so much better if we knew for sure. If you knew for sure.'

The cuckoo calls directly over our heads and I look up and see a flash of beautifully barred breast feathers.

'Are you even listening to me at all?' he demands hotly.

'You might as well go, and come back as quick as you can,' I say sulkily. 'Nothing is going to change much within a month,

I suppose. And people will only wonder if you refuse such a chance.'

'If you send for me, I'll come back at once,' he promises. 'For whatever reason. The moment you send for me I will come to you. Wherever I am. I have a new servant and he will carry messages for me, between you and me without telling anyone. His name is Glynne, you will remember that? And trust him when he comes to you?'

'I'll remember, but you will promise to go to the French coronation, and come straight home?' I ask him. 'No running after the dowager queen like that puppy Henry Stuart, Margaret Douglas's son.'

'I will,' he promises. 'I won't be long, a few weeks only.'

'All right then,' I say unhappily. 'Go.'

He produces from behind his back a small scroll and a purse of gold. 'This is for you,' he says sweetly. 'My dear wife. For any expenses you have when I am away. And this is my will. I leave you a thousand pounds worth of land. A thousand!'

'Oh, don't say it!' At once I am in floods of tears again thinking of Janey dying in the night, alone, without even saying goodbye to me. 'Don't say it. I don't want to inherit anything from you. I just want to live with you, not die. Everyone that I love dies, and now you are going away!'

'Keep it safe anyway,' he says, pressing it into my hands, 'and I will be back within the month to reclaim it from you.'

GREENWICH PALACE,
SUMMER 1561

The court hardly notices when Ned bids farewell to the queen, everyone is so busy with amusement. This is Elizabeth's

favourite time of year and every day there are balls and hunts and picnics. We ride out of Greenwich Palace down to hunt the water meadows that run beside the river. We walk in the gardens in the evenings and watch the early swifts and swallows fly round and around the high turrets and swoop over the waters. They dip into their own reflections, making a little splash as they part from their mirrored selves.

Elizabeth is as much in love with Robert Dudley as ever, quite unable to resist his outstretched hand to dance or to walk beside him, quite unable to resist his bullying when he threatens to go and live in Spain if she does not consult him as if he were her husband. He has regained all the ground he lost on the death of his wife with the queen, though he never will with the court. The country will never accept him as her husband and the great game of Elizabeth's life is to promise him enough to keep him close to her, without revealing to anyone else what she swears to him. I think her deception is far more disloyal and far worse than mine. At least I don't lie to Ned, though I have to lie to everyone else.

William Cecil is kinder and more attentive to me than he has ever been, as if he fears that Robert Dudley will persuade the queen to marry him, and the country will turn to me as her successor. People would far rather have me as queen than any woman married to a Dudley.

'You look very pale,' William Cecil says to me gently. 'Are you missing your beloved friend so much?'

I have to swallow my little gasp as I think he is speaking of Ned, but he has Janey in mind. 'I miss her very much,' I manage to say.

'You must pray for her,' he says. 'There's no doubt in my mind that she will have gone straight to heaven. There is no such thing as purgatory and no souls can be prayed out of it – but it is still a comfort to pray for the happiness of our friends in heaven, and God hears every prayer.'

I don't tell him how fervently I pray that Ned will come home soon. I just lower my eyes to the ground and hope that he will let me go away from him to the queen's rooms. Nobody cares how I look there. Actually, Elizabeth prefers it when I am pale and quiet.

'And do you miss her brother, the Earl of Hertford, too?' Cecil asks archly.

It is such an odd tone for such a serious man that I risk a quick upward glance. He is smiling down at me, his dark eyes searching my face. I can feel that I am blushing, I know that he will see it, and he will make up his own mind.

'Of course,' I say. 'I miss them both.'

'Nothing that you should tell the queen ... or me?' William Cecil hints gently.

I flash a glance at him; I will not be teased about this. 'You told me I should wait for the right time to speak to her.'

'I did,' he says judicially. 'And now would not be the time.'

I press my lips together. 'Then I will speak to her when you tell me that I may,' I say.

I will find the courage to speak to the queen, and summon Ned home so that we can face her together, as soon as William Cecil says the time is right. Until then, I am dumb with fear of her. I dare not tell William Cecil how far we have gone without either his permission or the support of Robert Dudley. Of course, Ned was sure that both William Cecil and Robert Dudley have a pretty good guess what we are about, and anyone would wager that a handsome young man like Ned and a beautiful princess like me would fall in love if they are allowed to spend every day together. So perhaps I should speak out soon, with the hope that William Cecil will take my part.

But what if William Cecil is not inviting my confidences but, on the contrary, warning me off marriage to Ned with this teasing tone? I wish he had been clearer before we were wedded and bedded and Ned gone away.

Worse still, I find that I am a little queasy in the morning and

I cannot eat meat, especially meat with fat, until the evening. It turns my stomach and that is odd, as I have always been hungry at breakfast time, coming to it ravenous after chapel and fasting. My sister Jane used to say that I was gluttonous, and I would laugh and say ... but it doesn't matter now what I used to say, since I will never say it to her again, and now I can only face bread and milk and sometimes not even that. Jo the pug sits on my lap at breakfast and eats most of my portion. I believe that my breasts are warmer and a little tender, too. I don't know for sure, and still there is no-one that I can ask, but I think these are signs that I might be with child. And then what will I do?

Lady Clinton, my lady aunt Elizabeth Fitzgerald, a kinswoman of mine who loved my sister Jane, stops me in the gallery and remarks that I am less merry without my friends the Seymours. She waits as if I should say something in reply. Lady Northampton, who comes behind her, says openly to my face that if I am in love with Ned Seymour then I would do better to tell the queen and have her order him to make an honest woman out of me. They stand side by side, Elizabeth's friends, Elizabeth's confidantes, a pair of harpies, as if they know everything, as if my precious secret is anything like their horrible old flirtations in the reign before this one, in the years before that, long ago when they were young and pretty and tender-hearted.

My cheeks blaze with shame that they should speak of Ned and me as if we were an ordinary couple, a pair of fools holding hands at the back of the court. They cannot know, they cannot understand, that we are deeply in love and, in any case, married.

'If he promised you marriage and left you, we should tell the queen,' Lady Clinton whispers. 'Everyone saw that you were inseparable, and then he suddenly goes away. I will speak out for you.'

I am horrified that they should think that I should have been a loose woman. I am furious that they think that I should be such a fool as to be abandoned by a faithless lover. I am heir to the throne of England! I am sister to Jane Grey! Is it likely that I would lower myself to lie with a man not my husband and have to rely on my aunts to bring him home to me? But I cannot tell them that we are married and that he went away with my permission. And I cannot bring myself to confide in either of the two old harpies (who are at least thirty) that I am a married woman with child. I choke back my rage and I just smile prettily, and say that I am missing Janey very badly indeed. They take the tears of rage for grief and they both say that she was a lovely girl and it is a terrible loss, and so we none of us say anything more about Ned.

It seems that everyone is in full summer happiness but me. Everyone is courting but me. Elizabeth and Robert Dudley are open lovers: they go everywhere together, sometimes they even hold hands where everyone can see. She treats him like a husband and an equal, and everyone knows that if they want an allowance, a pension or forgiveness for some crime, then a word from Robert Dudley is as good as the word of the queen since the one follows the other as if she had no choice in the matter, and no tongue of her own for anything but for licking his amorous lips.

He is lordly with his favour. She has given him huge sums of money, and licences to tax profitable trades. She has stopped short of giving him a dukedom but she pats his cheek and swears his family will rise again. Nobody now remarks that his wife died in the most suspicious of circumstances less than a year ago and that everyone blamed him. Nobody remembers that his father was executed for treason and his father before him. I remember it – but then it was my sister that Robert Dudley's father forced onto the throne and so on to the scaffold. Everyone else at court chooses to behave as if Dudley comes from the greatest of families and has always been trusted and beloved.

It's not so in the country, of course. I get secret messages from people assuring me that if there is an uprising against Elizabeth and her adulterous lover then they will support me. I barely even read them. I give them at once to William Cecil who says quietly:

'Her Majesty is blessed in so loyal an heir. She loves you for this.'

I want to say smartly: 'Well, she gives little sign of her love.' Or I want to ask: 'Does she love me enough to allow me to be happy? Or does she only love me so much that she keeps me on this rack of uncertainty?'

For though everyone knows I am the heir she still does not name me as such in an act of parliament, and now that Mary Queen of Scots has announced that she is coming back to Scotland, many people are saying that Elizabeth should name her as the heir and so make peace with her and with Scotland and France.

'Your friend Ned is well received in Paris and he writes to me that Queen Mary of Scotland will not ratify the peace treaty and insists on returning to Scotland, upholding her claims against the English throne,' William Cecil tells me. 'He has been a great intelligencer in the court of France for me. He has been greeted like a prince. He and my son Thomas have met everyone who matters in France, and Ned has told me much that I didn't know about the secrets of the court.'

'And when are they coming home?' I try to make my voice as light and as casual as I can.

'Soon, I hope. I have never known two young men spend more money,' Cecil says, telling me nothing.

I have to know that he is coming soon. I write to him, and when I get no reply I worry that he has forgotten his promises to me, that he is in love with someone else. I order that the servant Glynne is to be admitted to my rooms the moment that he arrives, but he never comes. I write again to Ned to tell him that still I know nothing for sure, but my queasiness has got better and this makes me think that I imagined it, and it meant nothing. He does not reply to that letter either. I have not had another course and certainly, I am fatter. I tie my stomacher more and more loosely and I swear that the curve of my belly gets greater every day. But I cannot believe that there is a baby in there. It seems like months and months since Ned lay with me and ran his covetous hand down my sleek flanks. It is half a year; for sure it has been so long that I cannot believe that there is a baby, yet I cannot stop myself fearing that there is.

My lady-in-waiting, Mrs Leigh, remarks upon my bigger breasts and my thicker waist, and I ask her how a woman knows that she is with child, and how soon a baby comes after a wedding night. She is so appalled that she frightens me, shock makes her eyes bulge and she whispers: 'My lady! For shame! My lady!'

I swear her to secrecy. She has been my lady-in-waiting for years; she should know that I would never be dishonoured. I tell her that I am a married woman and I show her my ring and my wife's kerchief. I tell her that I have Ned's letter of proposal safely in my jewel box, and his will in which he names me as his wife. I explain that the baby will be the next heir to the throne and she tells me that a woman can count how long it takes. She says it is ten months from your last course, and I will be able to tell if it is a boy or a girl by how it lies in the belly, and whether I crave sweet things or salt. If I feel seasick in the first months the baby will not die at sea. If I put away my kittens from my rooms he will be an honourable man. I think half of this must be nonsense, but it is all the help I have to hand.

I have to count on her to help me. She can work out with me when the baby would be born, if there is a baby there at all, she can help to hide my sickness. She tells me that there will be no difficulty in that, but right now, her sister is ill at home and they need her there. I give her leave to go for a week to help with the haymaking, and then she simply vanishes.

Like that! She never comes back to me though she has been in my service for years, and this makes me realise that I am in very great trouble indeed. If Mrs Leigh leaves me without warning, runs away from the court and profitable service because of my secret, then it must be a dangerous burden. I would have paid her a fortune to stay with me and help me – I would have given her all of Ned's purse of gold – but she would rather be far away. She must think me either horribly shamed or truly endangered, and either way she wants nothing to do with me, and I am all on my own once again.

If only I had someone to help me decide what I should do! I write again to Ned under cover of the English ambassador at Paris, though I don't even know if he is still at Paris. I tell him that the linnets are well and that Jo the pug is comically faithful to me as if she knows I need a friend. She has started sleeping on my bed, and I cannot stir without her coming to sniff my face. I tell him that the queen and Robert Dudley are as man and wife in the first dizzy months of marriage. I tell him that Mrs Leigh has run away and I have no-one to advise me. I say that I don't know for sure what condition I am in, but that I would be so much happier if he were here. I don't want to sound pitiful as if I am pleading for him to come home, but I really feel that I am alone with my worry and without a husband; and now I need him so much.

I get no reply.

I know that there are dozens of reasons why he should not reply but of course I fear that he has forgotten me or fallen in love with one of the French papists. What if the beautiful Dowager Queen Mary has taken a fancy to him and will take him to Scotland as her king consort, and I will never see him in London again? I write again, and though I wait and wait, there is no answer.

'My boy and your friend Ned Hertford are going on to Italy,' William Cecil remarks to me, as if it is pleasant news. 'Unless we summon them home. What do you think, Lady Katherine? Shall we tell them to come back and leave their amusements?'

I want to say: command him to come! Instead I look at the bows on my shoes over the smooth line of my stomacher, and I feel my itchy belly squeezed tightly against the boning. 'Oh, tell them to enjoy themselves!' I say generously. 'We are all happy here, are we not?'

William Cecil is not happy here. I can tell by the deep groove between his eyebrows, by the way that he sounds as if he is lying when he joins the light-hearted chatter of the court. He fears the coming of Mary Queen of Scots to her kingdom. He fears that Elizabeth, a queen, is planning to hand her throne on to another queen as if there had been no Adam made in Eden, as if women can name their heirs, as if their heirs should be women. He hates the idea of a papist heir to England – it will overthrow his life's work of bringing England to peace as a Protestant kingdom – but Elizabeth is entranced by the thought of her beautiful cousin so near to her. Cecil suspects that Queen Mary of Scots – or any papist – is his enemy in religion, determined to reverse his life's work. But he knows he has reached the limit of his power. He cannot persuade the queen to think of her cousin Mary as an enemy. He cannot persuade her to marry a suitable suitor. He cannot force her to be with child. She will not give the country a son. And I am so afraid that I will. I am so afraid that I am about to give the country a royal son and heir, and nobody knows but me. And I am not sure.

For a moment, I almost think I can tell him the truth. He keeps me from the other ladies with a gentle hand on my arm. 'Shall we send for the Earl of Hertford?' he asks me gently. 'Do you need him home, Lady Katherine?'

I throw my head back and laugh as merrily as Elizabeth when she is pretending to be carefree. 'Heavens, no!' I assure him. 'I am in need of no man, least of all the earl!'

We are boating on the river in barges, Elizabeth on her throne in the royal barge, musicians alongside, people watching from the banks. Robert Dudley is at her side as always, all her ladies, me included, are placed about the deck looking beautiful and privileged. Nobody notices the absence of Janey, nobody misses her but me. My sister Mary is like a dainty little doll, set on a high seat. She gives me a wink; nothing ever seems to trouble Mary. I think I might tell her that I am so afraid that I am with child and abandoned by my husband, but then I remember that she is my little sister, and that our older sister always tried to shield us from unhappiness and went to the scaffold, never speaking of doubts or fears, having written me a letter of good advice, the best advice she could give, under the circumstances. I will not be a lesser sister than Jane. I will not burden Mary with my worries.

Ambassadors, earls, lords sit around the great barge, drinking the best of wine and gossiping. I see Robert Dudley lower his dark head to Elizabeth and whisper in her ear and I see her turn her head and smile. They are so powerfully, so vividly in love that I suddenly forget that she is my most difficult cousin and I feel for her as another young woman in love. I can see that she yearns for him, from the way her head turns, to the way that she clings to the carved arms of her chair to stop herself from reaching for him. I think – I know this. I understand this. I have felt this too. And I look away before she can see the dangerous knowledge in my face.

'Indeed, it is a disgraceful spectacle,' someone says quietly in my ear, and I turn to Lord Pembroke, my one-time father-in-law, who stands beside me, observing me as I watch Elizabeth.

'Oh, I don't know,' I say, falling back on my reputation for innocence and ignorance, as if they were one and the same thing.

'Well, God bless you for that,' says the man who hustled me out of his house without a blessing, without a farewell.

From her perch on the chair, Mary gives me a smile and a nod, as if to advise me to do what I can with this unpromising material.

'We have missed you, in the House of Herbert,' he says pompously. 'I know my son regrets that he was parted from his pretty little wife.'

I have nothing to say to this sudden barrage of lies. I widen my eyes and keep mumchance, in order to see where he is headed.

'And I know that you liked him,' he insinuates. 'Childhood sweethearts, very pretty. Perhaps you could look on him with your favour once again. You are a great lady now, with perhaps a great future, but you will remember your youthful affections.'

There is so much here to deny that I put my hand over my stomacher where my belly presses hard, and I feel a little flutter, like a gurgle. I bow my head.

'So, here is my son Henry, as much in love as ever,' his father concludes and steps to one side to reveal, just as a masquer shows his dancing partner, Henry Herbert, healthier by far than the white-faced boy at our wedding day, handsome, smiling, and apparently deeply in love with me.

'I didn't expect this,' I say to him, as his father beetles away to kneel before Elizabeth.

'Forgive me,' Henry says abruptly. 'You know that I never wanted to leave you. You remember how quickly things happened, and that it was impossible to know what was right, and I was sick and I had to obey my father.'

Briefly, I close my eyes. I remember the terror and the chaos, and knowing that Jane was lost and that nothing could save her. 'I remember,' I say tightly. I remember well enough that they dropped me as fast as if I had burnt their fingers. But I remember that none of us knew what to do, certainly not the tentative youth that was my husband.

'I never thought that they would part us,' he says earnestly. 'I thought that our promises were real. I thought that we were married and that we would be husband and wife. I had no idea that we could be parted.'

I remember desiring him as a girl desires the idea of a husband. I remember the wonderful glamour and beauty of the marriage, my elaborate gown and the two-day feast. I remember him, sick as a dog, but trying to walk with me behind Jane and Guildford Dudley to the altar. I remember Jane, drawn as tight as a lute string, not knowing what she should do, what was God's ineffable will, her terror of the crown, her courage when she faced it.

I smile, thinking of my indomitable sister. 'Yes, I remember it all.'

He sees the smile and takes it for himself. 'You are the queen's heir now . . .' he begins.

'She has not named me to parliament,' I caution him, one eye on the throne where Dudley has almost inserted himself beside her, so they are all but entwined like snakes, she almost sitting on his lap.

'You are the only Protestant heir,' he amends. 'And the most liked by all the country. She called you her heir before all the court.'

I incline my head.

'If we were to marry,' he says very quietly to me. 'If we were to marry again, as we did before, and to have a boy, then that boy would be King of England.'

I have a strange feeling as he says this, as if my stomach had turned over with a sudden grip of nausea or bubble of wind. I think – can this be the quickening of the child as he is named to his great place? Like Elizabeth in the Bible? Saints and sinners save me, I think! If that was my baby moving then I have to be married, at once! And it might as well be Herbert as anyone. In fact, better Herbert than anyone, since he has come to me, since his father wants us to be married again, and Elizabeth can hardly forbid it since we were married before. It was an excellent match then, it is still good now. He wants it, his father wants it, the queen cannot forbid it . . . and I have to marry someone. Christ knows when Ned is coming home. Only His mother the Virgin knows why he does not answer my letters. She, like me, looked for a man to be the father of her child. She, like me, knew that she couldn't be too choosy. I have to marry someone if I have a baby quickening inside me.

The lurch in my belly is so powerful that I cannot believe that he does not see it. I reach out to him, he does not know that I am gripping his hand for support. 'Indeed, we have happy memories,' I say at random. I am sweating: he will see beads of sweat on my white face.

He takes my hand. 'I have never thought that we were not married,' he says. 'I have always thought of you as my wife.'

'I too, I too,' I say randomly. I wonder with sudden terror if this is the baby actually about to be born, if it is coming right now, before everyone. I must get to the back of the barge and find somewhere that I can sit down and grit my teeth and try to hold on, praying that this voyage of pleasure is over soon, and I can get to my room. I can't let it come here. I can't just void myself before the court! On the barge! On the royal barge! In my best dress!

He dips his head and shows me something in the palm of his

hand. It is my old wedding ring, from our long-ago wedding day. 'Will you take this back, for our betrothal?' he whispers.

'Yes! Yes!' I say. I almost snatch it I am so desperate for him to go.

'And I will send you my portrait.'

'Yes, yes.'

'And you will send me yours?'

'Yes, of course. But please excuse me now . . .'

'We are betrothed again.'

'We are.'

I am such a fool. That great heave was not birth but was quickening – but who knew that it felt so terrible? There's nothing in the Bible to warn you that it feels as if you are about to die. But now it has happened to me, I know what it is. I am definitely with child, there is no denying it even to myself. Often now, I have this strange sensation of stomach-churning terror. The baby moves without my will, so sometimes I am lying in bed and my swollen belly gives a little jump and squirm and I can actually see the belly move as if I had a kitten hidden under my nightgown. But it is not a kitten – I would know what to do with a kitten, there would be no objection at all to a kitten – it is a baby and one that I am not allowed to conceive or grow or birth. But whether I am allowed or not, whether I want it or not, this child is coming, like a terrible unstoppable force, like a cloud of rain that rolls across open countryside, dark and forbidding and quite uncontrollable.

'Are you all right?' Mary asks me, with the frankness of a younger sister. 'For you look as bloated as the queen when she is ill, and you are so bad-tempered these days.'

I long to tell her that I am in love with Ned but that I have heard no word from him. That he was supposed to go away for weeks but he has been gone for months. I long to tell her that we married, but he has deserted me and now I am with child and I can't even complain of his treatment of me, since the marriage was a secret, and the baby an even more terrible secret, and I cannot bear to keep it secret any longer. And, in any case, sometime it must be born and then my secret is over and I am shamed as low as a strumpet whipped at the cart-tail.

'I feel ill,' I say miserably. 'I feel so very ill. Oh, Mary, I wish I could tell you how very ill I am.'

She hauls herself up to sit on the window seat beside me, her little feet sticking out. 'You've not got a fever?'

'No, no, not an illness,' I contradict myself. 'I just feel ill.'

'You are missing Ned?'

'Not at all.'

She frowns at me, her pretty face puckered as if she cannot understand me at all. 'I have a friend, a secret friend, and I will not tell you his name; but I would never deny him.' She offers me her secret in return for my own. 'He says that he loves me and I know that I love him. I won't say more. This is just to show you that I can keep a secret, that I am a fully grown woman though very small. You can tell me that you love Ned and I can add it to my secret-hoard. You can share your secret with me.'

I give a little moan of despair at the thought of my sister getting herself into the same terrible state that I am in. 'Don't speak of him,' I tell her. 'Whoever he is, your secret friend. And don't speak to him. Don't keep him secret. Forget him. Don't even dream of him. And if he wants to marry you, then tell him you can never marry without the queen's permission.'

'She's never going to let me marry.' Mary dismisses the suggestion with a sulky little shrug. 'She'd be too afraid of me giving her a little heir to the throne. She doesn't want a Tudor prince four foot tall.'

I am so horrified at the thought of this that I gasp at her. 'But would you not have a child of normal size?'

'Who knows?' She shrugs her rounded shoulders again, a miniature coquette. 'Who knows how these things happen? At any rate, I shall be sure to pick a tall lover to even things up.'

'Mary, you cannot have a lover! You cannot even joke about it.

Swear to me that you will meet nobody. That you will put aside your secret.'

'Is this about Ned? Did you make a secret marriage?'

I clap my hand over her mouth and I glare at her. 'Don't say another word,' I say. 'Really, Mary. Don't say another thing. I have no secret and you must never have any.'

She pushes my hand away. 'Hey-ho,' she says indifferently. 'I'm not the flea in your bedding. No point pinching me. But I don't gossip either. The secret that you don't have is safe with me.' She wriggles to the edge of the window seat and makes a little jump to the floor. 'But Henry Herbert is no match for you, mark my words. He's a weathercock, that one: he goes wherever the wind blows. He does what his father tells him, and his father thinks of nothing but their family. Right now they think you will be named as heir by parliament, rather than Queen Mary, and take the throne when Elizabeth dies. That's why they're all round you as if they loved you. Don't think that they do.'

'I don't think anyone does,' I say bleakly.

Mary catches my hand and puts it to her cheek. 'I do,' she says. 'And I have a big heart. Bigger than Henry Herbert's, anyway.'

'He's my only hope,' I say bleakly.

'Are you really going to marry him?' she asks me incredulously. 'Because, I warn you, he is showing a picture of you all round court, and saying that the two of you are betrothed. People ask me. I have denied it.'

My baby stirs as if to disagree. I give a little gasp. 'I don't dare refuse him.'

'Has he given you a ring?' Mary enquires.

'Yes. My old wedding ring from before. He kept it. And he has given me a bracelet and a purse of gold to prove his sincerity. His father has given me a brooch from his mother.'

'Ask the queen for permission to marry him while we're on progress,' Mary advises. 'She's at her best when the court is out of London, and she and Dudley will be side by side all day – all night, too. Or why not ask Dudley to speak for you? He's a lover himself this summer; he's on the side of love against the world. He can't argue caution, he's rushing her into marriage as fast as he can. If it's what you want. Though why you should want it, I can't understand.'

I blink. 'I'm not even packed,' I say irrelevantly. 'I can't find Mr Nozzle's travelling basket.'

'I'll help you,' says my surprising little sister. 'Stop crying. Ned'll come home soon and reclaim you or you'll marry Henry. Either way you get a home and a husband. Somebody will love you for yourself. I do, anyway. What more do you want?'

ON PROGRESS: THE ROAD TO WANSTEAD, SUMMER 1561

We ride out of London and stop the first night at the palace of Wanstead where Lord Richard Rich, who abandoned Jane so promptly, welcomes us as the proud owner. Robert Dudley puts him to one side, lifts the queen down from her horse and carries her over the threshold as if it is his home, and she is his bride. Elizabeth laughs in delight and Richard Rich manages a thin smile.

The servants have unpacked our clothes and jewellery, but everything at Wanstead is so fine that we will use their linen, and gold and silver plates. I see Elizabeth eyeing the rich parkland around the great house and I know that the court will be hunting tomorrow. I will have to make an excuse; riding only ten miles has given me a stitch so painful that I can hardly stand when I am lifted down from the horse. I certainly can't gallop behind hounds.

'Letter for you.' One of the Rich servants in livery bows and offers me a letter with my name on the front.

'A letter?'

For a moment, I don't even take it. I stare at it with rising hope, then slowly, wonderingly, I put out my hand. I feel as if someone is handing me the key to escape from a prison of worry.

At last Ned has written to me – at last. Perhaps he has written from the coast and he has returned to England already and is riding north to find me. I am so glad to see his letter that I quite forget my resentment that it comes so late. It does not matter. Nothing matters. If he will come to me now we can confess, I can break my betrothal to Henry Herbert and we can tell the queen, and all will be well. As little Mary says, so wise for her years: a home and a husband, what more do I want?

But then I see it is not Ned's handwriting, nor his seal. As soon as I have it in my hand my hopes plummet. I leave the busy stable yard where the grooms are taking the horses from the court and turning them out into rich meadows, step into the garden where the trees make a cool shade over a stone bench and I can sit and rest my aching back and read my letter.

It is from Henry Herbert. It is quite dreadful.

Having hitherto led a virtuous life I will not now begin with loss of honour to lead the rest of my life with a whore that almost every man talks of . . .

I nearly drop the page. I think I am going to faint; I am breathless with horror. I read it again. He calls me a whore; he says that every man talks of me. I can feel my heart pounding and the baby in my belly has gone still, as if he too is frozen with horror at the insult to his mother.

'Ned,' I whisper miserably. I cannot believe that he should stay away and let this terrible thing happen to me. I cannot believe that our love affair should end up in this disaster: a baby in my belly and Henry Herbert – Henry Herbert of all people! – accusing me of being a whore.

*You sought to entrap me with some poisoned bait under the
colour of sugared friendship yet (I thank God) I am so clear
that I am not to be further touched than with a few tokens that
were by cunning slight got out of my hands both to cover your
abomination and his likewise.*

He knows I am with child. He does not name Ned but there
will be others quick enough to ruin Ned's good name with
mine. I have to return Herbert's gifts and beg him to keep silent.
Clearly, he is furious with me for trying to entrap him, and I
cannot in all honesty say that he is wrong and I am innocent. I
can't blame him for his outrage. I would have married him and
used his name to hide my terrible shame. And, of course, in my
heart I always knew that it would not have worked. I might have
given birth before I got to the altar. I would have had to tell him
the very moment that we were married and then he would have
been as furious with me as he is now.

But then I would have been his wife and my baby would have
had his name, and I would have won myself a refuge, even if it
were temporary. But anyway, what else could I do? I thought
that if I could just be a wife when I gave birth then that would
be enough for me. My baby would have a name, I would have a
husband. Now I will be openly shamed on the birth of my baby
and named as a whore by a young man that I tried to marry and
cuckold in the very same moment.

I drop my head into my hands and I cry into the page of his
cruel letter. I really don't know what I am going to do. I really
have no idea what I should do now, and at this very moment, the
baby gives a turn and sits heavily inside me, pressing on my belly
so that I have to hurry to the garderobe at once to piss again. I
think: my God, this is misery. I think: this is the worst misery
that I could imagine, and it is happening to me. I was so very
happy as Ned's wife and Janey's friend, as the queen's heir and
the saint's sister, and now I am thrown down so very low. Very
low. So low that I can't quite see how I will ever rise again.

It is not difficult to persuade the ladies of Elizabeth's chamber that I am not well. The strain in my face robs me of my girlish prettiness, and I cannot sleep at night, for the baby kicks and presses against me as soon as I lie down. I have dark shadows under my eyes and my beautiful creamy skin is spoiled with a rash of spots. Anyone would think me sick with a flux. I am swollen as if I had a dropsy and I am constantly aching in my back and in my groin. And every day, in attendance on the queen, I have to stand and stand while she sits and walks and dances. I have to curtsey with a straight back, I have to smile. I think that this is like a long torture, as bad as any instrument in the Tower, and that it would be better for me to confess and face my sentence than go on every day with these lies in my mouth and this constant pain. If they were racking me it could hardly be worse.

The progress moves onward, from beautiful house to welcoming host, Elizabeth as merry as a pig in clover with Robert Dudley at her side all day, dancing with her all evening and sleeping in an adjoining room at night. They are like young lovers, flirting and laughing, gambling and riding together. They are as happy together as Ned and I were – before she sent him away and condemned me to loneliness and shame.

I write to one of the maids left behind at Westminster and ask her to go to my chest in the treasure room, take out my jewel box and send me everything that Henry Herbert gave me. I must get his stupid portrait back to him, and the locket with a lock of his hair. I have spent his money so I cannot refund him.

PIRGO PALACE, ESSEX, SUMMER 1561

I hear nothing from my maid, and I am afraid that she has not had my letter, or she cannot find my things, or there is some muddle. Before I write again to tell her to hurry up and do as she is bid, the court arrives at my uncle John Grey's new house at Pirgo. He is touchingly proud of his house, a royal mansion, given to him by the queen. He believes that such a mark of favour to him must surely spill over to me. He gives me prominent roles in the entertainments for the queen; he wants me to lead the dances. He cannot understand why I shrink from her attention.

'And you're losing your looks,' he complains. 'What's the matter with you, girl? You've got fat. You can't overeat until you are named as royal heir and declared by parliament. The queen has no patience for gluttons. We all want a pretty heir who looks like a fertile girl. But you look exhausted.'

'I know. I'm sorry,' I say shortly.

For a moment I wonder if I can tell him that I am deep in a sin far worse than gluttony, but I look at his hard-chiselled face and I dare not tell him that yet another Grey niece has put herself on the wrong side of the throne.

'What's that you've got under your cape?' he demands suddenly.

'My cat, called Ribbon,' I say.

He does not smile at the pretty white cat. 'Ridiculous,' he says. 'Don't let my hounds see it, they'll tear it apart.'

'Letter for Lady Katherine,' his groom of the servery says, and hands me a letter with the Pembroke crest. 'Messenger waiting for a reply.'

'Oh, really?' my uncle cheers up in a moment. 'Henry Herbert writing to you, is he? His father spoke to me a little while ago. Said that they might think of renewing your betrothal. Open it up, girl.'

'I would rather read it later,' I say. My mouth is very dry.

He laughs. 'Oh, don't mind me,' he says, and turns to the groom and speaks of the arrangements for the queen's dinner while I break the seal and spread out the one page.

Without delay I require you, madam, to send me, by this bearer, those letters and tokens with my picture that I sent you or else, to be plain with you, I will make you as well known to all the world as your whoredom is now, I thank God, known to me and spied by many scores more.

I think I may be sick. I read the words and reread them. He knows I am on progress – does he imagine I carry his portrait with me everywhere? Poor fool: I suppose he does. How vain he is, I think wildly. How stupid. How glad I am that we're not going to marry, and then I think: oh God, if we're not going to marry, if he's going to name me as a whore, what am I going to do?

'All well?' my uncle enquires. 'You don't look too happy? A lover's tiff?'

'It's all well,' I say, stammering on the lie.

If Henry does not get his letters back and he announces that I am Ned's lover then I will fall from royal favour and my uncle and all my kinsmen will fall with me. Mary will have to leave court, and where will she go? We will not be paid as the queen's ladies: we will not receive bribes from petitioners, nor her favours. My ruin will be the ruin of my entire family. And where will this baby be born, and who will pay for its keep?

'It's all well.' I bare my teeth in a joyless smile. 'All quite well.'

'Good, good,' he says cheerily. 'We'll ask the queen for permission for you and Henry Herbert to marry, perhaps while she is staying here. If tonight goes well, and she is in a good mood, eh? You should see the size of my marchpane castle! If only they can carry it in from the subtlety kitchen without dropping it! I tell you, my heart will be in my mouth! It's time you were wed, young Katherine.'

'Not yet.' I swallow down bile. 'Don't speak to the queen yet, I pray you. My lord Henry is displeased with me about a little thing. I have to send him a token. If I could send my maid to Westminster she could find it for me.'

He laughs. 'Oh, young love! Young love! You make such difficulties for yourselves! You send him a pressed rose from my hedgerow and that will be more than enough for him, you'll see. And I will speak to the queen for you when she is in a good humour as soon as you give me the nod.'

'I'll nod,' I say foolishly. 'Don't speak till then. I will nod.'

He pats my shoulder. 'Go and change into your prettiest gown,' he says. 'We are going to give Her Majesty a dinner and an entertainment that she will remember for all her reign.'

'I'll go,' I say obediently. 'Thank you, Uncle. I thank you very much.'

'And put all your pets in the stables,' he says. 'I won't have them dirtying my new house.'

I keep Ribbon in his travelling box because he is terribly inconstant and will wander off; but I smuggle Jo the dog and Mr Nozzle the monkey into my rooms and give them the run of my chamber. God bless them, they are the only creatures in the world who care for me. I am not going to leave them in the stables, whatever my uncle says.

I get through the evening like a tired old actor, playing my part as my uncle's beloved niece, the queen's second-favourite cousin – after Mary Queen of Scots – her named heir, with the mindless accuracy of a sleepwalker. I cannot think what I can do. I cannot think who will help me. I cannot stop Henry Herbert naming my shame to his father, and then to the rest of the court. Even if I could find his damned keepsakes and send them to him in time, I doubt that would silence him, his pride is so wounded, his vanity so stung. So I have to think – if he speaks out and shames me, then the queen will know at once, and so will William Cecil and Robert Dudley and Lady Clinton and my uncle, and Catherine Brandon my step-grandmother and my aunt Bess St Loe; and everyone who has promised me their goodwill in the past will hate me for being a lewd girl and a liar.

I think: I have to tell someone who might be my friend and stand between me and the queen. I have to choose someone, from all these time-serving, two-faced, self-interested courtiers. I have to find one person that I can burden with my terrible secret, and hope that he will stand by me.

I could tell William Cecil – he is the best advisor to manage the queen, and he supports me as a Protestant princess and heir. He is opposed to any papist so he will always prefer me to Mary Queen of Scots or Margaret Douglas. I am the only Protestant princess. He is promised to my cause. But I cannot tell him. I simply cannot. I could not look into those brown eyes, as trusting and sad as a spaniel, and tell him that I have been lying to him for months, that I married in secret and lay with my husband and now I have lost him and he has gone off – who knows where, with Cecil's own son – leaving me to face the anger of the queen alone. It's too much. I can't say it. I cannot make myself speak the words. I am too shamed to confess to a man like William Cecil.

'Are you all right?' My sister Mary is at my elbow, looking up into my face. 'You look green.'

'Queasy,' I say. 'Don't look at me. I don't want anyone to look at me.'

'What is the matter with you these days?' she demands. 'You're as nervous as a foundling.'

I blink the sudden tears from my eyes.

'And you're always crying!' she complains. 'Has Ned left you?'

'Yes,' I say, and the word falls from my mouth like a stone as I realise the truth. 'He said that he would write; and he hasn't written. He said that he would go for weeks; and he has been gone months. He doesn't reply to my letters; and I don't even know where he is. So, really, I have to say that he has left me. He left me ages ago. And I don't know what to do without him.'

'Henry Herbert?' she suggests.

'He's furious with me for being in love with Ned. He knows all about that.'

She purses her pretty mouth. 'Can't you be happy without either of them?'

'We were promised to marry,' I say. Even now, I can't even tell the truth to my sister. 'I feel compromised.'

Mary laughs up at me. 'For God's sake! Our own sister died on the block for God's Word. That's what being compromised means. She died because she had given her word to God and would not retract it. Are you going to let your life be ruined for one little promise? A love promise? To a man? Just forget your promise! Break it!'

'This is nothing like Jane,' I say.

'Of course! We should try very hard to be nothing like Jane. We should live for joy and seek pleasure. The one thing that Jane's death should teach us is that life is precious and every day is a gift that we should treasure. Turn your coat! Turn your collar! Retract your promise!'

'That's not what she wanted to teach us,' I say, thinking of 'Learn you to die'.

'I don't think she was a very good teacher or a very good example,' Mary says boldly.

I am as shocked as if Jo the pug suddenly stood on her hind legs. I had no idea that my little sister had thought of this at all. I had always thought that she was too young to understand what happened to Jane and – to my shame – I had thought that her little stature meant that she did not hear all the discussions and debate that rage so far above her pretty hood.

Her dark eyes spark with irritation and then she smiles. 'I shall find my own philosophy and live my own life,' she tells me. 'And I shall fear nothing.'

She walks past me and someone asks her to dance. I see her

lining up with the other girls who are twice her height but not nearly as pretty, and none of them as wise. I think of her, not four foot tall but fearing nothing, and I think – I can't tell the queen, I can't bear to ruin Mary.

I think I will tell our Aunt Bess – Lady St Loe. She's not the most tender-hearted woman in the world, but she loved my mother and she promised me her friendship. She said at my mother's funeral that I could turn to her. She's a woman of vast experience, married to three men, and I have lost count of the number of her children. She will know the signs of pregnancy and when a baby is due. She must understand how love can drive you forward beyond where you should, perhaps, have gone. And she is friend and confidante to Elizabeth. If she takes my news well then surely she can confess for me and make it all right?

I have taken my decision, but I can't find the right moment, or even the right words. I don't dare speak out while we are under my uncle's roof: I cannot bear to risk the shame to him. If Elizabeth is angry she will be furious with everyone and I can't expose him to the whiplash of vitriol that she can unleash when she thinks she has been unfairly treated. So I wait, as the progress winds its slow way east, day after day, through humid days and summer storms – one night a thunderstorm so powerful that the chimneys rock on the roofs and everyone thinks that the world is ending – until we get to Ipswich, and then I have a pain, a new pain, which shoots from my crotch to my ribs, and I think, oh God, now I am splitting apart, and I have to tell Aunt Bess and get a physician or I will die of this secret as the baby bursts out of me.

MR MORE'S HOUSE, HIGH STREET, IPSWICH, SUMMER 1561

I wait till the night-time, though the court is so joyous and care-free in this summer season that Elizabeth does not go to her bed till nearly midnight. But when it is finally quiet and the servants are sleeping on the trestle tables in the great hall of the towns-man's house, or wrapped in their cloaks at his great fireside, I leave Jo snoring on my pillow, Mr Nozzle beside her, and the cat in his basket, and I creep to the St Loe rooms, tap on the door and when I hear Aunt Bess say: 'Who is it?' I tiptoe in.

She is sitting up in bed in a nightgown, reading her Bible by candlelight, a nightcap tied under her chin. Thank God, she sleeps alone. If she had a companion I could not have said a word. Her husband has gone ahead of the court. He is the captain of the queen's guard and chief butler, and he has to make sure that the next night's dwelling exceeds Elizabeth's demanding standards. So Bess, a wife of only two years, is parted from her husband so that Elizabeth can be with her lover in the greatest luxury that Sir William St Loe can organise. So do we all run around her, this difficult queen, as if she had not been raised in a little house, glad of hand-me-down clothes, with no name or title or friends.

'Who is it?' Bess asks, and then when she sees me she smiles: 'Oh, Katherine, my dear. What is it? Are you unwell?'

I close the door behind me and I go to the bedside.

'Aunt Bess . . .' I begin, and then I think, I cannot say anything. I cannot tell her anything. I cannot bring myself to say a word.

'What is it, Katherine? What is it, dear?' she asks. She looks concerned. I think, if I had a mother who looked at me like that I would be able to tell her anything.

'I ... I ...'

Her gaze narrows. 'What?' she demands. 'Are you in trouble?'

In answer, I part the heavy folds of my night robe. Underneath it, my white linen nightgown clings to my plumper breasts, my swollen waist. She can see the unmistakable curve of my swollen belly, the little pronounced dimple of the button of my belly, which has popped out despite my strapping myself down.

She claps both her hands over her mouth, and above her fingers her brown eyes widen in a silent scream.

'Good God, what have you done?' she whispers.

'I am married,' I say desperately.

'What? To Henry Herbert?'

'No, no, I only promised him when I was desperate, but he knows about this.'

'Good God!'

'I am married to Ned Seymour.'

'Are you?'

'Yes. But he has gone away and does not write to me.'

'He denies the marriage?'

'I don't know. I hope not.'

'Does he know of this?'

'I don't know. We weren't sure. Janey knew.'

'What good is that to anyone?' Lady Bess demands furiously. 'She's dead and he's missing. Does anyone else know? William Cecil?'

'No, no, I couldn't tell him. I couldn't tell Lady Clinton either, and I—'

'Why the hell tell me?' she hisses, her hands still at her face. 'Why the hell would you come and tell me?'

'I thought you would help me?'

'Never!' she says flatly.

'But, Lady St Loe – my mother – your old friendship? You promised me ...'

'I loved your mother and she was good to me when I married my second husband at your house, and then again when I married my third. Note that, child: married. Publicly married.

She would kill you rather than see you in this state and no husband to be found. She would not ask me to help you, she would bundle you out of court to somewhere in the country and pray to God that the baby is stillborn and that you can hide your shame.'

'Lady Bess . . .'

'I don't have credit,' she says as flatly as a Genoese banker refusing a loan. 'I don't have credit to carry you through this. Nobody does. Nobody has enough. You'll have to go away.'

'I don't want money . . .'

'You do,' she says. 'Desperately. And a home, and a husband and a sponsor to explain it to the queen. I have none of these for you, and if I did, I am not sure that I would extend all the credit I have in the world, for a stupid, stupid girl like you.'

I start to cry, weakly. 'But I have nowhere to go . . .' I did not dream that she would be angry with me. 'Where can I go? Aunt Bess, please! Don't you have somewhere that I can go? Can't I go to your house?'

Again she slaps her hand over her mouth to stifle the scream. 'A Tudor heir born in my house? A child half Tudor and half Seymour? Don't you know that she will see that as a plot? No! No! Don't you hear what I am saying? Elizabeth would throw me out of the court if she even knew we had been speaking, if she even knew that I know of this. Go. Go now, and don't tell anyone that you have spoken to me, for I will simply deny it.'

'But what am I to do?' I demand of her.

The shadows leap and fall on her frightened face as she reaches for her bedside candle. 'Go and hide somewhere, have the child, give it away – throw it away if you have to – and come back to court pretending that it never happened,' she counsels. 'And never tell anyone that you spoke to me. And be sure that I will never confess it.'

'Dear Aunt Bess, I beg you! Please don't blow out the candle!'

There is a puff and the room is in darkness.

Incredulously I stand in the dark, and then I stumble towards the door.

I go to my bed but I don't sleep. The baby has shifted again, I think it has dropped lower, for the swell of my belly is not so high. I think for a moment that perhaps it has died and is shrinking and that this might be the best thing for me. But then it squirms and kicks against me so strongly that I cannot pretend for even a moment that it is dead.

Besides, I have a sudden rush of love for the poor little thing. I don't want it dead. I can't wish it dead. When Lady St Loe said I should hope for a stillbirth, I thought her a monster. I thought she was beyond cruel. I will not give this poor little being away. I would not dream of putting a pillow over its little face and throwing it into a ditch. I will remember the puff of the candle and the darkness till I die. How could she? But there is no point in crying about Lady Bess when I have to think what I can do and where I can go.

I wipe my eyes and sit up in my bed. I have to do something at once: the pain is like a vice gripping my belly; something must be happening. Although Aunt Bess was clear that she would do nothing for me, she has given me an idea – I should get away from court and give birth to this child in secret, perhaps leave him with a kindly family and return to court. When Ned comes home, if he ever comes home, and if he still loves me, if all this has been a terrible mistake, then we can ask for permission to marry, announce that we are husband and wife, and produce the baby, the new heir to the throne.

Robert Dudley at least would be glad of that. It would give Elizabeth a male heir that she can nominate for the throne; it would leave her free to marry him. William Cecil would be happy to have a Protestant heir in the cradle. But I have to find somewhere to go into confinement where my secret will be safe.

I long to go to my old home of Bradgate, but everyone knows me there, and the news would get back to court as fast as a spy could ride. I wish I could go to Hanworth and be at Ned's home;

but his mother would not support our marriage when we asked her, I doubt she would welcome me on my own, and Janey would not be there, where she promised to be. I dare not go uninvited and I dare not tell Ned's mother why I need a home. I cannot tell my uncle, I cannot bring myself to tell him the truth, and I will not bring my disgrace to his new front door. I need someone who has vast lands, and many houses, who can give me a hideaway until my baby comes. Someone who can pay for a wet nurse, and bribe people to keep my secret. Someone who has the courage to hide me from the queen, someone who would take the risk of her displeasure to give her a Protestant heir.

I think it can only be William Cecil or Robert Dudley; no-one else has what Lady Bess calls 'credit', as if we were all misers, hoarding our reputations. I cannot bring myself to speak of courtship and secret promises to William Cecil. He is so old and so very respectable, he talks to me like a fond uncle. I would sooner confess to my real uncle Grey than tell William Cecil. Besides, he has asked me already and I have lied to him, barefaced, throughout this long pregnancy, and he will not forget that. But Robert Dudley has always been kind to me. He befriended Ned, he acknowledges my importance as the heir to the throne. He has recovered his reputation after murdering his wife; his credit at the court is the best in the land. He owns dozens of houses that the queen has given him – surely he can tuck me away in one of them? I decide that I will tell him in the morning, and I lie down again and try to sleep.

I turn around, and then around again. It's pointless lying in my bed. I heave myself like a beached whale to one side and then to another but I cannot get comfortable with the baby pressing down on my heart so I can barely breathe, and leaning on my belly so I have to get up again to piss in the night pot. My mind is racing and there is a thudding in my ears as if I am in danger. I will never sleep until I have confessed to Robert Dudley and he has promised me a sanctuary. He sleeps late, I am sure. I think that I will go to him at once, and tell him at once, and throw my fortune into his hands and my fate to his mercy.

My determination takes me to his door, and I tap on it quietly. It opens quickly, as if someone was alert on the other side, and Robert's manservant, Tamworth, looks out into the gallery.

'Lady Katherine!' he exclaims softly, and he steps out and takes my hand and draws me inside. 'Don't wait there, someone might see you.'

I close the door behind me, and I see someone stir in the big four-poster bed. 'Oh, welcome!' Dudley says, a chuckle in his voice, and he throws off the covers and stands beside the bed, stark naked as if he is expecting a lover. When he sees it is me, he starts back at my astounded face, pulling some of his bedding to tie around his waist. His naked shoulders are broad and his chest is muscled and strong. I cannot help but wonder who he was expecting, naked in his bed, so darkly handsome, dozing till she could come to him. I cannot help observing that he is well made, and I think any woman would be glad to have Tamworth show her to this bed, as he is obviously used to doing.

'You can go, Tamworth,' Dudley says shortly. 'Wait outside, keep the door.'

Tamworth throws his cloak around his night robe and goes out of the door. I hear the chair creak as he sits down in the gallery to guard our privacy and I note that he knows exactly what to do.

Robert glances to the other door to his bedroom. 'Keep your voice down,' he says.

'Is that the queen's room?' I can hardly believe that even on progress they are given adjoining bedrooms, and so all the gossip must be true.

'Never mind. Keep your voice down.' He goes quietly to the adjoining door and slides an oiled bolt to lock it shut. 'What do you want, Lady Katherine? You should not be here.'

'I am in trouble, I am in terrible trouble,' I tell him.

He nods. 'What?'

I hardly know where to begin. 'Ned Seymour and I were secretly betrothed,' I start.

His dark eyes are on my face. 'Foolish,' he says shortly.

'Then we married in secret.'

His gaze narrows. 'Madness.'

'Then he went to France and now Italy with Thomas Cecil.'

Now he says nothing, he just watches me.

'And I am with child.'

His jaw drops. 'Good God.'

'I know.' My voice trembles, but for once I don't weep. I think I have got to a place that is beyond tears. I am as low as I can be brought, telling a shameful secret to the queen's lover, in his bedroom after midnight. And this is the only way that I can think to survive this terrible series of events.

'Does William Cecil know?'

I think – this is how it is. I have become a counter to be played by great men.

'No, I came to you. Only you.'

'Well, you shouldn't have come to me,' he says bluntly. 'Not for a matter like this.'

'Who then?' I demand. 'For I have no friends, and I am an orphan.' I meet his critical dark gaze. 'I have no older sister to advise me,' I remind him, the man whose plotting led to her death. 'I have no father.' Thanks to you too, I think.

He takes a turn around the room, pulls a linen shirt over his head and a pair of riding breeches over his nakedness. 'You should have gone to the queen long before now.'

'Yes, but I can't go now,' I protest. 'I thought that you might let me live in one of your smaller houses, somewhere far away, and have my child.'

'Never,' he says. 'The scandal that would break about your head would be beyond your imagining. Everyone would think that it was my child, or that you were the queen giving birth in secret to my bastard. You would bring down the throne. Do you think—' He breaks off with a curse. 'No. You don't think, do you?'

He is right. I had not thought of that. I am incapable of thinking.

'You could not have chosen a worse moment,' he says almost to himself. 'The Queen of Scots returning to Edinburgh, the peace treaty not even signed by her . . .'

'It's coming,' I say flatly. 'Whether the Queen of Scots takes her throne or not. The baby is coming. I have to go somewhere.'

He runs his hand through his dark curly hair. 'When?'

I look at him. 'When what, Sir Robert?'

'When is your baby due? When will it be born?'

'I don't know,' I say. 'I don't know for sure. Soon I think.'

'For God's sake!' He forgets himself and raises his voice. 'You must know when you were wedded and bedded. You must have a general idea.'

'We were married in December, at his house,' I say. I smile at the memory of Janey and I slipping and sliding in the mud as we walked along the foreshore to Ned's house.

'Next month then,' Robert says.

'Will it be?'

'Something like that. It's usually nine months or so.'

'Is it?'

'You don't know? For the love of God! Have you not seen a midwife?'

I can't confess that we were lying together before we were married. 'How could I see a midwife?'

His irritation suddenly leaves him as he realises how very alone I am. I have no mother to advise me, my sister is dead, and I have not found a friend to replace Janey. I am brought so low that I have had to come to him. 'Yes, of course,' he says quietly. 'Poor little wench.'

'I hoped you would help me,' I say humbly. 'For my sister Jane's sake. She married your brother. It was your father's plan. Nothing has gone right for us since then.'

His gesture cuts me short. 'Not another word about her,' he says. 'And it doesn't behove you to cite her name. Not in your condition.'

'I am a married woman,' I say staunchly. 'She would not have condemned me for marrying for love.'

'Then where's your husband?'

I stammer. 'You know that I don't know.'

'Not heard from him at all?'

I shake my head.

Robert Dudley flings himself into a chair beside the fireside, but he does not invite me to sit down. I hold on to the high back of the other chair and lean against it. He picks up a knife from a side table and turns it this way and that, to catch the light, as he thinks.

'No question but that it is Ned's child,' he says. 'Tell me the truth now, absolutely.'

'No question,' I say, swallowing the insult.

'And when he comes home he will own it?'

'He cannot deny it.'

'And you have proof of your marriage?'

In answer I show him the chain around my neck, my betrothal diamond and my wedding ring of five links.

'I see you have a ring,' he says drily. 'Who were your witnesses?'

'Janey,' I say. 'But she is dead.'

'But there were others present?'

'Just the minister.'

'A proper minister, with a parish?'

'One that Janey knew.'

He nods. 'And you have letters from Seymour. Did he give you money? Did he give you deeds to land?'

'I have a letter of betrothal and his will names me as his wife and his heir,' I say proudly.

Robert nods.

'I have a poem,' I say.

He puts his hand over his forehead and rubs his eyes, as if he is trying not to laugh. 'Never mind that. Now listen, Katherine. I cannot send you into hiding. That would make things worse for you and very bad for me. I will tell the queen what you have told me and you will have to face her. She will be very angry. You should not have married without her permission – as an heir to the throne your husband is of tremendous importance to the safety of the realm. But it's done, and thank God, you could have done a lot worse. He's not a Spanish spy or a papist, he's got no claim in Scotland. He's of a good family – a reformer, thank God, and well liked – and you are with child, and if you have a boy then it eases some of the pressure on her.'

'She could marry who she liked, if she had a Protestant English boy heir,' I observe.

Dudley's dark eyes flash at me. 'So she could,' he agrees. 'But it is not for you to observe. Don't try to be clever. It is very evident that you're not that. So you are going to go to your room and, in the morning, wash your face and dress and do your hair and wait for me to send for you. I am going to wake the queen early, and tell her what you have told me.'

I am about to say that he cannot wake the queen, that no-one can enter her bedroom in the morning until she orders it. But then I remember the interconnecting door and I see that Robert Dudley can come and go as he pleases.

'Will you tell her that I am very, very sorry?' I say quietly. 'Ned and I fell in love. I love him still. I will never love anyone but him. I did not do it to offend her. I thought of nothing but how much I love him.'

'I'll do my best to explain,' Robert says shortly. 'But I can tell you now, she'll never understand. Go now.'

All morning I wait in my room for the summons to Elizabeth. I am sick with fear. I have been sick in the morning for months from the baby, now I am sick with fear of the queen. I wonder if I am ever going to feel well again, if I am ever going to be happy again. I think of my poor sister and how she waited to hear from this queen's sister whether she was to live or die, and I think that it is odd, and cruel, and incomprehensible that Jane should have died for her faith and that I should be scared to death for love, and that we will never be able to talk about this. I will give birth to her nephew, and he will never know her.

At midday one of the ladies, Peggy, puts her head round the

door and says: 'She's asking for you. We're going on the river. You picked a bad day to take off!'

'She wants me?' I am out of my chair and on my feet in a moment, ignoring the swimming sensation in my head.

'She just wants to know where you are. I said you had over-slept. But you'd better show your face.'

I take a glance at myself in my little beaten-silver looking glass. The gentle tones of the reflection show me a beauty: creamy skin, golden hair, dark eyes.

'Come on,' says Peggy, disagreeably. 'They're getting into the boats now.'

'She wants me to come out on the river?'

'Didn't I just say?'

I hurry behind her and the two of us go to the quayside. I cannot believe that Elizabeth is going to interrogate me while sailing on the river. I thought she would send for me the moment that Robert Dudley spoke to her. I cannot understand what is happening. Elizabeth has been in a bad mood since her arrival in Ipswich. The town is passionately in favour of the reformed religion, and Elizabeth has a hankering for the old ways of the Church. The ministers here have wives, and Elizabeth longs for a celibate clergy dressed in the richest of robes. She is such a silly mix of reform and papistry; she is not serious about her faith like Jane. They have promised her a water masque of boats, to take her mind off her complaints, and we all have to take our places on one of the great trading ships, to dine and watch the display that has been prepared for Elizabeth's amusement.

Robert Dudley is at her side and he meets my anxious enquiring look with an expression of complete blankness. Clearly, I am to seek no help from him. Elizabeth inclines her head to my curtsey but does not summon me to her side. She is neither angry nor sympathetic, she is like she always is – frosty. It is as if nothing has been said about my condition. For a moment I think that he cannot have told her anything, that his nerve failed him at the last moment. A little quieting gesture of his hand behind her throne warns me to say nothing and do nothing, and I curtsey again and step back.

The ship is anchored and the outgoing tide makes it pull against the hawser and rock and twist. It's a horrible movement, both side to side and up and down at the same time. It's far worse than rowing in a barge. I can feel the bile rise in the back of my throat and my mouth is filled with brine.

'We will dine,' says Elizabeth as if she can read my white face and knows that I am afraid that I will not make it through the day without vomiting. 'Ah,' she says. 'Oysters!'

The famous Colchester oysters are offered to the queen and she slides her eyes to Robert Dudley and says: 'Is it true that they inspire lust in the unwary?'

'Not only in the unwary,' he replies, and the two of them laugh together.

'Perhaps virgins like Lady Katherine and I should not taste them?' she says. The server, taking the hint, immediately proffers Elizabeth's great platter of oysters to me. With her dark gaze on me, I have to take one.

'It depends if you like the taste,' Robert explains. 'I, myself, can't get enough of it.'

She laughs and slaps his hand away from another shell, but she is watching me. I cannot refuse to eat a gift from the queen's platter, and I raise the shell to my mouth. The smell of seaweed and the sight of the gluey shell is going to be too much for me. I know I am never going to be able to eat it. I know I am going to disgrace myself before the court. I can taste the salt of hot bile in my mouth, I can feel my stomach churn and heave.

'*Bon appétit!*' the queen says to me, her sharp eyes on my green face.

'And to you, Your Majesty,' I say, and I open my mouth and pour it down and swallow it down. I close my mouth like a trap and I hold it.

The queen laughs so hard that she has to cling to Robert's hands. 'Your face!' she exclaims. 'Have another!' she begs me. 'Have more.'

I cannot speak to Robert Dudley privately till the evening, after chapel. I manage to get beside him as we take our places in the great hall. 'Did you tell her?' I demand.

'I told her; but she won't speak of it till we are back in London,' he says. He glances forward to the top table, where the queen's bronze head turns back to look for him. 'Excuse me.'

'Is she not angry? Will she forgive me?'

'I don't know,' he says. 'She says that she won't speak of it till London. What d'you think?'

I don't know what to think, except that every day of the progress must bring me nearer to my confinement and the only person who has an opinion on the matter – Robert Dudley (of all the midwives a young woman might choose) – thinks that it must be September. Thank God we will be back in London by September and the queen will tell me then what I am to do. Nothing could be worse than this daily ordeal of travel, these miserable nights of amusement, and this terror of discovery every day.

WHITEHALL PALACE, LONDON, SUMMER 1561

I am given permission to go ahead of the royal progress and return to London. Nobody says why, but I take it as a favour won for me by Robert Dudley, though he says nothing and the queen is as light-hearted as if he had not spoken. I go at once to the royal treasury rooms to find the tokens that Henry Herbert gave me as his pledge, but the box where I keep my precious papers – Ned's betrothal to me, his beloved will, and the Herbert love letters – is not where I left it.

'You took them with you!' my maid says. 'Because you said they were precious to you. So you took them on progress.'

'But I wrote to Tabitha to find them here, and she said they were missing. They weren't with me. We didn't take them.'

She looks puzzled. 'I am sure that I packed them. Are all your jewels safe?'

'My jewels are nothing to do with it!' I exclaim. 'I clearly remember telling you to take the box of papers to the groom of the wardrobe and have them stored in the jewel house for me.'

'Oh, that box!' she says, her face suddenly clearing. 'Yes, I took that for you.'

'Well, go and find it then. Why would you not fetch it at once?' Suddenly exhausted, I sink down to my bed and then there is a clattering knock on my door. I jump to my feet and open it myself. Outside is a captain of the yeomen of the guard and a couple of yeomen behind him.

'Lady Katherine Grey,' he says.

'Obviously,' I say sharply. 'Who asks for me?'

'You are under arrest,' he says. 'You are commanded to come with me to the Tower of London.'

'What?' I simply can't understand what he is saying.

'You are under arrest. You are to come with me to the Tower. You may bring three women to serve you. They are to follow behind us with whatever goods and clothes you require.'

'What?'

He steps inside the room without answering me and he bows, his outstretched arm indicating that I should go out through the open door. My baby turns in my belly under the hard stomacher. I go where the captain indicates. He puts his hand in the small of my back and I flinch away. I cannot bear to be touched. I don't want him putting his heavy hand anywhere near my belly where my baby suddenly kicks out and makes me give a little gasp.

'This way,' he says, thinking I am about to cry out. 'And no disturbance, if you please.'

I am very far from making any disturbance, I am blindly obedient, stunned like a heifer hammered between the eyes as it walks down the Shambles towards the butcher. My ladies are gathered like a flock of startled hens at the doorway to my presence chamber, eyeing me in horror as if I were taken with the plague and they want to draw back their skirts for fear of infection; but I hardly see them at all. I am blinded by my own shock.

'The Tower?' I say to myself, but there is no meaning in the words for me.

The captain goes ahead of me, and his men come behind. It is like a scene in a masque. I follow him. I don't know what else I can do. But I really don't know what is happening.

'I have to have my linnets,' I say suddenly. 'And my little dog. And I have a cat, and I have a monkey, a very valuable animal.'

'Your ladies will bring them,' he says solemnly, glancing over his shoulder to make sure that I am keeping up. I follow in his footsteps and he leads me out of the palace, through the privy gardens, and towards the river. I look around in case there is anyone I know who would take a message for me, but who would take a message? And, in any case, what would it say?

'Is this about the Spanish?' I ask. 'For I have not spoken with them, and I have told William Cecil everything that they have ever said to me.'

We go in silence through the gate to the pier. The queen's sergeant porter, Thomas Keyes, is on duty. He holds open the gate for us and he bows low from his enormous height to me. 'My lady,' he says respectfully.

'Mr Keyes,' I say helplessly.

The captain leads the way to the pier, and there is a barge at the steps, without livery. He puts out his hand to help me down the steps and I go carefully, conscious of my big belly and my weight tipping me forward. I walk up the gangplank and take my seat at the rear of the barge. An awning shades me from the afternoon sun and from anyone watching from the palace. I wonder wildly if William Cecil has fallen into disgrace, just as King Henry's advisors used to fall, and if it is a mistake to mention his name. 'I report to Robert Dudley also,' I say. 'I never fail in my loyalty to the queen, and to her faith.'

'My orders were to escort you. I don't know any more,' the captain says.

The crew cast off and raise their oars and then when the barge is pushed from the pier they dip them, all at the same time, in the water. The hortator beats one strike of the drum and they all pull together and the barge leaps forward, making me rock in my seat. Again and again the drum pounds softly and the barge rocks me to its beat. The sun on the water is dazzling, the baby is heavy in my belly. I am terribly afraid, and I don't know what I should fear. I wish that Ned were here. I wish with all my heart that Ned were here.

For once in my life, I have nothing to say, not a scream of protest, not even a flood of tears, not one word. I am so shocked I am struck dumb. Where Elizabeth sank down onto the steps at the watergate and wept in self-pity and made sure her words were recorded, I am silent. I disembark from the barge, I take the outstretched hand to help me up the steps. I go quietly, like a frightened child, to wherever they lead me, up the stone steps and through the garden gate into the front door of the lieutenant's house, the mansion house of the busy little walled village that includes both mint and armoury, treasure house and palace, prison, and place of execution.

They help me up the narrow staircase to a good-sized bedchamber at the front of the house and when I sink into a chair they go out and close the door quietly. Then I hear the key turning in the lock. It is not a long terrible grating sound – it is an oiled lock that has been used often. I am only another prisoner.

THE LIEUTENANT'S HOUSE, THE TOWER, LONDON, SUMMER 1561

When I get up in the morning and look through the leaded panes of the small window I can see the green where they built the scaffold and beheaded my sister. If I squint to the left I can see the chapel where they buried her severed head beside her slight truncated body. I sleep in the bed that was hers when she was queen, I cry into her pillows. I sit in her old chair. The tapestries that hang on the walls are those that hung in her bedroom.

On the other side of the Tower grounds, past the White Tower and out of sight, are the stables where she put her hand on our father's rein and begged him not to leave her. I can hear the clang of the gate that opened for him on that day. This is the place of my sister's crowning, betrayal and death. My father is buried here, too. This is where Elizabeth, with extraordinary cruelty, has chosen to imprison me.

She took her time like the heartless automaton that she is. She smiled at me on progress, she waved to the crowds along the route. She favoured me before the Spanish and the French ambassadors. She said nothing, not even to Robert Dudley when he told her the news that triggered her jealous hatred. She gave everyone – even me – to understand that I was still an heir, just as I was before he confessed to her, that I am her cousin, her lady-in-waiting, a favourite, a girl she regards as her daughter. Actually, she behaved as if he had said nothing, that she had heard nothing. It was as if no confession had ever been made, and Bess St Loe and Robert Dudley said nothing either.

She allowed me to return early to London and – when she could act easily and fast, secretly and unchallenged – she had me arrested and locked up in these three rooms, overlooking Tower Green, where the beheading of my sister plays over and over again in my mind's eye whenever I look out of the window.

Of course, she's not going to behead me. I am not so timorous that I imagine things are worse than they are. She is furious with me, but I have committed no crime. I will be held here, in moderate comfort, with my pets and my women, until the baby is born, until Ned comes home, and then we will both beg her pardon and be released, and we will have to live quietly at Hanworth until she forgets or forgives me. At the worst she will treat me as she does our cousin Margaret Douglas – with suspicion and dislike. Like her, I will raise my Tudor son, and laugh up my sleeve.

Like it or not, any boy of mine will be the next King of England; my rights will pass to him. This could make Elizabeth more kindly to me, as she can raise him as her heir, and then nobody can insist that she marry. But, since it is Elizabeth – a barren Tudor from a tyrannical line – it may make her angrier with me, as the prettier younger cousin who has done what she cannot. There is no way of knowing with Elizabeth. I cannot guess at her mind. I would never have imagined that she would imprison a woman about to give birth for doing nothing worse than marrying the young man she loves.

As she establishes her rule, the whole country and I learn that she is powerful and unscrupulous. I truly believe her to be a tyrant as wicked as her father, but I don't fear that she will do worse to me than hold me in this shameful imprisonment until the birth of my son. She means me to be humiliated, and she has triumphed. Indeed, she has brought me very low.

'Oh, no, she plans far worse than this,' Mary my sister says, climbing up into one of my high dining chairs, and sitting back, her little feet stuck out in front of her.

'What could be worse?' I ask.

Mary is my only visitor though the court has returned to London, and she is escorted by a woman who is certain to be spying on us and reporting everything we say. No-one else comes to see me. My ladies are allowed to serve me, my gowns have been sent to me, my plates with my family crest and my silver forks; my linnets from Janey are in their cage. I have half a dozen of Jo's puppies in their basket and Jo watches over them all as Ribbon the little cat watches her. Mr Nozzle the monkey is exploring the walls and fireplaces of the three rooms over and over, round and round, going from tapestry to mantelpiece, table to floor and back up high again. I feel worse for him than I do for myself, as Mr Nozzle loves a garden in sunshine and these rooms are always dark and stuffy during the day and cold at night.

'The queen has decided that there was a plot,' Mary says quietly. 'She thinks that the Spanish arranged your marriage with Ned and that they will turn her from the throne and make you queen and him consort, and your son will be raised as heir, as rival heir to the French candidate – the Queen of Scots.'

I stare at Mary. 'This is madness. Ned is as staunch a Protestant as any in England, and I am sister to Jane Grey! Nobody can think that we would turn papist for the throne of England. Nobody can think that we would join with the Spanish!'

There is a tap at the door and the woman spy is distracted. 'But she does,' Mary whispers quickly. 'Because it's exactly what she would have done herself. She would have done anything to become queen. She doesn't realise that everyone is not the same. She would never marry for love, so she doesn't believe that you did.'

'Someone must tell her that I meant no such thing!' I say. 'Robert Dudley must tell her. William Cecil will tell her that I always reported the Spanish ambassador to him!'

Mary shakes her wise little head. 'Oh Lord, it's worse than that at court! Now she suspects both of them, too. Robert Dudley because he knew of your marriage—'

'Because I told him myself! And he told her the very next day!'

'And Ned is in France and on his way to Rome. She thinks he's going to report to the Pope.'

'He's with Thomas Cecil! Does William Cecil think that his own son has gone papist?'

'Exactly, I told you, it's terrible at court. She says, over and over, why would the two of them go to Rome, if not to meet with the Pope? Did Cecil know? Is this his plot? It looks very bad.'

'Only if you think that everything is treason.'

The woman spy returns to her seat and looks from one of us to the other, fearful that she has missed something. We turn our bland pretty smiles on her.

Mary folds her little hands in her lap and looks at me steadily. 'That's exactly what she does think, all the time. Especially of us cousins.'

I stand up and I pull my flowing gown tight over my belly so she can see how big I am. Since the shame of my arrest I have gone into loose gowns and anyone can see that I am nearing my time. 'Do I look like a woman about to flee to Spain? Do I look like a woman capable of leading a treasonous army against the Queen of England?'

'Not to me you don't,' Mary says steadily. 'And I will go and talk to Cecil.'

'No, don't do that.' I am so afraid of Mary being arrested as a fellow plotter. If they are mad enough to arrest me, they are mad enough to accuse Mary, too. 'Don't do anything. Just stay quietly at court and serve the queen as best you can. Try to behave normally. And don't come again too soon.'

'You don't want to see me?'

I can tell that she is hurt. 'I don't want you endangered. I don't want another Grey girl in the Tower. Two is enough. We are both as innocent as Jane. I don't want you locked in here, where they killed Jane and torment me.'

She pushes herself to the edge of the chair and drops lightly on her feet. She goes to the window and stands on tiptoe to look out to the green where her sister died. 'I don't doubt that she is in heaven,' she says staunchly. 'I don't doubt that you married for love and not for strategy. I don't doubt that our destiny is to do what seems right to us, whatever people think.'

I close my eyes to block out the sight of the green. 'I am sure she is in heaven,' I agree. 'And I did marry for love, and I love him still. And of course we have to live according to our own conscience; but I do want you to be very, very careful with your appearance, your friends and your faith.'

'I am,' Mary says, fearful of nothing. 'I had permission to visit you from William Cecil and I have to report back to him how I found you. I am his spy as well as your sister. I think everyone is a spy for someone or other.'

'You can tell him everything,' I say. 'I have nothing to hide.' I catch the curious gaze of the woman spy who came in with my sister. 'I have nothing to hide,' I repeat.

'I know,' Mary says. 'I'll tell William Cecil that you should be released to Hanworth. You should have your Seymour baby there, in Ned's family home, and he should be christened in his own chapel.'

THE TOWER, LONDON, AUTUMN 1561

It is hot and airless in the lieutenant's small house, and I am not allowed out of my rooms, not to walk in the garden nor on the flat roof of the Tower where I could, at least, get a breath of air in the evening and see the sun set.

Every day the lieutenant of the Tower, Sir Edward Warner, comes to my room and asks me who knew that Ned and I were in love, and who knew that we were married, who witnessed the betrothal and the marriage, and who encouraged us to do it, and keep it secret.

He asks the same questions over and over again while Mr Nozzle paws at the stone walls and tears miserably at the frayed edge of the tapestry, swinging dolefully on the dangling hem as if it were a bell rope and he were tolling a mourning bell.

Over and over again I tell Sir Edward that we were two young people in love, the witness was Janey, that no-one else knew except perhaps the servants and, of course, the minister, and he writes it all down very carefully and says that the minister will be sought out and that I must hope that his story confirms mine. I say that my box of papers, which proves everything I say, is in the royal jewel house, and they will find it if they will but look for it. I say that I already told all this to Robert Dudley, and the lieutenant says that this has been noted. He asks what I told Bess St Loe, and I stammer, remembering the dark that followed the sudden blowing out of the candle.

'Bess St Loe?' I repeat, feebly.

'She has been arrested for questioning,' he says heavily. 'Indeed, I have interrogated her myself for her part in this conspiracy.'

'Good God, is she in here too?'

He nods. 'Under suspicion of treasonous conspiracy with you.'

'Sir Edward! That is so wrong! All I did was tell her that I was with child and beg her to help me for she had been a friend of my mother! God knows, there was no conspiracy. She cried out that I should never have come to her and ordered me from her room. She would not even speak to me in my trouble.'

He writes this down, very slowly, word for word. I have to bite my lip on my impatience. 'Sir Edward, I do promise you, this is just a story about love and perhaps folly, but when I see Ned—'

'The Earl of Hertford is on his way from France,' he tells me.

My knees suddenly weaken and I feel behind me for the chair, and I sink down. 'I must sit,' I whisper. I am breathless at the thought of seeing him again. I forget that we are in such trouble. I can only think that he is coming home to me. 'He's coming home?'

'He's ordered home for questioning.'

'Ask him anything!' I say triumphantly. 'He will say the same as me.'

'I will be asking him,' he says, dour as ever. 'For he is coming here. He is under arrest, too.'

They bring Ned in at dusk, under cover of darkness, and I can hear the heavy boots on the pavement below my window. There are many prisoners walking with him surrounded by guards, a woman with her head bowed and crying, clinging to the arm of another man, someone dawdling and protesting at the back, a man with his arm laid across someone's shoulder. There must be about a dozen of them, arrested all together.

At first I don't understand who these people are. Then I realise with growing horror that Elizabeth has ordered the arrest of Ned and his servants, his brother, his sister-in-law, my stepfather, Adrian Stokes, my servants, ladies from the queen's bedchamber, Bess St Loe's servants: everyone who ever knew me has been arrested for questioning. The queen is pursuing us as her father pursued the Pole family – down to the last little boy. The treasure house has been searched for my box of papers, my rooms have been stripped out and searched. Ned's boxes from France have been confiscated and his house in London searched from cellar to attic. With all the power of her huge spy system, Elizabeth has launched a massive operation to root out a widespread conspiracy. Cecil's spies are looking for a connection between supporters of my sister Jane, allies of Spain, enemies of Elizabeth, and anyone who would prefer a legitimate heir on the throne to a declared bastard. The queen has convinced herself that there is a plot, organised by the Protestants in England and the Spanish abroad, designed to put me on the throne of England and prevent Mary Queen of Scots from ever becoming queen and handing the country to her French family.

The guards around Ned pause at the gate of the lieutenant's house and then enter, disappearing from my view. I think they are bringing him into my rooms, to live with me, and I rush to the door as if I could throw it open, and then I remember I am locked in, and step back from it. I pull at my flowing gown; I am so afraid he will find my broad belly a shock. He loved the narrow curve of my waist – will he find me ugly in these last days of my pregnancy? I pat my hair, I straighten my hood. I go to sit in my chair and then I stand up again, by the fireplace. I could almost beat down the door in my impatience to see him.

Then I hear the terrible sound of them climbing the stone stairs that go past my rooms. They go past my door, they don't stop to come in, they go on up to the rooms on the floor above. I cry out in disappointment and I run to the door and press my face against it, trying to distinguish Ned's footstep, trying to recognise his breathing. I hear the door above mine open, I hear them go in, and the clatter as men drop bags, scrape the heavy wooden chairs on the stone-flagged floor, and then the slam of the door and the grate of the key in the lock and the noise of their feet on the stairs as they descend.

He is above me. If he stamped with his heel on the floor, I would hear him. If I screamed at the top of my voice, he would hear me. I stand for long minutes, my face tilted up to the ceiling, the puppies whimpering as if they are longing for him too, hoping to hear a word from my husband, home at last.

Every day now I have strange cramps and my belly stands out so firmly that I think the baby must be coming. 'I cannot go on like this,' I say desperately to Sir Edward. 'Do you want me to die in childbirth like Jane Seymour?'

He looks anxious. 'If you would only confess,' he says. 'If you would confess, then I could get you sent to your uncle, or to Hanworth, and the midwives could come.'

'I can't confess to what I have not done,' I say. I am crying for pain and self-pity. I am in a truly impossible situation, for who can ever prove to a Tudor queen that she is not in danger? All the Tudor monarchs think that they are in mortal danger, often without cause. King Henry saw imaginary enemies everywhere, and killed good friends and advisors from his fear.

'I married a nobleman for true love. I insist that I see my husband. You must at least tell him that I am here, on the floor below him, and that I am near my time.'

There is a tap on the door. Of course, my heart leaps as if it could be Ned: suddenly freed and coming to save me. Sir Edward looks at me suspiciously.

'You are expecting a message?' he asks.

'I am expecting nothing. I am hoping for mercy.'

He nods to the guard who stands by the door and he unbolts it and swings it open. It is one of the lieutenant's servants. 'What d'you want, Jeffrey?' he asks abruptly.

The man bows. He is holding a posy of late roses, red roses. 'These for the young lady,' he says. 'From the Earl of Hertford.'

They are a deep red, Lancaster red. Nobody at the Tudor court would ever offer a white rose. I put out my hand and Sir Edward fussily shakes them in case a note drops out. Then he takes the posy apart looking for a message, and asks me what red roses mean to me; if they are a signal. I say that they mean that Ned is thinking of me, imprisoned just one floor below him. We are under the same roof again, as we have not been for months. He knows now that I was with child when he left me, and how I have suffered in his absence. He is telling me that he loves me.

'That's all,' I say. 'He is a poet. Flowers are like words to him. Red roses tell me that he loves me still. Red roses are for true love.'

Sir Edward, for all that he is Elizabeth's gaoler and spy, cannot hide that he is moved. 'Well, you can keep them,' he says, finally handing them over.

'Thank you,' I say. I hold them to my lips. 'These are the most precious flowers I have ever had in my life. Will you tell him how glad I am to have them from him, and how happy I am that we are together again, even if it is here in prison, where both our fathers were once imprisoned? Will you tell him that I love him still and that I don't regret – that I will never regret – that he loved me and married me? Tell him that I pray every day that we will be together again as husband and wife, as we planned to be.'

He shakes his head. 'I'll tell him that you like the flowers,' he says. 'I can't remember the rest.'

'You could write it down,' I say, laughing at us both. 'You write down everything else I ever say or do. Why not this?'

Ned's flowers bloom, tucked in the ribbon at my wide waist. I put them in my hair, I put a bud under my pillow and I press the last one in the pages of the Bible at the Song of Solomon, the psalm about love. I have forgiven him as if he never went away. I have forgiven him for this perilous place. I love him. His judgement is good. He is my husband and we have done nothing wrong.

Mary comes to me again.

'Are you sure it is wise to come?' I say, bending over my broad belly to kiss her cheek.

'I come with permission, they want me to talk with you in the hope that you will say something incriminating,' Mary says without resentment, indicating a woman servant who curtseys and stands by the door, listening to everything that we say.

'But how did you get here?'

'I walked. Mr Thomas Keyes, the queen's sergeant porter, walked with us. He's waiting downstairs to take me back.'

I take no notice of the queen's spy. Everyone in the Tower reports on me anyway; I never say a word that is not noted. I am interrogated every day and they even listen to my prayers. They can listen all they like, all they will hear is that I love my husband, and so I should.

'Is Her Majesty in good health? I pray for her good health,' I say.

'I am sorry to say that she is not,' Mary replies. 'She is very tired and very weary. She cannot eat. I think she is very distressed by her fears about a conspiracy. She is convinced there has been a mighty conspiracy against her. And the Scots ambassador has come to London to press her to name their queen, Mary, as her heir – instead of you. Of course, that would be a terrible mistake. She is feeling beset.'

I bow my head. 'She must do as she sees fit,' I say demurely. 'But our line, from the king's sister, named as the king's heir, born in England and of the reformed religion, has the greatest claim.'

'She must do as she wishes,' Mary agrees. 'But she said to the Scots ambassador that naming her heir was like setting her winding sheet before her eyes. She said princes cannot like their own children.'

Mary meets my gaze with her most limpid look. I mouth the words, 'Quite mad!' and she nods in agreement.

'I wish I could beg her pardon and reassure her that she has nothing to fear from me,' I say for the benefit of the listening woman. We all know that no-one could say anything that would cure Elizabeth of suspicion and fear. 'I did a hasty act for love. She should see me as a fool perhaps, but not as her enemy.'

'She doubts everyone,' Mary says. 'She has imprisoned all the Seymours, and even our poor stepfather, Adrian, who is not responsible for us, and had no idea what you were doing at court. She is even afraid that William Cecil knew of your marriage and encouraged it.'

I am genuinely amazed that she would doubt the man who has advised her from girlhood. 'She should be sure that William Cecil never thinks of anyone but her. Of course he didn't know of it. Would he have sent Ned away from me and thrown me into despair if he had sponsored our wedding and wanted us to conceive a child?'

'That's what I said,' Mary says, nodding to the waiting woman as if to invite her to report on all of this. 'And she knows that I knew nothing about it either.'

'It was secret,' I say simply. 'We wanted a secret wedding, so no-one knew but Janey. I tell them over and over again.'

'Weary work,' my sister observes. 'Do they ask you every day?'

'Every single day they come in and I have to stand before them and they ask me over and over what we did and how we met and who knew.'

'They make you stand?'

I give her a wry smile. 'They may not torture a lady of the nobility but they can certainly give me pains. At least I have a midwife who comes to me now, and she says that there is nothing wrong.'

'Does she say when the baby will come?'

'She doesn't know exactly. Nobody knows. She thinks it will be soon.'

The woman at the door stirs and Mary says: 'I am not allowed to stay too long. I am only permitted to come and see that you are well, and that you have everything you need.'

'I need to see my husband,' I tell her. 'I need to see the queen.'

Mary makes a little pout and shrugs her shoulders. We both know this is said for the benefit of the spy. Mary is allowed to bring me some apples, but not my freedom.

'I will come again next week.' She bobs up from the stool and looks around at my pets. 'Does someone walk the puppies? There is a terrible smell.'

'There's hardly any smell,' I say. 'Anyway, it's the moat. And I hope that the lieutenant will let me out in the garden and then I can take them all out. If he does not let me live in comfort he will have to endure the smell.'

The days are very long, and my room is hot and stuffy. I play with the puppies and I whistle to the linnets, let them fly around the room and call them back to my hand. Mr Nozzle scrabbles painfully at the foot of the stone walls but then scampers up the chairs and takes a flying leap from one carved back to another. He jumps on the wall hanging and holds with one tiny black hand and then springs into my arms.

'And what will you make of a baby?' I ask him. 'You must be kind and not pinch him.'

I listen for Ned, and sometimes I hear his footsteps on the floor. He sends me little gifts and every morning and night he taps with his heel to send his love. They do not allow him to send me anything written, and they still question us both every day. I hear them troop up the stairs to his room and back down again after an hour. I think they are hoping to prove that we conspired together against the queen, but by the end of the month the lords that Cecil sent to question us seem to be as tired of their interrogation as I am. Without colluding, we tell the same story – the simple truth, and they have to believe that it was a marriage for love, that we had no thought that the queen would see us as anything but two young lovers incapable of resisting each other. Indeed, that was obvious to everyone from the beginning. Only the fearful Elizabeth thought it must be a conspiracy. Only the cold-hearted Elizabeth would look for an explanation when everyone else would see springtime and youthful desire and thoughtlessness.

THE TOWER, LONDON, AUTUMN 1561

I notice the questions change. No longer are they asking who knew of our plans, who were our friends at court, how often did I meet the Spanish ambassador? Now they are on another tack. They are starting to concentrate on who was present at the betrothal, who witnessed the wedding. They ask about servants; who prepared the cold meats that Ned had in his bedroom? Who served the wine? Who was the minister? They ask about Janey.

'So he was not known to you, this so-called minister?' Sir

Edward asks me. The panel of three men have allowed me to sit as I complained that I am weary and near to my time, and it is late in the evening.

'As I said when you first asked me.'

'He was not attached to a church?'

'I don't think so. Janey ran out and fetched him.'

'Fetched him from where?'

It sounds so unlikely when they question me like this. 'I don't know. I think she went to where the ministers preach, perhaps at St Paul's Cross. She just brought him back and he read the service and she paid him ten pounds.'

The man at the end of the table raises his head. 'Where did she get the ten pounds from?'

'I don't know!' I say impatiently. 'Perhaps it was her own money, perhaps Ned gave it to her.'

'How d'you know he was a minister of the Church at all?' Sir Edward asks portentously.

'Because he wore a furred gown like a minister from Switzerland?' I suggest impertinently. 'Because he came with Janey when she asked for a minister? Because he brought a Bible and read the marriage service? Because he said that he was? How else? Should I have asked him for a copy of his degree? Why would I doubt him? Why would you doubt him now?'

They exchange looks, they are uncomfortable and it makes me certain that someone has told them to pursue this new line of questions against their own wishes.

'And the ring?'

Proudly, I extend my hand to show them on the third finger of my left hand is Ned's pointed diamond that he gave me for our betrothal and his wedding ring with the five links. I wore them on a chain around my neck from our wedding day, now I have them on my finger. 'His rings,' I say. 'I have never been without them since my wedding day.' I press them to my lips.

Their grim expressions become more downcast. 'And the earl's written proposal, and his will before he left for France when he names you as his wife?' Sir Edward says.

He knows I do not have these. We all know that my papers are missing. My fool of a maid thinks that she took my box of papers to the treasure house with the other things that I wanted kept safely in London when I was on progress with the queen. But when she went to look for it, it was missing, and then I was arrested and now nobody can find it.

'I had it with my other papers,' I say. 'If I could just go to my rooms I am sure I could find it.'

'Your rooms have been searched,' he says as if I am some kind of criminal. 'And your boxes in the treasure house have been searched. Nobody can find any papers to prove that you were married.'

I make a gesture at my straining belly. 'I think it is obvious to anyone that I am married.'

Sir Edward clears his throat. 'The marriage could be invalid,' he says awkwardly. 'If it was not performed by a proper minister. The earl and his sister could have tricked you into a false marriage with a pretend minister and you are no more married than . . .' He breaks off as if he cannot think of an example of a famously deflowered spinster – though I wager it is the queen who pops into his mind.

'Sir Edward, you mistake your position,' I say quietly. 'Of course I am married. I am Lady Seymour the Countess of Hertford, and you should remember that I am of blood royal. Nobody may question my word.'

He ducks his head; these are difficult interrogations for him as well as me. 'I beg your pardon, I meant only that we have no evidence.'

'I need no evidence because I was there,' I insist. 'My friend Janey would never have tricked me in such a way. Why would she do such a thing when she wanted us married? Her brother is my true husband. He would never have betrayed me. Why should he do so? He wanted to marry me in honour, for love. That is what we did. Ask him yourself.'

'We do ask him,' the last man at the table says, looking up from his notes. 'But he is the only other person we can ask. You had no witness but his sister and she is dead, and we can't find this minister of yours, and we have no evidence in writing.'

'Then you will have to take my word, and the word of the Earl of Hertford,' I say proudly. 'And that should be enough for anyone in England. A marriage between two people in the sight of God is good enough for God and the law. You know as well as I do. We didn't even need a minister to make a true marriage, we chose to have one come in and read the marriage service but it would have been a legal marriage if we had said our vows to each other before God. We didn't need a witness, God saw that it was a good marriage. That's what we did. That is good enough for me, and it must be good enough for you, and for whoever has told you to question me like this.'

I am so tired by this exchange that when they are gone, trooping down the stairs and complaining to each other that they are getting nowhere, I lie down on my bed and I sleep till the early hours of the morning. My lady-in-waiting serves me with some bread and meat and small ale for my breakfast, and some plums, but I cannot eat anything. I feel restless and walk from one side of the room to another, looking out at the river and over the green. The baby has gone very still and – I am certain – sunk lower in my belly so I feel even more bulky and awkward.

I am puzzled by this new questioning. I wonder if they have decided to try to disprove my marriage, since they cannot prove a conspiracy. But what good would it do them to shame me? And who would ever believe such a thing of a young man so prickly about his honour as Ned? Who would believe that a young woman, sister of the sainted Jane, would not be married by a Protestant preacher?

Then, suddenly, as I look out over the river and the wheeling gulls, there is a sensation as if my bowels have turned over, a sensation so strong that I think I am about to die. I cling to a chair back and gasp out in pain. The agony is too much even for me to scream. My lady darts forward and then jumps back as there is a cascade of red water on the stone floor. Mr Nozzle leaps for a tapestry and swarms up it, the puppies dash into their box and whimper. Ribbon the cat sniffs at it and walks away, shaking a paw.

'My God, the baby is coming!' my lady says. 'Your waters have broken and you are not even in confinement!'

The pain goes as suddenly as it came and I could almost laugh at the thought that being locked in the Tower is not adequate confinement. Of course, I should be in a darkened room with two midwives with me, two ladies to serve me, a couple of maids, a wet nurse and rockers waiting to take the baby, a husband pacing between chapel and his dinner. Of course everything is wrong. But nothing is going to stop this baby coming.

'Tell the lieutenant of the Tower to send for the midwife, and see that someone tells the Earl of Hertford,' I say. I want to cry for sheer terror that I have to face this ordeal without my mother or my sister or any kindly loving woman. 'Tell him to pray for me and our child.'

She hammers on the door and it takes forever before we hear the slow steps of the guard mounting the stairs. 'Let me out! I have to see Sir Edward!' she screams to his murmured query through the thick door. 'The baby is coming!'

I manage to get to the corner where there is a plain crucifix on the wall and the open Bible before it. I manage to kneel and pray. I manage to wait as the pain comes again, and pray for the safety of the baby and myself, and I pray that the midwife comes soon, for God knows we need one person who knows what she is doing here.

As the midwife bangs the outer door and rushes up the stairs, I hear above me my husband, my true love Ned, hammer on his locked door. 'What's happening? What's happening?' I can hear him bellow, even through the thick wood of my own door.

'Ned! Ned! Our baby is coming!' I scream upwards at the beamed ceiling. Mr Nozzle dives for my unmade bed and puts his head under the pillow. I hear Ned's footsteps quickly cross the floor and then he shouts, muffled, as if he is pressing his lips to the stone floor of his cell, desperate for his words to reach me.

I can't hear what he says – his floor is quarried stone, cold and thick. But I don't need to hear him. I know he loves me, I know he will be in painful anxiety until I can send him a message that I am well and his baby thrives. And as the midwife rushes in and the door is slammed shut and bolted behind her, I find a little happiness in knowing that as I endure my pains down here, Ned is only one floor above, on his knees, his face pressed to his stone floor, listening for his baby's first cry, praying for me, his wife.

It is a long ordeal, though the midwife says it is quick for a first child and that she has sat with women who have endured this for days. I try to stop my ears to her gloomy predictions and her terrible stories of deaths in childbirth and stillborn babies, and my lady-in-waiting interrupts her to say: 'But her ladyship is doing very well!'

'Lady Katherine is doing as well as she can,' the old witch concurs.

I gasp as one of the pains ends, and I correct her: 'Lady Hertford,' I insist. 'I am the Countess of Hertford.'

'Whatever you say, my lady,' she says, her gaze sliding away from mine, and this makes me wonder again if someone is trying to prove that our marriage did not take place at all and she has been ordered not to address me by my married name.

I cannot think, my mind is so fogged with pain and fear as I walk up and down through the pains and then lie on the bed for a rest. I feel as if I am splitting open, a terrible sensation, as if I am being quartered without benefit of hanging. I think of Jane, going to her death only a stone's throw from this window, and I think of the agony that she must have felt when the axe came down, and I think perhaps I am dying in the Tower like my sister did, like my father did, and that all I can hope for, at the end of this agony, is that I will see them in heaven.

The midwife, who has been watching me walk and then pause to lean on a chair and groan through my pain, suddenly puts her spindle away and says: 'It's coming now. Best get ready.'

'What am I to do?' I demand wildly. 'What happens now?'

She laughs shortly. 'You should have thought to ask that before, Lady Katherine,' she says.

'Lady Hertford,' I hiss, claiming my married title with what might be my last breath. 'I am the wife of the Earl of Hertford.'

Roughly she pushes me to my hands and knees and, like a labouring mare, I groan and push as she commands and rest as she orders, and then I feel the strangest sensation, a slither and a wriggle, and she says: 'God bless you and help you, you have a boy.'

My baby, Viscount Beauchamp, is to be called Edward for his father and his forefathers. He can trace his line back to Edward III and beyond. Royal on both sides, his birth should be greeted with celebrations, with the salute of cannon and announcements all around Christendom, but they put me into my bed, and tuck him in beside me, and nobody even visits. They take him to be baptised in the chapel of the Tower and my poor little boy is christened in the font that stands over the tombs of his family. It is as if the mortuary of traitors at the Tower of London is our family chapel. His aunt is buried below the font, and his grandfather Grey. His grandfather Seymour is buried there, too. He is not even baptised by a minister, but by Sir Edward, the lieutenant of the Tower, his gaoler, because the god-forsaken Supreme

Governor of the Church of England, Elizabeth, will not allow
an ordained minister into the prison to bless the soul of her newborn cousin. This makes me cry. This is so low. She is so low. To
forbid a priest to bless an innocent baby. She is below lowness.

THE TOWER, LONDON, WINTER 1561–2

I cannot be unhappy with my baby cooing in his cradle and
smiling when he sees me. He is more amusing than any pet; he
is quite enchanting. Even Mr Nozzle sees that a prince has come
among us, and serves him with the same delighted surprise that
my ladies show when they run to fetch a scrap of cloth to lay on
my shoulder when he gives a little belch after his feed, or hold his
waving hands and tiny plump feet when I unstrap his swaddling
bands.

I feed him myself, as though I were a peasant girl, and I laugh
to think that Elizabeth, in her tyranny, has given me the greatest
joy I have ever known. If I had given birth to the little viscount
in a royal palace, where his birth merits, he would have been out
of my hands the moment he was born, and I should have lived
apart from him. He would have been kept in a royal nursery and
I should have been with the court – wherever it happened to be,
even if I had to be away from him for weeks. He would have been
raised to be a stranger to me and his first smile would have been
to his wet nurse. But since I am imprisoned and he – as innocent
as me – is incarcerated too, we are like little birds in a cage, singing and preening together, as happy as my linnets.

He nestles against me at night, he sleeps in my arms. I learn
to wake and listen to his quiet rapid breathing. Sometimes he
lies so still that I put my ear to his tiny button nose to convince

myself that he is alive and well, and that in the morning he will open his eyes, as blue as speedwell, and smile at me.

They tell me he is a good baby. Indeed, he never cries. But they tell me that I spoil him, by picking him up as soon as he stirs, by carrying him with me from one room to another, by holding him on my lap when I read or write, putting him to my plump breasts as soon as he pummels his little face into my bodice. The milk springs easily; the love comes, too. This is a happiness that I never dreamed could be. I did not know that it was possible to love a child so much that his birth is a delight and his life is a miracle, and nothing, nothing will ever make me regret him.

We call him Teddy. I put a blue ribbon from my window every morning so that his father, when he looks down from his own window, shall see that his son is well. I wish he could see what a handsome boy he is going to be. I wish he could see how the two of us, just as Janey promised, have made a baby of exquisite beauty. He has my fair hair and dainty features, he has Ned's long lean body. He is fit to be a prince. Of course, he is a prince. He is Elizabeth's heir and the next in line for the throne of England, whether she acknowledges him or not.

There were no Christmas gifts for this little boy from the court that he will command. Only Mary visits me, bringing a little music box that I recognise from the great receiving room at Hampton Court.

'I stole it,' she says frankly, winding it up and setting it before Teddy, who pays no attention at all.

'Mary!'

'I don't consider her to be the owner of the royal treasures,' she says bluntly. 'They're more yours than hers. If you are to be overlooked as the heir for having a child out of wedlock, why should I serve a queen that everyone knows is a Dudley whore? Born of the Boleyn whore?'

At once, I glance to the door but there is no waiting spy today.

'Exactly, nobody has come with me but Thomas Keyes, the sergeant porter, who was good enough to walk with me. He's waiting downstairs.'

'He's not listening?' I ask nervously.

'He does not spy on me. He is a true friend,' she says. She climbs up into one of the tatty chairs and shakes her head. 'It's all changed again. There's no spy on me. They don't care what you say any more. They accept that you acted in love and there is no plot to discover. They've given up questioning and they have released all the prisoners but you and Ned.'

I am so pleased, I clasp my hands together. 'They accept my marriage? We are to be released?'

'No, I think the plan is to deny it, and shame you.'

The disappointment is no surprise. I think I had known this was coming when they changed the questioning last year. But with a son in my arms and my husband under the same roof, I hardly care what people say about me. I know the truth, and I know what Ned is to me and I to him, and God knows. Who cares what Elizabeth says? As soon as we are free we can remarry and who will care then?

'Will they deny our marriage and then will she let us go?'

Neither of us needs to say who 'she' is. Elizabeth has become a monster in my mind. One Tudor queen took my sister, the other will take my good name.

Mary makes a little gesture with her hand that says maybe yes, maybe no. 'She'd do anything to keep you locked up, but she's running out of reasons. They reported the interrogations of the Seymours and of Aunt Bess, and of you and Ned, to the Privy Council, and it was obvious that the two of you married secretly for love. They looked for the minister who married you, but couldn't find him. I don't think they looked very hard. But anyway, you had exchanged vows and you have a ring. It's a private marriage. Elizabeth's mother had little more. The Privy Council have waited for days for her to invent some crime, or make up a law that she can claim that you have broken, but she says nothing.'

'Why doesn't she speak?'

Mary's pretty face is twisted with malicious giggles. 'Because she's afraid,' she whispers. 'Terrified. Half the country would prefer Mary Queen of Scots as Queen of England because they're papists, and the other half, the Protestant half, would prefer you now that you're married to an Englishman and have a son and heir. Nobody really wants her, a barren queen, especially one who is in love with a wife murderer.'

I give a little gasp at Mary's bitter description of Elizabeth and her lover, Robert Dudley.

'Well, they don't,' she says bluntly. 'And who can blame them? There's no more prosperity for the country than when Mary was on the throne, there's no greater peace. Now we're threatened by both France and Spain and our queen won't marry to get us an ally. Everyone has their own preference for the heir, and all Elizabeth has said is that we can't inherit because our father was executed for treason, and our cousin Margaret Douglas can't inherit because her parents weren't married. That leaves only Mary Queen of Scots, and she won't name her! What the people want is to know where they are, and who will be the next king, and if she won't tell them, then they'll decide for themselves.'

I glance towards the cradle. 'Teddy,' I say simply. 'It has to be Teddy. I come after Elizabeth, and Teddy is my son.'

'Of course,' Mary says. 'Everyone knows that. Which is why the Privy Council can't bring themselves to agree that she can keep you in prison for nothing. For all they know you're the mother of the next King of England. D'you remember what it was like as Queen Mary came towards London and all of Jane's court ran off towards her to tell her they were mistaken?' She laughs harshly. 'How very, very sorry they were?'

'I ran, too,' I tell her. 'Or at any rate, my father-in-law and husband did.'

'Mother ran. Father ran. Everyone begged her pardon. I was dragged along to make my curtsey. That's what Elizabeth fears. Everyone has to be friends with the heir, it stands to reason. So nobody dares to move against you until they are certain that you will never be the heir, and she won't say that either.' She puts her head on one side. 'Equally, no-one dares to speak for you for fear of her bad temper.'

'She can't disinherit me,' I say.

'She doesn't even dare to try. She speaks against us privately, but she would never bring it before parliament or even before the Privy Council. But Teddy . . .'

'The only way to disinherit Teddy would be to say that he was a bastard,' I say slowly.

'Exactly,' Mary says. 'So that's what that evil Tudor witch is going to do next.' She leans over the cradle as if she would be a good fairy against the evil fairy of the story. 'She's going to try to make out that this innocent boy is a bastard and unfit to inherit. It's the only way she can deny that he is her heir – declare him a bastard. That from her, who is a bastard known.'

Mary is quite right. In February when the ice is white on the inside of the window every morning and it is dark for twelve hours every day, Sir Edward taps on the door of my room and comes in with a bow.

'Your ladyship,' he says, by way of avoiding my maiden or my married name.

'Sir Edward?'

'I have come to tell you that you are bidden to Lambeth Palace tomorrow to be questioned by the archbishop himself.'

'What is he going to ask me?'

Sir Edward looks embarrassed. 'About the pretended marriage,' he says quietly.

'I don't know of any pretended marriage,' I say frostily.

He gestures to the paper in his hand. I see the royal seal and Elizabeth's own looping signature. 'It is called a pretended marriage here,' he says.

I smile at him, inviting him to see the bitter joke. 'It sounds like a very fair inquiry, doesn't it?' I say.

He bows his head. 'Your husband is to go, too,' he says quietly. 'But you are to travel in separate boats and not see each other.'

'Tell him that I love him,' I say. 'And tell him that I will never deny him, our love or our son.'

'You say your love?' he prompts me.

'My love and our marriage,' I say wearily. 'No-one will ever trick me into denying the truth.'

Matthew Parker – now honoured with the archbishopric of Canterbury as his reward for being one of the few churchmen who could bring themselves to support Elizabeth – was among those that put my sister Jane on the throne, but I don't expect him to favour me and defy the queen now. He married his wife the very moment that clergymen were released from their vows of celibacy, but I don't expect him to defend my marriage either. He was appointed by Elizabeth and he will never defy her. I won't find justice in the archbishop's palace at Lambeth, any more than in the Privy Council.

But the people of London are on my side. As my barge rushes out of the watergate with a swirl of dark river water and starts to beat upstream, I can see people pausing on the banks, peering towards the barge, and then, faintly, I can hear them shouting over the cold grey water.

The time chosen for my appointment was carefully judged to avoid this. The tide is flowing upstream and the barge goes swiftly with an icy wind behind it, but it is not fast enough to outpace the news that Lady Katherine, the bride of handsome Ned Seymour, is out of the Tower at last and going to Lambeth. By the time the rowers feather their oars to bring us alongside the quay at the palace, everyone on the horse ferry is crowded over to the side nearest my barge, and everyone on the riverbank and quayside is cheering wildly for me.

I stand up so that they can see me. I wave my hand.

'My lady, please come this way,' the archbishop's steward says nervously, but he cannot prevent me smiling to the crowd and acknowledging the shouted blessings.

'Fear nothing!' someone screams at me.

'God bless you and your bonny boy!'

'God save the queen!' someone else shouts, but they don't say who they mean.

I wave as if I take the blessing to myself and I go as slowly as I dare into the dark archway of the palace, so that everyone can see that I am a prisoner going in to questioning, that I am young – I am still only twenty-one – that I am beautiful. I am – as I have always been, as I always will be – the rightful heir for Queen of England, sister to the sainted Queen Jane, and now everyone is starting to think this, too.

LAMBETH PALACE, LONDON, WINTER 1562

I knew Archbishop Parker when he was all but chaplain to Jane's father-in-law, John Dudley. He and other reformers met constantly to discuss the theology of the reformed Church of England and Jane was in correspondence with their religious advisors. I dare say he never noticed me, I was so much the unimportant younger sister, but I remember him at Jane's court when she was proclaimed queen, and I remember him fading away as fast as the others, sliding from the Protestant queen to the papist – despite all his promises. Then I didn't think much of him as an advisor to a saint, and I don't think much of him as an archbishop now.

He has the impertinence to keep me waiting in his privy chamber, and when he comes in there is a dark-faced clerk with him, who sits down at a table without asking my permission, dips his nib in a pot of ink and waits to write down everything that I am to say. If I had failed to observe that they sent a discreet barge to fetch me, which flew no standard, if I had overlooked the chilly anteroom, and the cool greeting from my sister's one-time friend and co-religionist, I would know, from the poised nib of his clerk, that this is not a conversation between a spiritual advisor and a young woman who has had the misfortune to displease a bad-tempered queen. This is an interrogation, and he has been told exactly what to report. His difficulty – though he doesn't know it yet – is that I am never going to deny my honourable marriage, forswear the man I love, or condemn my child the viscount to a new title of Ned Seymour's by-blow.

Archbishop Parker looks at me gravely. 'You had better tell me all about this pretended marriage,' he says kindly. 'You had better confess to me, child.'

I take a breath to speak and I see the leap of hope in his face. If he can go back to Elizabeth and tell her that I have confessed to him that I am unmarried, that I was never married, then she will be pleased with him and continue to ignore the half-hidden presence of his own loyal wife, though she hates the idea of a married clergy. If he can tell her that I have a little ailing bastard in the Tower then she need not feel rushed into marriage and childbed herself. If he can assure her that the reform cause has no son and heir then she can promise Mary Queen of Scots that the inheritance of England is still unsettled, and dangle before that young woman the prospect of peace and inheritance.

'I will confess to you,' I say sweetly, and see the clerk dip the nib of his quill pen and wait, hardly breathing. 'Though I believe, my lord, that you and my sister Jane agreed that a trou-bled soul should confess directly to God?' I give him a moment to note that; and then I continue: 'However that might be, I confess that I loved a young man of noble birth and that both his mother and mine knew that we were in love and intended to marry. They were going to ask the queen for her permission when my mother died. I confess that we were betrothed before a witness, and then married before a witness, and by a minister, but without the permission of the queen. I confess that we laid together in the married bed and he used me as a wife. I confess that we have a handsome boy baby who is as copper-headed and wilful as any Tudor. I confess that I cannot understand why I am imprisoned nor why you invite me to confess to you.'

It's a robust start to a questioning that goes on all day, and the clerk scribbles page after page as the archbishop takes me through everything I have answered before. Clearly, there is nothing illegal about what we did. Their only hope is that I break down and lie for my freedom. After a day of questioning it is the archbishop who is drawn and pale, and I am flushed and furious. He demands that I lie on oath, and I refuse. More than this, I despise him for trying to force me, a young woman newly risen from childbed, to name my son as a bastard and my husband as a blackguard.

'We will stop for the day. I must go to pray, and you – madam – should consider your obstinacy,' the archbishop says weakly.

I give him a little nod of the head, as if I am dismissing him, and I turn for the door. 'Yes, do pray,' I recommend to him.

'I will see you again the day after tomorrow, and I hope then you will give me a true account,' the archbishop says.

I pause at the door as my guard holds it open for me, and he can hear what I say and repeat it all over London if he wishes. 'I have told you the truth today,' I say clearly. 'I will tell you the same tomorrow or whenever you ask me. I was married in honour, and my son is Viscount Beauchamp.'

THE TOWER, LONDON, WINTER 1562

By pressing my cheek to the cold glass and colder lead of the window in the lieutenant's house, I can see the steps leading down from the green to the watergate, and I wait here, with my cheek getting more and more chilled, from dawn till sunrise, when I see the guard come from our front door to take Ned to the barge.

My love, the only man I will ever love, is between four guards, two leading the way, two following behind as if they think he would escape and leave me and his baby imprisoned. I guessed that they would take him to Archbishop Parker today, the very day after my testimony, and I turn from the window when he has gone, and I go to my Bible and lay my frozen face on it and pray that he is true to me.

Of course he could be true and still make some mistake that allows the archbishop to find against us. If Ned has forgotten the minister's furred robe or his foreign accent then his account will not tally with mine. If he thinks to protect my reputation by denying that we were lovers before our marriage, then they will seize on his lie. If we differ on any point then they will try to make out that the marriage was false and our story concocted to save face.

I can't help but fear this. It is such a long time ago! A year ago, and we snatched at the time together and were so rushed. I have lost the papers, and Ned never knew the name of the minister. We have lost Janey, who was our only witness and only friend. It is so likely that Ned will forget something – he has been to France and Burgundy and Italy since last year, and then suffered the shock of being summoned home. But I have his two rings, and I have his poem by heart. No-one could truly think that this was all invented. But no-one really cares for the truth. All they want to do is to make my son a bastard so that Ned and I and Teddy can be bundled out of sight and shamed and forgotten.

They keep Ned all day. It is fully dark by the time they bring him back, and then they don't return him to the lieutenant's house. I am waiting for him to turn in at the gate, and I have a candle at my window and I am going to wave to him. But I cannot see him at all at first, only the bobbing flames of the torches of his guards as they lead the way from the dark archway towards the high White Tower, where it stands, bleak against the night sky. But he halts as he comes out from the archway, and puts back his hood and looks directly up to my window. I hold my candle out of the window so he can see the tiny light guttering in the wind and know that it shines for him, that I am true to him as I trust that he is true to me.

They speak to him to make him go on, and he raises his hand to me and goes past the lieutenant's house, past my doorway and across the green to the looming tower. Up the steps he goes to the entrance doorway and it opens as he comes near and bangs shut behind him and I know that he has said something, or they have made something up that allows them to keep him in the royal prisons, confined in a cell. He's not in the lieutenant's house any more, like an honoured lord confined under house arrest. Now he is in the tower where they keep the traitors, and torture them, too.

For four days we go back and forth to the archbishop and each time that he has seen Ned he asks me about another detail: some of them are real, some of them fabricated, I am sure, and some I simply cannot remember or never knew. I feel more and more troubled and my early defiance melts into fear. I beg him to understand that we were married, that we undertook a marriage in good faith before God. I beg him to understand that if I cite God as my witness, I cannot lie. I am sister to Jane Grey – am I likely to take the Word of God in vain? I hear my voice change from scorn to pleading. The archbishop looks less and less anxious, and more and more like a man who is getting the answers he wants. The clerk scribbles faster and faster. I dare not think what is going to happen next.

THE TOWER, LONDON, SUMMER 1562

Nothing happens. Painfully, nothing happens at all. I just have to wait. I think of Jane, living in the Partridges' house, waiting and waiting for Queen Mary to forgive and release her, certain that Her Majesty would be bound to forgive and release her – and then the priest coming to tell her she would die the next morning. Some nights I wake in tears dreaming that I am Jane, and that my time of waiting is ending, and that this dawn I will have to make the short walk to the green. But then I roll over in my bed and reach for my baby in his cradle, rosy from crying, hungry for his feed, his feet kicking with impatience, and I put him to my breast and feel him suckle and know that here is powerful innocent life that cannot be murdered, and that one morning, one day, I am going to take this little baby out to his freedom.

My little sister Mary visits me with a basket of new asparagus. 'Someone gave me this from his garden,' she says vaguely, heaving it up on the table. 'I thought the lieutenant's cook might steam it for you with some fresh butter.'

'He will, thank you,' I say. I bend to kiss her and she hauls herself up onto the window seat. 'Is that Ned's window?' she asks, looking across at the White Tower where a blue scarf flutters from one of the hinges.

'Yes. He puts out a scarf to show me he is well in the morning, and I do the same,' I say. 'If he was ill he would put out a white scarf, and if he is released he will fly nothing.'

She nods. She does not ask what standard will be flown from the window for bad news. Nobody in the Tower wants to prepare for bad news. Only my sister Jane had the courage to look forward to her death and write to me of learning to die.

'The court is leaving London,' she says. 'I'm to go, too. She's not being unpleasant. You would think I was nothing to do with you and no kinswoman to her at all. She treats me as any one of her ladies. She likes any one of them better than me; she gives Thomasina the dwarf more attention. I go everywhere with the court and I dine with the ladies. She barely speaks to me and she often fails to see I am there. But she treats others far worse.'

'Oh, who does she treat worse?' I ask, intrigued.

'Our cousin Margaret Douglas for one,' Mary says quietly. 'She's under house arrest at the Charterhouse at Sheen, suspected of treason.'

I muffle my gasp with a hand to my mouth. 'Another cousin under arrest? And in our old house?'

'They say that she was trying to get her son Henry Stuart married to Mary Queen of Scots.'

'Was she?'

'Almost certainly; but why should she not? It would be a wonderful match for him, an adequate match for her, and an English king consort in Scotland would be better for us than a Frenchman.'

'Is the whole family arrested?'

'Her husband is held here, I think, in the Tower. But her son has disappeared.'

I put my hands to my head as if I would pull my own hair. 'What? This is madness.'

'I know,' Mary says gloomily. 'Elizabeth is crazed with fear like her father. And I have to serve her. And I have to go wherever she fancies.'

'If only you could get away,' I whisper.

Mary shakes her head. 'They'd use it against you. No, I'll go on progress and pretend to enjoy it.'

I put my hand over hers. 'Where are you going this year?'

'North. We're to stay at Nottingham and she's commanded a masque. Everyone is in it. Me, too. I play an angel of peace on a swing. The masque is called *Britain and the King*. It goes on for three days.'

'Heavens.'

'It opens with Pallas on a unicorn,' she says. 'Elizabeth, I suppose. Followed by two women on horseback, Prudence and Temperance. Next day: Peace. Last day: Malice is thrown down and we all sing.'

I can't help but laugh at her gloomy expression and dour description. 'I am sure it will be beautiful.'

'Oh, yes, there are to be lions and elephants and all sorts. But the point of it is two women united, the friendship between two women. And the other message is that British kings inherit by blood, they're not chosen.'

'What does she mean? Is she sending a message to Mary Queen of Scots?'

'She's trying to. Elizabeth is telling Queen Mary that they are monarchs of Britain together, they can rule together: Mary in the north, Elizabeth in the south, and that Mary will be a sister queen and heir. She's practically promising her the throne. She says it is passed by inheritance to the closest heir. Not by choice, not by religion, not by will.'

I take three strides across the little room till I am brought up short by the table. 'Finally, she dares to openly deny me.'

'Still not open, still not denial,' Mary says angrily. 'The masque is not to be performed before the people. Nobody would understand it unless they had a classical education – I've had to explain it to half the ladies. She doesn't have the courage to declare herself. She is putting you aside by getting that spaniel Archbishop Parker to do her work for her; she is announcing it in a masque. She wants the court to know that you are not her heir, that you are shamed, that your son is a bastard; but she does not dare tell the country.'

'Oh dear God, Mary, has the archbishop declared that my marriage is invalid?'

'He has. And called that poor baby a bastard.' Mary nods grimly towards the cradle where my innocent son sleeps quietly, not knowing that he is being robbed of his name. 'God forgive him. She hopes that nobody will speak in support of a woman taken in lust, and nobody will turn out for a bastard baby. You are ruined, and he is disinherited. Ned, of course, is shown to be dishonourable.'

I pick up one of the puppies, and hold it under my chin for comfort. 'The archbishop is a liar,' is all I say.

Mary nods. 'Everyone knows it.'

For a moment we sit in grim silence.

'And I have to dance in her rotten masque,' she spits. 'I am in the train of Pallas on the first day, and I sit on my swing and then dance for Peace on the last. She knows what she is doing when she makes my dancing send a message to that papist Mary.

Me! Jane Grey's sister sending a message of hope to a papist heir of England.'

'She knows what she is doing,' I agree. 'She has cured herself of her fear of us. You will never have a son, she's sure of that. And now nobody will support my son, named as a bastard to an unchaste mother.'

'Oh, she's won,' Mary says dismissively. 'We weren't even conspiring against her and she has worked against us as if we were the vilest of enemies. Margaret Douglas was nothing but fanciful talk and ambition for her son, but she is named as a traitor, too. She's not much of a kinswoman, our queen. There's little joy in being close to her. D'you think she will free you, now she has ruined you?'

I get up and go to the window.

'What are you doing?' she asks as I swing open the casement.

'I am hanging out a black ribbon,' I say quietly. 'For bad news. Because nobody is going to call for my release now.'

The court leaves London and I think of Mary sitting on her swing as an angel of peace, and dancing for Elizabeth in the masque, which tells Mary Queen of Scots that she – a papist, a Frenchwoman – is to be Elizabeth's heir and that we are to be forgotten. I think it is hard for me, here in the Tower with the man I love imprisoned a hundred yards from my window; but it is perhaps even harder for my sister Mary, in smiling service to a woman that she knows is my enemy, her enemy, the vindictive enemy of every woman that she sees as a rival.

The weather grows warmer and I open my windows at night and hear the blackbirds in the orchards singing sweetly later and later every evening, as they court and build their nests. I put bells around Ribbon's neck so that she cannot hunt the nestlings, and I put my crumbled breakfast bread on the windowsill every morning and watch for the robin that swoops in and struts before the pane of glass, showing his red breast and claiming his place.

In the evening I study, reading the books that Jane left behind here in the lieutenant's library, studying the Bible that she sent to me, rereading her letter to me, to her friends and teachers, seeing her as both my sister and a heroine. I am trying to find her courage, her sense of destiny, in myself. She always knew that her feet were on a holy road whether they led her to the throne or the scaffold; she always knew that she was walking towards God. I am afraid she must have found me very light and foolish. I know better now, and I wish I could tell her that I know better now.

Teddy is thriving and only wakes once in the night to feed. I ask the lieutenant if we can go outside in the warm summer air, so that he can feel the sunshine on his skin, and he says that my lady-in-waiting can walk him in the garden or by the river every day.

'Nobody has told me that the innocent babe is under arrest,' he says, and I think I hear the note of resentment in his quiet voice and I think – this is what it is to be in the service of Elizabeth. You start hopefully on a course and then you find that she goes further than makes sense, further than you can bear.

I go to bed early, and I lie in the twilight as the room slowly darkens, and I wonder what will happen when Mary Queen of Scots replies to the message of Elizabeth's masque. Can those two determined rivals really make peace together? Will they be – as Mary once offered – two queens in one isle? Will they really make a great meeting together, and become friends? Might Elizabeth finally have found the one person, an equal, that she can trust?

And if they do meet, make friends, fall in love with each other's majesty, will I decline into such obscurity that Elizabeth releases Ned and me from our imprisonment? Is my greatest ambition now to be forgotten by everyone who said that I should one day be a queen?

There is a tap on the outer door, and the key turns noisily in the lock. I get up from my bed, throw my robe around my shoulders and go to unbolt it. My maid sleeps with Teddy, and my lady-in-waiting comes in every day. There is no-one to open my door from the inside through the night but me. This is no hardship – nobody ever comes at night-time after the dinner has been served. This must be a guard with a message, I dare not hope it is a pardon.

'Who's there?' I call a little nervously, but I cannot hear the reply as I slide back the bolts and when I open the door there is a guard and a taller man with his hood pulled so far forward that I cannot see his face.

I go to slam the door but he puts out a quick hand. 'D'you not know me?' he whispers. 'Wife?'

It is Ned, it is Ned, it is Ned my husband, handsome and smiling. He gives a nod to the guard and pushes my door open. He sweeps me into his arms and kisses my face, my hair, my closed wet eyelids, my lips.

'Ned,' I gasp. I cannot catch my breath.

'My love. My wife.'

'You are free?'

'God! No! I have bribed the guard for an hour with you. Kitty, I love you so. I have never stopped loving you. God forgive me for leaving you. I should never have gone.'

'Oh, I know! I know! I should have been clearer. But I knew you would come back. Did you not get my letters?'

'No! I had no letters from you! I could not understand it! I had only one, when I was ordered back, and they told me you were with child and under arrest. I had no idea what to do. The French told me I was safer staying with them than going home to face Elizabeth. They begged me not to leave them, but I could not abandon you here.'

'You did not get my letters? I wrote! I wrote often, begging you to come home. They cannot have gone astray.'

We look at each other, the truth dawning on us, the realisation that we have been surrounded by enemies.

'Ned, I wrote so often, it cannot have been an accident. They must have been stolen.'

'We've been surrounded by spies from the first,' Ned says,

drawing me to the bedroom. He throws off his hooded robe, tears off his jacket, and shucks his shirt over his head. He is thinner from his imprisonment, and his skin is creamy pale in the twilight. I am at once breathless with a desire as urgent as his.

'Oh, but you must see Teddy!'

'I will, I will, but first I must see you. I have dreamed of you for so long.'

We are through the doorway and at the side of my bed. I have not a moment of hesitation. I throw back the covers and get in. Ned leans forward, naked to the waist, and strips off my nightgown over my head. I fling up my arms and it ripples away.

'You swore to the archbishop that we were married?'

'I did! I never let him say we were not.'

He laughs shortly. 'So did I. I knew you would not betray me.'

'Never. I will never deny you.'

I reach for him and he pulls down his hose and comes towards me. We are urgent, passionate. We have been parted for more than a year; we were new lovers then, we could not get enough of each other. I have dreamed of this moment and ached for his touch. He hesitates above me, looking down into my rapt face.

'My love,' I whisper to him, and he falls on me like a falcon stoops on a lure.

We have only an hour together and when he stumbles from my bed and I help him pull on his shirt it reminds me of our wedding day when we dressed each other, fumbling with the laces, and Janey and I had to hurry home for dinner.

'Now let me see my son!' he says.

I lead him into the maid's room where our baby sleeps in his cradle beside her bed. Her hand is still outstretched so that she can rock him when he stirs. He sleeps sweetly, on his back, his hands clenched in little fists above his head, his cheeks flushed, a rosy little blister from sucking milk on his top lip.

'Good God, he is so beautiful,' my husband whispers. 'I had no idea. I thought babies were ugly. He has all of your beauty: he is like a perfect little doll.'

'He is as stubborn as you,' I say. 'He's not much of a perfect doll when someone crosses him. He bellows for a feed like a hungry lord, and will not bear any delay.'

Carefully we tiptoe back to my chamber. 'You feed him yourself?'

'There was no-one else to do it!' I laugh at his shocked face. 'I have raised him as if I were a poor woman with a baby at the breast. I have given him my own milk and my own love, and he thrives on it.'

He kisses my hands, my lips, my face, he kisses me like a starving man who would taste everything. 'You are an angel. You have been an angel to him and to me. Tomorrow night I will come again.'

'You can come again?' I can hardly believe it. 'How?'

He gives his adorable chuckle that I have not heard for so long. 'Since we are publicly named as sinful lovers, it seems that we are allowed to be together, though we were parted when we were husband and wife. Sir Edward gave me the nod as if to say that since we are punished so cruelly for sin, we may as well enjoy it. I slip the guard a coin, and he brings me to you.'

'We can be together?' I don't care if we spend the rest of our lives in the Tower if we can sleep in each other's arms and he can see his son.

'It's not how I hoped we would live, but it is the best we can do for now,' he says. 'And still I have hopes. Elizabeth cannot defy all her advisors, and William Cecil and Robert Dudley know that we are innocent of everything but love. They are our friends. They want a Protestant heir to the throne, and we have him. They will work against Mary Queen of Scots; they will never accept her. I don't despair, my love.'

'Nor do I,' I say, my courage leaping up at his words. 'I don't despair. I will never despair if I can be with you.'

THE TOWER, LONDON, SUMMER 1562

Against all the odds, against the royal malice, we are happy. Ned's mother sends him his rents and fees from his lands and interests, and so he is a wealthy prisoner. He bribes the guards and orders whatever we want. He comes to my rooms every evening and we dine together, play with our baby, and make love. The daytime becomes a time of waiting, when I study, care for our child, and write letters to my friends at court. Sir Edward, the lieutenant of the Tower, allows me to walk in his garden and I take the baby with me and put him down on a shawl on the sun-warmed grass so that he can kick his feet and watch the seagulls circling in the blue sky above him.

The night is when my real life begins, when the guard quietly admits Ned to my room, and we talk and read together. He watches me feed our son, swaddle him on his board, and hand him to the maid for the night, and then we dine well on delicacies that his mother has sent from Hanworth and treats delivered to the Tower for free, gifts from the people of London.

Every day Ned or I have a note or a letter from someone promising their support if we appeal against our sentence. Some of them promise that if we escape we shall find a haven. One or two even offer to raise an army and free us. All of them we burn at once, and never even speak of them. Elizabeth has ruled that we are sinners, she must not invent any worse crime to pin on us. We will not give her any excuse for a trial for treason.

But in any case, she is not attending to us this summer. Perhaps she thinks she has done all she can to ruin us and has turned her attention to other quarrels. She has arrested her dearest friend and lady-in-waiting Kat Ashley for recommending the suit of Prince Erik of Sweden. Elizabeth is more offended now by Kat recommending marriage than she was when Kat warned her that she was seen as a whore. Who can predict what will alert Elizabeth's fears? Nobody knows what she will do next. She has become so frightened and so cruel that she has imprisoned her own beloved governess, the woman whom she says was like a mother to her.

'On what charge?' I demand of Ned.

'No charge,' he replies. 'There is no charge. Elizabeth does not live within her own law. Kat Ashley is arrested on a whim. God knows what will become of her. Perhaps Elizabeth will name her crime, or perhaps she will be held for a few days, and then released and restored to favour. Maybe Elizabeth will order our release in the same letter.'

There are several of us, held for no reason, charged with nothing, victims of Elizabeth's jealousy or fears. My cousin Margaret Douglas is suffering interrogation, accused in a dozen muddled reports of spies, kept under close house arrest. Her husband, Matthew Stuart Earl of Lennox, is held here, somewhere in the Tower. We have never even seen him, either walking on the roofs or even looking out of a window. I am afraid that he is kept alone, and I know that he will fail under that sort of treatment. He has never been a favourite of the queen and his wife is a rival heir. He has not the spirit to survive the enmity of Elizabeth. Their son Henry Stuart is also too fragile to face her; it is as well for him that he has escaped to France. The court is buzzing with gossip that Cousin Margaret hired necromancers and soothsayers, that she has predicted Elizabeth's death, that she urged Mary Queen of Scots to marry Henry Stuart and unite England and Scotland under his rule—

'What?' I interrupt Ned. 'How does Elizabeth tolerate this? If Margaret has done all this, why is she kept at Sheen, as if she were guilty of some minor rudeness, while we are under lock and key in here, for doing so much less?'

'If they prove the necromancy charge against her they could burn her for a witch,' he says soberly. 'I don't begrudge her Sheen, if they are building such a case against her. They can take her from the Charterhouse at Sheen to Smithfield without even a trial if they prove she has used a witch to predict the death of the queen.'

The baby is in my arms, suckling and sleeping. He stirs as I tighten my grip on him. 'Could Elizabeth really bring herself to kill her own cousin?' I ask him very quietly. 'Could she bring herself to do such a thing?'

He shakes his head. He does not know what she might do. We none of us know what she might do.

'I have news for you,' I say, breaking the silence. 'I have something to tell you tonight. I hope it will make you happy.'

He serves me some early strawberries, a gift from a nameless friend, from the fields of Kent.

'Tell me.'

'I have missed my course and I think I am with child.' I try to smile but my lips are trembling. I am so afraid that he will be angry, that this will bring us into more trouble. But he drops his spoon, comes around the table and kneels at my side and takes me in his arms. This time his joy is unalloyed. He holds me, and little Teddy, in one warm embrace.

'This is the best news, the best news I could hear,' he says. 'To think that you are so well and so fertile, and I am so strong that we should conceive a child inside this terrible place that has seen so much death. Thanks be to God who has brought light out of darkness! It's like a miracle. It's like pushing back death itself to make a baby inside the prison walls.'

'You are really happy?' I confirm.

'God be my witness! Yes! This is wonderful news.'

'Shall we tell Sir Edward?'

'No,' he decides. 'We'll tell no-one. We'll keep it a secret like you did before. Can you hide it from your maid? From your ladies?'

'If I stay as slim as I did before, then nobody will know until the last months,' I say. 'I hardly showed at all before.'

'Let's choose when and where we tell,' he says. 'This is a powerful secret that you hold, let's save it to use as best we can. Oh, my love, I am so glad. Do you feel well? Do you think it is another boy?'

I laugh. 'Another heir for Elizabeth? Do you think she will be pleased to have another little royal kinsman?'

His smile hardens. 'I think she cannot go on denying our sons, and if we have two that makes the point twice over.'

'And if we have a girl?'

He takes my hand and kisses it. 'Then we will call her Katherine-Jane for her beautiful mother and her sainted aunt, and God bless all three of you, my daughter, her mother and her aunt, all wrongfully imprisoned here.'

THE TOWER, LONDON, SUMMER 1562

It gets hotter in the city and I am afraid of the plague. There is always illness in the summer, this is why the court goes on progress – so that the palaces can be cleaned and Elizabeth can hurry her barren body far away from any sickness. This is the first year that I have spent in London in summertime, and the stink from the river and from the moat around the Tower fills me with dread. You don't need to be a great physician to recognise the smell of disease. London smells of death and I am afraid to breathe the air.

Elizabeth's childhood friend and lady-in-waiting Kat Ashley is moved from the Tower for her safety. She is still in disgrace but Elizabeth won't let her beloved Kat be in the least danger. But we are left here to take our chances with the pestilential mists from the drains and the river. She leaves my baby here – where she knows there is disease.

'Should I write to William Cecil and ask him to move us?' I ask Ned one evening.

He has the baby in his arms and is singing him a little poem of his own making. The baby is cooing with pleasure as if he understood the rhyming words, his dark blue eyes fixed on his father's loving face.

'Not till we have news from court,' he says, glancing up at me. 'There are great changes happening and they will affect us. The queen was trying to make an alliance with the Queen of Scots, but in France there has been a terrible attack on the reformers. The Protestants are in open rebellion against the ruling Guise family and they are appealing to Elizabeth for her help. She was planning to meet with Queen Mary but now I think she cannot. Not even Elizabeth has the gall to publicly befriend a woman whose family are executing Protestants. When Elizabeth comes back to London in the autumn, the preachers and parliament will force her to agree that she cannot ally with France when they are stained with the blood of our faith. It is Mary of Scotland's own kinsmen, the Guise family, who have put men and women of our church to the sword in a merciless killing. Elizabeth cannot take England into an alliance with a daughter of Guise. Nobody would ever accept it.'

'If she gives up her alliance with Mary then there is no-one to be her heir but Margaret or me,' I observe.

'And his little lordship here,' his father says. 'If you will be so good as to pass your right to him. Lord Beauchamp is the next man in line. See how sternly he looks at me? He's going to make a great king.'

'She has named him as a bastard,' I say with steady resentment.

'Everyone knows it is a lie,' his father, my husband, says. 'I don't even consider it.'

THE TOWER, LONDON,
SUMMER 1562

The court returns to the palace at Hampton Court in the late summer and decides, reluctantly, that England must defend the reformers of France. Elizabeth despairs of an alliance with Mary Queen of Scots and screws up her courage to order the reinforcement of Le Havre to protect the Huguenot Protestants from the Guise army. Everyone expects Robert Dudley to command the English force, and there is much muttering of favouritism when the queen insists he stays at home, and sends his brother Ambrose in his place. Robert Dudley is too precious for her to risk, even in the sacred cause of a war to defend the country's religion.

This war could be the saving of us. Elizabeth is almost certain to release Ned to command a troop.

'The Earl of Lennox would be very glad to be released too,' Sir Edward, my gaoler, confides in me. 'Poor gentleman, he does not have the temperament to tolerate confinement.'

'I should think nobody enjoys it,' I say irritably.

'He complains very much at your husband's freedom, and that you can meet. He misses his own wife, Lady Margaret, very much. He weeps for loneliness in his room at night.'

'Then he should not have conspired against the queen,' I say primly.

'If he did so.'

'Yes, of course. But what is wrong with him?'

The lieutenant leans towards me, as if anyone can hear him but Mr Nozzle on my shoulder and Teddy in my arms.

'He is quite distracted, poor gentleman. He scrabbles at the door and cries for his wife. He says that the walls are closing in on him and begs me to open the windows.'

'He is going mad?' I ask.

'He's not right,' Sir Edward confirms. 'Some people cannot stand it, you know. And not all prisoners live as merrily as you and his lordship.'

'We're very grateful,' I say. It is true. We are as happy as the linnets in their cage, my husband, his baby, and me. And now I have the added joy of knowing that there is a new baby on the way as well.

THE TOWER, LONDON, AUTUMN 1562

I wait for a visit from my little sister, Mary, with increasing confidence that she will come and tell me that we are to be released, but she does not come. She sends me a note to say that they are still at Hampton Court and the queen has taken to her bed with some illness, the physicians have been called, but nobody knows what is wrong with her.

'No, it is worse than that, she is fatally ill,' Ned whispers, coming to my room early, kissing his son and handing him back to the maid. 'Come here,' he says, drawing me to the window seat where we can talk privately. Mr Nozzle leaps up and sits solemnly between us.

'Fatally ill? I thought she was just dropsical again?'

'I have friends at court who send me the news. It's serious, very serious. Kitty, the queen has taken smallpox. It is true: smallpox, and she is unconscious. Right now, she cannot speak or move. For all we know, she may have already died. She may be dead right now. The Privy Council is in emergency meeting.

I am getting messages all the time. They are trying to choose a successor if Elizabeth dies.'

'If she dies?' I choke on the words. She has been such a curse and a blight on my life that I can hardly imagine a world without her. 'Dies? Elizabeth might die?'

'Yes! Don't you hear me? She could die. It seems unthinkable, but it is more than likely. She has the smallpox, and she is not strong. She has taken to her bed and her fever is rising. The Privy Council has been summoned. They have to choose an heir if she will not speak. She is dumb with fever, she is wandering in her mind. They are calling for Henry Hastings, they are calling for Mary Queen of Scots or for Margaret Douglas.' He pauses, he smiles at me, his eyes are bright. 'But mostly, of course, they are calling for you.'

I take a breath. I think of the day that Jane was offered the crown and knew that she had to take it.

'Me,' I say flatly. I think of Jane and the terrible danger of ambition, I think of the temptation of the crown and the prospects for my son.

'Henry VIII's will names your mother's line after Elizabeth,' he says steadily. 'Not Margaret Douglas's mother, not the Scots line; your mother, and then you. Elizabeth said that inheritance should follow the natural order, but the Privy Council is not going to make Mary Queen of Scots, half a Guise, the Queen of England when we are at war with France and her family. The old king Henry's will named your line. King Edward's will named Jane and then you. There is only one Tudor Protestant successor. It's you. Everything points to you.'

I think. I take a breath and think of my son, and the baby that should be born a prince. My imprisonment has sharpened my ambition. I will not suffer for being an heir and not claim my throne. 'I am ready,' I say, though my voice trembles a little. 'I am ready. I can wear my sister's crown.'

He exhales as if he is relieved that I know my duty to my country, that I am prepared to take my place on the throne. 'Elizabeth could be dead right now, and they could be bringing you the crown. They could be on the barge from Hampton Court and coming down with the tide.'

'Coming to me here, in the Tower?'

'Here in the Tower.'

I think how terribly unlucky it would be to start my reign where Jane started and ended hers. And then I think what a trivial stupid thought this is. I should be preparing my speech for when they come to tell me that Elizabeth is dead. 'Could there be a war?' I demand. 'If I took the throne, would the papists rise against me?'

He frowns. 'Almost certainly not. They would have no support. Mary Queen of Scots can't invade us while France is in uproar, and her family cannot send French troops to support her. Margaret Douglas writes a war of letters but has no army, and no support in the country. She is under arrest herself and her husband is crying at the bars on his window, no help to her. Henry Hastings is from the old royal family and has no support. There is no-one else. This must be your time. This must be the very time for you.' He nods to the maid's closed door. 'And for him. The heir apparent.'

There is a quiet tap on the door and I leap to my feet, knocking the table and spilling the wine. 'Is it now?' I ask. I can feel my heart hammering and I think of the baby, safe and silent in my belly, and his brother just next door. I think that we are the new royal family and they may be bringing me the crown.

Ned crosses the room in three strides and opens the door. The guard is there, another man with him. 'A messenger, my lord,' the guard says respectfully. 'Said he had to see you.'

'You did right to bring him to me,' Ned says easily. The guard steps back and the messenger comes into the room.

I cannot take my eyes from the scroll in his hand. Perhaps it has the royal seal, perhaps it is the Privy Council informing me of the death of Elizabeth and telling me that they are on their way.

Ned holds out a peremptory hand. The messenger gives him

the scroll. It is a short scrawled message. 'Says I am to trust you,' Ned says to the man. 'What's the news?'

'The queen has named Robert Dudley.'

'What?' Ned's exclamation is so loud, his shock is so great, that I hear Teddy wail in the maid's room and she opens the door and peeps out.

'Nothing! Nothing!' I command, waving her back to the baby. I turn to the messenger. 'You must be mistaken. That cannot be.'

'Named him as Protector of the Realm, and the Privy Council have sworn to support him.'

Ned and I exchange incredulous looks.

'It's not possible,' I whisper.

'What does your master say?' Ned demands.

The man grins. 'Says that they won't argue with a dying woman but that your wife should be ready.' He turns to me and makes the deep bow for a royal. 'Says it can't be long. Nobody would support a Dudley, and nobody will have another Protector. The queen is out of her mind with fever. By naming Robert Dudley she has given the Privy Council the right to crown who they please. She is beyond reason; they cannot reason with her. Nobody will ever give the crown to him. The queen has denied her own line, she is a traitor to her own throne. Everyone knows it has to be Lady Hertford.' He bows to me again.

Ned nods, thinking fast. 'Nothing to be done until the queen has gone, God bless her,' he says. 'Any move we make can only be then. We are her loyal subjects as long as she draws breath. We will pray for her recovery.'

'Yes,' the man says. 'I'll get back to Hampton Court and tell my lord that you understand. You'll hear as soon as there is any more news.'

'We live in extraordinary times,' Ned says, almost to himself. 'Times of wonders.'

Of course we cannot sleep. We don't even lie on the bed together and kiss. We can't eat. We are both of us incapable of doing anything but walking fretfully around the two rooms and looking out of the window into the dark garden in case there is a torch bobbing towards us. I change my gown so that I look my best when the lords come with the crown. I put a cloth over the linnets so that they go to sleep and don't sing. The dogs are quiet in their box and I put Mr Nozzle into his cage. Without a presence chamber, without a court, we are as dignified as we can be. I sit in the one good chair and Ned stands behind me. We cannot stop ourselves posing, like actors in a masque, playing the part of majesty even while the messenger may be riding towards us to tell us that the script is ready, the play-acting has become real.

'I will reward the lieutenant of the Tower,' I remark.

'Not a word,' Ned cautions me. 'We are praying for the recovery of the queen, God bless her.'

'Yes,' I agree. I wonder if it is wrong to outwardly pray for someone and secretly hope that they die. I wish I could ask Jane: it is just the sort of thing she knows. But really, how can I want Elizabeth to live, when she has been such an enemy to me, and to my innocent son?

'I am praying for her,' I tell Ned. I think I will pray that she goes directly to heaven, and that there is no purgatory; for if there were, she would never escape.

We hear the first trill of birdsong, loud in our silent room, and then one by one the songbirds start to call for the day. A thrush sings a ripple of song, loud as a flute. I stir in my seat, and see that Ned is looking out of the window. 'It's dawn,' he says. 'I have to go.'

'With no message!'

'Any messenger will find me easily enough,' he says wryly. 'I'm going nowhere. I will be locked into my cell in the Tower. And if the message comes for you then they will send for me as soon as they have told you ...' He trails off. 'Remember, if anyone asks, you prayed all night for her health,' he says. 'You were here alone.'

317

'I will say that. And really, I did.' I cross my fingers behind my back on the half-lie. 'Will you come tomorrow night?'

He takes me in his arms. 'Without fail. Without fail, beloved. And I will send you any news that I hear. Send your lady-in-waiting to me at dinner time and I will whisper to her anything that I have heard from Hampton Court.' He opens the door and then hesitates. 'Don't be misled by gossip,' he says. 'Don't leave your room unless the Privy Council themselves come to you. It would be fatal if you were seen to accept the crown, and then Elizabeth recovered.'

I am so afraid of her that I actually feel a shudder at the thought of making such a mistake and having to face her with a genuine accusation of treason against me. 'I won't! I won't!' I promise him. I swear to myself that I will never be queen for nine days like my sister. I will be queen for the rest of my life or not at all. I cannot make it happen one way or another. Everything depends on the strength of a sickly woman of nearly thirty years old, fighting one of the most dangerous diseases in the world.

'And pray for her health,' Ned says. 'Make sure that people see you praying for her.'

We hear the door below open and the guard whisper hoarsely up the stairs: 'My lord?'

'Coming,' Ned replies. He gives me one hungry kiss on the mouth. 'Till tonight,' he promises me. 'Unless something happens today.'

I have to wait all day. The lieutenant of the Tower, Sir Edward, comes to visit me and finds me on my knees before my Bible. 'You will have heard that the queen is sick,' he says.

I get to my feet. 'I have been praying for her all day. God bless her and give her strength,' I say.

'God bless her,' he repeats, but his half-hidden glance

towards me shows me that we both know that if she slides from
unconsciousness into death then there will be a new Queen of
England and the little boy in the cradle will be Edward Prince
of Wales.

'You may like to walk in the garden,' Sir Edward offers.

I incline my head. 'We'll go now.'

I cannot sit still, and I may not go anywhere. I cannot concentrate on reading and I don't dare to daydream. 'Lucy, bring
Teddy's ball.'

I wait and I wait, starting up every time I hear the challenge
from the gatehouse and the big gates creak open, but there is
no more news from Hampton Court. Elizabeth is locked in a
long silent battle for her life, and the Privy Council are trading
favours to choose the heir to the throne. Nobody will consent to
Elizabeth's nomination of Robert Dudley for Protector. Dudley
himself – with his own father buried in the Tower in the chapel,
beheaded for treason – knows that it cannot be, though I swear
that his eager ambition, Dudley ambition, must have leaped up
when he first heard of it.

He will be favouring his family's candidate: Henry Hastings,
who married the Dudley girl in the round of weddings that saw
Jane and I married off to reinforce Dudley power. Even now,
eight years after Jane's death, the old Dudley plot for the throne
rolls on like a great watermill wheel incapable of stopping, that
turns one wheel and then another and then the great grinding
stone that shakes the whole building. The plot is set in motion,
the water flows, the mill wheel turns; but nobody will support
Dudley.

Nobody will openly support Mary Queen of Scots. She
is a papist and her kinsmen are making war on Huguenot
Protestants and mustering to fight English soldiers in Le
Havre. Overnight she has become England's enemy and she

will never recover her reputation as a ruler who will tolerate our religion. Very few people favour Margaret Douglas. For all that she is of the royal family she is widely known as a papist, imprisoned for the most diabolical of crimes. Nobody would accept such a woman as Queen of England. There is no-one else of blood royal and of the reformed religion but me. No-one else whose line was named by the king's will. I shall wear my sister's crown.

All day I hear this, like plainsong, in my head, as I play with Teddy in the garden and help him to stand and let him jump on my lap. All day I hear over and over again: 'I shall wear my sister's crown, I shall fulfil her dream. I shall complete the task that Jane started and there will be rejoicing in heaven.'

At dinner time I send my lady-in-waiting to wait on my husband. I send a basket of peaches by way of a gift and she takes them to his dinner table. She comes back to me, her lips compressed as if she is holding in a secret.

'My lady, I have a message.'

'What is it?' I hear in my head: I shall wear my sister's crown, I shall fulfil her dream.

'My lord said to tell you – thank God – that the queen has recovered. She has come out of her swoon and the spots have broken on her skin. He said God be praised she is better.'

'God be praised,' I repeat loudly. 'Our prayers have been answered. God bless her.'

I turn and go into the house, leaving Teddy with the maid, though he calls after me and raises his arms to be lifted up. I cannot let anyone see the bitterness in my face. She has recovered, that false kinswoman, that evil queen. She has recovered and I am still here in prison and no-one is going to come and set me free. Nobody is coming to crown me today.

THE TOWER, LONDON,
WINTER 1562

Elizabeth recovers as if the devil himself was nursing her with satanic tenderness. Jane's sister-in-law, who was Mary Dudley, nearly dies taking the pox from Elizabeth, and loses her famous beauty. I have no pity for her. It was she who took Jane by barge to Syon on the night that they made her queen. It was an ill-advised journey: and now Jane is dead and Mary will spend the rest of her life hiding her scarred face from the world, as if Dudley ambition has blasted their daughter's beauty.

The queen has recovered, but the country is in turmoil. Everyone knows that she was near death and no heir named, and now word is rapidly spreading, from the great houses of London into the streets, that she tried to make a traitor's son, a traitor's grandson, into the Protector of the kingdom. Our queen tried to make her lover into a tyrant like Richard III. People are horrified that she would fail in her duty by dying without naming an heir, and then betray her country to a favourite. People speak of other royal favourites and the danger of an unsteady king. Ned gets a stream of messages from his friends and my supporters who are guests at private dinners held in secret by the reformist lords, who swear that an heir must be named to the throne of England, and it must be me.

'William Cecil is determined that you shall be named as heir,' Ned promises me. 'He says that no-one has a better claim, either by religion or inheritance, that Elizabeth knows this, that everyone knows this. He says that you must be released. Everyone agrees.'

'Then why are we still here?' I ask.

We are seated together in my room, enfolded in the shabby chair that once served as Jane's throne. We are both half-undressed, warm from the bed, wrapped in a rug before the fire, sated with kissing and touching.

'I have to say that I've been in worse places.' He gathers me closely to him.

'I would spend every evening of my life with you like this,' I say, 'but not under lock and key. Elizabeth has freed Margaret Douglas and her husband, the Earl of Lennox. Why not us?'

'They're not freed,' he corrects me. 'He's been released to live with her but they're still under arrest. Elizabeth had to let him go to his wife because he cannot bear imprisonment.'

'I cannot bear imprisonment!' I exclaim. 'Perhaps she will let us go to live under house arrest. We could ask for it, if they will not agree to free us completely. I could have my baby under your roof at Hanworth.'

'When we are freed, I will never come back here again. Only once a year to lay a flower on the tombs of our family,' Ned promises.

'Not even for my coronation? It is the tradition.'

'We will make a new tradition,' he says. 'I am not having my son inside these walls again.' Gently he touches my rounded belly. 'Neither of them.'

'I like Windsor Castle best,' I say sleepily.

'Hampton Court,' Ned rules. 'And perhaps we shall build a new castle.'

'A new palace,' I correct him. 'We won't need a castle. The country will be at peace. We can build beautiful palaces and houses and live as a royal family among our people.'

'A godly peace at last,' he says.

'Amen.' I pause for a moment, thinking of a new beautiful palace that we might call Seymour Court. 'It will happen, won't it?' I ask. 'For we have had so many hopes and so much trouble.'

He considers. 'Really, I think this time that it has to. She truly has no other credible heir and this time she has gone too far even for her friends and advisors.'

THE TOWER, LONDON,
WINTER 1562

Ned and I have a prisoners' Christmas with gifts brought in from the city, and green boughs from the governor's garden. We eat like princes. The people of London leave presents at the gateway of the Tower every day: food and little fairings. I am so touched that they send gifts for Teddy. A London silversmith sends him a spoon with our family crest of angel wings engraved on the handle; a toymaker sends him a wooden hobby horse. He is most excited by this, though he does not yet have the skill to walk with it held between his legs. Instead he pushes it before him wherever he goes and commands me to say 'Gee up'. All he can say is 'Hee!' and his father complains that his first words should be '*À Seymour!*'

We dine alone, each in our own room, but Ned comes to my rooms as soon as the dishes have been cleared from his table and his servants have gone for the night. The guard lets him in and we go to bed for Christmas kisses. There has been no lovemaking since my belly grew big, but I rub my face against his naked chest and he strips me naked so that he can stroke the proud curve of my belly.

'Does it not hurt the child, strapping so tight?' he asks.

'I don't think so,' I say. 'I hid Teddy till the last months.'

'I am so glad to be with you this time.' He buries his face in my warm breasts. 'I must be the happiest man ever held in these walls.'

I chuckle. 'No carving in the stone? No counting of the days?'

'I pray for our release,' he says seriously. 'And I think it will come soon. The queen has to call a parliament if she wants money for her army in France. And the parliament will not grant her funds unless she names her successor. They have her trapped. All the lords of the Privy Council have been meeting privately ever since Twelfth Night and the strongest voices have been raised for you to be named as her heir.'

I breathe a sigh. 'They admit that we are married?'

'They always knew it,' he assures me. 'They just did not dare to deny her before. And in any case, they have made us both swear to our marriage before the Archbishop of Canterbury, who recorded that for the Queen of England. The Archbishop of Canterbury has heard our wedding vows. We could hardly be more married. Nobody can deny it now.'

I laugh out loud. 'I had not thought of that! What fools they are! To entrap themselves when they hoped to catch us.'

'Fools,' he says with the deep delight of a lover in the arms of his beloved. No-one else matters, no-one else is of value to the two of us, entwined in bed with the fire flickering on our half-naked bodies: 'Fools in a foolish world, exiles from this, our joy.'

THE TOWER, LONDON, SPRING 1563

Mary comes to see us, bringing me some fresh-baked little breads formed into the shape of men with currant eyes from the royal bakery for Teddy, her arms loaded with little gifts.

'Heavens, what are these?' I ask her.

She is laughing, spilling presents on the table. 'As I walked through the city people recognised me and gave me things for you. I was all but mobbed. My guard is showing the lieutenant all the things that he carried, to make sure there are not notes among them.'

'Gifts?' I ask.

'All sorts of little toys and fairings. The people love you. Everyone shouts out to me that you should be released and allowed to live with your husband. Everyone in England thinks you have done nothing wrong and should be freed. Everyone – I mean really everyone – from the ladies at court to the sluts of Smithfield.'

'They call for me?'

'I think they would march for you.'

We say nothing, looking at each other for a moment. 'No marching,' I say quietly. 'Anyway – praise God that you did not take the smallpox,' I say, kissing her. It is awkward for me to bend over and she notices it at once.

'It would be large pox on me,' she remarks. 'What's the matter with you? Have you hurt your back that you are so stiff?'

I wait till she has hauled herself onto the chair and then I put my finger across her mouth to prevent her crying out. 'I am with child,' I whisper in her ear.

She is wide-eyed in my grip until I release her.

'My God, how?' she demands.

I laugh. Mary is always so practical. 'Since they found against us, the lieutenant has let Ned come to me most nights.' I say. 'We bribe the guards and we spend all night together.'

'When do you expect the birth?'

'I am not sure. Soon, I think, within a month or so.'

She looks anxious. 'Katherine, you must keep it secret, for everyone is speaking of you at court. The people who call for you to be free would go mad if they knew you were carrying another baby in here. They would storm the Tower for your release and the guards would throw open the gates. I think Elizabeth will be forced to name you as her heir, recognise your marriage as valid and your son as heir apparent.'

'Really? I know the lords are advising her to name me ...'

'She attended parliament and in the church service before the opening the dean himself told her that she must marry, in his sermon! Then both Houses told her, one after another, that she must name her heir. They won't tolerate a deathbed nomination of Robert Dudley. She has gone too far now. She has lost the loyalty of the lords and the parliament by that mistake. She spoke to the lords in council very fair, and told them that it must be her choice, and they told her flatly that she must marry and make an heir or name one, that they wouldn't be commanded by her passions.'

I gasp at her. 'They never said that!'

'I can't begin to describe the scenes at court. She summoned Henry FitzAlan Earl of Arundel, and he said to her face in front of all of us ladies that if she was going to be ruled by passion then he and all the lords would prevent it.'

'He dared to say that to her?'

'He did. And he wasn't the only one. Everything is different since her illness. I can't tell you how much everything is changed. I think she feels that she betrayed herself. Everyone saw how much she loves Dudley. She put him before the good of the kingdom. The lords and her advisors think she has betrayed her country. Nobody trusts her now, nobody believed she would go so far as to name Dudley to rule England. Everyone feels she has shamed herself and let us all down.'

'What did she say to Henry FitzAlan?'

'She was so furious, she started to rage and then she burst into tears. You've never seen such a thing. We ladies didn't know what to do. She was speechless with tears and he just looked at her and bowed and went out and she flung herself into her bedroom and slammed the door as if she was a child in a temper. She didn't come out for the rest of the day – but she has never sent for him again.'

I look at Mary. I am quite stunned by this description of Elizabeth becoming a furious child instead of a commanding queen. 'My God, she has lost her power,' I say wonderingly. 'If FitzAlan can scold her, she has lost her power over her court.'

'And Robert Dudley has none. Did I tell you that on her deathbed she willed a fortune to his valet?'

'To Tamworth?' I ask, remembering the man who rose up

from his bed and went to guard the door without surprise or question, as if he had done it many times.

'On her deathbed,' Mary repeats. 'So now everyone says that it proves that he guarded the door while she was with Dudley. She is completely shamed and Dudley too.'

'Nobody supports him for Protector of the Realm?'

Mary makes a contemptuous face. 'Not one. Not even he speaks for himself. He says that Henry Hastings should be heir, but that's only because they are brothers-in-law. Not even Dudley dares to claim the Protectorship. It was the delusion of a fever and it shows that the only thing the queen thinks of when she is about to die is leaving her kingdom to her lover and hiding their secret shame by paying off his valet.'

'And the parliament will force her to name an heir?'

'They won't grant her the money for the army in France unless she does. They have her in a vice. She has to send money for her troops, and parliament will only give it to her if she names her heir – if she names you.'

'She can't name anyone else?'

'There is no-one else.' Mary's eyes are bright. 'I can't tell you how many friends I have at court now. You would think I was six foot tall. Everyone is my friend and everyone has been heartbroken for you. I have dozens of messages for you. Everyone knows that it has to be you. Even Elizabeth. She will have to announce it any day now.'

I pause for a moment so that I can feel my triumph. 'It's certain, Mary? I can't stand another false hope.'

'It's certain,' she says. 'She will have to name you. She has to name someone, and there is no-one else.'

'And release me,' I say.

'Of course release you,' my sister confirms.

'And Ned, and name him as my husband.'

'She has to. She cannot put a woman's whim against the will of the parliament. She has publicly promised that she will take advice, and name her heir, and nobody advises anyone but you.'

'Is she very scarred by the pox?' I ask, thinking of Elizabeth's frantic vanity.

'She's doing all she can to overcome it. She has only a few marks on her face and she's painting them out. They cut her hair when she was in the fever, so she's wearing a wig of red horsehair. But she looked well when she went to parliament in her scarlet robe trimmed with ermine. One or two said that she looked so young and healthy she could give them an heir next year if only she would marry now.'

'But she'll never marry at their bidding,' I predict.

Mary shakes her head. 'I would swear that if she can't have Robert Dudley, she'll never take anyone. Most people think she showed that herself, naming him as her heir.'

'Then why does she not understand that I had to marry for love?' I ask. 'If she is in love so deep that she would risk her kingdom? Why does she not sympathise with me?'

Mary shakes her head at the plaintive tone in my voice. 'Because she's not like you,' she declares. 'You don't understand her. Everyone thinks she's a woman blown about by passion, that her heart comes first. But she's not. She's a woman who feels her passions but is not shifted by them. She's determined and she's selfish. She'll never give Robert Dudley up, but she'll never marry him either. She loves the throne more than him. He still thinks she will be unable to resist him but I think he's wrong. He'll find he has the very worst of the bargain: always close to Elizabeth, but never on the throne.'

'You make her sound like a tyrant,' I whisper.

Mary raises her arched eyebrow. 'She's a Tudor,' she says. 'They're all tyrants.'

I gasp and put my hand to my belly where I have felt a great heave. I bend over, panting with pain.

Mary is instantly alert. She jumps down from the chair and reaches up to put her hand on my bent back. 'What is it? What is it?'

'Something moving,' I gasp, waiting in case the pain comes again. I straighten up. 'Dear God, a terrible spasm.'

'Is the baby coming? Is it due?'

'How am I to know when it is due?' I say wildly. 'I can't see a wise woman or a physician.' I can feel the sensation coming on again and this time I hold the arms of the old throne and pant like a dog as the pain rises and falls. 'No, I remember this,' I say when I can get my breath back. 'It's coming now.'

'What can I do?' Mary rolls up her sleeves and looks around the room.

'Nothing! You must do nothing!' I am well enough to know that Mary must not be found here, assisting at the birth of yet another heir to the throne of England. 'You must go, and say nothing about it.'

'I can't leave you here like this!'

'At once! And don't say anything about it.' I am holding my belly tightly in my hands, as if I would delay the remorseless movement of the baby and the irresistible rhythm of the pains. 'Go, Mary! As soon as you are safely away I will send my maid to the lieutenant and he will get me a midwife. But you can't know of the birth. You'll have to wait with the court for news and then act surprised.'

She almost dances on the spot in frustration. 'How can I leave you? My own sister? Without help? Here? Where Jane . . . where Jane . . .'

'To keep yourself safe,' I gasp. The pain is coming again. I feel the sweat stand out on my face, all over my belly. 'I care for your safety so much. I swear I do. Go, Mary, and pray for me in secret.'

I am bent over the chair so she stretches up on tiptoes and kisses my face. 'God bless you and keep you,' she whispers passionately. 'I've gone. Call your maid at once. Send me news without fail.'

She tiptoes from the room and the guard lets her out and shoots the bolts behind her. I wait for a few moments, riding another wave of pain, and then I shout: 'Lucy! Come to me!'

There is complete uproar. The rooms are stripped for a child-birth and the Tower guards go running around the city looking for a midwife who can come at once, and a wet nurse in milk. The Tower servants drag in a day bed to my bedroom and tie a rope to the posts of my bed for me to pull in my labour, while I stride up and down the rooms and clutch the back of a chair when my pains come. They are coming quickly now; I can hardly recover between them. The dogs are everywhere underfoot, and Mr Nozzle sits on the top of the wooden shutter and watches me with concern in his twinkly brown eyes. I send a message to Ned, and when I glance out of my window as I walk back and forth, trying to ease the constant ache in my back, I see that his scarf has been replaced at his windowsill. He is flying the Seymour standard and I laugh aloud at his joy, and have to steady myself by bracing against the wall.

My lady-in-waiting, Mrs Rother, comes in, white as her linen, and a fat red-faced woman follows her. 'My lady,' Mrs Rother says. 'I had no idea! If you had told me we could have prepared. This is the best midwife we could find in a hurry.'

'Don't mind me!' the woman objects, speaking in the sharp accent of a Londoner born and bred.

'I don't mind,' I assure her. 'I hope you will care for me and my baby. This is my second birth.'

She holds my hands in her comforting meaty grip as the servants behind me make up the day bed with clean linen, and bring in jugs of hot water, clouts and sheets, and linen torn up into swaddling cloths.

Lucy holds Teddy on her hip. 'Should I take him out?' she asks nervously. 'And shouldn't the dogs go out?'

I am suddenly overcome with tiredness. 'Yes. Put everything to rights,' I say to Mrs Rother and Lucy. 'I want to lie down.'

They guide me to the day bed and let me rest between my pains. 'Tell my lord that I am well,' I whisper to Lucy. 'Tell him I am merry.'

The baby is born that evening, a beautiful boy, just as I prayed. They pack my bleeding parts with moss and tie my breasts up with linen and let me lie in the tattered big bed. They have found a wet nurse and she sits beside me and feeds him. We show him to Teddy who points and says, 'Hee!' as if to tell the baby to gee up. But Ned is not allowed to come to me.

The lieutenant of the Tower, Sir Edward, whispers through the half-open door from the presence chamber, 'I have sent your news to the court, Lady Hertford. I am afraid that they will be most surprised.'

'Thank you,' I say, leaning back on the pillows. I am dizzy from drinking the mulled birthing ale. I know that the court will be more than surprised. Those who want a secure Protestant succession will be delighted – that's almost everyone. Those who measure my claim will see that it is redoubled. Only Elizabeth will begrudge me this beautiful baby and resent my happiness. We will have to wait and see what she will do in her revenge.

She moves swiftly and spitefully. The lieutenant of the Tower, Sir Edward, is locked in his own dungeon, and Ned is commanded to appear before the Star Chamber to answer charges of deflowering a virgin of the blood royal in the queen's house, breaking prison, and ravishing one of the blood royal for a second time.

As he leaves the Tower to face his accusers I drape the Seymour standard over my windowsill, so that he can see that his babies and his wife are well, that we honour our name and that we will never deny it.

Of course, he does not deny us. But I don't know what he says, nor how he bears his interrogation, till I get an unsigned note from Mary, written in unrecognisable script.

*The Privy Council announced that you are the heir on the very
day that they got news that you were with child. There was
uproar, but it proves your marriage and strengthens your claim.
Ned did well before the Star Chamber and swore that you were
man and wife. He's to be fined a greater sum than anyone could
pay – and stay in prison indefinitely. The people of London
are calling for your release, singing ballads and comparing you
with our sister Jane. They demand the freedom of your sons,
they are calling the boys the new blessed princes in the Tower.
Send me news of your health and the babies. Burn this.*

THE TOWER, LONDON, SUMMER 1563

I christen my baby Thomas Seymour but no-one is allowed into
the Tower for his baptism. His godparents are two of the Tower
guards, who give him his name at the font in the Tower chapel
as my lady-in-waiting holds him. They bring him back to me
with his little soul saved, but there is no-one to church me. I
think that I am surely a good Protestant, for here is another of
the sacraments of the old Church that I am refusing. I get up
out of bed and wash myself and change my linen and pray in
private, and it is done.

I can get no news except the court gossip that Mrs Rother
brings me. She tells me that my cousin Lady Margaret Douglas
and her fragile husband, Matthew Stuart, are living quietly at
their home, keeping their heads down as Elizabeth's displeasure
blows over them. Now that they are freed – who were guilty of so
much – the people of London are even angrier about my imprisonment, and now people start to say that my sister Jane was with
child in the Tower, just like me, and her baby was killed when she

died. I hate the way they use her name, but I am touched that they remember her as a martyr and say she would have given them a boy and an heir for England. They say that I, too, am unjustly imprisoned. The very people who called for 'Our Elizabeth' to be a saviour for the reformed religion in England now swear that she has become as bad as the persecutors were before. They say that she is torturing the sister of their Protestant martyr. Her army has failed in France, and failed to defend the Protestants, and now her defeated troops are straggling home, wounded, unpaid, miserably mutinous, their ranks ravaged by a terrible outbreak of plague.

But the most extraordinary news comes not from Mrs Rother, but from my little maid Lucy, who had it from the poor lieutenant's cook, who had it from one of the royal cooks, direct from the royal dinner table. In an attempt to reverse the opinion of everyone, and make her a safe choice of heir, Elizabeth is going to order Robert Dudley to marry Mary Queen of Scots.

It drives me quite mad not to be able to tell this to Ned, imprisoned in the White Tower and unable to come to me. He would laugh and laugh with me over this insane proposal. Elizabeth must have lost her mind to think of proposing her shamed lover to another queen, especially one who is so grand and on her dignity. Mary Queen of Scots has been offered Don Carlos – the heir to Spain. Why would she consider one of Elizabeth's subjects? And one so tainted by such scandal? But Elizabeth is so desperate to avoid my rightful claim to the throne that she has hatched this impossible plot so that I can be put aside in favour of a shamed favourite and a papist Frenchwoman, whose family has just defeated our English army.

Elizabeth goes further. She proposes that she and Mary shall somehow live together, that she and Dudley and Mary shall all live together in some great palace. They shall be two queens sharing a court, sharing an island, and presumably Robert will be shared, too. It is an extraordinary, scandalous, mad idea, and I imagine the Privy Council, William Cecil, and Robert Dudley himself tearing their hair out of their heads.

Apparently Elizabeth writes letters to Mary (the city is full of gossip): flirtatious letters, like those written from a lover to his mistress. She is going to send her a diamond ring, like a betrothal ring. She promises eternal love and friendship. She says that if Mary is ever in need or in danger, she shall summon her potent fellow queen and Elizabeth will come to her – without fail. Elizabeth is doing what she does best – encouraging lust for her political ends.

And then – just like her father, who favoured one man over another, so that they would hate each other – Elizabeth now turns to Margaret Douglas, our disgraced cousin, and shows the world that she prefers her to me as an English-born heir. Lady Margaret never had to face her accusers like I did. The testimonies of those who said that she employed soothsayers and necromancers to foretell Elizabeth's death have all been dismissed. She was released from prison without a stain on her character and now up she pops at court, received with favour, her son the pretty boy Henry Stuart, back from France, towed everywhere in her broad-beamed wake, like a dainty sailing ship after a barge. Margaret Douglas suggests to everyone that Henry Stuart would be a suitable husband for the Queen of Scots – the very idea that gave royal offence earlier! – but now it can be spoken, now it can be considered. Robert Dudley, for one, will favour such a misalliance, if only to spare himself.

It is madness to ask what a madwoman thinks. It is folly to interrogate a fool. But really – what is the queen thinking, that she would forgive a traitor, jeopardise her own throne, lose her lover, and name her enemy as an heir; just to prevent me coming to the throne after her death? I have always found her inexplicably vindictive; now I find her completely insane. Why would she risk everything to stop me being honoured? Why is it so important to her to humiliate and punish me?

I can only think that she has fallen into the jealous mood of her childhood, when she lived in a constant state of anxiety as to who was favoured by her father. First she queened it over her half-sister, Mary Tudor, who was forced to wait on her when she was a little child, and then Elizabeth was mortified when the tables were turned and Mary was favoured. She saw her despised half-sister take the throne, acclaimed by everyone in the first months of her reign. Elizabeth has always been rivalrous of other women: I imagine she hated her stepmothers, then her half-sister, then poor Amy Dudley, and now me. She must hate me with a really terrible vengeance if she will sacrifice Robert Dudley in marriage to another woman to keep me from a title. I begin to think that she is as mad as her father.

But this only makes me fear her more, and I wish I could talk to Ned about my rising concerns. This is no longer a matter of politics, of strategy. This is not a queen avoiding an heir that she fears would draw the attention of the court away from the throne, this is a woman going to the ends of the earth to spite a rival. She is ready to lose the love of her life and nominate the enemy of her country as her heir, in order to keep me from a chance at the throne, and to prevent me living happily with Ned and our children. How she must hate me to go to these lengths! How she must hate the idea of a happy marriage with beloved children, if she would ruin herself to spoil my life. And how far might she go, to take vengeance on me for being younger, prettier, happier, and a better heir than she was?

I don't forget seeing her malice to her half-sister, Mary. She watched her die, and tormented her as she died, flirting with her husband and refusing her any comfort. I don't forget that Amy Dudley died alone at home and that her murderer was never named, but that Elizabeth knew of her death before it was announced. Elizabeth's rivalry is something a woman should fear. I think of my cousin Mary Queen of Scots and pray that she never falls into Elizabeth's power as I have done. I think of Margaret Douglas and think it is a miracle that she has been freed. I begin to wonder if Elizabeth is as fatal to her kin as her deadly father was to his.

THE TOWER, LONDON,
MIDSUMMER 1563

The weather becomes terribly hot and the sun beats on the stone walls of the Tower till they are too bright to see and hot to the touch. The moat is a sluggish stinking ditch filled with dung and offal, and the tides do not cleanse it but stir up the filth, and then retreat, leaving rotting seaweed and dead fish. In the evening I can smell the stink of decay from the river, and the terrible sickly smell of the city.

The lords are demanding that Ned and the babies and I be released from the Tower and allowed to live in the country. Every summer there is sickness in London, but this year is likely to see plague. The returning troops from France, poor and defeated, are terribly diseased, and there is no provision for them. They lie around the streets to beg, coughing and spitting into the open drains that run sluggishly down the centre of every street, blocked with rubbish. It is dry weather, with long airless days, so there is no rain to wash away the pestilential filth, and no breeze to blow the sickly miasma from the streets.

Lucy comes to me white-faced and tells me that her mother, who lives outside the walls of the Tower and does my washing, has taken to her bed. She has the terrible swelling in her armpits and the buboes in her groin that indicate the plague. Lucy is shaking with fear. 'She washed your linen only yesterday,' she says. 'I brought it in myself. I put it on the baby.' She is trembling with distress. 'God spare us, your ladyship. I would never have done it! I did not know! What if the baby takes the plague?'

Lucy's home is nailed up and marked with a red cross on the door. Lucy is not allowed in to see her mother, everyone is barred out. The sick woman tosses and turns on her bed, alone in her house. She will live or die in a lonely vigil; but she knows that she is most likely to die, and her daughter cannot even take her a mug of clean water. Sufferers with the plague pray for death as their fever rises and the swellings on their body make them cry with pain, but nobody can go to them.

'I have not seen my brother,' Lucy says fretfully. 'He's in service to the Duke of Norfolk.'

'Then perhaps he's out of the city with the court,' I say helplessly. 'Perhaps they're safe at Windsor with the queen.'

'Shall I take the baby's linen off again? And wash it again?'

My newborn child has been in linen from a plague house for half the day. 'Yes, do,' I say uncertainly, 'and burn herbs, Lucy, at the doorway and windows.'

Elizabeth, the heartless queen, takes no risks with her own health though she leaves me and my little boys in the heart of the pestilential city. She locks herself up at Windsor Castle, and no-one is allowed to go from London to her court. She even has a gallows built on the edge of the town to hang anyone who dares to approach. A gate and her giant sergeant porter is not enough for Elizabeth – she has to be guarded by a hangman – but she leaves me and my babies here, in the most diseased place in England.

The worst thing is never knowing why one person catches the illness and another is spared. In a good year a whole street can be well, and one person, perhaps in a little house in the very middle, will die. But in a bad year the whole street will go dark and only one little house, surrounded by death, will burn a candle and use whatever preventatives they can buy. As the heat of August goes on and on it becomes clear that this is a bad year, one of the very worst. The parishes have to send out carts to fetch and bury the dead every night and they report that perhaps as many as a thousand people are dying every week.

Every day I am more terrified for myself and for my boys, and for Ned in the tower. 'Keep away from the boys,' I say anxiously to Mrs Rother and to Lucy, to anyone who comes into the Tower from the diseased city. 'I will care for them today. And throw away all the linen that has come from the Thames washerwomen. And clean up the room, sweep the floors and make it sweet.'

Lucy looks at me with sulky resentment. Her grief for her mother has soured her. 'Your son Thomas slept with his wet nurse,' she says. 'The clout he has on was hemmed by my dead mother. If you think the plague comes from touch, the boys may have it already.'

I give a little moan of fear. I think that if I lose either of my sons I will die of grief. I think: this is what Elizabeth was hoping for. She has prayed that I will die, and my sons will die, and nobody will be able to fix the blame at her door. I will be like Amy Dudley, her victim that everyone has forgotten.

I put out a blue scarf from the window so that Ned can see that we are well, and I stand by the window till I see the answering flutter of blue on his wall. I know he will be pacing the floor in his fury, writing to all of our friends at court. A bad year for plague makes imprisonment in the Tower a death sentence. Here, in the very heart of the city, encircled by a stinking drain, every cloth that we wear and everything that we eat comes from the diseased city and is handled by half a dozen people before it gets to us.

I write to William Cecil myself and beg him to send Ned and me and our babies out of the Tower to the country. I have never, in all my life, willingly spent the summer in London. I dare swear that neither has he. Nobody with a country house or even a little cottage stays in the city during the plague months.

All day long I wait for an answer; but none comes. I think that Cecil must have already left the city, gone to his beautiful new house at Burghley, or perhaps he is safe in Windsor Castle with the merry court, hiding behind the guards at the entrances to the town, the gallows waiting for anyone who seeks shelter with the privileged few. How shall I survive this summer if everyone goes away and forgets about me? How happy Elizabeth would be to come back to London in the autumn and find that I am dead and buried in a plague grave, my babies' little swaddled corpses thrown in with me.

I don't know whether to close the windows against the dangerous miasma that breathes off the river, or fling them open to try to keep the stuffy room cool. In the evening, when the babies are asleep, I wrap my head and shoulders in a shawl and walk in the lieutenant's garden. The newly appointed man, Sir Richard Blount, who has replaced poor Sir Edward, watches me from his window. A guard stands at the gate. I feel terribly tired, and I wonder if it is a sign of the plague. If exhaustion and a sense of foreboding swell up before the buboes, then I may not see the dawn.

I am about to turn and go back into the house when I hear a clanging noise. It is not the tocsin bell of alarm, it is a deeper tone with a crack in it, clattered by an irritable hand. I can hear the creak of cartwheels as the sound comes closer, as if a cart, ringing a bell as it goes, has entered the gateway and is making its way around the guardhouse and the little village of the Tower where the servants live. Again and again the bell rings and then I hear the cry that comes between each clang of the clapper.

'Bring out your dead! Bring out your dead!'

God help us, the plague cart has come inside the Tower itself. There must be plague in the servants' cottages, or among the grooms at the stables. I pull the shawl over my mouth and I go quickly indoors and bolt the door as if I would lock out death itself.

I get a note from Mary, it is damp with vinegar. Someone has sprayed it with stale wine in the hope of preventing the plague clinging to the paper.

We are at Windsor; but you are not forgotten. The lords insist that you are not kept in the Tower in a plague year. They tell Elizabeth that it is a hidden death sentence. Keep everyone at a distance and let no-one touch the boys but yourself. I believe you will be freed within a few days.

I wash the boys' linen myself. I take Teddy out to play in the early morning: the midday sun is dangerously hot for a Tudor like him with his fair skin and copper hair, and the evening mists carry disease. I wash our own plates, but the water comes from the well in the Tower, sometimes I can see it is cloudy with dirt, and there is nothing I can do about the dinners that come from the lieutenant's kitchens. The baby suckles from a woman who may have tainted milk. I have no way of knowing, but I dare not starve him by sending her away now. Lucy continues to be well and I watch her for any sign of faintness or fever and discourage her from coming and going. Mrs Rother sends a message that her sister is ill, and that she is going with her to the country. She says she is sorry to abandon me but she dare not delay. The villages outside London are closing their doors to anyone from the city, and if she does not leave now she will have to sleep in outhouses with sick people fleeing sickness.

I watch Ned's window and every day there is the blue kerchief that shows me that he is well. I give one of the guards a silver penny to tell Ned that none of us is sick, and we hope to be released. He sends me back a poem:

> My love is not blighted by plague
> Nor burnèd by the sun
> My love is constant through all days
> Until our freedom's won.

I sprinkle it with powder before I take it from the guard's hand and I read it at arm's length. The words I hold in my heart. I burn the paper.

THE TOWER, LONDON,
SUMMER 1563

In the early morning, while it is still cool, I can hear the tramp of many feet coming up the stairs to my rooms, which means a visit from Sir Richard, the new lieutenant of the Tower. I stand beside my tattered throne, Mr Nozzle on my shoulder, Thomas in my arms, Teddy beside me, his hand in mine. Lucy stands behind me. I think we look more like a poor family of plague-struck beggars than the royal heirs of Elizabeth's nightmares.

The door opens and Sir Richard comes in and bows. 'Forgive me,' I say, 'but the guards must stay outside. I am afraid of the plague.'

'Of course,' he says. He gestures to them and they step backwards. 'I am glad to say that you need fear no more. You are to be released.'

I am so flooded with joy that I cannot hear him. 'What?'

He nods. 'Yes, my lady. You are to be released from the Tower. You can leave today. You can leave this morning.'

'Released?'

'Yes,' he confirms. 'Thanks be to God – and to the mercy of our sovereign lady the queen.'

'God bless her,' I whisper. 'I can go when I wish?'

'I have horses ready for you, and a wagon for your goods.'

I gesture at the chipped table and the tattered chairs. 'I have nothing worth taking. Lucy can pack our clothes in a moment.'

He bows. 'I will wait for your command,' he says. 'You should go as soon as possible, before it gets too hot.'

'And the Earl of Hertford comes with me?' I ask as he reaches the door.

He bows again. 'His lordship is released also.'

'God be praised,' I say. 'I thank the merciful God for answering my prayer.'

We are packed and ready to travel within half an hour. I won't allow anything to delay me. The well-worn furniture can come in the wagon behind us, along with a trunk of clothes. The linnets will come in their cage shrouded with a shawl, and Jo the pug with her heirs in a basket, a net tied on top so they are kept safe in the open wagon. Mr Nozzle will go in his cage in the shade. I shall have Teddy before me on my saddle and the wet nurse will carry Thomas strapped before her. Lucy will ride pillion behind a guard and if Teddy gets tired she can take him in her arms.

I imagine us riding into Hanworth, the cleanliness of the house, the brightness of the sunshine, the sweetness of the air, with Ned's mother, Lady Anne, on the front steps waiting to greet her grandson, a Tudor-Seymour boy, the heir to the throne of England.

Sir Richard is in the Tower yard with the loaded wagon and a guard. When they see me coming they mount up and then I see my husband, Ned, coming under the arch of the stables, surrounded by his guards. He crosses the yard in four swift strides. Before anyone can stop him he takes my hands and kisses them, searching my face for my rising blush of desire, then he takes me into his arms and kisses me on the mouth. I feel a rush of love for him. I put my arms around him and press against him. Thank God we are reunited at last, and tonight we will sleep in the same bed. I could cry for relief, and thank God our worries are over.

His face is as radiant as mine. 'My love,' he says. 'We are spared the plague and reunited. Thank God.'

'We will never be parted again,' I promise him. 'Swear it.'

'Never parted again,' he promises me.

'Now, you must see your boys before we set off.'

Teddy remembers his father, despite these long days of separation, and jumps towards him, his arms outstretched. Ned snatches up his son, and I see how small my boy is, when he is held in his tall father's arms, against his broad chest. Teddy puts his arm around his father's neck and holds his face against his cheek. Thomas gives the gummy beam that he shows to everyone, and waves a sticky hand.

'How handsome they are, how well they look! Who would have thought that we would have brought such bright blooms from this dark place?' Ned says. 'Truly, it is a miracle.'

'It is,' I say. 'And now we will start our married life with two boys, two sons and heirs, in your family house. We are going to Hanworth, aren't we?'

'Yes. We have to thank my mother for this release. I know that she has been writing constantly to William Cecil about us. She will want us at home.'

The lieutenant comes to my side. 'My lady, we have to go now if we are to make the journey without too much fatigue for the children. It's going to be very hot later.'

'Of course,' I say. I take hold of Teddy's plump little bottom but he tightens his grip on his father and insists: 'Teddy – Dada! Dada!'

'Will Teddy ride with me?' Ned asks. 'I don't think we'll get him off me without a crowbar.'

'Do you want to ride with your dada, on his big horse?' I ask him.

Teddy lifts his beaming face from his father's neck and nods. 'Teddy – Dada. Hee-up.'

'Teddy can go before his father, and when he wants to rest he can be carried by Lucy as she rides pillion,' I suggest.

'Your lordship's horse has cast a shoe,' the lieutenant says to Ned. 'Farrier is shoeing him now. He'll be a few minutes more. Best to let her ladyship start her journey so she can rest as she pleases. You'll catch her up on the road; the wagon will be so slow.'

'Very well. Teddy can wait with me and we'll catch you up. I'll hold him steady,' Ned promises me. He kisses me again, over our little son's head. I have a moment of rare joy when I embrace my husband and my elder son together, my hand on my husband's shoulder, the other around my little boy.

'I'll see you on the road.' I cup my hand around my son's cheek. 'Be a good boy for your dada and keep your hat on.'

'Yeth,' my boy says obediently, his grip tight on his father's neck.

'He's choking me,' my husband smiles. 'Don't fear he'll fall off. He's clinging on as if he was Mr Nozzle.'

I kiss him again and then I climb on the mounting block and into my saddle. Everyone is mounted and waiting for me. I wave my hand to Ned and my son, and follow the guards out of the stable yard. 'See you in a little while!' I call. 'See you soon.'

The horses' hooves clatter on the cobbles of the main gate. We ride under the arch of the gateway and, as the shadow falls on me, there is a deafening roar. Beyond the gateway, the lane is lined by the guards of the Tower and the bridge over the moat is massed with the Tower servants. As I ride past, the guards present arms and salute, as if I were a queen riding out to take my throne, and I emerge into the sunshine into a blast of cheering as the servants throw their hats in the air and the women curtsey and kiss their hands to me. I am free at last; I can smell it on the breeze and in the joy of the cry of the seagulls.

I smile and wave at the Tower servants, and then I see that beyond the bridge and the furthest gatehouse the citizens of London have somehow heard that we are free, and there are people being pushed back from the roadway by the guards, cheering, and even holding up roses for me.

I go through them all as if I were leading a royal procession. I am still fearful of the plague so I don't stop to take any flowers, and besides, my guards, stern-faced, push their way through the crowd that parts before them. But the fishwives and the street-sellers, apprentice girls and the spinsters and brewsters, all dressed in their rough work aprons, defy the guards and throw roses and leaves down before me so my horse walks on a trail of flowers and I know that the women of London are on my side.

We wind our way past Tower Hill and the scaffold that stands there, where my father ended his life, and I bow my head to his memory, and remember his hopeless struggle against Queen Mary. I think how glad he would be to see one daughter, at least, riding from the Tower to freedom, her baby beside her and her noble husband and heir following behind. It's bitter for me to think of him, and the death that he brought on Jane, so I turn my head to the wet nurse as she rides pillion behind the guard with Thomas strapped against her, and I beckon her to ride beside me so that I can see my boy, and feel my hope for the future.

That's when I notice that we are riding north instead of west and I say to the officer riding ahead of me: 'This isn't the road to Hanworth.'

'No, my lady,' he says politely, reining his horse back. 'I am so sorry. I didn't realise you had not been told. My orders are to take you to Pirgo.'

'To my uncle?'

'Yes, Lady Hertford.'

I am so pleased at this. I will be far more comfortable with my uncle in his beautiful new house than at Ned's home at Hanworth. His mother may have written to Cecil for her son, maybe she even persuaded the queen to release us, but I have had no good wishes from her, not even after I had given her two grandsons. I would far rather that we stay with my uncle in his family home than with her, as long as he has forgiven me for the deception I had to practise on him.

'Did he invite me?' I ask. 'Did he send a message for me?'

The young man ducks his head. 'I don't know, your ladyship. My orders were to take you all to Pirgo, and see you safely there. I know no more.'

'And Ned knows to follow us? He thought we were going to Hanworth.'

'He knows where you are going, my lady.'

We ride for about two hours, through villages where the front doors are resolutely closed, past inns with bolted shutters. Nobody wants anything to do with travellers from London. Everyone on this road is fleeing from infection and when we pass people walking, they press back against the hedge so that not even our horses brush them. They are as afraid of us as we are of them. I stare at them, trying to see if they have any signs of the plague on them, and the wet nurse gathers Thomas closer to her and pulls her shawl over his face.

When the sun is overhead, beating down on us, it is too hot to ride on. The commander of the guard suggests that we stop and rest in the shade of thick woodland. The wet nurse takes Thomas and feeds him, and the rest of us dine on bread and cold meat and small ale. We have brought everything from the Tower kitchens; I have to pray that the food is not infected.

'I need to rest,' I say. I think that if Ned left shortly after us he will catch up now and I will be able to doze with him in the shade of the trees and for the first time in our lives we will be able to be together without deception. I will sleep in his arms and wake to his smile.

'Make sure that someone watches out for my husband, his lordship, on the road,' I caution the commander of our guard.

'I have sentries posted,' he says. 'And he will see your standard from the road.'

They spread carpets and shawls on the forest floor and I bundle my riding cape under my head. I lie down and close my eyes, thinking that I will rest for a moment and that soon I will hear the sound of Ned and his guards riding towards us. I smile sleepily, thinking how excited Teddy will be at being on a great courser, riding with his father, outside the walls of the Tower for the first time in his life. I think of his tight grip on his father's neck and the tenderness that Ned showed when he held him close.

And then I sleep. I am so relieved to be out of the plague-stricken city that my worries slide away from me. It is the first sleep that I have had in freedom in two long years and I think the air is sweeter when it does not blow through bars. I dream of being with Ned and the children in a house that is neither Hanworth nor Pirgo, and I think it is a foreseeing and that we are going to live happily together in our own house, the palace that we said we would build when I am queen. I sleep until Mrs Farelow, the wet nurse, gently touches my shoulder and wakes me, and I know that it is not a dream, that I am free.

'We should be getting on,' she says.

I smile and sit up. 'Is Ned here yet?'

'No,' she says. 'Not yet. But it is a little cooler.'

There are a few scattered clouds over the burning disc of the sun and a cool breeze from off the hills. 'Thank God,' I say. I look at the wet nurse. 'Did he feed well? Can we go on?'

'Oh yes, your ladyship,' she says, getting to her feet. 'Do you want him?'

I take my beloved baby boy into my arms and he beams to see me. 'I can almost feel that he is heavier than this morning,' I say to her. 'He is feeding well.'

'A proper London trencherman,' she says approvingly.

The guards bring up the horse and the commander has to lift me into the saddle. I think that Ned will lift me down at Pirgo – he will surely have caught up with us by then – and I take up the reins and we ride forward.

It is pearly evening twilight by the time we ride up through the parkland to the big gabled palace of Pirgo. My uncle comes out of the great front door to greet us, his household, servants, retainers and companions lined up on the steps. It is a welcoming greeting, but he is not smiling; he looks anxious.

'My lord uncle!' I so hope he has forgiven me for lying to his face; surely he will see that I could do nothing else.

He lifts me down from my horse and he kisses me kindly enough, as he always did. I gesture to the wet nurse and to Thomas. 'And this is your newest kinsman. His royal brother, the viscount, Lord Beauchamp, is coming behind us with his father. I am surprised they have not joined us but his horse cast a shoe as we were leaving and they had to come later.'

He only glances at my baby and then returns his attention to me. 'You'd better come inside,' is all he says.

He tucks my hand in his arm and leads me through the great double doors at the front of the house into a grand presence hall. His wife is nowhere to be seen, which is odd, as I would have expected her to greet me. After all, I am a countess, and now the declared heir to the throne of England.

'Where is Lady Grey?' I ask a little stiffly.

He looks harassed. 'She sends her courtesies and she will come to you later. Come in, come in, your ladyship.'

He leads me upstairs and through an impressive presence chamber, then a second smaller room, and finally to a privy chamber with a good-sized bedchamber behind it. I know these rooms: they are the second-best rooms. Elizabeth stayed here in a better suite. I think I will insist on the best rooms, but before I can speak, he closes the door and presses me into a chair.

'What is it?' I ask him. I have a sense of growing dread that I cannot name. He is usually so confident and yet he looks uncertain as to what he should say. He tends to be pompous, yet now he seems to be at a loss. 'My lord uncle, is there something wrong?'

'Did they tell you that Lord Hertford is coming here?' he asks.

'Yes, of course. He is riding behind us,' I reply.

'I don't think so. I have had word that you are to be housed here alone.'

'No, no,' I contradict him. 'We were to leave the Tower together this morning. He was only delayed because they were shoeing his horse. He is coming behind us and he is bringing Teddy – our son, little Lord Beauchamp. Teddy insisted on riding with his father. He will take him up before him on his saddle-bow. I expect they are taking so long because Teddy wants to hold the reins.'

Again, he hesitates, and then he takes both my hands in a cold grip and says: 'My dear Katherine, I am deeply sorry to tell you that your troubles are not over. You are not released and Lord Hertford is not free either. You are not to be housed together. He is being taken to Hanworth where his lady mother will be responsible for his imprisonment, and you have been sent here where I have been ordered to keep you a prisoner.'

I am so astounded by this that I can say nothing. I just look at my uncle and I feel my jaw drop open. 'No,' I say simply.

He is unblinking. 'I am afraid so.'

'But she freed me, at everyone's request, so that I could leave the city because of the plague!'

Neither of us needs to say who 'she' is.

'No, she did not. She was persuaded by the whole of the court that you could not be left in the Tower in such danger, but she has not pardoned you, nor forgiven you, and she has certainly not freed you. You are to be kept here, by me, as much a prisoner as if you were still in the Tower in the charge of the guards. I have orders that you are to see and communicate with no-one but the servants of my household and they are to prevent you from leaving.' He pauses. 'Or even going outside.'

'Uncle, you cannot have agreed to this? To be my gaoler?'

He looks at me helplessly. 'Would it have been better to refuse, and leave you to die of the plague in the Tower?'

'You are imprisoning me? Your own niece?'

'What else can I do if she orders it? Would it be better if she put me in the Tower with you?'

'And Ned? My husband?'

'His mother has promised to keep him within two rooms of her house. He is not pardoned or forgiven either. His own mother is guarding him.'

'My son!' I say in a rush of panic. 'Oh my God! Uncle! Our little boy, Teddy. I let him ride with Ned thinking they were following. Where is Teddy? Is he coming here? Are they sending him here to me?'

My uncle, pale with his own distress, shakes his head. 'He's to live with his father and grandmother at Hanworth,' he says.

'Not with me?' I whisper.

'No.'

'No!' I scream. I run to the door and wrench at the handle but as it turns and the door does not open I know that my own uncle's servants have already locked me in. I hammer with both my hands on the wooden panels. 'Let me out! I must have my son! I must have my son!'

I spin round and I snatch at my uncle's arm. He fends me off, his face white.

'Uncle, you have to make them send Teddy to me,' I gabble at him. 'He is not even two years old! He has never been away from me. He's not like a royal boy who has spent his life with servants: we have never been parted! I am his only companion, I have mothered him night and day. He will die without me! I can't be parted from him.'

'You have your baby,' he says feebly.

'I have two children!' I insist. 'I bore two children, I must have two children! You cannot take one from me. You cannot allow her to take my son from me! It will be the death of me, it is worse than death to me. I have to have my boy.'

He presses me down into the wooden chair again. 'Be still, be calm. I will write to William Cecil. He remains your friend. The Privy Council are working for your freedom: this might be a matter of only days. Everyone knows that you are the heir by right, by blood, and named so by the Privy Council. Everyone knows that you cannot be kept imprisoned indefinitely.'

I am silent, and he watches me as I twist round in the seat, hiding from his anxious gaze, and put my face against the wooden back of the chair. 'She has taken my husband from me and now she takes my son?' I whisper brokenly. 'Why would she save me from death, if she makes my life worse than death? I have to be with my boy. He's only little – he's not yet two years old. He has to be with me. I have to have him with me. How will he manage without me? Who will put him to bed?'

I raise my head and I look at my uncle's face, twisted with his distress.

'Oh God,' I exclaim. 'He will think I have abandoned him. He will think that I have left him. His little heart will break. He has to be with me. I cannot live without him. I swear to you, I will die if he is taken from me.'

'I know,' my uncle says. 'Perhaps she will relent. Certainly, she must relent.'

I raise my head. 'This is beyond cruel,' I say. 'I would rather have died in the Tower of plague than lose my son.'

'I know.'

PIRGO PALACE, ESSEX, AUTUMN 1563

My uncle and I are writing a petition to the queen. He comes to me every day and we make little touches to it. She is a scholar; she likes fine writing. She is not the student that my sister Jane was, but a well-turned phrase will always catch her attention.

We send a first draft to William Cecil to look over, and it comes back to us with his comments scribbled in the margins, and we rewrite it again. It has to be perfect. It has to convince her that I am truly sorry for marrying without permission. It has to persuade her – without being at all argumentative – that I maintain that I am married to my lord, and that our two babies are legitimate heirs. It has to assure her that – though I am my mother's heir and the great-granddaughter of Henry VII – I will never challenge Elizabeth during her lifetime, nor claim the throne at her death without her authorisation. If it were possible to assure her that she would never lose her looks, never age and never die, we would add a paragraph to swear to that, too.

I have to somehow convince her that I am the complete opposite of herself. She is so vain she cannot conceive someone to be unlike her. She can only imagine a world in her image. But I am completely different. I let my heart rule my head, while she is always calculating. I have married for love, while she is selling the man she loves into marriage with Mary Queen of Scots. I have two beautiful baby boys and she is barren. And the biggest difference between us is that I don't want the throne of England, I don't even want to be named heir at this price – and it is all she ever wanted since her childhood when she was named bastard and excluded from our direct line of succession, and it is all she cares about now.

I dare not presume, Most Gracious Sovereign, to crave pardon for my disobedient and rash matching of myself without Your Highness's consent; I only most humbly sue unto Your Highness to continue your merciful nature towards me. I acknowledge myself a most unworthy creature to feel so much of your gracious favour as I have done. My justly felt misery and continual grief doth teach me daily more and more the greatness of my fault, and your princely pity increaseth my sorrow that I have so forgotten my duty towards Your Majesty. This is my great torment of mind. May it therefore please Your Excellent Majesty to license me to be a most lowly suitor unto Your Highness to extend towards my miserable state Your Majesty's further favour and accustomed mercy, which upon my knees in all humble wise I crave, with my daily prayers to God to long continue and preserve Your Majesty's reign over us. From Pirgo the vi of November 1563. Your Majesty's most humble, bounden, and obedient servant.

Finally, my uncle and I send the finished petition to Robert Dudley as our friend and the queen's principal advisor. Oddly, his own fate hangs in the balance, just like mine. He may find himself in the extraordinary position of being the lover of the Queen of England and the husband of the Queen of Scotland, he could be a king consort as his brother nearly was. Only a Dudley could hope for such an outcome to ambition and desire: only an Elizabeth could imagine it.

What we don't know is what Queen Mary can imagine. We all have to wait to see if the shame of taking her cousin's cast-off lover is a price worth paying for being named as heir to the throne of England. We are all waiting to see if Elizabeth can bear to raise Dudley to the position of Earl of Leicester so that he can plausibly marry a royal, and then send him away. We are all waiting to see if the Privy Council will demand that Elizabeth names me as heir, as she promised them she would follow their advice. Robert Dudley promises to put our petition when the time is right, when she is ready to listen. We all know that only Robert Dudley can summon the queen's agreeable mood, only Robert Dudley can seduce her into happiness; but is he so potent that he can prevail upon her to be generous? Can he make Elizabeth – the Supreme Governor of the Church – forgive like a Christian?

He cannot. This is perhaps the first thing that she has ever refused him. We all thought that she could not resist him, that she could refuse him nothing. But this small thing, this sensible, kindly, common-sense act of pardon, is beyond her. She knows that I am breaking my heart, parted from my husband and my son, kept in isolation in my uncle's house, forced to depend on him to pay for my food and for my clothes. My baby is imprisoned with me for no fault of his own, my little son torn from me, and my husband held prisoner by his own mother. Elizabeth knows that this is cruelty to two noble families, and an offence against the laws of the land and justice. She should release us – we are no threat to her and want nothing but to love each other and be together – and she will not do it.

It seems that I will live and die in prison for the crime of marrying my lover, because Elizabeth Tudor could not marry hers. This is jealousy taken to an extraordinary degree. This is fatal malice, and when I receive her refusal I fear that only death will release me. Like all Tudors she invokes death. Her sister killed my sister. She will kill me. This can only end in death: mine or hers.

BOOK III

MARY

WINDSOR CASTLE,
AUTUMN 1563

Elizabeth, merry as a blackbird in a rose hip hedge, rides early in the morning and all her ladies have to go with her, merry or not, like it or not. I am high on a big hunter and I ride without fear as I have done since I was a tiny child at Bradgate. My father always put me on a full-sized horse and told me that if I held the reins firmly, and made sure that the horse knew who was in command, it would not matter if I sat a little askew in the saddle because of the twist in my spine, and if I spoke clearly and firmly then it would not matter that I am light and small. He told me that I can have a great presence even though I am of little height.

While Jane, my oldest sister, wanted to stay indoors with her books, and Katherine always wanted to play with her menagerie of little animals in the garden or in her room, I was always in the stables, standing on an upturned pail to groom the big horses, or clambering up the mounting block to sit bareback on their warm broad backs.

'You can't let something like being born small and a bit twisty stand in your way,' my father would say to me. 'We're none of us perfect, and you're marred no worse than King Richard III, and he rode out in half a dozen battles and was killed in a cavalry charge – nobody ever told *him* he couldn't ride.'

'But he was a very bad man,' I observe with the stern judgement of a seven-year-old.

'Very bad,' my father agrees. 'But that was his soul, not his body. You can be a good woman with a body that is a little short and a spine that is out of true. You can learn to stand straight as a yeoman of the guard, and you can be a beautiful little woman. If you never marry, then you can be a good sister to Jane and Katherine, and a good aunt to their children. But I don't see why you shouldn't marry and make a good marriage when your time comes. Your birth is as good as any woman in the kingdom, better than everyone but the king's children. Truth be told, it doesn't matter if your spine is out of true, if your heart is not.'

I am glad of his faith in me, and that he taught me to ride as well as anyone. He was the first to set me the task of standing straight and tall and I have trained myself to do so. I have long days in the saddle behind Elizabeth and her ridiculous master of horse, and nobody ever thinks to see if I am keeping up or if I am tired. I ride as far and as fast as any lady of the court, and I am braver than most of them. I never slump in the saddle or grimace when my back is aching at the end of a long day. I never look to Robert Dudley as a hint that he might turn Her Majesty for home. I never expect any help from either of them, and so I am never disappointed.

It is not the riding that wearies me, but God knows I am tired to death of Elizabeth, and when we clatter over the cobbles at the great gate of Windsor Castle and the sergeant porter, Thomas Keyes, looks up at me with his concerned brown gaze I nod to him with a little smile to tell him that I am exhausted only by this queen, not saddle-sore but heartsore.

For all this happy time as the heat of summer goes on into autumn, while Elizabeth is spending her mornings at the hunt, and her middays at picnics and boating on the river, her evenings with plays and dancings and disguisings, my sister is imprisoned by our uncle, confined to three rooms with her baby, torn from her beloved son and stolen from her husband.

Nothing troubles our royal cousin! Everything gives Elizabeth pleasure. She revels in the warm weather while London swelters and the plague spreads across the kingdom. Every village on every road out of London has a cottage with a cross on the door and people dying inside. Every riverside house along the Thames has its watergate locked and barred so that no barges from London can enter. Every city in the kingdom is digging a plague pit for the bodies, and every church praying that the plague passes over their congregation. Every healthy house bars its doors to travellers, everyone is fearfully hard-hearted. But none of this troubles Elizabeth. She flirts with Dudley in the heat of the day and slips through to his bedroom any night that she pleases, while my sister cries herself to sleep and dreams of freedom.

Thomas Keyes has to stay on duty at the gate of the castle and may not help me from the saddle, but there is always one of the young men of court quick to my side to lift me down. They know that my sister and her two boys are the next heirs to the throne; they know that my rank is acknowledged by the queen. None of them knows how great is my influence, and what I might do for them if they please me. I hardly notice them. My only smile is for Thomas Keyes, the queen's sergeant porter, he is the only man that I would trust in this rivalrous pit of two-faced serpents. Thomas gives me a private nod as I go by, and I know that I will see him later in the day when Elizabeth is entertained by someone else and forgets to look for me.

'Where is Lady Mary?' she asks as soon as she is off her horse, as if she loves me dearly and has missed me all day, and I step forward to take her beautifully embroidered leather riding gloves. Someone else takes her whip and she holds out her white hand to Robert Dudley, who leads her out of the sunlight into the cool dimness of Windsor Castle where breakfast is served in the great hall and the Spanish ambassador is waiting to greet her.

I take the gloves to the royal wardrobe rooms, dust them with a little perfumed powder and wrap them in silk, and then return to the hall to take my seat at the table for the ladies-in-waiting.

Elizabeth sits at the top table with the Spanish ambassador on one side and Robert Dudley on the other. I sit at the head of the table for the ladies, I am her cousin, I am the daughter of a princess of the blood. We all bow our heads for grace, which Elizabeth defiantly hears in Latin to show her scholarship more than her piety, and then the servants bring in the ewers and bowls for us to wash our hands. Then they bring in one great dish after another. Everyone is hungry from the morning in the saddle, and the great joints of meat and fresh-baked loaves are served to each table.

'Have you heard from your sister?' Bess St Loe asks me quietly.

'I write, but she does not reply,' I say. 'She is allowed to receive my letters, though my uncle has to read them first, but she does not reply.'

'What's wrong with her – oh! not the plague?'

'No, thanks be to God, it has not reached Pirgo. My uncle tells me that she will not eat, and that she cannot stop crying.'

Aunt Bess's expression is tender. 'Oh, my dear.'

'Yes,' I say tightly. 'When the queen took her child, I think that she broke Katherine's heart.'

'But she will forgive her, and she will reunite them. She is gracious. And Katherine is the only heir of our faith. Elizabeth must turn to her.'

'I know,' I say. 'I know that she will in time. But these are hard days for my sister while we wait. And it is cruel to her two little boys, who have never known anything but confinement. Would you speak to the queen?'

'Perhaps they, at least, could be released ...' Bess starts, and then breaks off as the queen rises from the breakfast table and says that she will walk with the Spanish ambassador and Robert Dudley in the walled garden. Three ladies are to walk behind her, the rest of us are free for an hour or two. We rise and follow her out of the hall and curtsey as she goes through the garden door, Robert Dudley offering his hand on one side, Álvaro de la Quadra on the other. Elizabeth is where she loves to be – at the centre of attention with a man on either side. I think that if she were not a queen she would certainly be a whore. As they pass through, and the door is closed behind them by the guard, I slip away in the opposite direction, to the main gate. It is bolted shut against the plague, but there is a handsome guardsman on duty inside at the wicket gate. As I approach he bows and offers his hand to help me clamber through the narrow doorway.

Thomas stands on guard outside the bolted gate, arms folded over his broad chest, a huge man in the Tudor livery, the queen's sergeant porter. I feel myself smile for the first time today at the mere sight of him.

'Lady Mary!' he says as I bob up at his elbow. He drops to one knee on the cobbles so that his face is on a level with mine, his brown eyes loving. 'Are you free for long? Will you sit in the gatehouse?'

'I have an hour,' I say. 'She's walking in the garden.'

Thomas orders one of the guards to take his place and leads me to the gatehouse where he watches me climb into his big chair beside his table. He pours me a glass of small ale from the pitcher in the little pantry, and takes a seat on a low stool close by, so that we are head to head.

'Any news of your sister?' he asks.

'Nothing new. I asked Robert Dudley if he would speak again to the queen and he says that it is no use, and it only angers her more.'

'You have to wait?'

'We have to wait,' I confirm.

'Then I suppose our business must wait, too,' he says gently.

I put my hand on his broad shoulder and finger the Tudor rose on his collar. 'You know that I would marry you tomorrow if I could. But I cannot ask Elizabeth for anything now, not until she has pardoned Katherine. My sister's freedom must come first.'

'Why would she mind?' he asks wonderingly. 'Why does a great queen like her mind so much about your sister? Is it not a private matter of the heart? The Earl of Hertford carries an honourable name, why may your sister not live as his wife?'

I hesitate. Thomas has the simple views of an honest man. He stands at the gate every day and is responsible for the safety of a most contradictory queen. There are those who love Elizabeth and would die for her, who beg entry to her castles so that they can see her, as if she were a saint, so that they can go home and tell their children that they have seen the greatest woman in Christendom, laden with jewels in glorious majesty at her dinner. Then there are those who hate her so much for taking the country further and further away from the Church of Rome, they call her a heretic and would poison her, or knife her, or set a trap for her. Some visitors despise her for her promiscuity, some suspect her of adultery and some even accuse her of using black arts, of being malformed, of hiding a bastard child, of being a man. Every man and woman of every shade of opinion passes under Thomas's thoughtful gaze and yet he persists in thinking the best of them, trusts them as far as is safe, guides them homeward if he thinks they might be a danger, and believes that people are on the whole as good and kindly as himself.

'I don't know why Elizabeth cannot tolerate Katherine's marriage,' I say, measuring my words. 'I know that she fears that if Katherine is named as her successor then everyone will desert her and Katherine will plot against her, just as Margaret Douglas, another of our cousins, does. But more than that, it's not just Katherine – Elizabeth doesn't like anyone marrying; she doesn't like attention on anyone but herself. None of us ladies-in-waiting expect permission to marry. She won't even allow us to talk about it. Everyone at court has to be in love with her.'

Thomas chuckles tolerantly. 'Well, she's the queen,' he concedes. 'I suppose she can have her court as she likes it. Shall I come in this evening when I have locked the gate?'

'I'll meet you in the garden,' I promise him.

He takes my little hand in his huge paw and kisses it gently. 'I am so honoured,' he says quietly. 'I think of you all day, you know, and I look for you coming in and out of my gate. I love to see you riding by, so high on your horse and so pretty in your gowns.'

I lay my cheek against his head as he bows over my hand. His hair is thick and curly and it smells of the open air. I think that in all of this dangerous uncertain world I have found the only man that I can trust. I think that he does not know how precious this is to me.

'When did you first look for me?' I whisper.

He raises his head and smiles at my childishness, in wanting the story repeated. 'I noticed you when you first came to court when you were not even ten years old, a tiny little girl. I remember seeing you on your big horse and fearing for you. And then I saw how you handled him and I knew that you were a little lady to be reckoned with.'

'You were the grandest man I had ever seen,' I tell him. 'The queen's sergeant porter, so handsome in your livery, and as tall as a tree, as broad as a trunk, like a great oak tree.'

'Then when you were appointed as a lady-in-waiting I would see you come and go with the court, and I thought that of all of them, you were the merriest and sweetest lady,' he says. 'When your sister went creeping out through my gate, with her hood over her fair hair and I knew she was seeing a lover, I nearly thought to warn you; but you were so young and so pretty I could not be the one to bring worry into your life. I didn't dare to speak to you at all until you started to say good morning to me. I used to look forward to that – "Good morning, Captain Keyes," you said. And I would stammer like a fool and I couldn't say a word in reply.'

'That's how I knew that you liked me,' I tell him. 'You spoke clearly enough to everyone else but with me you were as tongue-tied as a boy. And you blushed! Lord! What a big man to blush like a schoolboy!'

'Who was I to speak to such a lady?' he asks.

'The best man at court,' I tell him. 'I was so glad when you offered to walk with me, when I went to visit Katherine in the

Tower. When you said you would escort me, and that the streets were not safe. I was so glad to have you at my side. It was like walking beside a great calm shire horse: you are so big that everyone just gets out of the way. And when I saw her, and she was in such distress that I would break down and cry with her, and then I would come out and you would be waiting for me, and I felt comforted just by your being there, like a mountain. I felt that I had an ally. An ally as big as a castle. A strong friend.'

'Certainly a tall one,' he says. 'I would do anything for you, my little lady.'

'Love me always, as you do now,' I whisper.

'I swear that I will.'

He is quiet for a moment. 'You don't mind my being married before?' he asks quietly. 'You don't object to my children? They live with their aunt at Sandgate but I would be glad to give them a loving stepmother.'

'Would they not look down on me?' I ask awkwardly.

He shakes his head. 'They would know you for a great lady even when they bent low to kiss your hand.'

'I should like us to have children,' I say shyly. 'First I will care for yours, and then perhaps some of our own.'

He takes my hand and holds it to his warm cheek. 'Eh, Mary, we are going to be happy.'

We are silent together for a moment, then I say, 'you know, I have to go now.'

He rises up from the stool to his full height and his head brushes the ceiling. He is nearly seven foot tall from enormous boots to curly brown hair. When I stand beside him my head is level with his polished leather belt. He opens the door for me and I go to the great barred gate of Windsor Castle and he opens the wicket gate inside it.

'Till tonight,' he whispers, and closes it gently behind me.

WINDSOR CASTLE,
CHRISTMAS 1563

My love gives me a gold ring set with a tiny ruby the colour of true love, a deep red. I give him a thick leather belt to go around his broad waist. I work it myself with a shoemaker's awl and I carve my name and my family crest into the thick leather. He can wear it turned to the inside, so that nobody knows but the two of us. When I give it to him and he takes it from the little silk bag that I have made, he blushes to his ears, like a boy.

I am so pleased with the ring he has given me. It fits my finger like a wedding band and he says I must wear it on my wedding finger when I am alone, for it is a pledge of his love to me and we are promised to one another.

'I wish we could marry and live together at once,' I whisper to him. I am sitting on his lap, his great arms around me. He holds me as tenderly as if I were a child, and yet I feel the pulse of his desire for me as a woman when I put my fingers on his strong wrist.

'I wish it, too,' he says. 'The moment that you say the word I will fetch a priest and witnesses and we will marry. Or we can go to a church. I don't ever want you to face the questioning that your sister has suffered. We will have witnesses and we will have our betrothal in writing.'

'They don't care about me,' I say resentfully. 'I am so small in Elizabeth's eyes that she does not even fear me. It's not as if I am like my sister, with half the courts of Europe making advances and weaving plots. My marriage is a private matter: it should make no difference to her whether I am married or single, whether I have a houseful of children or only you to love.'

'Then shall we marry in secret?' he asks hopefully. 'Do you dare?'

'Maybe next year,' I say cautiously. 'I don't want to remind the queen of her anger against Katherine. I am hoping that the council will persuade her to set my sister free this month. Some scholars are making enquiries that will prove her to be the heir, and prove her wedding was valid and so her sons are legitimate heirs. I can't think about anything else until that is written and published.'

Thomas nods. He has a great respect for the learning of my family, the more so since Jane is now recognised as a theologian and her published writings are read everywhere. 'Are you writing any of the book?' he asks.

'Oh, no,' I say. 'It is all being done by a senior clerk in the chancery, John Hales. He has seen the original king's will and says that it clearly names my mother and her line as heirs after Prince Edward and the princesses. Hales has proved that our grandmother's marriage was a good one, so our line is legitimate and English-born and Protestant. Now Katherine's husband, Ned Seymour, is paying for the opinions of clergy overseas to show that he and Katherine's marriage was valid too, with private vows, and their sons legitimate. When all the evidence is brought together, then John Hales will publish it and the country will see that Katherine is proven heir to the queen: legitimately born, and legitimately married.'

Thomas hesitates. He is a man with little education but he has much knowledge of the world, and he has been in charge of the safety of the palace and the queen since Elizabeth came to the throne. 'Now, pretty one, I am neither a lord nor a clerk but I'm not sure that this is so wise. The queen is not a woman that ever feels obliged to follow what everyone else thinks. Even if the whole country thinks one thing, she'll still go her own way. Remember the time that she was the only Protestant princess to stand for her faith, when her sister was Queen of England? She didn't change her mind then, even though the whole country seemed to be against her, from the queen and all

the Spanish downwards. It'll take more than a book to persuade
her, I reckon.'

'She did conform,' I say stubbornly. 'I can remember her
myself, going into Mass and moaning about it.'

'Coming out of Mass early,' he reminds me. 'Complaining
of sickness. And showing everyone that she would not stomach it.'

'Yes, but William Cecil is sponsoring this book,' I insist. 'And
Robert Dudley. What William Cecil thinks today, the queen
announces tomorrow. In the end, she'll take his advice. And he
and his brother-in-law and all his advisors have commissioned
this book, and will see it published. The queen will have to
name Katherine as her heir when the whole of Christendom
says she was truly married and all the Privy Council say she
is heir.'

We hear the clock strike the hour. 'I have to go,' I say, barely
stirring from his warm embrace.

He lifts me down from his lap and, leaning forward, he
straightens my gown and pulls the creases from my sleeves. He
is as gentle as a lady's maid. He touches my hood and tweaks my
ruff. 'There,' he says. 'The prettiest lady in the court.'

I wait for him to open the door to the guardroom and glance
out. 'All clear,' he says, and he steps back to let me out.

As I cross the courtyard from the main gate to the garden
stairs, my cape wrapped around me against a sprinkling of
snow, I have the ill luck to meet the queen herself, coming in
from playing bowls on the frozen green. She has her red velvet
hood trimmed with ermine pulled up over her ears. Her hand is
on Robert Dudley's arm, her cheeks rosy with the cold and her
eyes sparkling. I step back and curtsey, sliding my ruby ring from
my finger into the pocket of my cape before her quick dark gaze
spots it. 'Your Majesty.'

Thomasina, the queen's dwarf, follows them and makes a
comical little face at me, as if to ask me where I have been. I
completely ignore her. She has no right to express any curiosity
about me. I don't have to answer to her, and if she prompts an

enquiry from the queen then I will find her afterwards and tell her to mind her own tiny business.

'Lady Mary,' Elizabeth says with an unpleasant tone. I cannot think what I have done to offend her, but she is clearly displeased. 'Are you honouring me with your attendance at my dressing for dinner tonight?'

I can feel Robert Dudley's reassuring smile rather than see it. I dare not look directly anywhere but into Elizabeth's sparking dark eyes. 'Of course, Your Majesty,' I say meekly. 'And the honour is mine.'

'Remember it then,' she says nastily, and sweeps past me. I curtsey and when I raise my head I catch a quick sympathetic smile from Robert Dudley and a cheeky wink from Thomasina. He follows in the queen's wake. She lingers.

'Someone's writing a book about your sister,' she informs me. 'That's why she's so furious with you. She's just heard about it. Apparently, it's going to say that your sister will be the next Queen of England. You will be sister to the queen and aunt to the next king. Fancy a dwarf just like me so close to the throne.'

'I'm nothing like you,' I say coldly.

'Oh, do you think you will be taller with a great crown on your sister's head?' she asks, smiling. 'Will her elevation make you grow? Will you rise up higher if she makes you a duchess?'

'I don't know what you are talking about.' I turn away but she catches at the skirt of my gown in her little square-palmed hand, so like my own.

'What is it?' I say crossly. 'Let me go. D'you think we're going to brawl in the yard like page boys?'

'There are some that would pay good money to see it,' she says cheerfully. 'But I have always made my living as a miniature lady, never as a merry dwarf.'

'And I have never made my living at all,' I say grandly. 'And my height has nothing to do with anything. I'll thank you to let go of my gown.'

She lets me go, but her impertinent smile never falters. 'There is a book indeed, Lady Mary,' she says shortly. 'The scholars are putting it together, piece by piece. A page stolen from the chancery to show that your family was named as heir by Henry VIII, evidence of marriage to show that your line is legitimate, proof that all three of you, Lady Jane, Lady Katherine and you, are English-born, Protestant and royal.'

'Don't you speak of Jane,' I say warningly.

'Buried in a coffin as big as a child's!' she says jeeringly, and I turn on my heel and stride away, but I can hear her pattering after me and she dodges around me and blocks my way.

'You want to know the rest of this,' she tells me. 'Listen, for your own good. The scholars' reports from France and Spain all name your sister Katherine as the rightful heir. The queen is furious. If it was you commissioned the report you'd do well to warn your clerks to make themselves scarce. You could tell your uncle to take a trip to France for his health. You'd better keep your head down and stop running off to kiss the sergeant porter.'

I bite off a gasp of shock.

'I see a lot,' she adds quickly. 'You know how. Nobody pays any attention to us.'

'And why would you warn me?' I demand. 'When you live in her shadow?'

'Because we're both dwarfs,' she says bluntly. 'We are both small women in a very big and dangerous world. We have a sisterhood of shortness, even if you want to deny it. So I say to you – don't offend her. She's furious enough with your family as it is.'

She gives me a cheeky little nod of the head, as if to drive the point home, and then she turns and skips across the yard, looking like a little girl running after a teacher, and I see the door to Elizabeth's privy stair bang behind her.

WINDSOR CASTLE,
SPRING 1564

I serve Elizabeth all through the bitingly cold spring with meticulous courtesy and though she snaps her fingers at me for her fan, and complains that I scratch her neck when I tie her sapphire necklace, she can find nothing else to say against me.

I never even glance towards Thomasina the dwarf to thank her for the warning, and when a movement in the dance puts us side by side, I change my place if I can. I don't acknowledge the sisterhood of tiny feet. I don't subscribe to a stunted sorority. Of course I can recognise my features in Thomasina, in her rolling gait on her short legs, in the constant turn of her face upwards so that she can follow a conversation that is going on far above her head. I guess that her back aches like mine after a long day in the saddle, and that we both hate it when people address us as children, mistaking stature for age or wisdom. But I will never indicate that she and I are of the same mould. There is a coincidence of appearance but that is all. Should Elizabeth claim cousinhood with every redhead? Should Lady Margaret Douglas be sister to a horse? Appearance means nothing compared to breeding. I am all royal and no dwarf; I am all Grey and no pretty toy. I am an heir to the throne of England and Thomasina is an heir of nothing more important than short bones.

But one evening, in early spring, we go to dinner and I see that William Cecil is absent, which is unusual, and Robert Dudley's flattery and good humour are a little forced. Elizabeth bristles like a cat that has been caught in a shower of water tossed from a chamber window; everyone can see her irritability. No-one but Thomasina the dwarf seems to know who has been so foolish as to cross Elizabeth, and I cannot bring myself to ask her.

When the tables are being cleared, Robert Dudley bends over the queen's hand and I see her nod to her clerk, who gives him a sheaf of papers. He bows and takes them, and starts to leave the hall. I sidle round, against the walls, unnoticed by anyone as my head disappears behind the high-backed chairs, and I meet him just inside the great doors, and slip out when they are opened for him.

'Lady Mary,' he says, bowing to me. The doors close behind us, hiding us from the view of the court.

'Is there some trouble?' I ask him frankly.

He bends down low so that he can speak quietly to me. 'Yes. Someone – I imagine the French ambassador – has put a book in the hands of the queen that supports your sister Lady Katherine's claim to the throne.'

'Lady Hertford,' I say, giving her married title.

He scowls at me. 'Lady Katherine,' he repeats. 'This is not the time for you to be asserting a marriage that the queen has ruled is invalid.'

I look into the dark face of the man whose own marriage would have been ruled invalid, if his wife had not been conveniently murdered instead.

'We know the truth,' I say staunchly.

'And the authors have published what they think is their truth,' he replies evenly.

'Didn't you commission the book?' I demand, knowing that he did.

'No,' he lies. 'And those who are associated with it will suffer. The queen has issued a warrant of arrest for your uncle John Grey, for John Hales, the author, for Robert Beale, his clerk, for Edward Seymour's stepfather, Francis Newdigate. Even for Nicholas Bacon the Lord Keeper, who gave his opinion in favour of your sister.'

I go cold with shock. 'My uncle arrested? The Lord Keeper

arrested? But what about Katherine?' I clasp my hands on his sleeve. 'Oh, Sir Robert! They're not taking her back to the Tower, are they?'

'No.'

'But where is she to go, if my uncle is taken from his home? Are they leaving her there with Lady Grey? Or is she released? Oh, Sir Robert, is she released?'

'No.' He straightens up. 'Lady Mary, I have to leave about Her Majesty's business. I have to send out guards to arrest these men for questioning.'

I look up the long handsome length of him. 'You, arrest them? You, who had nothing to do with the book, now arrest them?'

'Yes,' he says concisely. 'As the queen commands me to do.'

There is no point complaining that he always does whatever the queen wants, that he never opposes her. You don't get to be a favourite at a tyrant's court without beheading your principles every day. All I can do is to try to keep him on Katherine's side.

'Sir Robert, this is cruel to my sister and to her little boys. They have done nothing. She has done nothing. Someone else commissioned this book – perhaps even friends of yours – but she did not. Someone wrote it – not her. Someone published it – not her. Can't you ask for her to be free? Even if you have to arrest these others?'

He shakes his dark head. 'The queen won't listen to me about this,' he says. 'She won't listen to anyone. She has the right to grant pardon only where it pleases her.'

'Margaret Douglas our cousin has been forgiven for far worse!'

'That is Her Majesty's decision. It is within her power.'

'I know that!' I say. 'She is—'

He throws his hand up to remind me that he cannot hear anything that is critical of the woman who rules us both.

'She is determined,' I continue, and as he turns and goes I whisper to myself: 'Determined to be vile.'

I am at the gatehouse with Thomas Keyes, who is watching the gate and the guard on duty from the little window, when I hear the clatter of horses, and Thomas says: 'That's your sister's advocate, under arrest, poor fellow.'

He lifts me up on to a stool so I can peep out of the window to see, and not be seen. Hales rides in on a poor horse and behind him I see another man, his face downturned, in the centre of an armed guard.

'My God! And that is my uncle John. John Grey, who was keeping my sister!'

Thomas leaves me, taking up his black staff of office. I hear his shout of challenge and then he opens the gate to them, admits them, and comes back to me, putting his great staff back in the corner and loosening his leather belt.

'But what have they done?' he asks me, his kind face puzzled. 'Is it just for writing their book?'

'Yes,' I say bitterly. 'You know my uncle would never do anything against Elizabeth. He has been loyal to her forever. And John Hales himself says that all he was trying to do was to prove the case for a Protestant to succeed. He wasn't calling for Katherine to take Elizabeth's place, just for her to be named as heir if Elizabeth should die without a son.'

'The Privy Council will see that,' Thomas says hopefully.

'Unless they close their eyes very tight,' I say bitterly.

GREENWICH PALACE,
SUMMER 1564

Elizabeth summons me to her bedchamber as she is dressing for dinner. She is seated before her table, her mirror of Venetian glass is before her, her red wig planted on its stand, candles all around her while her ladies meticulously, carefully paint her face with ceruse. She remains perfectly still, like a marble statue, as the mixture of white lead and vinegar is spread flawlessly from her hairline to her neck and down to her breasts. Nobody even breathes aloud. I freeze like all the other statues in the room until she opens her eyes, sees me in the mirror and says, without moving her lips where the ceruse is drying, 'Lady Mary, look at this.'

Obedient to the downward cast of her eyes, I step forward and when she blinks her permission, I take up the little book that is open before her.

The title is the *Monas Hieroglyphica* and the author is John Dee. It seems to be dedicated to the Holy Roman Emperor and the long preface challenges the reader to consider that the symbols of the planets are meaningful in themselves, and can be read as a language or as a code.

I look up and meet Elizabeth's dark gaze in the mirror. 'Look through it,' she orders through her closed lips. 'What do you think?'

I turn the small pages. They are covered with designs and astronomical symbols and tiny print explaining what each one means, and how each fits with each other. I can see that there are some mathematical pages, demonstrating the connection between the symbols, and some that look more like philosophical writing, or even alchemy.

'I can't understand it at first sight,' I say frankly. 'I should have to study it for many days to understand it. I am sorry, Your Majesty.'

'I can't understand it either.' Elizabeth exhales and a puff of white powder blows against the mirror. 'But I think it is an extraordinary work. He brings together the symbols of the ancients, and the studies of the Muslims – he speaks of a universal world that exists alongside this one, behind this one, that we can sense but rarely see. But he thinks that these symbols describe it, and there is a language that can be learned.'

I shake my head in bewilderment. 'I could read it carefully, if you wish, and write a digest,' I offer.

She smiles only slightly, so as not to crack the paint. 'I shall read it with the author himself,' she says. 'He is at my command. But you can sit and listen to our learned conversation, if you wish. I just wanted to see what you made of it, at first sight.'

'I have not had the privilege of your learning,' I say tactfully. 'But I should be glad to know more. If I might listen to you, I am sure I would understand more.'

'But I hear on all sides that your sister Jane was such a scholar,' she says. 'I hear that Roger Ascham is telling everyone that she was the greatest scholar of her time. He's writing a book memorialising her. Everyone seems to want to publish these days – don't they have enough to do?'

'He met her only once or twice,' I say, swallowing the desire to defend Jane against this old jealousy. 'He hardly knew her.'

'I studied with the queen Kateryn Parr, too, remember,' Elizabeth says, brooding over long-ago rivalries.

'And I,' says Lady Margaret Douglas from the back of the room, desperate to join in and remind Elizabeth of her kinship. Elizabeth does not even turn her head.

'I am sure she never read anything like this book by Doctor Dee,' I say, trying to return Elizabeth to the present.

'Yes,' she says. 'I dare say she would not have understood it.'

They paint her lips and darken her eyelashes and her eyebrows. They drop belladonna into her eyes to make them darken and sparkle. I stand holding the book, waiting to see if I am dismissed. This is not my night to serve her; it is not my night to paint the whited sepulchre that is this old queen. Tonight I should be free to do what I wish; but she keeps me here while she worries if I am clever enough to understand something that is unclear to her, fretting that my long-dead sister was a better scholar.

'At any rate, you don't think it is heresy?' She rises from the table and they hold the skirt of her gown to her feet so that she can step in, and they can draw it up and tie it at her waist.

'I could not give an opinion,' I say guardedly. 'Your Majesty would be the best judge of that. But I have always heard you speak well of John Dee.'

'I have,' she confirms. 'And I am glad he has come back to England with such learning! I shall start to read his book tomorrow. You may join us.'

I curtsey as if I am most grateful. 'Thank you, Your Majesty. I shall look forward to learning from you both.'

John Dee, dark-eyed, dark-gowned like a scholar, is surrounded by papers. Each one scrawled with a symbol, one pointed to the other, each one annotated with a dozen little notes. I see that he draws little hands with an accusing finger towards a paragraph that he wants us to note well. Elizabeth, his book open on her lap, sits among this scholarly storm, her eyes bright with attention. Thomasina, like an exquisitely dressed lapdog, kneels at her feet. I sit on a stool to one side; I will never cringe on the floor while Elizabeth sits.

John Dee speaks of the symbols of the stars, whatever is shown in the heavens is matched by what happens on the earth. 'As above, so below,' he says.

'So can you foretell the marriages of princes?' Elizabeth asks.

'With great accuracy, if I had their dates, time, and location of their birth, which would tell me their astral house,' Dee replies.

'Is that not astrology?' I ask him, warningly.

He nods at my caution. 'No, for I am not looking to foretell harm,' he says. 'It is illegal to foretell the death of a prince, but it is harmless to foresee their happiness.' He turns his bright look on Elizabeth. 'May I choose the best day for your marriage, as I did for your coronation?'

Elizabeth laughs affectedly. 'Not mine, good philosopher. You know that I am not that way inclined. I have just been forced to disappoint the archduke Ferdinand. I told him I would rather be a spinster milkmaid than a married queen!'

'Celibacy is a calling,' John Dee replies, and I fight to keep my face grave at the thought of Elizabeth as a nun. I don't dare to look at Thomasina, who keeps her head down.

At a little distance from our charmed circle the ladies sigh with boredom and shift position. The courtiers stand against the walls, talking among themselves, and one or two lean back against the panelling for weariness. Nobody is allowed to sit, though John Dee has been reading from his book for two hours.

Dee takes up another page and shows it to the queen as William Cecil enters the room quietly and bows.

'Forgive the interruption to your studies,' he says in a low voice. 'But you wanted to know as soon as the Queen of Scots gave permission for Lady Margaret Douglas's husband to enter Scotland.'

The boy my pretty kinsman Henry Stuart, yawning in a corner, catches the whisper of his mother's name and looks up, but Elizabeth and Cecil are head-to-head.

'Queen Mary has never agreed?' she exclaims, hiding her beam behind a painted fan.

Cecil bows. 'She has.'

She takes his sleeve and pulls him closer. Only Thomasina and I can hear their whispered conference. 'But I only asked because I was certain she would refuse him admission to his Scots lands,' she whispers. 'I only asked in order to distract and trouble Mary while she was negotiating with Don Carlos of Spain.'

'You have won more than you intended, then,' Cecil says smoothly. 'You have outwitted her. For she has given permission to both the Earl of Lennox and his son to enter Scotland, and as papists they are certain to divide her from her Protestant advisors. Shall they go, or would it be safer to keep the youth here?'

Elizabeth beckons to Henry Stuart Lord Darnley, a fair-headed boy as beautiful as a girl. He is a cousin of mine, since he is the son of Lady Margaret Douglas, but I can't say we share much family feeling. I have never liked his mother, who revels in Elizabeth's unfairness – she goes free while my sister is imprisoned; her stock rises while my sister's falls. I swear that she thinks of herself as heir to the throne while everyone knows that it should be Katherine.

Henry Stuart himself came back from France to serve like a little bird in the cage of court: he warbles away to please the queen but the cage door never opens. His mother would put him anywhere that he might be seen: she thinks he is irresistible. It is an open secret that she hoped he would marry Mary Queen of Scots but the queen managed to resist his rosy-lipped promises in the first days of her widowhood. Now he bows low to Elizabeth, and he nods to me; but we neither of us waste much time on the other. He is a vain young man with little interest in any woman of any size. What he knows to perfection is how to please older indulgent women who enjoy the company of a pretty boy, like his mother or the queen. All he likes for himself is to get drunk and range around the town looking for trouble with other pretty boys. Either way, I do not attract his attention, and he does not waste any on me.

'You may tell your father that he has his passport from the Queen of Scots, at my request,' Elizabeth says to Henry Stuart. He flushes like a girl and drops to one knee. Elizabeth smiles on him. 'Will you want to go to Scotland with him?' she asks.

'Not to leave you!' he exclaims, as if his heart might break. 'I mean, forgive me, I spoke too swiftly. I will do whatever you command, whatever my father commands. But I don't want to leave this court for another. Does one go from the sun to the moon?'

'You will have to go, if your father needs you,' Elizabeth rules.

His eyes shine as he flicks his long fringe out of his eyes; he is as adorable as a golden spaniel puppy. 'May I not stay?'

Elizabeth reaches out to him and sweeps the blonde locks from his rose-petal face. 'Yes,' she says indulgently. 'I cannot spare you. Your father, Lord Lennox, shall go and settle his business on his lands and you shall stay safe as a little bird in the nest with me.'

Cecil raises his eyebrows at the queen's doting tone, and says nothing. Henry Stuart presumes to catch Her Majesty's hand and presses it to his lips. Elizabeth smiles and allows him to take the liberty.

'I shall never leave you,' he swears. 'I couldn't bear it.'

Certainly, I know that he won't, for Thomas Keyes has orders not to let him out of the gate. But this is the masque of courtly love, and that is more important than any mundane truth.

'I know you never will,' Elizabeth purrs, like a fat cat with the pleasure of his attention.

'I am not like Robert Dudley! Isn't he going to Scotland to marry the queen?' Darnley asks, dropping poison on the sugarloaf.

Elizabeth's face convulses under the paint. 'He goes for love of me,' she rules.

WHITEHALL PALACE, LONDON, AUTUMN 1564

James Melville, a softly spoken Scots charmer, deployed by Mary, his queen, to inveigle Elizabeth into declaring her as heir, comes to our court at the end of the summer. The days are warm, but the nights are getting cooler; the leaves are changing colour and blazing in bronze and gold and red. Elizabeth, who loves the hot weather, lingers over her summer pleasures and insists that we go out on the royal barge to see the sunset on the river, even though the twilight brings a cold wind down the valley.

The queen summons the Scots diplomat to sit beside her throne at the centre of the barge. I am on one side, Kat Ashley, restored to favour, on the other. Thomasina the dwarf is standing on a box in the prow so that she can see the flow of the silvery stream ahead. I turn my gaze away from her. I don't like to see her standing up like a child to wave at the fishermen, at the rowers of the wherries.

Elizabeth is head-to-head with the Scots advisor. Whatever she is saying, she hopes to keep it secret. But I can read his discreet smile as clearly as my sister Jane could read Greek. I know exactly what she is telling him – she is telling him that he has to persuade Mary Queen of Scots to marry Robert Dudley, and in reward she will be given my sister Katherine's rights: she will be named as Elizabeth's heir. She is promising him that Katherine will be kept under house arrest until that day, that any campaign for her will be silenced, that any publications will be suppressed. Elizabeth is favouring Mary Queen of Scots as her heir and my sister will be ignored by everyone until it is agreed.

I dare not glance across at Kat Ashley, who must disapprove of this madness as much as Melville, as much as William Cecil, as much as the reluctant bridegroom, Robert Dudley himself. I dare not look at any of the ladies for fear of someone winking at me. None of us think that when the moment comes for him to leave, Elizabeth will bring herself to let her lover go. None of us think that Mary will be grateful for a cast-off. None of us think that Robert Dudley – even with his immense ambition – will dare to reach as high as a queen who is not already compromised by his lovemaking. But Elizabeth gives every appearance of being determined; and she whispers and whispers earnestly to the Scots ambassador, until, finally, he nods in agreement, bows, and steps back.

Elizabeth leans back in her chair and smiles at her beloved Kat. 'He'll do it,' is all she says. 'He will convince her. And she will take Dudley.'

'I can see why Melville will try – for the great prize of seeing his queen as heir to the throne of England. But will Dudley do it? Will you?'

Elizabeth turns her head. 'I can trust no-one but Robert with her,' she says in an undertone. 'And I trust her with no-one but him. If she were to marry Don Carlos of Spain or the French duke, then we have an enemy at our back door, and papist priests pouring across the Tweed. But Robert will save me, as he has done before. He will marry her and master her.'

'But you will have to let him go,' Kat says gently. 'You will have to send him into the arms of another woman.'

'Perhaps it won't be for a while,' Elizabeth says vaguely. 'It will take a long time to arrange, surely? And we might all stay together sometimes. We could have a northern court at York, or Newcastle, or Carlisle, every summer, for all the summer. We could have the Council of the North and Robert could command it. Certainly, once she is with child, he could come home to England.'

'With child,' Kat repeats, her eyes on the queen's face. 'She is young and fertile. They say that she is crying in her bed at night for a husband. What if she falls in love with Sir Robert and they make a child of love? Have you thought how you will feel when you hear that she is carrying his baby? How do you think he will feel when his wife is carrying the Dudley heir to the throne of Scotland and England? Don't you fear that he will love her, then? Wouldn't any man love his wife then?'

I can see Elizabeth grow paler under the paint on her face. I guess that her stomach is churning with jealousy. 'He should father a prince,' she defends her own idea. 'He is a man entirely fit to own a kingdom. And perhaps it will take so long that she will be past her childbearing years before they are married.'

'She's twenty-one,' Kat says flatly. 'How long do you think you can stretch it out?'

Elizabeth pulls a fur over her shoulders and turns a furious face towards me. I flinch from her dark glare. 'Anything is better than her sister,' she says abruptly, nodding her red head towards me. 'I won't have a rival in my sight. I won't have my heir setting up house with a Seymour, quartering royal arms on her heraldry, while everyone flocks to her side. I won't have a young woman like Katherine Grey in my court, and everyone making comparisons.'

WHITEHALL PALACE, LONDON, AUTUMN 1564

Nobody believes that the queen intends to part with Robert Dudley. But she persuades James Melville that she means it, and William Cecil makes preparations for a meeting of Scots and English commissioners at Berwick to sign a marriage agreement and an alliance. Thomasina the dwarf looks at me with a hidden smile as if we two, who see Elizabeth when she is not showing off her dancing, or her music, or her scholarship to the Scots ambassador, know more than these men who are obliged to admire her. To make her favourite a worthy suitor she decides that he has to be Earl of Leicester and Baron Denbigh, and all the court attends the great hall to watch Robert Dudley, the son of a traitor and the grandson of a traitor, kneel before the queen and arise an earl. Queen Mary must be assured that Elizabeth loves Robert Dudley like a brother, and respects him as a temporal lord. But Elizabeth cannot even complete this charade without spoiling the scene. As he kneels in homage she caresses the back of his neck. The Scots ambassador sees it; we all see it. She might as well announce to the world that she loves him and he is completely under her thumb. It is impossible: Mary Queen of Scots will never take Elizabeth's leavings when they are not even pushed to the side of her plate. It is as if Elizabeth's spittle is still on him.

WHITEHALL PALACE, LONDON, WINTER 1564

I am hurrying into court one evening in November with a cold mist coming off the river and a haze of drizzle around the torches in the courtyard when Thomas looms out of the shadow of the doorway to the main gate as if he has been waiting for me.

'Thomas!' I exclaim. 'What are you doing here? I can't stop. I have to go to the great hall.'

His big face is scowling, his bonnet is crushed in his great hand. 'I had to see you.'

'What's the matter?'

'It's trouble for you,' he says miserably. 'Oh, Mary, God knows that I wish I could spare you.'

I swallow down my fear. 'What is it? Not Katherine? Not one of her boys?'

He drops to one knee so his head is level with mine. 'No, thank God, she is safe as a little bird in a cage. It is your uncle. He has died.'

'She has beheaded him?' I whisper my greatest fear.

'No, no. It's not that bad. They say it was grief.'

I feel myself go still and quiet. He was never a loving kinsman – but he suffered imprisonment for supporting Katherine, and he was a good guardian to her. Now that he is dead she has lost her guardian. And another of our family has died through the disfavour of a Tudor. Truly, they are hard masters to serve, impossible to love.

'God save his soul,' I say without thinking.

'Amen,' says Thomas devoutly.

'But what about Katherine? Oh, Thomas. Do you think the queen will free her now? She can't stay at Pirgo without him.'

He takes my hand and holds it between his broad palms. 'No, pretty one. That's the bad news on top of bad news. They're sending her to William Petre. I myself saw the guard ride out to fetch her, as if she were a prisoner likely to break out. They're not freeing her, they're moving her, and will keep her even closer.'

I frown. 'Sir William Petre? Is he still alive? I thought he was sick. He must be a hundred and two, at least.'

He shakes his head. 'He's not yet sixty, but they're putting a heavy burden on him. Perhaps he was the only one who lacked the skills to wriggle out of it.' He looks at me, his big face creased with concern. 'It might be all right. He has a pretty house; she may like it there. Her little boy may be allowed to play out in the gardens.'

'Where? Where does he live?'

'Ingatestone Hall in Essex. You've been there, do you remember it? It's halfway to New Hall.'

'I have to see her,' I say with sudden determination. 'I have to go and see her. I can't stand this any longer.'

I wait until Elizabeth has finished the dinner and danced with the new earl, Robert Dudley. He exerts himself to charm Elizabeth and make her laugh, and everyone continues to congratulate them on his rise to greatness, and her good judgement in recognising the extraordinary value of this man. But has she done enough to persuade Queen Mary to have him? Baron or not, earl or not, Mary Queen of Scots will not have Elizabeth's cast-offs without a firm promise that she will be given my sister's rights, and the conference at Berwick between the Scots and English advisors is struggling to make an agreement. Elizabeth is determined that Mary shall marry Robert Dudley and be named as her heir. Mary insists that the inheritance comes before the marriage. Nobody asks how two queens who trust each other so little can make a lasting agreement.

But at least Elizabeth is in a happy mood tonight. I hold out her satin nightgown, warmed before the fire, as someone else serves sweetmeats and a third lady-in-waiting brings sweet wine for her, while the grooms of the bedchamber stab the bed and look underneath it for enemies, as if we truly believe that she is going to spend more than ten minutes in there once the door is shut. I wait till she is settled in her chair by the fire and she has everything that she might want, and I go towards her and kneel.

'Don't go any lower, Lady Mary, or you will fall under the log basket,' she says, and everyone laughs. I feel Thomasina's steady gaze on my face as I am insulted before them all. I rise to my full height. Even now I am only level with Elizabeth's unfriendly eyes.

'Your Majesty, I ask you for a very great favour,' I say quietly.

'Have you thought carefully?' she asks. 'Before asking me for a great favour?'

'I have.'

Her eyes dance with amusement. *'Which of you, though he took thought therefore, could put one cubit unto his stature?'*

I flush scarlet as everyone sycophantically laughs at the queen's wit. 'I want to add lustre to your reputation for mercy, not height to myself,' I say quietly. I can feel Thomasina's eyes on my face as if they would burn me.

The good humour is wiped from the queen's face as if she had taken a sponge to the white lead. 'I can think of no-one who deserves my mercy,' she remarks.

'My sister Katherine,' I say very quietly. 'We have lost our uncle, her gaoler. I have just learned that he has died of grief at Your Majesty's displeasure. The turning away of your beautiful countenance has killed him. I know that Katherine my sister does not eat, and cries all day. She suffers, too, under her great queen's disfavour. I fear that she has not the courage to live without your goodwill. I beg you, at the very least, to let me visit her.'

She takes just a moment to consider my petition. I see that Thomasina is holding her breath. Her ladies wait. I wait.

'No,' she says.

I can only write to Katherine.

My dear sister,

I hope that you can be comfortable at Ingatestone, and that your little boy brings you joy. I know you will have heard comforting news from Hanworth. Your oldest boy and the earl his father are both well, and long to be with you again.

I am well at court, and Her Majesty is so filled with grace and tenderness, so judicious with her great power, that I don't doubt you will be forgiven some day soon. I do ask for you.

Oh Katherine, I miss you so much.

With love

Your sister

Mary

WHITEHALL PALACE, LONDON, WINTER 1564

While I wait and hope for a reply, Sir William Cecil walks beside me in the gallery one day, shortening his long stride to my little paces, and bending down so that he can see my face.

'I hear that you have written to your sister?'

I imagine he read the letter the minute that I gave it to my page and asked him to deliver it to Katherine at Ingatestone. Indeed, the last paragraph was written for the queen to see.

'Yes,' I say guardedly. 'No-one told me that I was not allowed to write to her. I was enquiring after her health and assuring her of my sisterly love.'

'The letter was perfectly allowable,' he assures me. He stops and, with a little tip of his head, invites me to sit beside him in a window seat, where he can see my face without stooping. I pull over a low stool and use it as a step to climb up. He knows that I do not want assistance, and when I am settled, he sits beside me.

'I have sorrowful news for you about Lord Hertford,' he says.

My first thought is that my brother-in-law has died. I think that the news will be the end of my sister. I grit my teeth and say nothing. I raise my eyes to his face and wait for him to speak.

'He has been taken from the care of his mother and sent to live with Sir John Mason in his house in London,' William Cecil says.

'Why?'

The old courtier shrugs his shoulders as if to tell me that he cannot say, and anyway, I know as well as he does that there will be no good reason. Elizabeth has no cause for her spite against Ned and his little boy, my sister's son, except that he was at her court and fell in love with another woman. 'I am sorry for it,' he says heavily.

'And Teddy, the little boy, goes with his father?'

Cecil bows his head. 'No.'

I could hardly speak for distress. 'Where has she taken Katherine's boy?'

'He is left with his grandmother at Hanworth. He can live more freely with her in his family home.'

'Raised as an orphan?'

'In his family home, by his grandmother. He will be safe under her guidance.'

'My God, Katherine will be heartbroken!'

Elizabeth's advisor knows all about heartbreak. He only nods.

I steady myself. 'Is there anything we can do?' I ask quietly. 'Anything? Is there anything we can do to get them all back together again?'

'Not yet,' he says gently. 'But I have some hopes.'

'What?'

'If the Scots marriage between the queen and Robert Dudley is given up, then the Scots queen will never be named as heir to England. Our queen will see that she has no heir but Lady Katherine.'

'And is the marriage between the Queen of Scots and Robert Dudley given up?' I ask.

Cecil chooses his words. 'The Scots have called the bluff,' he says quietly. 'They have said that they will accept him, if their queen is declared heir to England. They have invited him to Edinburgh, but now that it comes to it, I think Her Majesty won't order him to go. We cannot deliver Robert Dudley. He will stay in England.'

This is enormous news that William Cecil tells me so quietly. Once again, there is no Protestant heir but my sister. As I take a shuddering breath I see that William Cecil is watching me.

'Whatever Her Majesty wishes,' I say humbly.

William Cecil nods his approval. 'I am sure she will judge rightly.'

He draws a letter from inside his black velvet jacket. 'This came first to me, as it must. But it is for you. I am sorry there is no good news.'

I look at the broken seal. It is from Katherine. I smile at her defiance. She is using the Seymour seal of angel wings on her folded letter. The seal has been broken and the letter read. Sir William's spies see everything. He gets to his feet, bows to me, and leaves me to read my letter from my sister.

Dearest Mary,

I thank you for your letter and your good wishes. I am afraid they come too late for me. I think my heart is broken at being parted from my husband and my darling boy and I can neither eat nor sleep. My marriage, which started with a feast in bed, is ending in hunger and lonely wakeful nights.

I know that you and all our friends have done your best to explain to Her Gracious Majesty that I meant no wrong, and that all my offences were for love, not for gain.

I hope that I may be freed, and my little boys. If I should die,
Mary, I do pray that you will care for them and tell them how
much I loved them, and their father. I hope that you can find
happiness and perhaps love. If you have a chance of either I
hope that you can take it.

Farewell, good sister
Katherine

WHITEHALL PALACE, LONDON, SPRING 1565

The pretty boy, Henry Stuart Lord Darnley, is granted a passport to join his father in Scotland and Elizabeth agrees that he
can go. His journey is enthusiastically proposed by Elizabeth's
two advisors, Robert Dudley and William Cecil, for their own
selfish reasons. Robert Dudley would send the devil himself to
Scotland to marry the queen if it left him safe at home, and Cecil
believes that Henry – French-speaking, cultured, beautifully
mannered, the cousin who has been pressed on her ever since her
widowhood by our cousin Lady Margaret Douglas – will distract
the queen from trying to unify and rule her people. He predicts
that Henry Stuart will cause endless trouble.

Nobody but his mother thinks that the Queen of Scots will
take the handsome youth seriously; Elizabeth never would. But
Cecil thinks that Henry Stuart and his father, the Earl of Lennox,
befriending all the Scots lords, irritating the powerful preacher
John Knox, stirring up old rivalries and claiming his wife's
Douglas family lands, will confuse matters in Edinburgh beyond
Mary's management. The fiercely Protestant Scots lords will hate
the effete papist French-speaking English boy and will conspire
against him, breaking the fragile support that Mary has won.

Robert Dudley, for his part, is desperate not to be banished to Scotland and married off to a woman who must despise him as an adulterer and a wife murderer. He knows that, whatever she says now, Elizabeth would never forgive him marrying another woman. He is gambling everything on her inability to let him go. He urges her to send Henry Stuart to take his place, as a diversion in Mary's court – nothing more.

Nobody suggests that pretty Henry Stuart Lord Darnley might be a suitable husband and advisor for Queen Mary, that he might hold her loyal to England and serve as an English ambassador and wise advisor. He's not yet twenty years old and he has spent his life under the heavy hoof of his papist mother, alternately indulged and scolded by her. He has been raised as a courtier, he is charming and pleasing and amusing and good company. But nobody thinks he can act like a skilled diplomat with his first loyalty to England. Everyone believes he is nothing more than a time-wasting folly.

I think that they underrate him. I believe his sweet face hides an avaricious heart, and his fair looks might charm the lonely French queen, surrounded as she is with hearty loud men of action, insisting on their rights. We are not all Elizabeths: desiring a man who looks more like a horse thief than a nobleman. But neither Cecil (though he has studied her likes and dislikes since she was a girl) nor the dark Robert (who has been her preference for as long) can make the flight of fancy to imagine that another woman might find a different sort of man far superior. I think young Henry has great charm, if you like a pretty doll – but as something of a pretty doll myself, that is not surprising.

Even I cannot say I am an admirer of Lord Darnley, and I see him leave court without regret. He is so excited by his freedom that he forgets his mother's rivalry with mine, and smiles at me for the first time ever. 'As my star rises, I will remember your sister,' he says sweetly enough. 'Who can doubt the favour that the queen is showing our side of the family? You and your sister will become unimportant and I will speak for you.'

'She is sorely in need of friends,' I say steadily. 'But all our trust is in Her Majesty.'

He waves to the court that has gathered to see him leave. He bows as gracefully as a dancer and turns and leaps from the ground into the saddle. His horse curvets, he holds it on a hard rein and sits well as it rears. He doffs his hat and kisses his hand to Elizabeth and she smiles graciously on him. He really does look as handsome as a mounted angel. I wonder how long after he is out of sight she will regret letting him go.

Less than a month is the answer! I could laugh if I were not standing, straight as a poker, tall as a broadsword, as she rages up and down her room. Sir William Maitland, the Scots queen's advisor, arrives from Edinburgh, carrying the extraordinary request from Queen Mary to marry Elizabeth's noble subject – Henry Stuart Lord Darnley. Elizabeth goes white with anger and retreats to her privy chamber. Cecil and Dudley go in and out like anxious jacks-in-the-box. In: to listen to Elizabeth shouting in rage that Henry Stuart is false as his mother, Margaret Douglas, as his father, Matthew Stuart Earl of Lennox, and that Mary is a fool and he will break her heart and ruin her chance of ever being named as heir to England. Out: to meet with the lords of the Privy Council and see if there is any legal contrivance, any forbidden relationship, any device by which they can refuse permission for the marriage or – if it has already taken place – declare it void.

It is as good as a play for me – a savagely comical play – to see how these great men set to work to destroy a woman's innocent desire. They think of nothing but the advantage of their own course, the victory of their own policy. They think nothing of a woman in love, a young woman, without advisors, a lonely young woman who has a handsome young man thrown at her in a court riven with anger, and has nowhere else to turn.

'It's not even as if he were a very admirable young man,' I say to Thomas Keyes. It is a cold afternoon and we are seated either side of the fire in his private room, over the watergate. One of his officers is on duty at the main gate. The winding mechanism for the portcullis of the watergate is on the other side of the wall and nobody can raise it without Thomas's permission. He has some wine in a pot and, as I watch, he gently takes the poker from the red-hot embers and seethes it in the wine. The hiss of the boiling liquid and the scent of mulled wine fills the room. He pours me a cup and takes one for himself.

'A dainty little nobleman,' he says. 'But, I fear, not one that walks in the ways of the Lord.'

This is an extreme condemnation for Thomas to make – my Thomas, who never speaks ill of anyone. I look at him over the top of my cup. 'Why, what do you know of him?'

He smiles at me. 'I keep the gate,' he reminds me. 'Nobody comes in without me seeing them. I know who visits him – and they're not the best sort of men. And I often see him. He comes down to visit my soldiers,' he says shortly. 'To drink with them – when they are off duty. I won't say more than that; it is not fitting.'

I am agape at the scandal he is hinting. 'You never told me anything like this before.'

'It's not fitting that I should speak of it,' he says. 'Nor that you should hear. My betrothed does not deal in gossip.'

I beam at him. 'You have a very high opinion of me, Thomas. The court's principal currency is gossip. You have just given me a fortune of scandal if I chose to sell it.'

He nods. 'Oh, I am rich in scandal. Don't you think I let people in and out at all hours? I hear everything; but I don't repeat it.'

'I am glad of it,' I say. 'For I could not be here if I thought you would ever tell.'

He shakes his head. 'Not me.'

'Have you taken any messages from Sir William Petre? Or heard any news of my sister?' I ask him.

'I know only what you do: that she is low in spirits, that he is a poor host, a tired and sick old man. He is ordered to keep her close and not spend money on her. It is an unhappy household.'

The thought of Katherine, who was always so light-hearted and playful, sunk under grief in a poor house, makes me lower my head and gaze into the red embers as if I would see a happier future for her there. I feel her sadness like a weight on my own shoulders, the pang of her hunger in my own belly.

'Good times must come,' Thomas says encouragingly. 'And as for us ... can we not marry, even in secret, and be together? We cannot make matters worse for your poor sister or her bairns, surely? And the queen is absorbed in the affairs of the other queen: she will not trouble herself about us?'

I look at his broad honest face, warm in the firelight. I am so tired of refusing him, I am so tired of caution and unhappiness. I am so tired of being the despised little sister to the saint in the Tower and the martyr of Ingatestone that I put out my hand to him.

'Yes,' I say. 'Let the two of us be happy at least.'

WHITEHALL PALACE, LONDON, SUMMER 1565

I am encouraged to be bold because my stock at court is rising as Elizabeth becomes more and more resentful of her other cousin, the papist cousin, the false-faith cousin, the two-faced cousin, the old cousin, the irritating cousin, the ambitious cousin, the hypocrite cousin Margaret Douglas, who has earned all these epithets for sending her husband to Scotland with Elizabeth's permission and her pretty son after him, and, between the two of them, rising up to the throne of Scotland and looking set to take it.

After days of sulking and spiteful comments Elizabeth tells Margaret Douglas that she must stay in her rooms at court and see no-one, and after a week of this cold treatment she signs a warrant for her arrest. Lady Margaret will not be kept, this time, in a beautiful house in comfort, but instead takes the short voyage by barge to the Tower of London. She is guilty of nothing more than the crime of having a handsome son who went to Scotland and now refuses to return. There is no charge laid against her, there cannot be: she has committed no treason or crime. They are imprisoning her in the Tower only to frighten her boy to run back to his mother. They are holding her as bait for her son.

But it does not work. Elizabeth's family is made of sterner stuff than she ever calculates. My sister, parted from her husband and her son, will not call one a blackguard and the other a bastard. Margaret Douglas, imprisoned in the Tower, will not order her boy home to be imprisoned with her. She sets up her little household in the Tower and waits for good news from Scotland. Surely, the Queen of Scots will not allow her future mother-in-law to be imprisoned; surely the ambassadors of France and Spain will not allow Elizabeth to persecute a renowned papist? Margaret Douglas, a tougher old warhorse than her sensitive husband and butterfly son, settles down to outlast Elizabeth's persecution.

The queen and all her court are invited to one of the greatest weddings of the year: the marriage of Henry Knollys, the son of Catherine Carey, Elizabeth's cousin and first lady of her bedchamber. She is a great friend of my step-grandmother, Catherine Brandon, since they are both staunch Protestant believers and fled to Europe rather than live under Queen Mary. They came back at the same time to Elizabeth's court and were welcomed by her with open arms. Of course, because of their religion, they idolise my sister Jane and I always feel myself to be a smaller inferior version of the great Protestant martyr. But despite this preference, I count them as my friends, especially my step-grandmother, Catherine Brandon, the Duchess of Suffolk.

Now Catherine Carey's son Henry is to marry the famously rich Margaret Cave at Durham House and Elizabeth has insisted for weeks that we parade her best gowns before her, so that she may choose the richest, hoping to outshine the bride and everyone else.

Elizabeth's passion for Mary Queen of Scots has turned to a hatred, quietly stoked by William Cecil, who points out that Mary can now never be heir to the throne of England: she has proven herself disobedient, she has proven herself unreliable and she has turned up her pretty nose at Robert Dudley.

The pretty youth Henry Stuart Lord Darnley, ordered home to England, denies his former devotion to Elizabeth and defies her, refusing to return. Elizabeth is beside herself at the disobedience, the disloyalty, and – above all, in my opinion – the infuriating preference. The young man prefers the genuine love of a beautiful queen of twenty-two, to the relentless demanding vanity of her cousin of thirty-one. There is no surprise in this to anyone but Elizabeth. In her rage, Elizabeth swears that the title of heir will never go to the papist queen, that her papist cousin Margaret Douglas is now her enemy, and her husband and son are worse than traitors.

I hold up one set of heavily embroidered sleeves and then another. She likes neither of them. I set them down and hold up another pair. This could take all day. The royal wardrobe is filled with ornate gowns, sleeves and kirtles. Elizabeth orders new every season, and nothing is ever thrown away. Every gown is powdered and stuffed with lavender heads and hung in a bag of linen to prevent moth. She could consider hundreds in her determination to mar the happiness of a bride on her wedding day. Dressing is easier for her ladies: we are to wear either black or white. Only the queen is to blaze in colour among us, only she is to be admired.

But I do not care what gown is chosen, nor what I am commanded to wear, for I am not going to be there. The wedding day of Henry Knollys and Margaret Cave is going to be my wedding day, too, and I am more sure of my happiness than I am of theirs. I am marrying a man that I know and love and trust, their marriage is arranged by their parents and licensed by the queen, who would not permit it if she thought there was any passion or love to be had. All admiration must come to her, not to any other woman.

Finally, the queen makes her choice of sleeves and it is the turn of another lady to open the jewel boxes so that she can select her necklaces, her chains, her earrings and her brooches. Only when everything is laid out and compared one with another, only when we all agree that she will be the richest, the best-dressed, the most beautiful woman present, do we start to prepare her for dressing.

Her thinning hair is carefully brushed and tied up on the top of her head in a scrawny bun. Mary Ratcliffe, the maid of honour with the steadiest hand, comes forward with a pot of fresh-mixed ceruse, and Elizabeth sits still, closes her eyes, as Mary paints the white lead and vinegar from her plucked forehead to her nipples in painstaking gentle strokes. It is a long process. The queen's neck, back, and shoulders have to be painted too; the gown she has chosen is low cut and there can be no ugly smallpox scars showing through the glowing white.

When the queen's cheeks are dry, Thomasina stands up on a stool and dusts rouge on the hollow cheeks, and paints carmine on the narrow lips. My aunt Bess comes forward with a brown crayon and draws in two arched eyebrows.

'Lord! What I do for beauty!' the queen exclaims, and we all laugh with her, as if this were amusing and reasonable, and not an absurd daily chore for us.

With immense care, Bess St Loe pulls the great red wig over Elizabeth's greying hair, as Elizabeth holds it at the front of her head, and then looks into her mirror to approve the effect.

She throws off her dressing gown and sits on her chair, naked but for her richly embroidered smock, one foot extended for her silk stockings.

Dorothy Stafford bends and carefully rolls them up to Elizabeth's knees and ties the garter.

'Do you know what fortune Margaret Cave will bring the family?' Elizabeth asks her.

'Lady Catherine told me that she is to inherit all her father's land at Kingsbury, Warwickshire,' Dorothy replies.

Elizabeth makes a little grimace as if she thinks what she would have done, if she had been an heiress like that, instead of a bastard set aside for the true heir. Behind the painted smile, her face is sour.

The queen stands as her ladies press the bodice to her belly, and then go behind her and start to thread the laces through the holes, pulling them tightly. The queen grips on the post of the bed to brace against them. 'Tighter,' she says. 'None of you pull as well as Kat.'

Elizabeth's former governess Kat Ashley is absent from her duties for once. She has taken to her bed complaining of short-ness of breath and fatigue. Elizabeth visits her every morning, but really misses her only when her laces are pulled. Only Kat will heave at them so that Elizabeth's stomacher lies completely flat on her empty barren belly.

Dorothy Stafford holds out the farthingale for Elizabeth to step into it, and pulls it up over her slim hips and ties it at her waist and then settles a satin roll on top. 'Are you comfortable, Your Majesty?' she asks, and Elizabeth makes a face as if to say that she is suffering for the benefit of England.

I step forward, proffering the chosen sleeves as Elizabeth steps into the kirtle. While one of the ladies ties the kirtle behind I lift up the sleeves and Elizabeth puts one arm through, and then another. Then she laughs, as she always does, and says: 'Lady Bess, you tie my sleeves on. Lady Mary will never reach.'

I smile as if I have not heard this a hundred times before, and Aunt Bess ties the sleeves to the bodice as Dorothy helps the queen into the gown itself.

We are like an army of ants trying to move a dead rabbit. We gather around her, pulling the puffs of the inner sleeves out through the ornate embroidered slashes, fastening the hooks and eyes, settling the gown over the farthingale and roll so that it rides high around her hips. When we fall back she says, 'Shoes,' and young Jennie goes down on her knees to tie the bows on Her Majesty's best shoes.

She stands while we drape her with jewels and pin them safely. She says she will wear a cape over everything to go down the river to Durham House, and we arrange the hood over the towering red wig. She stands high above me, I see her as a created monster, half of horsehair and satin, sea pearls and white lead. I think: this is the last day that I will fear you. I will seek my own heart's desire, as my sister did, perhaps as both my sisters did, as you never dare to do. Pray God I am indeed so small that you do not stoop to notice me. Pray God that since I am neither your rival in looks nor threat as heir, I can marry a nobody, as my mother did, as my step-grandmother has done, and hide my name in his. Like my step-grandmother who was Catherine Brandon but is now Catherine Bertie, I shall lose the great name of Grey and be called Mary Keyes.

Elizabeth goes towards the door to the privy chamber. We ladies are expected to follow without delaying to look at our own reflections, or straightening our own gowns. I go behind her, as my rank requires. In the absence of the disgraced Margaret Douglas I am first at court. I am going to slip away when everyone gets on the barge.

We walk through the privy garden to the pier and there is the father of the bride in earnest argument with the new Spanish ambassador, Don Diego Guzmán de Silva. They start apart as they see Elizabeth, and then Sir Ambrose Cave explains that the French ambassador was dining with him before the wedding and is now refusing to leave. He will not give way to the Spanish ambassador. Clearly, the queen cannot walk into a diplomatic squabble – least of all when everyone knows that France and

Spain are vying against each other to support the Queen of Scots against her loving cousin in England.

For a moment I think that Elizabeth will throw one of her tantrums and none of us will attend the wedding, and I will have to send to Thomas and tell him that our wedding, too, will have to be cancelled. But then I see him towering head and shoulders over every other man at court, at the privy garden gate, waiting to make sure that the queen safely boards her royal barge. His warm dark gaze rests on me and then passes, expressionless, onwards. I am so relieved that he knows, that he understands, that he will not make a play out of anger and disappointment as these foolish ambassadors are doing.

William Cecil is deputed to solve the problem. He and Sir Nicholas Throckmorton, the queen's ambassador to Scotland, go together to Durham House to clear the way for the queen. My Thomas is to walk with them. I see them go through the gate, Thomas holding the gate for the two great men, and following behind them with quiet respect.

The queen is unusually patient. From this I know that she is determined to attend Henry Knollys' wedding. Elizabeth wishes it and will make great allowances to ensure that she is not crossed. She takes a seat, and someone fetches the musicians, who come tumbling out of the palace, thinking that they had finished work for the day, and they play for her, while the court stands around and chats to each other, alert for her attention, restless as waiting horses. In less than half an hour the garden gate opens again and my Thomas ushers in Sir William and Sir Nicholas, who are both smiling.

'Please,' William Cecil invites the queen. 'Please embark in your barge. The French ambassador has left his dinner to oblige us all and you can make your entry to the wedding.'

It could not be better for me. Everyone is so eager to go after the delay that nobody notices me at all.

I touch Mary Ratcliffe's arm. 'I cannot come. I have such an ache in my belly, I couldn't trust myself in the chapel,' I say.

'Shall you ask permission?'

'She doesn't care,' I say certainly. 'I won't chase after her and delay her again. If she asks for me, tell her I was sick and begged to be excused.'

The court heads down to the pier, we can hear the shout as the rowers present the oars. 'Go on,' I say. 'Don't keep her waiting now!'

Mary scutters away and I am left in the empty garden. I turn and go back indoors to the palace, and on an impulse, I return through the privy chamber and into the queen's bedroom.

I am strangely tempted to meddle with the things. There are so many beautiful things spread everywhere – the pots and paints on the table, the jewels in their boxes, the ribbons and the laces, like toys in an overstocked nursery of a spoiled child. The servants will come in soon, to clean and tidy and put everything to rights, but in the meantime I am undisturbed. I take the empty pot of ceruse and I paint a little under my eyes. I rub it off at once. It is such a bright white, it makes me look like a masquer. It does nothing for my looks; I do not have pockmarks and wrinkles to hide.

I take off my hood and let my hair down and brush it gently, smoothly, with the queen's gold-backed hairbrush. The bristles glide through my fair hair and it tumbles to my shoulders. I put down the brush and plait it carefully, using my own hairpins to coil it closely against my head, so my hood can go on top. I think, tonight Thomas Keyes will take off my hood and let down my hair, and I spray it with a little oil of roses that Elizabeth keeps on her table and I sniff at the warm sweet smell.

I make sure that I pull my fair hairs from her hairbrush, where they gleam among the thin wisps of grey, and then I put it back, exactly where her lady-in-waiting laid it down. I dab a little carmine on my lips and admire the effect; I powder a little rouge on my cheeks. I take up Elizabeth's pencil and colour my eyebrows, as she does. This is too strong, and I rub it off again with the heel of my hand. I feel wonderfully naughty, like a child playing at a wealthy mother's dressing table.

I can tell from the silence of all the rooms that the whole court has gone to Durham House, and so I rise up from the table and smile at myself in the silvered mirror. There are jewels belonging to the queen in boxes all around the room but it does not occur to me to steal anything. I am Jane Grey's sister, I am Katherine Grey's sister: she is the rightful heir to all of this. All this is ours; I don't doubt I will sit here by right one day.

I have invited three of my kinswomen to dine with me: Margaret Willoughby, my favourite cousin, and the two Stafford girls. I can trust them to keep my secret; but I will not risk their being blamed for my wedding by having them as witnesses. Instead, I send for my maidservant, who was taking the absence of the court as an excuse for her own holiday, and she comes to my rooms in an excited rush, wondering what I want from her. I tell her to wait and she will see. Then there is a tap on the door and she hurries to open it, and there, filling the doorway, his head bent under the lintel, is my love, my great love.

'It is nine o'clock,' he says, and we hear the clock strike to prove his punctuality. 'Are you ready, my darling?'

I get to my feet and I put my hand out to him.

'I am ready.'

'And no second thoughts?' he asks gently. 'Are you sure?'

I smile at him. I don't need rouge to make me flush with desire. 'I am sure,' I say. 'I have loved you for so long, Thomas. I will be proud to become your wife.'

He bows his head and takes my hand and we lead the way, with my three friends and the little maid, Frances, following, through the deserted palace to Thomas's rooms above the watergate.

His rooms are crowded: his brother is here and several of his friends. Thomas has hired a priest, who is waiting with his prayer book open. I turn and say to my bridesmaids: 'You must all go, and wait outside. If anyone ever asks you, you can say that you were not witnesses, you were outside the door.'

We are all giddy with nerves. They laugh as they go out, and I giggle, too. Then I turn back to Thomas and know the seriousness of what we are about to do.

'And are you sure?' I ask him in reply. 'For the queen has quarrelled with all her other heirs. Of all her kin I am the only one left at court. She might embrace us as family, or hate us. She might be glad that I have lost my great name; or she might hate me for my happiness. I cannot predict her.'

'I am sure,' he says. 'Whatever comes. I am sure that I want to marry you.'

'Then let us begin,' says the priest. He starts the words of the marriage service that I thought I would never hear read for me. He holds out his prayer book to Thomas, who places a golden wedding ring on it, small enough for my finger, and Thomas and I promise to love one another and be faithful husband and wife till death parts us.

Of course, I think of my sister. She did not ask me to witness her wedding; she was protecting me just as I am protecting my kinswomen by leaving them outside the door. But I have read all the evidence from the trial of her marriage, and from the inquiry into her husband, and I know of Ned's room with the wines and the food laid out, and Janey Seymour as their only witness, and how when the priest left them they went to bed together and fell asleep and had to jump up and dress each other and she had to run back to court. I know how much she loved him, and that nothing would have stopped her from marrying him. I know what it has cost her, and I know that I am choosing as she did – to marry a man for love, to live life to the full, and to take whatever comes from the malice of Elizabeth. Because I won't learn to die, nor live my life as if it were half a life. I want to be a wife and perhaps a mother. I want Thomas as my husband more than I want to survive in this arid twilight court. I am twenty years old. I am ready for life. I want love, I want a real life, I want a husband.

We eat dinner together, Thomas's family and mine. Thomas proudly presents his son from his first marriage, and I greet him as his new mother. Thomas introduces his brother and his best friend who insisted on being a witness, and an old friend of his in service to the Bishop of Gloucester. They are a little in awe of me and my grand cousins, but crowded together in a small room, sharing a secret celebration, a feast with wine, any shyness melts away, and Thomas is so steady and warm and respectful that nobody can feel awkward. Very soon we are talking animatedly and laughing and saying, 'Shh, shh,' though the court is far away, celebrating a grander wedding, though, I dare say, not one with more love.

His best friend says to me: 'I have not seen him so happy ever. I never thought he would be happy again after the death of his first wife. I am so glad for him. Truly, you have blessed him.'

His son says to me: 'I am so glad, we are all so glad that Father is happy again.'

Thomas says to me: 'You are my own.'

Conscious of the time, and the possible return of the queen, they don't stay after they have dined and drunk our health. Thomas sees them out of his gate and his men are surprised that he is not keeping the gate until the queen returns. 'Not tonight,' he says quietly, and no-one questions him.

As he sees his guests through the front gate, and my kinswomen back to their rooms, I lock the door and undress. I don't know whether to leave my smock on or off. I have brought a nightgown for this very night, which is rather fine, but I don't know whether to sit in it before the fire or get into bed naked. I laugh at myself, worrying about such a thing, when I have married the man I love without the permission of a famously jealous queen, and I have far more to worry about than this; but still, I am a bride on my wedding night. It is natural for me to fret about these details. I want to please him, I want him to take a breath when he sees me, in embroidered silk at his fireside or half-naked in his bed. I want us to take joy in each other.

I am half in, half out of bed when he tries the door and so I have to throw on my beautiful cherry-red silk nightgown, and hurry to open it, so when he comes in I am neither wanton in bed nor regal at the fireside, but blushing and flurried and unprepared.

He is carrying a tray of wine and some little cakes.

'Not more food!' I say.

'I am no small man,' he says with a smile. 'I need to keep up my strength.'

'I like you just as you are,' I say. 'God knows, I would think you would be enough for me as you are. I don't mind you weak with hunger.'

'Try this,' he begs me, and it is the sweetest almond pastry from the queen's own kitchen, whisked up for us as a favour by one of her own subtlety cooks.

'It's delicious,' I say with my mouth full. 'But does the cook know the occasion?'

'I said that I was dining with the most beautiful girl I have ever seen,' Thomas said. 'He offered himself to make her a little pastry.'

I sip the wine. Thomas looks at me.

'Shall I get into bed and you come to me?' he asks gently. 'It shall be just as you command.'

I realise that I have been anxious. I realise that I have been nerving myself to be brave. I realise that I have been frightening myself about nothing, that here is a man who loves me truly. That here am I, who love him. Whatever comes of this wedding and bedding we will meet it together, with true love.

'I am coming,' I say, and I untie the sash at the waist of my nightgown and drop it, fearlessly, to the floor. I see his eyes take in my rounded breasts, my tiny waist, the slight turn of my spine that forces one shoulder before another. Apart from that little twist, I am flawless, a beauty in miniature. I shake my head and my hair falls forward, hiding my blushing face, smelling of roses.

'Come at once,' he replies, and he strips off his breeches, pulls off his shirt and holds out his hands to me. He lifts me, naked as

I am, into the high broad bed. He comes after me, rolls towards me like a felled tree, takes me in his arms and holds me against his great chest. 'My darling,' he says tenderly. 'My love.'

I don't stay all night with my husband. I am back in my own rooms by the time the court comes home and my ladies undress me and put me to bed without realising that I only joined the court as they returned. Frances the maid takes my shoes without a flicker of expression. I think I will lie awake, sleepless from joy, but as soon as my head is on the pillow I fall asleep and I don't wake until the girl comes into the room with the logs to make up the fire.

It is my morning to wait upon Elizabeth and so I get washed and dressed and hurry to the royal rooms, and only when I am halfway there do I catch myself up and think: he loves me. He held me last night like a man drowned in the deepest of loves. He has married me. He loves me. I am his wife.

It is like a song that goes on and on in my mind all day. As Elizabeth sees ambassadors, rides out with Robert Dudley, comes back hungry for her breakfast, flirts with the Spanish ambassador in the hopes of persuading him that she has serious thoughts of marriage, and then wins money at cards before leading the court in to dinner, all day, I think only: he loves me. He held me last night like a man in the deepest of loves. He has married me. He loves me. I am his wife.

When the court has finished dinner and they are clearing the hall for dancing and a troop of tumblers, I go down to the front gate and there is Thomas, tall as a tree, admitting the citizens of London who have come to see the dancing.

'Good day, Lady Mary,' he says to me aloud. 'Good day, Mrs Keyes,' he says to me quietly.

'Good day, husband,' I say, smiling up at him. 'I have come to see if I should come to your room secretly, when the court is asleep.'

'I should think so,' he says, pretending to take offence. 'Indeed, I expect you. I expect very obedient behaviour from my wife.'

'You shall have it,' I promise him. I see one of William Cecil's men approaching the gate, and I smile at Thomas and slip away. 'I have given you my word.'

The first night we sleep undisturbed till dawn in each other's arms. When his head lies beside mine on the pillow we are as equals, his broad forehead against my little one, his gentle kiss on my smiling mouth. His long legs stretch down to the bottom of the bed, his feet extend over the edge, and I occupy only the top half of the bed, but side by side, with the curtains drawn around us, we are equals, we are one.

The second night I wake at midnight to hear the Westminster Abbey bell tolling over and over, the low haunting note that says that someone has died.

'Elizabeth,' I whisper in my moment of waking, the wish coming before the words, the wish coming before the thought. I wake to joy as I half dream, half believe that it is the announcement of Elizabeth's death and my sister will be Queen of England.

Thomas hears the mourning bell too and springs out of bed and ducks to avoid the roof beams. 'I must go,' he says, and scrambles into his livery. I get up, too, pulling on my shift.

'Shall I do your laces?' he turns, halfway to the door.

'I'll manage. You go,' I say briefly. I know that he will be desperate to do his duty, to guard the gate against whatever bad news is coming.

He leaves his room at a run and I throw a shawl over my head like a poor woman and go down the stairs and across the yard. I think I will get to my rooms unseen but there, coming out of the ladies' rooms, is Thomasina. In one glance she takes in my half-dressed state, my tumbling hair. But she has no time for comment.

'It's for Kat Ashley,' she says over the insistent tolling of the bell. 'God bless her. We've lost her.'

'Lost her?' I say stupidly.

'She has died. She was failing fast. The queen is heartbroken,' Thomasina says. 'She left the dancing and ordered the bells to toll and the court into mourning. She says that Kat was like a mother to her.'

'She was,' I agree solemnly; but I think: and even daughterly devotion didn't stop Elizabeth arresting Kat and holding her in the Tower.

I dash into my room and cram on my hood and then rush to the queen's rooms to find her presence chamber shaded, with the shutters closed and everyone exchanging the news in hushed voices. Inside the private rooms the favoured courtiers whisper low-voiced remarks. Many people will miss Kat Ashley; but everyone knows that this leaves a vacancy among Elizabeth's ladies that an ambitious woman might fill, and a gap among her advisors that someone will seize.

I go to the bedchamber door. Aunt Bess, looking weary, comes out as I wait outside. 'Will you take over from me for an hour?' she says. 'She wants two of us in there all the time to sit with her and grieve.'

I nod and go in.

The room is shuttered and the fire is lit, it is dark and stuffy. Elizabeth is lying in bed, sheets drawn up to her chin, fully dressed, only her shoes slipped from her feet. Her ruff is crumpled around her neck, her eyes are smudged with paint, the ceruse is smeared on her pillow, on her askew red wig. But in her grief she looks almost like a child. Her suffering is as naked as any orphan in the streets. Elizabeth is always alone though she fills her court with flatterers and time-servers; and now, with the death of the woman who has been at her side since childhood, she realises it all over again. Kat Ashley came to her when she had lost her identity. She had been a beloved princess, the daughter of an adored wife, then she was put away, forgotten, her title and her name taken from her. When Kat Ashley first came to the little girl she found a child all but destroyed. She rebuilt her pride, she taught her a love of scholarship and of faith. She taught her to survive and be cunning, to trust no-one. Kat was the only woman in the world who loved Elizabeth then, and now she has gone. Elizabeth turns her face into the pillow to muffle her shaking sobs, and I think – yes – now she is alone indeed, now perhaps she will understand what it is to love someone truly and be taken from them. Now perhaps she will have pity on Katherine, an orphan, parted from her husband and son.

William Cecil himself comes to the queen's rooms, waits for me to come out to the privy chamber and asks me to take a message in to the queen in her bed.

I hesitate. 'She is seeing no-one,' I say. 'And Blanche Parry is to be the first lady of the bedchamber.'

He bends down so he can speak quietly in my ear. 'It would be well that she heard this first from you,' he says, 'since I cannot enter.'

'I'm not your best choice for bad news,' I say reluctantly. I can feel a sense of dread in my belly, although I think there can be nothing wrong with my sister: William Cecil would not torture me like this if Katherine were ill. 'What's happening?'

'Henry Stuart Lord Darnley has married the Queen of Scots,' Cecil says quietly. 'Keep your voice down.'

He does not need to warn me not to exclaim. I know how disastrous this is for England. I keep my expression blank as well. 'Henry Stuart?'

'Yes. And she has made him king.'

Now my face is frozen like a mask. Mary Queen of Scots must be madly in love, or simply mad, to give the crown and the throne to a youth who could be bought for a sovereign. I guess that she so wanted to be the wife of a king once more that she thought she would make one, choosing to ignore that Henry is a born courtier without any touch of the regal.

William Cecil admires my stillness, and goes on: 'She has put herself far beyond any possibility of succeeding to the English throne – a papist and now with a weak husband. She is no threat to us. We would never have accepted Dudley as a King of England coming in at her side; we certainly won't have Darnley. We will not have a papist king and queen, and not even the French will support her, married to a man like him.'

'It is her undoing,' I whisper. 'She has thrown away her future for a boy.'

'Yes,' Cecil confirms. 'Clearly she has been persuaded that he and his father can defeat her enemies. Already they have persuaded her to raise an army to make war on her own people, on the Protestant lords: her own people of our religion. She has made herself into our enemy. So for England, there is only one possible heir left. Mary Queen of Scots is a declared enemy to our religion, Margaret Douglas is her mother-in-law, your sister is the sole remaining heir. The queen will see this now, so take her the news yourself, and stand before her while you tell her, so that she knows what a faithful family she has.'

Elizabeth's fury with her rival queen quickly replaces Elizabeth's grief. She rises from her bed, orders a private funeral for Kat Ashley, and then storms into the Privy Council demanding that they make war on the Scots.

There is a rebellion in Scotland. The Scots queen's half-brother the Earl of Moray has turned against her. Though he welcomed her to Scotland and advised her earlier, he is a staunch Protestant and cannot stomach a papist queen with her papist jumped-up king. Although Elizabeth has no real interest in fighting for religion, she decides to support the bastard James

Stewart Earl of Moray against his ordained queen and half-sister. She sends him a fortune in gold to pay his followers and every messenger brings us news of his treason and demands for more help. The Privy Council ask each other, even ask us ladies, what the queen is doing, supporting a rebel against a crowned queen, sending money but not sending an army, doing enough to encourage him but not enough to ensure his victory. The French ambassador comes to court in a cold rage and says that if Elizabeth supports Protestant rebels against a legitimate half-French papist queen, they will intervene also . . . and all of a sudden, Elizabeth loses her heart for the Protestant cause and the bastard rebel; all of a sudden she remembers her loyalty to a fellow queen. To overthrow one woman in power is to threaten every woman in power. Suddenly, Elizabeth is an ally.

Besides, all the news we have from Scotland is of the young queen's triumph, and Elizabeth hates to be on the losing side. Queen Mary raises an army and she leads it herself, she pursues her half-brother in a series of running battles and finally chases him over the border. From our garrison in Newcastle-upon-Tyne he begs for reinforcements, he limps south to London, a frightened man, and Elizabeth astounds him with a strong reprimand for disloyalty to his queen and half-sister. Thomasina and I exchange one bland look as Elizabeth leaves Moray and the Protestant cause in Scotland in ruins, and the court baffled as to what she really wants.

She does not surprise me. For there is no sense in how she treats me, or how she treats Katherine and her little boys. Elizabeth is driven by fear and she takes sudden anxious decisions and then reverses them. Mary Queen of Scots will never be heir to England now, but still Elizabeth does not recognise my sister, as fearful of a powerless woman in captivity as she is by an armed rival on her border. She will not release my sister, who may die under house arrest, if she cannot be reunited with her husband and little boy. The court, the Privy Council, the queen's allies, even her enemies look in vain for consistent strategy from Elizabeth. They do not see that it is spite not strategy that drives her against her cousins: my sister and Queen Mary. It is rivalry, not politics that persuades her. I know this, for all her cousins suffer from her spite and rivalry: me too.

WHITEHALL PALACE, LONDON, SUMMER 1565

I am lying in Thomas's arms, listening to his steady breathing, watching the sky in the window opposite his bed slowly grow from dark to pale and then blush with the peach and pink of the rising sun. I don't stir, I don't want to wake him; I want this moment to never end. I feel a deep sense of peace and joy with this big man beside me, his arms around me, his breath warm on the back of my neck.

There is a sharp little tap-tap on the door, and I am instantly alert and frightened. Nobody knows that I am here; I must not be found here. I raise myself up in the bed and at once Thomas is on his feet and out of bed. He sleeps like a sentry – he is always ready to wake. He moves like a big cat, silent on his broad feet, and I snatch up the sheet and hold it across my nakedness and jump down from the high bed. I step back into the room, so that I cannot be seen from the doorway. Thomas pulls on his breeches, glances to see that I am hidden, nods at me to stay quiet and still and speaks to the bolted door. 'Who goes there?'

'It's Thomasina, the queen's dwarf!' comes the urgent hiss. 'Open up, Thomas Keyes, you great fool.'

He hides a smile and unbolts the door, barring it with his arm. She does not have to duck her head to slip into the room and she sees me. 'I knew you would be here,' she says breathlessly. 'It's true then. You're married. You'd better get dressed and come at once. She knows.'

I gape at her. 'How?'

She shakes her little head. 'I don't know. She asked for you the moment she woke this morning, God knows why, and then they found you were not in your bed.'

'I can make something up.' Frantically I pull on my gown, Thomas ties my laces. 'I can say I was visiting a sick friend.'

'Here, let me,' Thomasina says, pushing him aside. 'Great lummox. I must go. You can't be found with two of us in your room, Thomas Keyes! That would be a scandal indeed!'

For the first time ever, I don't correct her. I don't say there are not two of us here, there is one princess and one dwarf, we are not two of the same thing. I don't pause in cramming my feet into my little shoes, and tucking my stockings in the pocket of my cape. She has come to warn me because she believes in our sisterhood, one little woman helping another in a dangerous world. I won't deny my affinity with her again. She has been a friend to me now, and a sister.

'Who told her?' I demand. I fold up my long hair and cram my hood on top. Thomasina is quick and skilled with a couple of pins.

'One of the maids,' she said. 'She didn't dare do otherwise. She just said you weren't in your bed. Not where you are. But we've all known that you two were courting for months. Are you married?'

'Yes.'

'Without permission from the queen?'

'There's no law against it,' I say pedantically. 'There *was* a law but it was repealed.'

She laughs at me. 'The queen doesn't need a law to express her displeasure,' she says. 'Ask Margaret Douglas. Ask your sister. God help you.'

She dives out of the door. 'Hurry up!' I hear her call, and the patter of her feet down the stairs.

Thomas shrugs on his billowing shirt and reaches for his livery jacket. 'What should we do?' he asks me. 'Shall I come with you to the queen?'

'No. You can't come anyway if she's in her bedchamber.'

'I have served her loyally since she came to the throne,' he remarks. 'She knows that I am faithful.'

I compress my lips on my opinion of Elizabeth's regard for her faithful servants. Ask Robert Dudley what rewards there are for serving her faithfully, ask William Cecil. 'I'll remind her of that, if she says anything,' I promise him.

I reach up on tiptoes and he bends down for a kiss. It is not a kiss for luck or a quick peck. He puts his arms around me and he holds me closely. He kisses me with passion, as if we may never kiss again. 'I love you,' he says quietly. 'Come to me at the gate as soon as you can, to tell me that things are well with you. Or send me a message that all is well.'

I show him a brave smile. 'I shall come as soon as I can,' I say. 'Wait for me. Wait for me.'

I go at a run to the queen's presence chamber. Already it is filling up with petitioners and visitors who hope to catch her fleeting attention as she walks through to chapel. Half of them will be asking for clemency or pardon for men or women arrested for heresy or treason or suspicion. The prisons are crowded with suspects, the court crowded with their families. The Privy Council believe that the papists will rise against Elizabeth in support of Mary Queen of Scots. They believe that my cousin Margaret Douglas was conspiring with France and Spain to put her papist son and a papist queen on the throne. It has become a fearful country, a suspicious country, and now I am afraid and under suspicion too.

I go through the crowds to the door of her privy chamber. People make way for me – they know that I am one of the Grey girls. I see glances of pity from people whose own lives are so endangered that they have come to court for help. People under the shadow of the scaffold are pitying me. There are two guards on the doors to Elizabeth's privy chamber. They swing open the doors for me and I go in.

Most of the queen's ladies and some of her maids-in-waiting are already in attendance and clearly they are all talking about me. A terrible silence falls as I walk into the room and look around at these women who have been my companions and friends for eleven years. Nobody says a word.

'Where is Blanche Parry?' I ask. She is the new first lady of the bedchamber; she will know how much trouble I am facing. Lady Clinton nods her head towards the closed door.

'She's with Her Majesty. She is much displeased.'

There is a ripple of talk but no-one speaks directly to me. It is as if they dare not address me for fear of the contamination of treason. Nobody wants to be known as my particular friend, though almost all of them have been proud to call themselves my friend at one time or another.

'Is it true? Are you married, Lady Mary?' one of the younger maids blurts out, and curtseys and colours red to her ears. 'Begging your pardon,' she whispers.

I don't have to answer her, but I am not going to deny it now. I am never going to deny my marriage or the man I love. Part of me thinks – but this is quite absurd! I have one sister executed for claiming the throne, and one sister imprisoned for falling in love – and here am I, with a ring in my pocket and a private marriage, neither claiming the throne nor marrying a noble.

'Is she very angry?' I ask.

Someone makes a little whistle like calling up a storm.

'Am I to go in?'

'You're to wait here,' Lady Clinton says. 'She'll send for you.'

'I'll go to my room and change my hood,' I say. Nobody says that I may not go and so I go out through the doors again, through the presence chamber and the furtive glances, and up the narrow stairs to my rooms. My maid, white-faced, brushes my hair and pins my hood without saying a word. I don't speak to her.

When I go back to the privy chamber someone has called William Cecil and he is standing in the window bay talking to my step-grandmother, Catherine Brandon, and Blanche Parry. Everyone else is waiting at a polite distance, straining their ears to hear, not daring to step closer. When I come into the chamber, Sir William looks up and sees me. He gives me a weary smile and I go across the room and look up at him. My lady step-grandmother stands behind me, as if she would advocate for me.

'Now here's a to-do,' Sir William says gently, and I think – thank God, at last someone who knows that this is a marriage for love, that means nothing except to us who love one another. It will offend the queen since all love but her own heartless play-acting offends the queen. But here is a sensible man who knows that it is of no importance in the greater world.

'I am sorry that I did not ask permission,' I say quietly.

'You are married?' he confirms.

'Yes, to Mr Thomas Keyes.'

A suspicion of a smile crosses the old statesman's face. 'I think he must be the biggest gentleman of the court and you the smallest lady.'

'John Dee would say that we were the opposites that make the whole,' I observe.

'The offence is very great,' Sir William says, nodding to the closed chamber door.

'The offence is very small. Her Majesty may take great offence, but there is no cause.'

He bows his head at my correction.

'Am I to go in? I can explain it was nothing but a private matter.'

'I would take her in . . .' my lady step-grandmother offers.

Blanche shakes her head. 'She won't see you,' she says shortly. 'She is very angry, Lady Mary. This, on top of everything else . . .'

'This is nothing,' I say staunchly. 'And everything else – if you mean my sister's marriage to a young nobleman – was no ground for offence either. The marriage of Mary Queen of Scots is a matter of national importance but nothing to do with us. My sister and I were acting as private individuals.' I look around at the other ladies of the bedchamber. 'Are none of us ever to marry?'

William Cecil clears his throat. 'You're to go to Windsor,' he says. 'While Her Majesty makes inquiry.'

'I will speak for you,' my lady step-grandmother says.

'Inquiry into what?' I demand. 'There was a marriage, held in private. There were witnesses. His family was there, a maid was witness for me. There was a priest who will attest that the wedding was valid. You need hold no inquiry to know everything. I will tell you everything. Mr Keyes will tell you everything.'

William Cecil looks tired. 'Perhaps. But Her Majesty wishes you to go to Windsor while she holds an inquiry.'

I take his hand and look up at him. 'Sir William, you tell us that there is a plot by the Spanish to finance the Queen of Scots. The Queen of Scots has married the heir to the throne of Scotland, and defeated the Protestants that were rebelling against her. Is this the time for you and the Privy Council to worry about me?'

'Little me?' he suggests with a smile.

'I could not be a smaller person at court. The affairs of my heart could not be of less importance.'

'She insists,' he says gently. 'Pack your things.'

I would go straight to Thomas at the gate but two ladies go with me to my rooms to help me to pack my books, my papers, and my clothes and jewels. Then when I am ready to leave, there are two guards at the door and they take me down the privy stair to the watergate. I look for Thomas at the great gate of the palace but he is not there and his deputy on duty does not look up so I cannot gesture. The room above the water-gate where we lived together as man and wife shows no lights at the windows; the shutters are closed. Either he is in there, under arrest in darkness, or they have taken him somewhere else already.

'I want to see my husband, Thomas Keyes,' I say to the guardsman beside me. 'I insist.'

'My orders are that you will go by barge to Windsor,' he says.

'The sergeant porter,' I remind him. 'Of military rank and unimpeachable honour. I insist that you let me see him.'

He bobs his head down towards me. 'They've taken him into the city,' he says, very quietly. 'He's already gone, my lady.'

WINDSOR CASTLE, SUMMER 1565

I am kept in three good rooms overlooking the upper ward of Windsor Castle. The outer door is locked at night but during the day there is a guard set outside and he will walk with me if I want to go out to the royal garden. I am allowed to walk anywhere inside the castle walls but I am not allowed out. The rooms are spacious and I have my two ladies-in-waiting and three maids. These are better rooms than Katherine had in the house of the lieutenant of the Tower, and more freedom than Jane had there. I am so glad not to be held in the Tower – that would be unbear-able. I could not tread the same track as my imprisoned sister, I could not wake to see the green where my martyred sister was killed. At least this is better than that.

I live quietly, I attend the castle chapel twice a day, walking there with the guards before and behind me. I read, I study, I sew, and make music. There is nothing to do, but at least I am not on my knees to a tyrant who hates me.

I write to my sister Katherine that I, too, have married for love and I, too, meant nothing wrong by it but to be happy with a good man. I write that I, too, have offended the queen by this but that I hope that she will forgive me, and forgive Katherine, too. I give it to the commander of the castle but I don't know if it will get beyond Cecil's spies to my sister.

I write to Thomas Keyes. This is a harder letter. He is no poet like poor Ned Seymour. Our courtship was never one of words and pretty sayings. So I write briefly and I don't expect anyone to deliver my letter to him. If I am writing only for the spies, it does not matter. Thomas does not need assurances of my love, nor I of his. We are lovers, we are married, we know each other's heart. However brief the letter he knows that I love him as passionately and as powerfully as the greatest poet, though the lines are short.

> *My dearest husband,*
>   *I am being held at the pleasure of Her Majesty at Windsor Castle, I hope she will pardon us both very soon, as soon as she learns that we meant no ill by our marriage and only hoped for our happiness.*
>   *I miss you very much. I love you very dearly. I do not regret our marriage (except that it has displeased the queen). You are the heart of a heartless world. – your wife, Mary*

The trees in the park are as bright as the queen's bronze, copper, and gold chains, and the flowers in the herb garden lose their colour and their petals and become tatter-headed sticks. The summer ends in long warm days and every day I climb the circling steps to the top of the tower where I can see the river and the boats coming to and fro. Although I always look for it at sunset, the royal barge never comes for me.

The commander of the castle stops me as I walk back to my

room one evening and says that I am to pack and leave the next morning.

'Am I released?' I ask him.

He bows his head to hide his embarrassment, so I know that I am not. 'To stay with Sir William Hawtrey,' he says quietly. 'A brief stay, I understand.'

'Why?' I ask bluntly.

He bows again. 'My lady, they don't tell me.'

'But why Sir William Hawtrey?'

He makes a helpless little gesture. 'I know nothing more than that I am to escort you to his house.'

'It seems I am to know nothing, too.'

CHEQUERS, BUCKINGHAMSHIRE, AUTUMN 1565

It takes us all day to ride from Windsor, over the river and through the Chiltern Hills, and my happiness comes back to me as soon as I am on horseback and looking around at the green horizon, the stooks of straw in the fields, and the neat little villages where people come out to stare at the guards and at me, and my groom who rides beside me, and my maid who rides pillion behind one of the guards.

We carry no standard so nobody knows that I am a prisoner of the queen. This is another sign of Elizabeth's fears. She does not want the country to know that she has arrested yet another of her cousins for no good reason. From the very start of Katherine's imprisonment people have demanded that Katherine should be free, and complained that Margaret Douglas cannot be held because her son has married the queen's rival. But I don't expect anyone to call my name as they called for Katherine or called for Jane. There is no-one who will ride to my rescue: my friends are all at Elizabeth's court, in her power. My family is lost to me. My dearest and most trustworthy ally is my husband, and I don't know where he is, nor how to get a letter to him.

Sir William Hawtrey, a good old man of nearly forty-five years, with his wealthy young wife standing behind him, greets me at the doorway of his handsome house of Chequers and takes me by the hand to lead me inside. He treats me with an odd mixture of deference – for I am sister to the only heir to the throne – and anxiety – for he has been forced to agree to keep me as his prisoner.

'This way,' he says pleasantly, leading me up the stairs to the north-east wing. He opens a door to a tiny room, big enough for a bed and a table and chair. At once, I recoil.

'Where are my rooms?' I ask him. 'I cannot stay here.'

'The queen commanded it,' he says uncomfortably. 'I think you are just staying for a night or two. There was no other room that was secure . . .' His voice trails away.

'Sir William,' I say earnestly, 'I have done nothing wrong.'

'I am sure,' he says gently. 'And so you are certain to be pardoned and recalled to court. This is just for a little while, a night or two.'

I look round. My maid hovers on the threshold; there is hardly room for her to serve me.

'Your maid will be housed nearby, and she will sit with you during the day, and serve your meals,' Sir William says. 'You are to walk in the garden as you wish, for your health.'

'I cannot live like this,' I say.

'You won't have to!' he assures me. 'This is just for a short stay. I don't doubt that she will forgive you, and you will return to court.'

He makes a gesture again, ushering me into the room, and I go in. I have a horror of him touching me. I hate to be pushed about, or lifted up. Nobody must ever think that they can just pick me up and place me where they want me to be without my consent. I go to the little window and pull up a stool so that I can stand high enough to look out over the parkland. It is beautiful, like Bradgate, like my home. Dear God, it feels like years and years since Jane and Katherine and I were children at our home.

I can see the sunset in the little square panes of my high window. It is a beautiful evening, the sun going down and the moon rising. I wish on the moon, as I have done since I was a little girl and my sister Jane told me that it was pagan nonsense and I should pray for my desires and not throw away my thoughts on vain wishing. The evening star sits like a little diamond on the horizon and I wish for my freedom on the star, too, and for Thomas on every star in the sky.

The tap and then the noise of the opening door behind me makes me turn. It is poor Sir William looking weary and troubled. 'I just came to make sure that you had everything that you need.'

I nod my head without answering. It was a mean dinner, and he knows it. One of royal blood should be served with twenty courses. I ate tonight like a poor woman.

'I shall write to the queen and ask her to release me,' I say. 'Will you take my letter and see that it gets to her?'

'I will,' he says. 'And I will add a petition of my own. She must show mercy to you, and to your sister, and to your cousin Lady Margaret. And Lady Margaret's younger son.'

I am alarmed for the little boy. 'You can't mean Charles Stuart? He cannot have been arrested? He's only a child.'

His face is unhappy as he nods. 'He's being held in a private house in the North.'

'He's only ten years old!' I exclaim. 'His mother is in the Tower of London, his father and brother in Scotland – why would the queen not leave him at his home among his servants and friends? He's not strong, and he is all alone in the world. He is no threat to anyone. He must be lonely and frightened as it is, all on his own at home. Why put him in a strange house and declare him a prisoner?'

There is a silence. We both know why. As a warning to all of us that the queen's displeasure will fall on us and even on our children, even on innocent babies. As a warning to all of us that she is a Herod. She loves none of her kin until they are dead and she can honour them with a funeral. She likes none of her cousins anywhere but in prison. She loves them in the tomb.

Sir William shakes his head. 'For sure, I pray that she will release all her cousins soon.'

I write to William Cecil to ask him to represent to Her Majesty that Katherine and I have never spoken one word of conspiracy against her, that – unlike the Queen of Scots or Lady Margaret – we have never spoken of our closeness to the throne. We have both fallen in love, but this is no crime. We have married without her permission but this is not illegal.

I get a brief unsigned note in reply saying that my sister and her little boy are well at Ingatestone, her elder son is with his grandmother at Hanworth, her husband still imprisoned in London. My husband, Thomas Keyes, is in the Fleet Prison. The anonymous author of the note says that the queen will be approached to release us all into more generous keeping – especially Thomas Keyes, who is very confined. The matter will be put before the queen 'as soon as is convenient'.

I sit in my little room with the note in my hand for a long time before I come to my senses and thrust it into the embers of the fire. I understand that the queen is still in such a vile mood that nobody dare suggest anything to her, not even William Cecil. I know something else – which I knew already – that she has no kindness or generosity to me or to my sister. And now I know that Thomas is suffering for me.

I wonder exactly what the writer means by 'very confined'. I am afraid that they have put Thomas into a small room. There are cellars in the Fleet Prison that are low and damp. The rats run across the floor. Have they put my handsome big-boned husband in a cage?

He will be shamed, I know, to be imprisoned in the Fleet Prison – the common gaol for criminals, forgers and drunkards. When Sir William comes the next day, before the serving of my poor dinner, I ask him if he has any news of Thomas Keyes.

I recognise his anxious look now. His gaze goes to the floor, his face folds into lines of worry, he touches his silvery grey hair. 'I have no news, I have only heard gossip,' he starts.

'Please tell me,' I say. I can feel a pain extending from my belly to the back of my throat and I realise this is grief and longing. I love Thomas and I have been his undoing. I never thought that I would wish that we had not married, but I will learn to wish it, if he is suffering for my sake.

'Please tell me everything you know, Sir William.'

'They have put him in the Fleet Prison,' he says. 'But at least winter is coming and the plague season is past us.'

So the letter is true, as I knew it was. Thomas's prison is on the River Fleet, the dirtiest river in London. It will be damp and bitterly cold in winter. Prisoners have to pay for their own firewood, for blankets for their bed. If Thomas's family do not send him money and food he will starve. He's not a young man; he will get sick, held in close confinement there.

'They have given him a very small cell,' Sir William says very quietly. He glances around my little room, the small space either side of the bed, the table and chair tucked into the corner, the small high window and the cramped interior. 'Of course, he is a very big man.'

I think of Thomas as I first saw him, standing tall before the great gate of Whitehall Palace, his thumbs tucked in his shining leather belt, his broad shoulders set square, his towering presence, his grace. For a big man he is light on his feet, a quick thinker. I remember how he smiles when he sees me, how he drops to one knee to talk to me.

'How small is his room?' I can't imagine what Sir William is telling me. 'How small exactly?'

He clears his throat. 'He can't stand up in it,' he says reluctantly. 'He has to bow over. And he is too long for it as well. He can't lie in his bed stretched out. He has to fold up.'

I remember Thomas, his feet sticking out of the foot of his bed. He is nearly seven feet tall. They have not imprisoned him; they are crushing him.

'He will be in pain,' I say flatly.

'And they don't feed him,' he says, shamefaced. 'He is hunting game and little birds with a slingshot from his cell window so that he has meat to eat.'

I put my hand to my mouth to hold back a retch. 'It is a death sentence,' I say quietly.

Sir William nods. 'I am so sorry, my lady.'

So, she has won. I will deny my marriage and beg her for pardon like a slave. She can have me as her court dwarf, as her eunuch. If she will release Thomas before he is crippled I will agree never to see him again, and never mention his name. I write to William Cecil a letter in which I humble myself to the ground. I beg for forgiveness as if I am a sinner of the most vicious disposition. I say I would rather die than displease her. I sign my maiden name, my old name, Mary Grey. I do not mention Thomas. I show that he is nothing to me, that I have forgotten him, that our marriage never was. And then I have to wait. I have to wait to see if she is generous in total victory, though she has never been generous before.

CHEQUERS, BUCKINGHAMSHIRE, WINTER 1565

Agnes Hawtrey has no great kindness for me, since my keep comes out of her housekeeping, and her neighbours who visit her for Christmas cheer may not meet me. She gains nothing from having me in her house; she cannot even exhibit me. But since I am the only person other than her old aunt and cousin who would appreciate the gossip that she hears from London, she has to come to me for she is bursting to speak.

'I have to tell you,' she says. 'I have to tell someone – though you must never tell my lord, nor anyone, that I have spoken with you about the queen.'

'I won't hear anything treasonous,' I say quickly. 'I cannot listen.'

'This isn't treason and it's general knowledge,' she says quickly. 'Lord Robert Dudley has proposed marriage to the queen and she has agreed to marry him at Candlemas!'

'No!' I say. 'You must have heard it wrong. I would have sworn she would never marry him, nor anyone.'

'She will! She will! They are to marry at Candlemas.'

'Where did you hear this?' I am still sceptical.

'It's widely known,' she says. 'Sir William told me himself, but I also had it from a friend of mine who has a cousin in service to the Duke of Norfolk, who swore that the marriage must never take place, but cannot prevent it. Oh!' She suddenly starts as the thought comes to her. 'What about you? If she marries will she release you?'

'There is no reason why she should not release me now,' I say. 'I am hardly a rival to her for Lord Robert's affections. But certainly, if she is married and if she were to have a son there would be even less reason to keep me confined or my sister. If she marries, perhaps she will allow her ladies-in-waiting to marry, too.'

'What a wedding it will be!' she exclaims. 'Surely, she will have a pardon for prisoners for her wedding.'

'Candlemas,' I say, thinking of Thomas, cramped in his cold cell, lying on the damp floor, starved. 'That's not till February.'

CHEQUERS, BUCKINGHAMSHIRE, SPRING 1566

There is no Christmas feasting for me at Chequers. I am afraid that there is no joy for my sister at Ingatestone, nor for her husband in London at Sir John Mason's house. Perhaps Teddy at Hanworth gets a fairing from his grandmother for Christmas, perhaps a gingerbread man; but he will know by now that he will never get a Christmas blessing from his mother or father. I know that my husband, Thomas, will be desperately cold and starved. As the weather grows colder and it snows in January I think of him, bent over his little window, peering out to see if he can catch a sparrow for the morsel of meat on its little bones. I expect he traps and eats rats. I think of him sitting over a tiny fire of kindling and trying to get warm. I think of him hunched in his bed at night, and the strange agony of never being able to stretch out, standing all day with his shoulders bowed, sleeping with his legs folded up.

I hear that there is little joy in the court in London either. Elizabeth has been thrown down into a jealous despair at the news from Edinburgh that her rival queen and cousin is with child. Mary Queen of Scots and her young husband Henry

Lord Darnley are about to give Scotland a royal heir, and England yet another child with a claim to Elizabeth's throne. When Sir William tells me this, I have a rare moment of being glad that I am far from court. I cannot imagine the torment that the ladies-in-waiting will suffer at Elizabeth's hands if Queen Mary has a boy. I so wish I could be with Katherine and hear her giggle at the thought of it. As fast as Elizabeth denies her heirs, we give birth to new ones. It would be funny if it were not so bitter.

Robert Dudley remains confident that Elizabeth will marry him at Candlemas, according to her sworn word; but January comes and goes and then Candlemas passes him by, without Elizabeth's consent. I don't know how she puts him off – probably with another promise or another convincing delay – but her chaplain preaches a sermon that Candlemas no longer exists, it is now a heresy, so perhaps Robert's betrothal day disappears with the old tradition.

Elizabeth's irritable rivalry turns to fear when Queen Mary announces that she is the rightful Queen of England. The question of who should be named as heir to Elizabeth is suddenly made irrelevant as Queen Mary declares Elizabeth to be a usurper. She has the support of the new pope, Pius V, to make such a claim, and so all of Europe turns against Elizabeth. The Spanish support Queen Mary for her faith, the French support her for family reasons, and half of England would rise for her if she came over the border at the head of a papist army. She could lead a holy war into the heart of England and win the throne by right and with the blessing of the papist Church. Of course, all I think, as I am allowed into the icy garden for a short half-hour walk, is that my offence and Katherine's offence is diminished even more in comparison with the declaration of war from Queen Mary. But I know that the announcement will have plunged Elizabeth into jealous terror. She will not be able to think of anything else. She will not speak of anyone else. She will have mercy for no-one.

I write to William Cecil, reminding him that Katherine and I have done nothing to further our claim to be Elizabeth's heirs, that we will never claim our rights. That we are Protestants, co-religionists to him and to the queen, that if she is threatened by papist cousins she can turn to us for our friendship; she can show everyone that she supports our shared religion. We can stand beside her, before the court. We can support her claim to the throne in the country. At the very end, I write that I beg him – if nothing else – to allow Thomas Keyes a bigger cell and permission to walk outside.

I renounce him, I write. *Let our marriage be annulled as if it never was. I will never see him again if you will just let him go.*

Again, I sign myself Mary Grey, denying my love, denying my marriage, denying my very self. Again I wait for news.

I feel that I am a fool that I did not foresee what would happen next. William Cecil's spies play with Lord Darnley as if he were a little lapdog like my sister's pug Jo. They train him, they teach him tricks. First, they taunt his fragile manhood, saying that he is not truly a king if he obeys his wife, and now she is denying him the title of king. They swear that she depends not on him, the man set by God over her; but on her advisor, her secretary, David Rizzio. They hint that she obeys the Italian, that she prefers him to her young husband, even that she lies with him; perhaps the baby that she is carrying is his and no Stuart. They fuel his drunken corrupted young mind with fantasies of lust and betrayal, so that he bursts into her bedchamber with a loaded pistol that he points at her pregnant belly and demands that she give him Rizzio. Of course, Cecil and Elizabeth would not care if the gun went off and killed the baby and queen in one fortuitous accident. Darnley the pretty boy, with half a dozen companions, drags the queen's secretary from her privy chamber as he screams for mercy, clutching at her gown, and they stab him to death on the queen's private stair. A horrible death, a terrible plot. This is how Elizabeth and her advisor deal with grave political challenge. I should be glad that my sister and I are only imprisoned.

I hope that my brother-in-law, Ned Seymour, may be released. His gaoler, Sir John Mason, who hated him so much, has died and the council cannot find a replacement. No-one wants to be the guardian of a nobleman of England held without charge and without good reason. I ask Lady Hawtrey if her friend at court thinks that the queen is likely to send Ned to imprisonment with Katherine. It would transform her confinement to be with him. I hear every month that she is sinking deeper and deeper into loneliness and sorrow. Agnes says no – Elizabeth would not risk another Seymour son, another heir to her throne. But I think she must be wrong. Surely Elizabeth, with such news coming from Scotland, must release Ned and then the rest of us? She must show the country that she supports the Protestant cause against the papist claimant.

For Queen Mary has strengthened her cause and twisted the plot all around. She has cleverly turned her husband, that weak boy Darnley, in a full circle. She has denied her fear and horror that he should attack her and kill her loyal advisor, and has pulled him from the drink-sodden embrace of his treacherous friends. Now he is all against them, and he denies that he had any part in the attack on his wife and her murdered advisor. Queen Mary herself rides out against the traitors and wins back the support of the Protestant lords of Scotland. She is quick and courageous and defeats her enemies and befriends others. Elizabeth, trying to keep her footing in this difficult dance, is now telling everyone that she is grieved by the terrible events in Scotland and fearful for her dear cousin's safety. Publicly she urges Mary to take care, especially in her pregnancy.

Of course, this fools no-one; but it makes everyone wonder

if Mary Queen of Scots will dare to bring her victorious force south and invade us across the border. She has named Elizabeth as a bastard and a usurper. She has seen that Elizabeth is her enemy who gets her way by assassination and dark counsel. Queen Mary has learned her own strength. What will she do next?

I can't help but wonder if she will march on England and the papists rise to greet her as a liberator and saviour. And if she were to come, and if she were to win, would she free her other cousins? First, she would free her mother-in-law, Margaret Douglas, but then – why not me and Katherine? Would she, with a baby of her own, be merciful to my little nephews? I am breathless at the thought that it might be a papist queen who frees the sisters of Jane Grey. For sure, she could not be a worse cousin or queen to us than Elizabeth has been.

CHEQUERS, BUCKINGHAMSHIRE, SUMMER 1566

Every day starts earlier and I watch the trees from my window show a haze of the lightest green that slowly grows to a vibrant spring bursting of leaves. When I walk in the garden I wear a shawl around my shoulders instead of a heavy cape, and the bird-song is loud all around me. One morning I hear a cuckoo so loud and so distinctive that for a moment I am back at Bradgate and Katherine is pulling me by the hand and jumping over the furrows of a newly ploughed field, saying, 'Come! Come! Perhaps we will see him. A cuckoo is good luck.'

I have such a longing to be free in this season. I see the rabbits under the greening hedges and the hares loping through the mists of the bowling green in the early morning. I hear the foxes bark at night and the owls calling love songs from one high chimney pot to another. I am so conscious of my own youth and my own freshness in this young season of bursting life. I can't sleep at night with desire for Thomas. We had so little time together and yet my skin remembers every touch. I want to love my husband. I want to lie against his long bulk. I don't care where we live, I don't care if we are poor, I don't care if we are disgraced. If I could be free with him I would be happy.

And then I hear some good news, perhaps the start of joy for me, as slight and light as the greening trees which burst into leaf. Katherine's gaoler, Sir William Petre at Ingatestone, is too ill to keep her in his house any longer. Perhaps God has not forgotten us heirs. There is Ned without his gaoler, and now Katherine, too. I really think it possible that my sister might come to me, or that we all might be released and kept under house arrest together. Surely it would be cheaper and easier to hold us under house arrest in one house? I write to William Cecil saying that I should be so much happier if we might be imprisoned together. That, surely, it would be more convenient for Her Majesty if we were in one place, that my sister would need fewer attendants for I would care for her little boy, I would see that she ate, I would be company for her.

And more economical, I write winningly. *For we could share our fires and our servants.* I ask him if he will request it of Her Majesty, and also that Thomas Keyes might be released to live with his children in Kent. *I will undertake to never see him, and he will promise never to see me. But it is worse than bear-baiting to keep a great man like Thomas in a cramped cell. It is not Christian charity. You would not keep a big ox in a small pen like this. He has done nothing but love me, and he would never have spoken if I had not encouraged him.*

I receive one of Sir William Cecil's rare replies. He writes that my sister Katherine is to go into the keeping of another loyal courtier dug up from obscurity, almost in the grave from old age: Sir John Wentworth who lives at Gosfield Hall. She will live in the west wing, she will be served by her ladies. Her son Thomas, who has never known life out of imprisonment, who has never seen an open sky in all his three years, will remain with her.

As for Mr Keyes, he is to be allowed to walk in the yard and stretch out his long legs, William Cecil writes with a glimmer of his old humour. *The queen is disposed to show him mercy, and there are many who urge forgiveness for you and Lady Katherine in these troubling times. I am foremost.*

I am not quite sure what especially Cecil means by 'troubling times', since these are the only times we have known since his protégé came to the throne, but in June I hear that the worst thing for Elizabeth has finally happened: the Scots queen Mary has given birth. Even worse for Elizabeth, who urged Mary's husband to fire a gun into her belly, the young woman has survived the birth. Worse still, it is a healthy baby. And worst of all for Elizabeth: it is a boy. The papist cousin, just like the Protestant cousin, has a healthy son and heir to the throne of England. Elizabeth, thirty-two years old, unmarried, unloved, now has two cousins with boys in the cradle. She cannot deny them all.

What she does, of course, is what she always does. She runs away and pretends that it is not happening. The Chequers cook is friends with a royal groom and we hear all about the fine celebrations at Kenilworth, when Robert Dudley throws his fortune at the feet of his queen and most elusive lover. Apparently there is a whole new wing of rooms built just for her visit, and masques and hunts and a specially commissioned play and fireworks. After his disappointment of Candlemas he is throwing himself into another attempt at wooing. This year he has left court in a rage or in despair twice, and both times she has humbled herself to beg for his return. It is clear to everyone that she cannot live without him. He must be wondering if it is clear to her.

I sit in my tiny room and I think of Elizabeth my cousin watching fireworks reflected in the great lake at Kenilworth, and I try to damp down the bitterness of my rage. I am not a melancholy prisoner like my sister Katherine, I do not give myself up to grief. I cannot forgive Elizabeth for her insane treatment of us. I think of her as a malicious madwoman and when I write one of my regular letters pleading for forgiveness, promising my undying loyalty, I am lying like all of her courtiers. She has made a court of liars, and I am the worst.

CHEQUERS, BUCKINGHAMSHIRE, AUTUMN 1566

I hear that, once again, she keeps Robert Dudley uncertain; but this is just as I predicted. I believe he will always be on the threshold of marriage with her and never be able to jump over. I believe that she will never marry anyone. I swore it years ago, I would swear it now. She will always hold him close enough to ruin his life, but never close enough to ruin hers. She returns to London from Kenilworth and now she has to call a parliament. She needs funds. She is spending a fortune causing trouble in Scotland: spying and rebellion never come cheap. But parliament will not grant her money without a promise about the succession. They see that they have the chance to dictate to her. The Protestant parliament wants only one heir – my sister Katherine, with her Seymour son to come after her.

One day, when I am walking in the garden and admiring the blazing colours in the trees of the parkland, and the whirl of golden leaves around my feet, I see a square of white on the path before me. I pick it up in a moment and unfold it.

Your friends will speak for you and your sister. Neither of you is forgotten. England knows its heirs.

I tuck it in my pocket and when I get back to my room I burn it in the empty grate and mash the ashes with a poker. I find I am smiling. Perhaps soon I will be able to walk across a room that is wider than twelve feet. I will walk in a garden and out through the garden gate. Perhaps next spring I will hear a lucky cuckoo in Bradgate Park.

My unwilling host comes to me in my little room. He is wearing riding breeches and boots, a warm cape over his arm, a hat in his hand, he is not shamefaced, he is beaming. He bows low to me as I am seated on my single chair before the open window. At once, I am as alert as a deer scenting the wind for the smell of hunting hounds. What is happening now?

'You see, I am going away. I am going to London,' he says.

I nod, keeping my expression calm and interested while my thoughts whirl.

'I beg of you to stay quietly in my house while I am gone,' he says. 'If you were to take advantage of my absence to attempt to leave, the queen's displeasure would fall very heavily on me and on my wife. I dare not face it. You understand.'

'I have nowhere to go, and no-one to meet; and I would not expose you or my sister to such trouble,' I promise him. 'I don't doubt that the queen would punish my sister and my nephews if I were to escape.'

He bows again. 'Besides, I hope to return with good news for you and Lady Hertford, your royal sister,' he says.

I note that he gives Katherine her royal recognition and her married title. 'Oh, really?'

He glances behind to make sure that there is no-one lingering beside the open door. I close the window and turn to him. At once we are conspirators, guarding against spies.

'I am called to parliament,' he says. 'We are going to insist that the queen names her heir. Only parliament can raise taxes for her, and we can stipulate the conditions. For once we are all agreed, we have not been divided by advisors from court, and we are united with the House of Lords. We will insist that she name her heir, and that her heir be Lady Hertford and her son.'

I could leap up and clap my hands; but I sit like the princess I am and I incline my head. 'I am glad to hear it,' is all I say.

'When you are released –' he says 'when', he does not say 'if' – 'I hope you will tell your sister, Lady Hertford, that I have been as good a host to you as I was allowed to be.'

'I will tell her that,' I say fairly. 'And I will tell her that you went to London when you were called and that you spared no effort to join with the others to persuade the queen to name my sister as her heir.'

He bows as low as to a member of the royal family.

'And,' I add, 'I would be very obliged if you would visit Mr Thomas Keyes in the Fleet Prison and insist that he is released.'

'I will raise it with my fellow members of parliament,' he promises. 'Of course, no man should be held without charge.' He waits in case I have any other instructions. 'Should I speak to anyone at court on your behalf?'

I smile at him. I am not going to name my friends or my few kinswomen. I will incriminate no-one. 'Let it all be done in the open,' I say. 'Speak of me and of my sister to everyone.'

In my guardian's absence I am allowed to walk and sit in the garden. I study and I write, I read my Bible and I draw. I even attempt some frescoes on the walls of my room, remembering the carvings made by the Dudley boys in the stone chimney breast of the Tower all that long time ago. I think that if Katherine and I are released, and she is named as heir and we are restored to our home, then this long painful story of family disloyalty and loss of love will be ended and the innocent children will be freed. I think of the little nephews and I pray that they will both grow up in their father's beautiful house, under the care of both their parents, knowing themselves to be rightful heirs to the throne, certain to take their place. I think Katherine will be a good Queen of England: she will not usurp her powers or use spies and torture to get her way. Her boy who comes after her will be an honourable Protestant king, a Seymour Tudor king like my poor cousin King Edward.

After a week Lady Hawtrey receives a letter from her husband and brings it to me in my little room. She taps on the door and comes in when I call 'Enter!'

'My husband has sent a letter from London to tell me how they go on,' she says, curtseying very low. 'I thought that you would want to know the news.'

'I do,' I say. 'Please sit down.'

She takes a stool by the fireside and I stay in my dining chair so our heads are level. She unfolds the letter and looks through it.

'He says that the House of Commons have joined with the House of Lords to remonstrate with the queen and that there have been angry scenes,' she says. 'Both Houses are determined that Lady Katherine shall be named as the queen's heir. The Privy Council agree with parliament. The queen has quarrelled with the Duke of Norfolk, with Robert Dudley and the Earl of Pembroke.'

I listen intently. These are the queen's key advisors and

friends; the Earl of Pembroke was Katherine's former father-in-law. I would never have thought he would have risked disagreeing with the queen over Katherine. None of these men stands to gain anything from the recognition of Katherine. Elizabeth has to see that they are doing this for the good of the country. Nor would any one of them speak against the queen unless they were certain of success.

'Now she has forbidden them to come to her presence chamber,' Lady Hawtrey reads. She looks up at me. 'That's extraordinary, isn't it?'

'Yes,' I say tersely.

'She summoned thirty men from the House of Commons and would not allow the Speaker to come to her,' Lady Hawtrey reads. 'My husband says that she shouted at them.'

I turn my head to hide a smile. I imagine the provincial members of parliament were terrified before the queen, who could arrest them without warning, and hold them without trial. But they didn't weaken. They insisted on their right to advise her, and their advice was that she must marry and get an heir, and name one now.

Lady Hawtrey takes up the last page. 'He's coming home,' she says. 'He says the work is finished. He says they are victorious.'

'She named Katherine?' I whisper disbelievingly. It is the only outcome open to Elizabeth if the Houses have stood, united, against her. 'She has named her?'

Lady Hawtrey folds the letter and hands it to me. 'See for yourself. She has sworn it. They have granted her the subsidy and she has promised that they shall decide on her heir.'

She looks at me. 'They have won her to agreement,' she says. 'Did you think that they would?'

I give a trembly little laugh. 'I did not dare to hope, all I could do was pray for it. They have been courageous and she has been persuaded to do the right thing at last.'

She shakes her head in wonderment. 'She is an extraordinary woman, she is answerable to no-one.'

'She is answerable to God,' I say steadily. 'And He will ask her for Katherine, and for her boys, Teddy and Thomas, for her husband, Ned, even for Margaret Douglas and her little boy Charles, and for me and Thomas Keyes. The God who promised us that not a sparrow falls will ask the Queen of England where her cousins are tonight.'

CHEQUERS, BUCKINGHAMSHIRE, WINTER 1566

Queen Mary of Scotland has collapsed and is mortally ill in her troubled kingdom after an attack of the spleen. She has been unconscious for hours, they are warming her cold body. God knows what will happen. Her son and heir is still a little baby – if she should die there will be nobody to defend him. They say that her last words were asking Elizabeth to be his Protector.

She might as well ask a cuckoo to protect the eggs that are alongside it in the nest. She might as well ask an owl to protect a mouse. But I see the skill in it; even on her deathbed Mary is outwitting Elizabeth, trapping her with the bait of a royal boy. If Elizabeth agrees to be the Protector of the heir of Scotland she is recognising kinship. Elizabeth, greedy for influence in Scotland, still torn between love and hate for her more beautiful younger rival queen, cannot resist. I receive a short unsigned note in a hand that I don't recognise and conclude it is from William Cecil.

The queen is to stand as godmother to Prince James of Scotland.

That's all; but it is the end of my hope. Elizabeth has broken her sworn promise to parliament and to her lords. She has chosen Mary over Katherine, papist over Protestant. She thinks she has seen a chance, dangled before her by Mary, who may be on her deathbed but still has more wit in her cold little finger than Elizabeth has in all her endless cunning. Queen Mary has offered her baby as bait and Elizabeth has jumped into the trap. In the hopes that Mary is dying she will claim the motherless boy as her own. He will be her adopted son and the next King of England.

I send Katherine a Christmas letter but I have nothing to give her. In reply she writes to me and encloses a chain of gold links.

I have this, as I have so many little gifts, from my husband, who sends me his love in letters and treats. Our little boy Thomas is well and growing. Our oldest son Teddy is with his grandmother at Hanworth and she tells Ned that he is well and strong and a happy carefree child. We all pray for our freedom and for yours. I am lodged with good people who do what they can to comfort me as I enter another year, my sixth, in captivity. I am weary of it, and sad, but I believe that next year, perhaps in the new year, we will be forgiven and released. I hear the Queen of Scotland and our good queen are to come to an agreement which will make you and I their subjects and loyal cousins. I long to see you, my sister. Farewell.

I reread the letter over and over until I have it in my memory, and then I burn it in the little fireplace in my room. I wear her chain of gold around my neck and think that this little thing comes from a woman who has the rights to the treasure house of England.

It is not my only Christmas gift. My hosts give me some ribbons and my maid trims one of my shifts with some pretty lace. I give Lady Hawtrey a sketch of the garden from my window. If I could see more, I would draw more, but even my sight is confined.

CHEQUERS, BUCKINGHAMSHIRE,
SPRING 1567

Lord Darnley, that wildly vicious son of my cousin Margaret Douglas, is dead. The boy that no-one ever thought would make good has made a terrible end, naked and strangled in the garden, his house in ruins behind him. Someone – and everyone is saying that it is the Protestant lords – blew up his house, Kirk o' Field, with gunpowder and caught him as he fled. He was not a youth that was ever going to die in his bed – a murderer who threatened his own unborn son and wife, a twisted child spoiled by his mother's ambition – but everyone is shocked that he should die such a death, and horrified by what this means for the Queen of Scots, only just recovered from her illness and now widely suspected of murdering her husband.

Elizabeth, hardly concealing her delight at the disaster that has blown up the agreement between her and the Scots queen, just as the house Kirk o' Field has been blown apart, is now ostentatiously filled with pity for the vicious boy's heartbroken mother. Our cousin Lady Margaret Douglas is released from the Tower and allowed to stay with Thomas Sackville at Sackville Place. Her little boy Charles joins her, to comfort her in her terrible loss. The death of her syphilitic murderer son somehow excuses her own treason. Lady Margaret is set free; Katherine and I, innocent of anything, are kept imprisoned. Elizabeth can think of nothing but how she should respond to our cousin Queen Mary.

While the rabid Scots preachers declare that no woman can hold power, Elizabeth is driven to support her cousin. But she cannot do it wholeheartedly. She publishes advice to the Scots queen pointing out the contrast between herself – the celibate queen – and the scandalous newly widowed, twice-married queen. A copy of this letter even reaches me at Chequers, and I read it amazed that the queen calls herself a faithful cousin and friend, says that she is more sorry for the danger to Mary than for the death of Darnley, and that Mary must preserve her honour rather than look through her fingers at those who have done her the favour of murdering her husband, 'as most people say'.

I don't know whether or not 'most people' ever said that Mary was the murderer of Darnley before Elizabeth's damning defence, but I am very sure that everyone will say it now. I see the hand of William Cecil all through this: the murder in the night-time garden, the smearing of the reputation of the papist queen, the sudden leap of Elizabeth into confidence and pretend pity. The death of Darnley has ruined Mary, just as her marriage to him ruined her. It has ruined the agreement that she was making with Elizabeth, just as William Cecil planned.

This was not a quiet murder done on an out-of-the-way shallow flight of stairs with a packed jury to return a verdict of accidental death. This was a huge explosion in the heart of Edinburgh in the middle of the night with the queen having refused to sleep with her husband in the doomed house that very evening. As if she knew, people say. As if the gunpowder was packed by someone she knew.

Even locked in my room, even confined to the garden, the rumours reach me. The kitchen at Chequers is sizzling with gossip, the stable-yard lads are great supporters of the Scots lord: James Hepburn Earl of Bothwell, who has always fought for the Protestant cause, whose ways are simple and direct and violent. The laundry maids are filled with pity for poor Lord Darnley, blown up in his bed, or strangled by the barbarian Scots lords at the behest of his wicked wife. All spring the scandal gets more and more outrageous and elaborate until in April we hear that Mary Queen of Scots has run away from her capital city, and in May that she has married the man who killed her husband: James Hepburn the Earl of Bothwell.

CHEQUERS, BUCKINGHAMSHIRE, SUMMER 1567

Compared with this new disastrous marriage of the Queen of Scots, my love match with Thomas Keyes and even Katherine's with Ned Seymour fade into minor indiscretion. We fell in love with honourable men, who were free to marry. Nobody even knows if Bothwell has a wife. But Queen Mary marries him without any sign of shame, dressed in fanciful mourning wear: a black patterned velvet gown embroidered all over with gold and silver thread.

I ask Lady Hawtrey to be sure to find out about the gown and it is indeed gloriously expensive black velvet with real gold embroidery and a scarlet undergown! She is a bride and a widow at once. She may be a murderer, certainly she is marrying a murderer. She is ruined in the eyes of the world, French, Spanish and English, papist and Protestant. She has destroyed herself. Clearly, she cannot be heir to England.

I wait for Sir William to come to me and tell me that I am to go free. William Cecil's long secret campaign against the Scots queen, his secret plan for our succession, is finally fulfilled. There can be no reason for my sister and me to be held any longer. Sir William Hawtrey tells me that Robert Dudley's brother Ambrose visited Ned Seymour, defying the order that says that my brother-in-law is to have no visitors; and assured him that my sister Katherine will be named as heir, and the Dudleys will support her.

I am restless in my stuffy room. I open both the windows and look out. When I go out for my walk I pace up and down in the pretty midsummer garden, going round and round the outer path like a ferret circling its cage. Every time I hear hoofbeats I think it must be the queen's messenger coming to set me free. It cannot be long now.

Lady Hawtrey tells me the gossip from London. Lady Margaret Douglas's husband, the frightened father of Lord Darnley, has run away from Scotland, and been allowed into England. He is invited to court and Lady Margaret is free to join him. He tells of a Scotland which has turned to rebellion. The Scots lords are against Bothwell and against their queen. Queen Mary – Bothwell's victim, Bothwell's wife – cannot keep the authority of a queen. Just as Elizabeth always feared, a married queen is reduced to the level of her husband. Mary came to Scotland a royal French widow in a dress of the brightest white. She cannot hold the country as Bothwell's wife in seductive black with red petticoats. They treat her with outward respect, but they imprison her in the island castle of Lochleven. My sister's rival, who was so free and powerful, is now a prisoner just like us.

And, just like us, our imprisoned cousin is now dependent on the goodwill of Elizabeth. Nobody else can order the Scots lords to respect their monarch. No-one else has an army on the border, spies in place, and most of the lords as paid retainers. But instead of commanding the restoration of a fellow queen, Elizabeth listens to our other cousin, Margaret Douglas, who demands justice for the death of her son: the execution of her daughter-in-law, and the possession of her grandson, the little heir. All these righteous claims to humiliate the Scots queen have great appeal for Elizabeth, but she cannot pursue them.

More than any other belief, Elizabeth believes that the law of the land does not apply to queens. She wants everyone to think that a queen might make mistakes – might make fatal mistakes in her personal life – and still be fit to rule. If people say that a queen cannot be in love with a married man, where would that leave Elizabeth and Robert Dudley? If people say that an unwanted husband or wife cannot be mercilessly killed, then what adjustment should be made to the coroner's verdict of the accidental death of Amy Dudley? Elizabeth would like the baby Stuart in her keeping, would like to see his father's death avenged; but the safety of his mother as a queen is sacrosanct. Nothing matters more to Elizabeth, the daughter of a beheaded queen, than everyone understanding that queens cannot be beheaded. No queen can be beheaded in England ever again.

CHEQUERS, BUCKINGHAMSHIRE, SUMMER 1567

It is the Scots lords who end the stalemate, they don't understand the English queen and they ruin their own cause by accident. They announce that their queen, Mary, her royal will broken miscarrying twin boys in her island prison, has agreed to surrender her rights to the throne. They have made her abdicate in favour of her son and she has agreed to be as nothing, a prisoner with no title. They think this is their triumph but it turns Elizabeth against them in a moment. Now she refuses to recognise the little Prince James as King James VI of Scotland. She says he cannot be used to displace his mother, the little boy may not usurp his mother's throne, a queen cannot be thrown down by her lords. Never, never, never can an heir be put in the place of a monarch – it is the greatest fear of her life. She rails at Cecil, she swears that Queen Mary's dethronement shall not be allowed. Queens shall be treated with respect, they cannot be judged and found wanting. She will take England to war to defend her fellow queen, Mary.

Now Elizabeth turns on her loudly demanding newly restored cousin Margaret Douglas. Lady Margaret insists that her daughter-in-law Mary Queen of Scots be imprisoned forever, or brought to trial and executed for the abominable crime of husband-killing. It hardly matters to her, as long as the baby is brought to England and Lady Margaret can call herself the grandmother of a king and see him inherit the thrones of Scotland and England.

William Cecil plays his long game; he keeps quiet. Outwardly he agrees with the queen that an attack on a fellow royal cannot be borne, but he points out that any invasion of Scotland would probably lead to the Scots lords assassinating the queen at once. They would panic, he says smoothly, looking into Elizabeth's panic-stricken face. Far better for England to register a temperate protest, negotiate with the self-proclaimed regent, Lord Moray, Mary's faithless half-brother, and try to get the baby sent south when it is convenient.

Of course, the Protestant lords of Scotland are never going to hand their prince over to a dyed-in-the-wool papist such as Margaret Douglas. Of course, Lady Margaret, having ruined one son, should never be entrusted with another. Elizabeth is so frustrated by events that she will not speak to her great advisor or her beloved cousin; and I have more grounds than ever to predict that she will turn towards us. She has to turn to us. What other family is left to her?

CHEQUERS, BUCKINGHAMSHIRE, SUMMER 1567

There is Katherine, imprisoned at Gosfield Hall, innocent of any crime, beloved by half of England, her boy being raised as a royal Seymour in hiding. There is Mary, imprisoned at Lochleven, probably a murderer, certainly an adulterer, hated by half of England and a horror to her own co-religionists, her boy held by her half-brother, her husband on the run. Who is the better choice of heir? Which is the better choice for England? Of course Elizabeth in her monstrous perversity supports Mary and calls for her release.

The Scots take her money but make no progress, Cecil smoothly blocks any hopes of an English invasion of Scotland. Elizabeth's resolve falters. Cecil suggests that she goes on progress, Robert Dudley promises her an idyllic summer – why should she not be happy? Elizabeth sets the disaster of her cousin to one side and rides out beside her lover, running away from trouble again.

CHEQUERS, BUCKINGHAMSHIRE, SUMMER 1567

The swallows arrive in the gardens of Chequers and fly low in the evening. I can hear the nightingale singing in the wood at twilight. Summer is the hardest time to be imprisoned. I feel as if everything is free and living its life, singing at dusk, but me. I feel as if every living thing is seeking its mate and finding joy – everything, everyone – but me and my sister.

I am very low this evening. I usually try to read, or decorate my cramped room with drawings on the walls, or study my Bible or my sister Jane's writings, but this evening I stand on a chair at the open window and rest my chin on my hands and look out over the darkening horizon to where the solitary star comes out like a pinhead of silver against a dark blue silk gown, and I know that I am far from my family and far from my friends, and I will never see the man that I love again. Never in this life.

I can feel my face is wet with my tears and I know that this is no way for me to spend the evening. I will feel no better for this in the morning, I will have learned nothing by diving to the depth of my sorrow. I am not the sort of woman who says that she always feels better for a good cry. I rather despise that sort of woman. I usually keep myself busy and occupied, and avoid moments of grief for my loss of liberty and the loss of my sisters and the terrible blight that has been laid on our family because we were born Tudor. I pat my face with my sleeve and I search in myself for Jane's holy certainty, or even my mother's flinty determination. I cannot be tender-hearted and vulnerable like Katherine or I will simply despair like her.

I am about to swing the window shut and put myself to bed to try to sleep through to another day, so that these lingering lonely hours of the night are escaped. I reach out and put my hand on the latch of the window and then I hear horses coming down the road, several horses, perhaps six, a troop of men riding down the London road to Chequers. These are the hoofbeats that I have waited for. I strain my ears to listen. Yes, definitely, they have not gone past. They turn in towards the house and now I am leaning out of the window, staring into the half-light to see if there is a standard going before them, and whose colours are coming at a brisk trot at this time of the evening.

If someone has come for me, out of the summer dusk, some-one determined to see us free, someone taking a chance with

Elizabeth on progress and Cecil snatching a week at his new home, then I will go with him, whoever he is. If he takes me to poverty in France or Spain, if he involves me in danger and rebellion, then I will go. I will not spend another summer here, caged like one of Katherine's linnets. I will not stay. I don't care if we die as we ride to the coast, or if our ship is captured and sunk at sea. I would rather drown than spend another night in this little bed looking at the white ceiling and my scratched drawings on the walls. I would rather die tonight than live another day in prison.

The riders come around the bend in the track and now I can see them. The Tudor standard goes before them. It is no outlaw, but a message from Elizabeth. It is brought by a lord riding among his guard on the queen's business. At last, at last, this must be my freedom. It can only be that she is setting me free. Any other command and it would be a single messenger at a leisurely pace. At last, God be praised, God be praised for it, she is setting me free and I am going to ride out from this damned house and I will never set foot in it again.

I slam the window shut and jump down from the stool. I shake my maid, who is dozing in a chair. 'Do my hair,' I command her. 'Give me my best hood. Sir William will knock on the door at any moment. Open it to him. He is coming to tell me that we are to be set free.'

She flings open the chest and brings out my hood and I stand with my heart pounding as she pins up my blonde hair, and then straightens my hood on top. I take my wedding ring off my finger, kiss it and put it on a chain and tell her to fasten it round my neck. She tightens the laces of my gown at the sleeves and on the kirtle, and I hold my arms wide like a little doll, so she can settle the bodice into place, and just as she says, 'Perfect, your ladyship,' there is a knock on the door and I meet her eyes and smile and say: 'At last. God be praised. At last.'

I take my seat on my chair and she opens my door, curtseys to Sir William and steps back to present him to me. He comes into the room and bows low. Behind him I see the captain who led his men to the front door; his bonnet in his hand, he bows as he sees me and I incline my head.

'Lady Mary,' Sir William bows. 'Here's a sudden change.'

I cannot stop myself smiling. 'I heard the horses,' I say.

'They have come to take you from us,' Sir William says, flustered. 'With no warning, of course. But we will be sorry to see you go, your ladyship.'

I wriggle to the edge of the chair and drop to my feet. I put out my hand to him and he goes down on one knee to kiss it. 'God bless you,' he says huskily. 'God be praised that you are free.'

'You have been a kind host,' I say. 'But of course, I am glad to go.'

'You are to pack your things and leave in the morning,' he says. 'I hope that will be convenient.'

I would walk out of here and leave the old bed, the chair, the little table and the stool tucked underneath it. I would leave my clothes and walk out barefoot in my shift if I could go to Bradgate tonight.

'Perfectly,' I say.

The commander of the guard behind Sir William bows and says: 'We will leave after breakfast, your ladyship. At seven of the clock, if that is convenient to you?'

I incline my head. 'Perfectly,' I say again.

Sir William hesitates. 'You don't ask where you are going?'

I give a little laugh. I had thought only of my freedom. I have dreamed so long of getting out of here that I had not thought of my destination. I had thought only that I was riding out of that stone gateway and that I can go anywhere. I will want to go to London and visit my husband, Thomas, if he is still imprisoned. If he has been freed I shall go to wherever he is – Kent, I suppose. I hardly care. All I want is my freedom. I want to be on the road, I hardly care where it leads. 'Of course, I should have asked. Where am I going?'

'To your step-grandmother, the Duchess of Suffolk,' he says. 'To her house in London. I will escort you.'

It makes no difference to me. I want to go to London to get Thomas freed, and my lady grandmother Catherine is one of the last of my family still alive. I have always liked her, and she is a woman of great worldly experience – a favourite of a king whose favour was deadly. It is quite right that I should go to her, and when my sister is released she should join us too.

'And my sister?'

'I don't know what is proposed for her ladyship,' Sir William says. 'But we can hope.'

I note that we can publicly hope now. I note that he is hoping. I am to join my step-grandmother, I am going to free my husband. No doubt I shall see Robert Dudley or his brother Ambrose, since they are now taking an interest in our freedom. I shall see William Cecil; I shall visit Katherine and my little nephew and obtain their freedom. At last Elizabeth has seen reason and learned that she cannot support Mary Queen of Scots over my sister and me. There can only be one heir of Elizabeth and that is Katherine my sister. We will take our places in the world again. We will be free, we will be reunited. We might even be happy. Why not? Katherine and I have always had a happy temperament. We will be free to be happy once more.

CHEQUERS TO LONDON, SUMMER 1567

We leave in the pearly light of an English summer morning, the best time of day of the best season in England. The sun has risen behind a bank of pale clouds that lie like cream ribbons on the Chiltern Hills and we ride east, into the golden light on the old Roman road that goes straight as a sword, Akeman Street.

We ride in a small procession: the vanguard, then a little gap so I am not riding in their dust, then me and Sir William and the commander of the guard, and behind us, the rest of the men. We stop after a couple of hours to water the horses and to eat, and Sir William asks me if I am weary.

'No,' I say. 'I'm well.'

It's a lie. Already my back is aching and my legs are sore from being astride on the saddle, for I ride as my father taught me: I won't go pillion, seated like a country girl behind some dolt. I ride my own horse, and I straighten my back to sit proudly in the saddle; but I have been cooped up in a tiny room for so long that I have lost my strength and energy. But I have not lost my will to live or my passionate desire for freedom. I would rather die of the pain, cramped in the saddle, than confess that I am weary, for fear that the commander would say that we must go back to Chequers and make the journey when he can find a litter. Nothing will get me back into prison. I will ride with chapped hands and bleeding legs rather than go back into that little room and the view from the window of that square of sky.

It is like being born again, with the sky arching above me and the wind blowing gently against my cheek, the sun ahead of us. I ignore the pain in my back and the ache in every bone in my body. I can smell the honeysuckle and the wild bean flowers in the hedgerows. When we ride over the high hills where the sheep are grazing I can hear a lark soaring high above me, singing a leaping cadence with each beat of his tiny wings. Swallows swoop and circle over the village ponds, people stare and wave from the fields, dogs run and snap at the horses' heels. When we overtake a pedlar on the road he swings his pack to the ground and begs me to stop and take a look. I am dazzled by the sights and sounds of the everyday world: I never thought I would see them again.

We halt for dinner at midday, and at four in the afternoon the commander brings his horse beside mine and says: 'We will stop for the night at Headstone Manor at the village of Pinner. They are expecting us.'

I am immediately alarmed. 'I won't be confined,' I say.

'No,' he says. 'You are free. You will have your own bedroom and a privy chamber, and you will dine in the hall with our hosts, if you wish. This is not a new prison.'

'I won't be tricked,' I say, thinking of Katherine leaving the Tower to live with her uncle and thinking that her husband was joining her.

'I swear that I am to take you to the Duchess of Suffolk,' the commander assures me. 'But we couldn't do the journey in one day. We will have a half-day's ride tomorrow morning.'

'Very well,' I say.

My host, Roger, Lord North, greets me with every sign of respect. Clearly, they are welcoming the sister of the heir to the English throne. His wife, Winifred, makes a muddle of her curtsey, bending overly low, trying to show the proper respect to a royal, trying to get down lower so that her head bows to me, but I laugh it off and she shows me to my bedroom. Two maids from the house have poured hot water for me to wash, and my own maid has a clean gown from my little bag of belongings.

I dine on my own in the guest room rather than at the high table in the hall. I feel shy after so long – nearly two years! – of confinement. And I suspect that there will be spies as well as well-wishers among the diners in the hall. I am not ready for the jostle and noise of a great hall. I have been so lonely for so long that I cannot get accustomed to many voices, all talking at once.

We wake, attend chapel, and take breakfast early the next morning and at nine, by the clock over the stables, we are on the road again. My horse is rested and, though my legs are bruised and stiff, I am filled with such a delight in freedom that I beam at the commander of the guard and when we come to a stretch of straight dry road I tell Sir William that we can canter.

It feels as if I am flying, I am going so fast. I bend forward and urge the horse on and the thundering of the hoofs and the flying mud and the wind in my face make me want to sing with joy. I am free, I know I am free. I am free at last.

The little villages as we approach London are accustomed to travellers coming and going down Watling Street, and they look for the standard, and when they see the royal flag they recognise me and call out my name. The commander rides closer beside me.

'We were told not to draw attention to ourselves,' he says apologetically. 'Would you be so good as to wear the hood of your cape over your head, my lady? There's no point in inviting a crowd.'

I pull up my hood without a word of complaint, and I think that goodwill to the queen must be at a very low ebb, if a cousin as lowly as me can be a danger if seen on the road.

'Where is your sister? Where is Lady Katherine and her bonny boys?' someone shouts as we ride towards the entrance at the east of the city.

'Where are the little princes?' someone calls, and I see the commander of the guard grimace. 'Where are the Seymour boys?'

I pull my hood further forward and I ride close to him. 'It's a question I ask too,' I say drily to Sir William.

'It's a question I may not ask,' he tells me.

THE MINORIES, LONDON, SUMMER 1567

We clatter up to my step-grandmother's house at the Minories. It was actually once our house. I can remember my father telling me it was a gift to us from the young King Edward, and I remember shrinking back from the massive dark wood door and the echoing stone galleries of the former monastery. We lost it when Jane was killed, of course – when we lost everything.

My step-grandmother Catherine, a serene and beautiful woman of nearly fifty, is coming out of the hall, dressed in her travelling cape. She starts to see us, on our sweaty horses at her London door.

'Mary! My dear! I thought you were coming next month! I was told you would be here next month.' She beckons to one of her liveried grooms and says: 'Help Lady Mary down from her horse, Thomas.'

The man helps me dismount and then my lady grandmother kneels down to kiss me warmly. 'I am so glad you are released, and into my care,' she says. 'Welcome, child. You look pale. It's not surprising.'

She looks up at Sir William. 'How is this? They told me you would bring her to me within the month. I am leaving now to go to Greenwich.'

Sir William heaves himself down from the saddle and bows. 'The guard came to escort her without notice the day before yesterday,' he says. 'Orders. But her ladyship has been desperate to be free any day this past year,' he continues. 'It would have been cruelty to keep her another day. I don't think I could have kept her another day to be honest. She has earned her freedom, God knows.'

A shadow passes over my step-grandmother's face. She turns to me: 'But you know you are not freed?'

'What?'

She turns to Sir William. 'She's not free,' she says again. 'She is in my care. She is released into my keeping.'

Sir William swears and turns to his horse to muffle his oath. He turns back to us and he is flushed red with anger and there are tears in his eyes. 'Not freed?' he repeats. 'On whose orders is this—' He bites off words that might be treasonous. 'I thought she was to come to you as her lady grandmother, and then to go wherever she might please. I thought you were receiving her and taking her back to court.'

'Come in,' my lady grandmother says, conscious of the waiting servants and the people loitering in the street. She leads us into the great hall inside the house and then turns aside to the porter's room for privacy. There is a table and a chair, and a writing stand for messages and accounts. I lean against the table, suddenly exhausted.

'My dear, sit down,' she says kindly to me. 'Sir William. Will you take a glass of ale? Of wine?'

I cannot bear to sit. I feel as if I sit they will slam the door and never let me out again. I stand awkwardly, my back aching from the two-day ride, filled with a painful sense of dread. 'Am I not free?' I can hardly speak, my lips feel swollen and stiff as if someone has slapped me hard in the face. 'I thought I was free.'

She shakes her head. 'You are in my keeping, like your poor little nephew is in the keeping of his grandmother at Hanworth. But the queen is not releasing you. I have had to promise to keep you confined.'

'I can't,' bursts from me. I can feel the tears coming and I give a shuddering sob. 'Lady Grandmother, I can't be confined. I have to be able to go outside. I can't bear being kept in a little room like a doll in a box. I can't bear it, Lady Grandmother. I will die. I swear I will die if I cannot ride out and walk out and go freely.'

She nods, her face pale. She glances at Sir William and says: 'You kept her very close?'

He shrugs angrily. 'What could I do? I was ordered to let her walk in the garden only as much as her health required. But I let her go out all day, every day, as much as I could. They ordered that she should have one room, a small room, and one maid, and no messages or visits or friends. She was not even supposed to speak to my servants. I was not supposed to speak to her at all.'

My lady grandmother turns to me. 'Don't cry, Mary,' she says firmly. 'We'll do what we can. And at least you are in my keeping and can live with me and my children: Susan and Peregrine. And we can talk freely and study and write and think.'

'I have to be free,' I whisper. 'I have to be free.'

My step-grandmother looks at Sir William. 'I was leaving just now for Greenwich,' she repeats. 'Lady Mary may come with me. Does a train of wagons with her goods follow you? Or will you send everything directly to Greenwich?'

'She has next to nothing,' Sir William blurts out. 'She came to me with almost nothing. A few bits of tapestry, a pillow or two.'

My step-grandmother takes it in, looking from him to me. 'So where are her things? Where is her inheritance? Her mother was a princess of the blood, she had a great house filled with treasures. This is a wealthy family. They owned houses and lands and licences and monopolies. Where are her gowns and jewels from court?'

Sir William shakes his head. 'All I know is she came to me like a poor woman, and they sent nothing after her. I will deliver to you all that is hers. I am very sorry that it is not more, my lady.' He nods his head to me. 'I will give you anything you need from Chequers,' he offers. 'Just ask.'

'I want nothing,' I shake my head. 'I want nothing but my freedom. I thought I was free.'

'You shall have something to eat and then we will go down the river to Greenwich,' my lady grandmother rules. 'And then we shall see to your rooms and your furniture and your clothes, too. Her Majesty will provide what is missing, and I shall speak to William Cecil myself about providing for you and setting you free. Don't fear. You will be free, my dear, I swear it: you and your sister and her boys, too.'

I look at her, this woman who has been exiled and persecuted for her faith, this woman who married beneath her so that she might freely love and freely live. 'Please help us, Lady Grandmother,' I say quietly. 'I will promise anything to the queen if she will set me free. And Katherine, my poor sister.'

Stepping aboard the Suffolk barge is like stepping back into the past when I used to sail downriver with the court to Greenwich or watch the green meadows going by as we went upriver to Richmond. It is a hot day and a heavy heat sits over the stinking city but it is pleasant to be in the centre of the stream with the silk awning fluttering in the cool breeze that blows upriver from the sea. The seagulls cry overhead and all the bells of London peal out the hour as if they are celebrating my freedom. My spirits rise as we go past the familiar stone walls of the Tower and the yawning waterside entrance of the portcullis at the watergate. At least I am not making that slow walk into the prison rooms. I am in my step-grandmother's keeping, but I am going to a royal palace in her barge, and the sunshine is on my face and the salt-smelling wind is blowing in my hair, and I can see more than a small square of sky.

The river widens as we come towards Greenwich and then I see the Tudors' favourite palace – our favourite palace – like a dream shore, as if it were floating on the water, the quayside golden in the sunshine, the great doors standing open. It looks so rich and friendly and peaceful I cannot believe that this will be anything like imprisonment – not in this beautiful house with the doors standing wide to the rich gardens, greens and orchards.

Elizabeth is not here. She is on progress at Farnham Castle at Guildford, and only a few servants are in attendance, engaged in the great work of sweetening the rooms, cleaning out dusty old rushes and laying fresh green leaves and herbs in all the public rooms. My lady grandmother's servants are expecting her and they line up before her apartment in the palace and bow to me as I walk in with her. I had almost forgotten how many servants it takes to service one set of rooms, one demanding woman. I am so used to my cramped room and my one maid, I am so used to a window onto a small square of sky and silence. My lady grandmother leads the way into her private hall, takes her seat on the raised dais and gestures to me that I am to sit beside her. They wash our hands with a silver jug and ewer, and bring us cold small ale and a plate with fruits and meat, and the steward of the Greenwich household reports to my lady grandmother about the running of her apartment here, the absence of one of the grooms without permission, the rise in the price of wine.

I have no appetite. Her sharp eyes watch me as she listens to her steward and, when he has finished and bowed and stood back, she says: 'You must eat, my dear.'

'I am not hungry,' I say.

'You must be,' she insists. 'You had that long ride, and then the voyage on the river. Your triumph is to survive and thrive, you know. To fast and to fail is to do your enemies' work for them.'

'I have no enemies,' I say staunchly. 'I made none when I was in service to the queen, and I married a man for love who was free to love me. I have no rivals nor enemies and yet I have been imprisoned for two years. No-one has accused me of anything, no-one has borne witness against me. No-one has reason to hate me.'

She nods. 'I know. We cannot speak of it here. But anyway, you have to eat. Your course must be to survive . . .'

She does not say 'and outlive Elizabeth', but we both know that is what she means.

'I will,' I say. I give her a little smile. I see in her determination – a survivor's willpower – a model for myself. 'You did.'

She makes a little foreign gesture, a shrug from her famously beautiful Spanish mother. 'A courtier has to know how to survive. I was born and raised at court and I hope to die between silk sheets, in favour.'

'I can count on a tremendous funeral,' I say bitterly. 'Wherever I die. The queen loves to honour her family when they are safely dead.'

She gives a little snort of laughter. 'Hush,' she says. 'If you can laugh then you can eat. They tell me your sister is in deep grief and starving herself. That's not the way to victory. I shall write to her and give her this advice, too. It is what my friend the queen Kateryn knew, it is what your mother knew. A wise woman lives long and hopes for change.'

GREENWICH PALACE,
AUTUMN 1567

My rooms at Greenwich are adequately furnished and the queen herself sends me some silver pots for the ale and wine, after my step-grandmother provides William Cecil with a list of the things that we need. I don't think she minces her words as she rails about my poverty. I don't think she spares her assurances of our good housekeeping skills. My step-grandmother lost all her good things in the years of exile while she travelled in Europe, one step ahead of the papist spies who would have dragged her back to England for a heresy trial. Now she is determined that neither she nor her family will suffer again. She is high in favour at Elizabeth's court and she awaits the return of the court to Greenwich when she will argue for my freedom. She is confident that I will be released, that Ned will be allowed to go to Hanworth, that my sister Katherine and Thomas will join him and Teddy, that the family will be freed and reunited. She believes that Elizabeth's genuine devotion to the Protestant faith will overrule Elizabeth's perverse, persistent love for her papist cousin, her lingering family loyalty to Mary Queen of Scots, her fearful defence of the rights of queens, even for one who has done so little to deserve it.

'Be brave!' the duchess says brightly to me when she sees me wearily walking in the gardens, looking out at the river where the ships spread their sails and drop the tow ropes and look as if they are ready to fly away, free as the birds that circle their masts. 'Be brave! You will go where you please next spring, I swear it. I will speak for your husband, for your sister, for your brother-in-law and for those two innocent little boys. Your life will not end in prison, like that of your poor sister Jane. You will be freed, believe it!'

I do believe her. Her husband, Richard Bertie, bends down and kisses my hand and tells me that good times will come. Everyone suffers in this troubled world, but God rewards those who are faithful to Him. He reminds me that my step-grandmother was summoned home when her religion became the faith of England, and overnight she was no longer a damned heretic but one of the chosen.

'Besides,' my lady grandmother tells me, 'Elizabeth cannot create a force for Mary Queen of Scots. She has given the Clan Hamilton a great bribe, but they will not raise an army for Mary. She has demanded that the countries of Europe starve Scotland out. But not even the French, Mary's former family, will support a trade blockade on Scotland. Without Spanish support, without the French, Elizabeth can do nothing for her cousin: she cannot act on her own.'

'Or at any rate she dare not,' Richard Bertie supplements quietly.

My lady grandmother laughs and slaps her husband's hand. 'It is not in the interest of England to restore the papist queen to her throne,' she says. 'The queen, our queen, will never work against the interest of her Protestant country. Wherever her heart yearns to be, she always has a steady head. You can be sure of that.'

'I can be sure of William Cecil,' Richard Bertie says. 'His heart doesn't yearn for a papist in trouble.'

'And in the meantime,' I ask, 'what is happening to Mary the former Queen of Scotland?'

My step-grandmother shrugs her shoulders as if to say: 'Who cares?' 'She is imprisoned,' she says. 'She must miss the son that she handed over, she must grieve for the babies that she lost. She must know that she has been a fool. My God, she must regret with all her soul that she married that vicious boy and then allowed his murder, and then married his killer.'

'I don't know that there is any evidence that she murdered Lord Darnley,' I put in.

My step-grandmother raises her eyebrows. 'Then who did?' she asks. 'Whoever benefited from the death of that worthless young man if not his abused wife and her lover?'

I open my mouth to argue but I fall silent. I don't know the truth of the matter, I don't know what my dangerous and beautiful cousin might or might not have done. But I know that she, like Katherine and me, will hate her prison, beating against the bars like a frightened bird. I know she will be like us, determined to be free. I know that she, like us, will do anything to be free. In that is our only power. In that we are a danger to ourselves.

I think that Katherine and I have a chance. The luck that has run against us ever since Jane went upriver to Syon in the Dudley barge, and did not resist them when they crammed the crown on her little head, has turned at last. My sister is suddenly liberated by the death of her old guardian and keeper. This event comes as a surprise only to those who hoped to put my sister away, and never think of her again. Poor old Wentworth was more than seventy years old, he objected to the cost of her keeping, he pleaded that he could not be expected to do it, and now he has escaped his duty into the long rest of death.

I am so accustomed to bad news that I feel only dread when I see my lady grandmother come towards me, down the raked gravel path in early September with a single sheet of paper in her hand. I fear at once that something is wrong. My first thought is of my husband, Thomas Keyes, imprisoned in the Fleet, and my second is for my sister Katherine and her little boy.

I run towards her, my little boots crunching on the stones. 'My lady grandmother! Is it bad news?'

She tries to smile. 'Oh, Mary! Do you read minds like a dwarf in a fair?'

'Tell me!' I say.

'My dear, sit down.'

I grow more and more frightened. We go to a little stone seat in a bower of a golden-leaved hedge. I clamber onto the seat to satisfy her, and I turn to her. 'Tell me!'

She unfolds the letter. 'It is your sister. It is your poor dear sister.'

It is a letter from the executor of the old man's will, a man of no importance, caught up in great events. He writes to William Cecil to say that the widow Wentworth cannot take the charge of Katherine and her son, though she loves her as dearly as a daughter. Tentatively, Mr Roke Green says that he has no instructions as to where Katherine should go, or what the queen wishes for her. He is too poor himself, he lives in too small a way to house such a great lady. He himself is a widower, though if he had a wife they might offer her a poor refuge. Surely nobody could allow her to come to him, without a lady of the house to attend her, and his house is small and cramped and he himself is a poor man. But still – but still – this is his third letter and no-one has told him what is to be done! While Katherine's next destination is being decided by the great men of the queen's court, while Katherine has literally nowhere to go – shall he invite her to his own house? This is not to suggest any sympathy, any prejudice for or against her cause or her claim. But she is young and frail, beautiful and terribly thin, starving herself and in despair of ever seeing her husband and child again. She hardly gets out of her bed, she rarely stops crying. May Mr Roke Green put a roof over her head while the queen, in her wisdom, decides what shall be done with this poor weak lady? Because she cannot stay where she is, and she will die if they continue to neglect her.

I hold the letter out to my lady step-grandmother. 'She has nowhere to go,' I say flatly.

Her face is alight. 'So he says.'

'Yet you look pleased?'

'Yes, because this is our chance to free her, I think.'

I can feel my heart suddenly race. 'You think they might allow it? Will you invite her here?'

She smiles at me. 'Why not? As we have been warned, she has nowhere else to go.'

My lady grandmother writes to the queen, writes to William Cecil, writes to Robert Dudley. The court is at Windsor Castle. They are delaying their return to London, the weather is so fine, everyone is unwilling to come back to face the demanding question of how to support the Scots queen – a cousin! a monarch! – without opposing the Scots lords, our co-religionists. Elizabeth does not know what to do and would rather avoid the problem by staying at Windsor and flirting with Robert Dudley. My lady step-grandmother has to write to a court that has no appetite for thorny difficulties. So she offers them a solution, a simple solution: that Katherine shall come to live with her grandmother and bring her little boy with her. Ned shall be released to his mother's care at Hanworth. Thomas Keyes will be sent to his family in Kent. We should all be bound over to make no trouble, to send no letters, to correspond with no powers or factions; but that we should live as private citizens, and – since we have committed no crime – we should be free.

She sends the letters: to William Cecil at his beloved new home, Burghley House, to Robert Dudley, dancing attendance on Elizabeth at Windsor, and to the holidaying queen herself, and we wait, with hope, for a reply.

It comes promptly from William Cecil. The two secret lovers Dudley and Elizabeth must have decided that they will leave it to him to write to us. Their happiness, their freedom in the harvested dusty gold fields of England, shall not be troubled. The weather is fine, the hunting good, they neither of them want to deal with affairs of state. Elizabeth is celebrating that she has another year of keeping Dudley in thrall. I know Robert Dudley will speak in favour of Katherine's release, but only when he feels that he can do it without causing trouble. He will not allow anything to disturb the queen's happiness when she is happy with him.

William Cecil writes in his own hand that Katherine may not come to us yet. He writes 'yet' and he underlines. For this season she is to be housed with a good loyal man, Sir Owen Hopton at Cockfield Hall, Suffolk.

'Good God, who is he?' my step-grandmother demands irritably. 'Where do they keep finding these hopeless nonentities?'

'At Cockfield Hall, Suffolk,' I say, reading the letter over her shoulder. 'Look at this . . .'

I point to a brief sentence. *Her Majesty insists that Lady Katherine and her son are kept totally isolated. Neither receiving letters, gifts, guests, visitors or emissaries from foreign powers.*

My step-grandmother looks at me. 'What do they imagine she would do?' she demands of me. 'Don't they know that she is so sad as to barely speak? That she is eating so little that she is exhausted? That she rarely gets up from her bed, that she weeps all the time?'

I gulp down my grief at the thought of my sister, alone again, and moved even further away from me. 'Did you tell them?'

'Of course I told them. And anyway, Cecil knows everything.'

'What does the queen want of us?' I demand. 'Does she just want us to die in confinement and silence, in some little out-of-the-way place where no-one will complain if we just die of sorrow?'

My step-grandmother does not answer me. She looks blankly at me as if she has nothing to say. I realise that I have spoken the truth in passion and she has no will to deny it.

The court returns to Hampton Court, but my step-grandmother is not ordered to attend.

'I don't want to be the cause of your disgrace with the queen,' I say to her. 'I know you have to think of your own children, Peregrine and Susan; I know that you have to keep them safe. You can't have your household being tainted with the disfavour that follows Elizabeth's cousins.'

She tilts her head on one side and gives me her wry smile. 'I have faced worse, you know,' she says. 'I served the queen who taught Elizabeth all the scholarship that she now demonstrates with such pride. I served the queen who showed Elizabeth how to rule. I served the queen who wrote the prayer book and taught Elizabeth – and your sister Jane – their theology. I served her when she faced a charge of heresy and treason. I never forget Kateryn Parr, and I am not going to be afraid of Elizabeth now.'

'I'm afraid of her,' I confess, and I feel a sudden strange release from the defiance that has been a thread through the weave of my life since I was first deployed as a pawn in my family alliances, a little girl too young to give consent, given away in an alliance with Arthur Grey. 'I won't pretend to be brave. I am afraid of her. I think that she will be my undoing. I think that she already has been. I think that she wishes my death and that of Katherine, and that she always has done.'

My redoubtable step-grandmother gives me her brightest smile. 'Survive,' she reminds me. 'Survive and hope for better times.'

These are not better times for those of our religion in France. The king, dominated by his family – the Guise family – persecutes those of our faith until they rise up in a holy religious uprising. Of course, England, the primary Protestant power, should send the Huguenots arms and money, should send them an army to overthrow their papist rulers. But Elizabeth, as always, can only go halfway in any duty. She knows that she should prevent the papist rulers of France from murdering and destroying her co-religionists. But the Protestants of Scotland have overthrown her cousin the Guise French queen and she cannot tolerate that threat to royal power. She knows she should be the enemy of the Pope who – it is said – will declare her anathema: a figure to be despised, who can be legally killed. But it is a Protestant leader in Scotland, John Knox, who calls her and Mary Queen of Scots a 'monstrous regimen of women' unfit to rule, and urges all right-thinking men to rise up against them. Elizabeth is so piqued by this disrespect, so muddled in her thinking, that she hates John Knox worse than the Pope, and thinks that she should stand in sisterhood with Mary Queen of Scots as a fellow queen against him.

I send a note to my sister, carried by Richard Bertie's most faithful man, hidden in the foot of his hose. I don't doubt by the time it gets to Katherine it is smelling ripely of his sweat. I don't know if she will be able to reply. I don't even know if she will live to see it. I don't know how she is.

> *Dear Sister,*
> *I pray for you, my dear Katherine, in this time of our trouble. I am living well and kindly treated by our step-grandmother the Duchess of Suffolk at Greenwich. I live in her rooms and I am allowed to walk in the gardens and beside the river. I cannot see visitors, but I enjoy the company of Peregrine and Susan.*
> *I write constantly both to Queen Elizabeth and to the lords of the court for our release, and for the freedom of Ned Seymour and my poor husband Thomas Keyes. Please don't reproach me, even in your thoughts, for marrying him. He is such a good man, Katherine, and he loves me so much. Our marriage has been a disaster for him. I would have it annulled if it would rescue him from prison. But for no other reason.*

I hear that you are frail and weak. Please, please, fight
for life. Eat, walk, play with your son. We have to live,
Katherine. It was Jane who said 'learn you to die' and
that was only when she was under an inescapable sentence
of death. She was wrong. We don't have to learn to die. I
want to live. I want you to live. I am going to live. I pray to
God who hears all our prayers, and for whom we are more
important than the little sparrows that fall, that you and I will
live and be together one day. When I see the sparrows in the
hedges around the water meadows below Greenwich Palace,
I think of Janey's linnets and your love of wild things and I
pray that we will all be as free as the little birds one day.

I will not write – Farewell Good Sister – for I pray to see
you soon and that we will both be well and happy –
M

Bertie's man tells me he gets the letter into her bedroom in a
stack of wood for the fire, but there is no way of knowing if she
has read it, and there is no reply.

GREENWICH PALACE,
WINTER 1567

There is no summons to court at Westminster, not for my lady
grandmother, nor for her children, nor for me, but the gossip
seeps downriver from servant to servant, carried by pedlars,
brought by candle-sellers, and volunteered by milkmaids.
Everyone in London, including us, knows that Elizabeth is preparing to marry at last, and her choice has fallen on Charles II
the Archduke of Austria, son of the late Holy Roman Emperor,
Ferdinand.

It will be a mighty alliance, joining England to the great power of Europe, the Habsburgs. It will make us safe from invasion from any of the continental powers, inured to the enmity of the Pope. It will mean that we are restored to our place in Christendom, no longer a heretical outsider to the faith of Europe. We can aid Mary Queen of Scots or not, as we like. Her fall or her rise will not threaten us when we have the Habsburgs as our allies.

We will achieve this at almost no price. Elizabeth would not have to change her religion, the country would not change its religion. She would not have to put him, as a husband, above her. This is not to be a king consort. He is a younger son: he knows all about coming second. Best of all, perhaps, the archduke would not change his religion, he would practise his faith in private, there would be a chapel in every royal palace and a priest would travel with him. He would hold a Mass but not force it on any other. We would show, as we should, in this country, which has been papist and Protestant and papist and Protestant, turn and turn about with one ruler after another, that we can live in harmony. That there is one God; but different ways of approaching Him. That God's will is that we should love one another. Nowhere does Jesus say that we should persecute one another to death. No passage in the Bible required Jane's death, no law of man nor God requires our imprisonment.

But I am not tempted by this glittering prospect for my cousin Elizabeth. If I were free I would not waste a moment of my time on it. Elizabeth persuades her council that she intends to marry the archduke. She would never persuade me that she will ever put a man in Robert Dudley's place; but the Privy Council are hugely relieved at this solution to the inheritance question – and then – to further divert them, she asks them for their opinion and advice.

This is mostly to satisfy those lords and commoners who demanded last year that she name a successor and insisted that it be a legitimate Protestant – my sister Katherine. Now

Elizabeth, like a marketplace mountebank who charms coppers out of the pockets of the credulous, says that she has taken their advice that she must marry, that she is minded to marry a papist Habsburg, that the happy couple will (no doubt) conceive an autumn child, so she need name neither Mary Queen of Scots, trapped on her island, nor Katherine, locked up with Sir Owen. But Elizabeth can promise that she will have a baby, a beautiful son, who will be the nephew of the Holy Roman Emperor and the grandson of Henry VIII and all the world can rejoice that love has found a way, where hatred could not, to bring papistry and Protestantism into harmony once more and everyone can be happy – except, of course, Katherine and I, and Mary Queen of Scots. We will all three be left in imprisonment forever, and (hopefully) forgotten.

In scraps and words, the gossip comes from London and goes on beyond us – all over the kingdom. Though Elizabeth the queen is apparently willing and prepared to marry for the sake of the country, though she has convinced the Holy Roman Emperor that she will take his brother, the council is divided and, using their uncertainty as her shield, Elizabeth hides her determination to live and die a single woman. Her cousin Thomas Howard Duke of Norfolk says that there can be no danger to the kingdom but much benefit in marrying such a great prince, and his faith is no obstacle. The archduke has made such offers, and given such promises, that we can live with the queen's husband as a papist who receives Mass in private. Not so, says the rest of the council: Francis Knollys, that staunch Protestant; Robert Dudley, that staunch Dudleyist. The Protestant lords Sir William Herbert the Earl of Pembroke and Sir William Parr the Marquess of Northampton join together to warn the queen that the country cannot tolerate a papist husband, will not drink the health of a half-papist baby in the cradle. Robert Dudley suggests that a foreign suitor is unattractive, too. Someone tells the queen that he is ugly, that all Habsburgs have terribly weak chins, does she want to marry a man who looks like a squirrel?

Just before Christmas, Elizabeth sends to the Holy Roman Emperor and finally says that she cannot marry his brother the archduke Charles. Of course, the entire Habsburg family is hugely offended, and all of papist Christendom sees England as stubbornly and persistently heretical. It would have been better for us all if she had never gone through the charade of pretending that she was willing. Now they see us as perfidious. The French, who are persecuting every Protestant in their realm, are particularly bitter, and Elizabeth is without an heir once more, except for the deposed Queen Mary in her prison and my poor sister, in hers. We are back where we always seem to be – playing with the inheritance of the kingdom so that Elizabeth can remain free to love Robert Dudley.

GREENWICH PALACE, SPRING 1568

Sir Owen Hopton, Katherine's new gaoler, writes to William Cecil begging him to send a London physician into Suffolk. My sister, weaker every day from starving herself, is now desperately ill.

Dr Symondes has been sent to see the Lady, Cecil writes diplomatically, leaving it unclear who has taken the expensive decision to send the best doctor in London to my sister. *But this is not his first visit and he is not optimistic. We should pray for her soul.*

'I have to go to her,' I say to my step-grandmother. 'You must write to Cecil and ask for permission for me to be at her side. He will not refuse. He will know she cannot die alone. I have to go.'

She is pale with anxiety. 'I know. I know. I will write to him, you can write yourself, too, and we will send it at once.'

'Can I start without permission? Can I go now?'

She clasps her hands together. 'We dare not,' she says. 'If the queen should hear that I let you leave my house without permission, you would be taken from me, and who knows where they would put you then?'

'She's dying!' I say flatly. 'Am I not allowed to say goodbye to my dying sister? The last of my family?'

She thrusts a sheet of paper at me. 'Write,' she says tersely. 'And we will leave as soon as we are allowed.'

We don't get permission. We get a bundle of papers forwarded to us by William Cecil's office. On the top he has written a note in a steady hand. *I am afraid that even if you had set out at once, you would have been too late. Lady Katherine is dead.*

I look at my step-grandmother as if I cannot believe that such news should be told me in such brevity. Not one word of sympathy, not one word to recognise the tragedy of the loss of a young woman, aged only twenty-seven. My sister. My beautiful, funny, loving, royal sister.

My lady grandmother unties the ribbon around the papers and says: 'It is an account of her last hours. God bless her, the pretty child. Shall I read it to you?'

I climb on to the window seat of her privy chamber. 'Please do,' I say dully. I wonder that I don't cry, and then I realise that I have spent my life in the shadow of the scaffold. I never expected any of us to survive Tudor rule. My lady grandmother smooths the paper on her knee and clears her throat. 'It says that she prepared to die as the household begged her to fight for her life. She wasn't alone, Mary – Lady Hopton was with her and told her that with God's favour she would live. But she said it was not God's will that she should live any longer, and that His will should be done and not hers.'

She glances at me, to see if I am finding this unbearable. I know that I look calm; I feel nothing but an icy despair.

'Early in the morning, just as it was getting light, she sent for Sir Owen Hopton and asked him to take some messages for her. She begged the queen to forgive her for marrying without permission, she said, *Be good unto my children and not impute my fault to them.*' My step-grandmother glances up at me again. I nod for her to go on.

'She asked for the queen to be good to Lord Hertford, her husband, and said: *I know this my death will be heavy news for him.* She asked for him to be freed, and sent him her betrothal ring, a pointed diamond, and a wedding ring with five links.'

'I remember it,' I interrupt. 'She showed it to me. She always kept it with her.'

'She has given it back to him and a mourning ring as well.' My lady step-grandmother's voice is choked. 'Poor girl. Poor sweet lovely girl. What a tragedy! It says here that she prayed him to be – *even as I have been unto him a true and faithful wife, that he will be a loving and natural father to my children.* It says here that she commissioned the mourning ring with her portrait months ago – she must have known she was dying. She had it engraved for him.'

I am hunched up now, on the seat, my face to my knees, crouched like a hurt child, my hands over my eyes. I would almost put them over my ears so I cannot hear my sister's last loving words. I feel as if I am sinking down into the deeps of loss. 'What does it say?' I ask. 'What does the ring say?'

'*While I lived – yours.*'

'Is that all?' I ask. I think I must have arrived at the very ocean bed of sorrow. It is as if the deeps have closed over my own head.

'It says that they rang the bells for her and the villagers prayed for her recovery.'

'Did she say anything for me?'

'She said: Farewell, Good Sister.'

I hear the words that Jane said to Katherine, that Katherine now says to me. But I have no-one to bless. Now that Katherine has gone there is no sister for me. I am an orphan alone.

'Then she said, *Lord Jesus receive my spirit*, and she closed her eyes with her own hands and she left us.'

'I don't know how to bear this,' I say quietly. I push myself to the edge of the seat and I drop down to the floor. 'I really don't know how to bear it.'

My lady grandmother takes my hands but does not crush me in her arms. She knows that the grief I feel is far, far beyond the reach of any easy comfort. 'The Lord gave, and the Lord hath taken away; the Lord hath done his pleasure, now blessed be the name of the Lord,' she tells me.

Of course, our cousin the queen gives Katherine a magnificent funeral. How she does love a funeral, especially family! Katherine is buried in the village church at Yoxford, far from her home, far from the resting place of her mother, far from her husband's family chapel; but Elizabeth orders the court into mourning and manages to paint an expression of grief on her false face. Seventy-seven official mourners attend from court, along with a herald and court servants, Katherine's arms are displayed in the chapel on banners, pencils and banner-rolls. Everything that can exalt a Tudor princess is done for her. Katherine in death is recognised and honoured, as in life she was persecuted and ignored.

Elizabeth does not allow me to attend. Of course not. She only loves her heirs when they predecease her. The last thing she wants is someone pointing out that if Katherine was a Tudor princess then her little sister is one too – and the last of the line. The last thing she wants is a live cousin, especially when she is ostentatiously mourning a conveniently dead one. My step-grandmother is allowed to say the farewell to Katherine in death that she was forbidden in life, and she goes and comes back very sombre and says that it is a tragedy of her life that she has to bury children.

I stay in my room in a fury of grief. I can hardly breathe from grief at the loss of my sister and my hatred for the queen. I hardly eat: the household has to persuade me to take something once a day at least. I think it would matter not at all if I were to die for I could not say goodbye to my sister nor can I care for her children. I cannot be with my husband nor care for his children. Elizabeth has made me as lonely as she is, an only child as she is, an orphan as she is. I think her heart must be as small as mine, her imagination stunted to the age when her mother died and nobody knew who she was. I may be small but I am not – as she is – deathly petty.

I think I will not even get out of bed until my lady step-grandmother taps on my door and says: 'We have a visitor. Will you not come out to my presence chamber, and see who has come to see you?'

'Who?' I ask sulkily, not stirring from the pillow.

She puts her head around the door with a little smile, the first I have seen for a month. 'Sir Owen Hopton, Katherine's keeper, has come to see you. He took Katherine's boy Thomas Seymour to join his brother and grandmother at Hanworth. He took her wedding rings and messages to Ned Seymour. And now he has come to see you.'

I throw back the covers and jump down from the bed. My maid comes in behind my grandmother with my little gown and sleeves and hood. 'Ask him to wait, I am coming,' I say.

My lady grandmother leaves me to hurry into my clothes and follow her into her presence chamber. A tall weary man is standing before her, his cap in one hand, and a wine glass in another. On the floor near the door is a box and a tall muffled cage. He puts down the wine and the cap and bows as I come in, his hand on his heart.

'Lady Mary,' he says. 'It is an honour.'

I recoil as he kneels to me as if I were a queen. 'Please get up,' I say.

'I am so sorry for the news I bring,' he says, getting to his feet but stooping so that he can see my face. 'I learned to love and revere your sister in the short time that my house was blessed with her presence. Both my wife and I were very grieved at her death. We would have done anything for her. Anything.'

I see that I have to put my own grief aside to answer him. The death of a princess is not the same as a private loss. 'I understand,' I say. 'I know you could have done nothing to save her.'

'We did everything we could,' he says. 'We made sure that she could eat. She had no appetite but we served her from our own kitchens, though there was no money provided for her delicacies.'

The thought of Elizabeth's vindictive penny-pinching sets my teeth on edge but I smile up at him. 'I am very sure that she found a kind final home with you,' I say. 'And if I should ever come to happier times myself, I will not forget that you were kind to my sister.'

He shakes his head. 'No, I seek no reward,' he says. 'I didn't come for thanks. To know her was to know a great lady. It was a privilege.'

It is a bitter joke to think what Katherine would make of her ascent to greatness. There is no-one but her who would share the sour wit with me. I can only nod.

'I have brought you some of her things,' he says. 'Her husband, the Earl of Hertford, said that I should bring you some of her books, a Bible and some grammars. The earl said you should have the Italian grammar that was dedicated by the author himself to your oldest sister, Lady Jane Grey.'

'Thank you,' I say.

'And I brought you this,' he says a little more shyly. I see my lady step-grandmother's gaze go to the cage at the back of the room.

'Not the monkey!' she says.

For the first time in weeks I feel that I could laugh, however inappropriate the occasion. While everyone will remember the tragedy of my sister I will also remember her silliness and her charm. That her executor should make his sorrowful way around England with a box of books and a caged pet is so typical of the young woman, who was such a mixture of grand passion and funny whims.

'What do you have for me?'

'It *is* the monkey,' he says, with one eye on my lady step-grandmother, who audibly says: 'Absolutely not!'

'We really can't keep it ourselves, and the Duchess of Somerset said that she would not have it at Hanworth.'

'And I won't have it here!' my grandmother insists.

He pulls the cover off the cage and there is Mr Nozzle, sad-faced as always, seated in a corner, like a little pagan god, shivering at the cold welcome. I swear that when he sees me he recognises me and comes hopefully to the door, making a little gesture with his black-tipped fingers as if to turn a key.

'There now, he knows you. He hasn't wanted to come out since his mistress died,' Sir Owen says encouragingly. 'He's been pining for her like a Christian.'

'Nonsense,' comes from my step-grandmother's great chair, but she does not forbid me opening the cage and Mr Nozzle – an older and I think sadder Mr Nozzle – comes out with a bound and jumps into my arms.

'I will keep him if I may?' I turn to her.

'You girls!' she says, as if Jane and Katherine and I are still children together, begging for unsuitable pets.

'Please!' I say, and I hear Katherine's voice in mine. 'Please, he will be no trouble, I promise.' I remember a sunny day in Jane's bedroom and Katherine refusing to put him out of the door, and lying about his lice.

'Well, keep him,' she says indulgently. 'But he is not to tear things, or make a mess in my rooms.'

'I will keep him clean and tidy,' I promise her. I can feel him take tight hold of my thumb in his little hand as if we are shaking on an agreement. 'She did love him so very much.'

'She had a loving heart,' Sir Owen remarks. 'She had a very loving heart.'

Someone has trimmed his little jacket with black ribbon so he is in mourning for the young woman who loved him. His sorrowful eyes look at me, and I tuck him into the crook of my arm.

'What of her cat and dog?'

His downcast face droops further. 'The cat is old now, and lives in our stable yard. They're not loyal, you know. I didn't think to catch him and bring him.'

'No,' my step-grandmother says hastily. 'Indeed no. We don't need another cat.'

'And the little pug, Jo . . .' he hesitates.

'You've never brought her, too?'

'Alas, I couldn't,' he says.

'Why?' I ask, but I think I know.

'She was at the bed all through Lady Katherine's last days. She never left her side, she never ate. It was a little miracle. Her ladyship said that she should have her meat put down on the floor of her bedchamber. She noticed her little dog, she did not forget her, even while she was preparing herself for God.'

'Go on,' I say.

'She slept on the foot of her bed, and when her ladyship closed her eyes with her own hand, she made a little noise, like a whimper, and laid her head down on her ladyship's feet.'

My step-grandmother clears her throat, as if she cannot bear this mawkish scene.

'Truly?' I ask.

'Truly,' Sir Owen says. 'We had to take the body, you understand, and embalm it and seal it in lead. It was all done as a princess should be buried, you know.'

I know. Who should know better than me?

'The little dog followed the body like the first of mourners, and we were all too tender to push her away, to be honest with you. We didn't mean any disrespect, not to the Lady Katherine, God knows. But she always let her little dog run after her everywhere, and so we let her follow, even though her mistress was gone.

'On the day of the funeral, there was a beautiful hearse, very dignified, covered with black and cloth of gold, as is fitting, and the herald went before and seventy-seven mourners from the court came behind, and my household and many many local people, and gentry from far afield. Her ladyship was there, too; everything was done beautifully.' He bows to my step-grandmother. 'Everyone followed the hearse to the chapel, and the little dog followed, too, though nobody noticed her at the time, what with the banners and the herald and the honour from the court and everything. I wouldn't have allowed it, if I had noticed, but, to tell you the truth, I was as grieved as if she had been my own daughter – not to be disrespectful – I never forgot her estate. But she was the most beautiful lady I have ever served. I don't expect to see her like again.'

'Yes, yes,' my step-grandmother says.

'She was laid to rest in the chapel and a handsome stone put on her grave, and the banners and the pennants all displayed around, and then everyone went home after they had said their prayers and blessed her. Nobody prayed for her soul,' he specifies, one eye on my staunchly Protestant kinswoman. 'We all know there's no purgatory now. But we all prayed that she should be in heaven and free from pain, and then we all went home.

'But the little dog didn't come home with us. She stayed in the chapel on her own, funny little thing. And nobody, not even the stable lad who took such a fancy to her, could get her away. We offered her a bit of bread to come, and even meat. She wouldn't eat anything. We tied a bit of string round her neck and pulled her away but she slipped her collar and went back to the chapel to sleep on the tombstone, so we let her. She closed her eyes and she put her nose under her paw as if she was grieving. And in the morning, poor little thing, she was still and cold, as if she chose not to live without her mistress.'

I look at my step-grandmother and I see the same twist in her mouth that I know I am showing. I am biting the inside of my lips so that I don't cry over the death of the little pug, so that I don't cry for the death of my sister, so that I don't cry for the ruin of my house, and all for no reason, for no reason at all.

We are all silent for a moment and then Sir Owen speaks. 'But I have the linnets coming behind in the wagon,' he says, suddenly cheerful.

'Not Janey Seymour's linnets!'

'Their babies, or perhaps their babies' babies,' he says. 'She had them nesting and breeding and we had to give some away and keep some as she ordered. But I have a bonny cage of singing linnets for you, coming after me in the wagon.'

THE MINORIES, LONDON, SPRING 1568

Bess St Loe, our family friend and sometime ally, pulled off a triumph last year that makes me smile whenever I think of her. Aunt Bess buried her third husband and walked as a great heiress to the altar for the fourth time – but this time she surpassed herself – she netted George Talbot Earl of Shrewsbury and is now the richest woman in England second only to the queen, owning almost all of the Midlands of England.

It would take a sadder little woman than I not to laugh aloud at the tremendous progress that Aunt Bess has made. Once she was a friend and a hanger-on at Bradgate, now she is a countess. Aunt Bess, born a poor girl and widowed young, glad of my mother's favour, is now a great woman by her extraordinary business sense, and by marriage. Of course, I think that her good luck might serve me. A landowner such as Aunt Bess with thousands of houses at her command and acres of farms and villages could very easily house me in one of them. She is trusted by the queen, she could guarantee that I would not run away or plot with the Spanish, nor anything else that the queen pretends to fear, in order to keep me in captivity. If Aunt Bess will say one word for me (though I don't forget that she never said anything for my sister Katherine) then I might yet be a free tenant near Wingfield Manor, Tutbury Castle, Chatsworth House, or any of the other half-dozen houses that she owns. If she were to be my landlord I would need no guardian, I would liberate my step-grandmother from her duties and Elizabeth's irritable disfavour, I would be far from London and quite forgotten, and I could be free.

I tell my step-grandmother that I am thinking that Bess might speak for me to the queen and might offer to house me, and she encourages me to write to the new countess and ask her to use her influence with the queen – for she is still a lady-in-waiting, though now considerably higher up the ranks. I think that a little house, a very small house in a mean village, might be a source of great happiness to me. I might have Thomas Keyes' children to live with me, even if I could never see him. And Mr Nozzle would like a little orchard, I am sure.

GRIMSTHORPE CASTLE, LINCOLNSHIRE, SUMMER 1568

Elizabeth our cousin bears her grief for the loss of my sister Katherine so well that the court comes out of mourning in a month, and the May Day revels are among the merriest that have ever been. She recovers so well from her anxiety for her cousin Mary Queen of Scots, still held in prison, that she exchanges letters with Mary's captor and the guardian of her little boy, Lord Moray – the Queen of Scots' treacherous half-brother. When Elizabeth hears that he has opened the royal treasury and is selling off Mary's famous jewels to the highest bidder, she overcomes her much-praised anxiety for her cousin and makes an offer. His shocking betrayal and theft from his own half-sister and ordained queen ceases to trouble Elizabeth, who outbids everyone to win the auction for a six-string necklace of pearls beyond price. I think of Mary held in Lochleven Castle as I am held at my step-grandmother's house at Grimsthorpe, and think how bitter it must be to her to learn that the cousin that she thought would rescue her has struck a deal with her captor and is wearing her pearls.

But my cousin Mary wastes no time counting her losses and mourning for her miscarried babies. Later in the month of May we learn that she has broken out from captivity, broken out like a woman of desperate courage, and I think – I wish I had the bravery and the money and the friends to do the same. Mary rows herself over the lake, disguised as a page, raises an army, and challenges her false half-brother to meet her on the field of battle. Elizabeth should send an army in support – she has loudly promised one – but instead she sends her best wishes, and they are of little effect. The Queen of Scots is defeated. This was her last throw, and now she is on the run and nobody knows where she is.

She must be somewhere in the wild country of Scotland. The battle was outside Glasgow, in the west, not a country that she knows, nor one where she is likely to have friends. Her husband and greatest ally, Bothwell, is missing. Her cousin Elizabeth does nothing to help her. Mary is quite alone. We hear nothing for days, and then we hear that she rode thirty miles after defeat in battle, thirty miles by night over rough ground in darkness. She has found a safe hiding place, an abbey where they love their queen and her faith. If the English were to come to her aid now, it could still be all changed about in a moment. Mary could regain her throne; Elizabeth could have a beautiful cousin as a neighbouring queen once again.

We know this, even my step-grandmother and her family and I, exiles from the court, at my lady grandmother's house at Grimsthorpe, in Lincolnshire, know this, because the whole country knows that Mary has called on Elizabeth and sent her a token. It is an object of such power that Elizabeth cannot refuse. It is the ring, the diamond ring that Elizabeth gave her five years ago when she swore eternal love and friendship and said that Mary should send to her in case of need, and that she would not fail her.

I follow this story – all the world follows this story – as if it were a breathless tale published in printed sheets and sold by balladeers. It is an irresistible story of one great queen swearing infallible aid to another, and now the promise is called in. I cannot wait to hear where Mary is. I cannot wait to know what she will do next.

I think Elizabeth must send her help. She should have sent an army to support Mary when she first broke from her prison. But now – our cousin is free and defenceless, now she sends the ring that will summon Elizabeth's support without fail. Elizabeth has to be true to her public oath, has to rescue our cousin the queen.

There is no news of any special grant going to Scotland. But of course, Elizabeth could send secret funds and tell no-one. There is certainly no army mustering, for we would know of that, even tucked away here in the country. I think that perhaps Elizabeth will meet with the Privy Council and persuade them that they must support the Queen of Scots, so that majesty itself is not threatened. I think that perhaps she will call parliament and name Mary as her heir – finally take herself to that sticking point of naming her – so that the Scots can see that they may not attack Elizabeth's kinswoman and heiress, that it is in their interest to return her to her throne so that Mary can pass on her title to her son and finally the thrones of Scotland and England will be united.

There are rumours that the French will snatch her from the coast of Scotland. She is their kinswoman and she is desperate. And if they rescue her before we do, and the Queen of Scots is in French hands, how shall England be safe from attack? Will she not make another marriage to a great prince and win back her kingdom and remember her cousin Elizabeth as a disloyal breaker of a sacred oath, an unreliable ally, a false kinswoman? Will she not think of the English as false-faith enemies? Will she not take the throne by force that should have been offered her by right?

Everything points to Elizabeth saving our cousin and restoring her to her throne. There are compelling reasons that she must do so. There is no good argument for any other course of action. As a kinswoman, as a fellow queen, as one who has given her sacred word, Elizabeth must help Mary. She cannot refuse.

But still we hear nothing. I write to my aunt Bess on my own account, asking if, at a convenient moment, she will ask the queen if I might be set free to live in one of her houses. I ask it for the love I know that she bore my mother and that she promised to my sister. And I ask her also for news. Does she know what is happening about my cousin Mary Queen of Scots, and is she to be rescued? Does she know any news at all?

Before I have any reply to my letter my step-grandmother comes into my private room where I am reading Latin with a lady-in-waiting and says: 'You'll never ever guess what has happened now.'

I jump down from my chair, frightened at once. I have not lived a life where good news is expected. 'What is it?'

'Mary Queen of Scots has crossed the Solway Firth, left Scotland and landed in England and written a public letter to Elizabeth saying that she expects to be returned to Scotland at once, with an English army in her support.'

I think that I should be excited. It is another bold brilliant move. Mary is forcing Elizabeth's hand. Elizabeth cannot prevaricate, as she always does, when our cousin is so bravely decisive. But I don't feel excitement; I feel dread. 'Has the queen replied?'

My lady grandmother is bright. 'My husband, Richard, is with the court at Greenwich and he says that Elizabeth and Cecil are hammering out the terms. Elizabeth says that Mary must be restored to Scotland with a strong army. The Scots must know (everyone must know) that they cannot throw down a queen. William Cecil agrees, so the Privy Council will agree. Nobody will argue that a queen can be destroyed by such as John Knox, on our very doorstep. Parliament will have to vote funds, an army will have to be raised. Queen Mary will be sent home to Edinburgh and Elizabeth will have to send an army to fight for her.'

'She will do that?'

'She's done it before. She sent an army to Scotland against the Catholic regent. She won that battle. She knows it can be done.' My lady step-grandmother reflects. 'And besides, it won't come to that. The Scots lords don't want a battle with England. Half of them are in our pay already. If Elizabeth and Cecil muster an army the Scots will know that they have to take their queen back and make peace with her. It was Bothwell they couldn't stomach; many of them truly love Queen Mary.'

'I like to think of her as free,' I say. 'I know that she is a papist and perhaps a sinner, but I am glad she is out of Lochleven Castle and free, whatever happens next. I think of her often: as beautiful as Katherine, near to her in age, and I like to think that she, of all of us cousins, is free.'

There is one Tudor cousin who does not celebrate the freedom of Queen Mary. Our cousin Margaret Douglas, vengeful as a harpy, dashes with her husband, the Earl of Lennox, to court, both of them draped in deep perpetual mourning for their son the wastrel Henry Stuart Lord Darnley, to fling themselves at Elizabeth's feet in tears: they must have justice for their son. Queen Mary is his killer, she must be sent back to Scotland in irons, she must be tried for murder. Elizabeth must arrest her, she must be burned as a husband-killer.

The queen is impatient with her cousin. Darnley went to Scotland at his mother's bidding, and refused to come home to England when he was commanded by Elizabeth; she will never forget that. He took up arms against his wife; we have all heard that he held a primed pistol to her pregnant belly. He was certainly a victim of the Scots lords, who hated him; but there is no certain evidence that Queen Mary was involved in the plot. And anyway, Margaret my cousin should know by now that Elizabeth has a resilient conscience. How does she think Amy Dudley died?

Elizabeth explains, gently enough, that the Scots cannot try their queen, no people can put their ordained monarch on trial. Equally, Elizabeth has no authority over Mary. They are both queens and Elizabeth cannot arrest Mary or imprison her. Queens make the law, so they are above the law. She is certain that Mary will have a full explanation when she meets her mother-in-law. It is a private matter between them. In short, nobody cares very much what Margaret Douglas thinks. To be honest, nobody ever has.

But it makes me uneasy, as the days get warmer and I have no reply from Aunt Bess, Countess of Shrewsbury as she is now, and no news from court that I am to be moved anywhere else. It makes me uneasy that I am still a prisoner, held by my step-grandmother, and at the same time, my cousin Mary Queen of Scots is in the safekeeping of Sir Francis Knollys at Carlisle Castle. It seems that Elizabeth has no accusation to bring against either of us, her cousins; but both of us are still imprisoned. Does she think she can hold us both till we die of despair like Katherine?

Elizabeth sends Mary some clothes; she has nothing but the riding dress she escaped in. But when they come to unpack the parcel it is little more than rags: two torn shifts, two pieces of black velvet, two pairs of shoes, nothing else.

'Why would she insult her cousin the Queen of Scots?' my step-grandmother asks me. 'Why would she treat her with such contempt?'

Both of us look at the tattered footstool and the two ragged tapestries that have been my household goods for so long, at the battered cup that Elizabeth sent from the servery for my use.

'To warn her,' I say slowly. 'Like she warned Katherine, like she warns me. That we are poor without her favour, that we are prisoners without her favour. She may say that she cannot arrest another queen, but if Queen Mary is the guest of Francis Knollys and cannot leave, then what is she if not Elizabeth's prisoner? Do you think Cousin Mary understands the message? That she is a prisoner like me?'

GRIMSTHORPE CASTLE, LINCOLNSHIRE, SUMMER 1568

The Privy Council meets at Greenwich Palace and announces that Mary Queen of Scots will have to face a trial. She cannot be returned to Scotland by an English army without her innocence proved. She must be accused of killing her husband and the penalty for killing a husband – a crime of petty treason since it is a rebellion against the natural order as well as a murder – is death by burning. Amazingly, Elizabeth does not reprimand the council for disagreeing with her – which tells us all that they are her mouthpiece – saying what she does not dare. But Elizabeth does rule that Mary may not come to court to explain her actions, as one queen to another. She says that she and Mary cannot meet, that the Scots queen's reputation is sullied by the rumours. The idea that a woman guilty of adultery cannot attend Elizabeth's court would be funny if it were not so terrible when applied to our kinswoman Mary. How will she ever get a fair hearing if she is not allowed to speak? And if the Privy Council, that chorus inspired by Elizabeth and Cecil, are saying that she must be tried for murder without being able to speak in her own defence, then those two have surely decided that she is guilty and must die.

But Mary is too clever for them. She rejects the scraps of

velvets and the old shoes, she calls it 'a cold calling', and Sir
Francis, embarrassed with rags in his hands, says there has been
some stupid mistake from the groom of the wardrobe. Mary
says that she is a queen: she wears ermine, she is royal. Nobody
should send her clothes for any rank less than royalty. And –
equally – no-one can try her, she is an ordained monarch: only
God can judge her.

Elizabeth backs down, swiftly and speedily, as only Elizabeth
can. She writes to her cousin that it is not to be a trial, for – of
course! – a queen cannot be put on trial. It is an inquiry into the
behaviour of the Scots queen's half-brother Lord Moray. She is
not accused: he is. They will inquire if he has been treasonous,
and then restore her. They will clear her name and return her to
her throne. She will be freed of scandal and able to take her son
into her keeping again.

'She will be free,' I say. 'Thank God that at least she will be
free.'

In July I finally receive a reply from my aunt Bess. She writes
to me under her new seal, a lion rampant. I smile as I look at it
and break the seal. I like to think of my aunt Bess with a rampant
lion as her crest, it's very apt.

*Dearest Mary, I am sorry that I cannot give you a better
answer for I should be glad to have you at my home (at any
one of my many homes!) for the love that I bear your mother
and yourself, dear Mary. But before I could ask the queen if I
might house you, she has asked me to undertake a greater task
than keeping you. My husband the earl and I are to take a
house guest – perhaps you can guess who? And we are to keep
her safe, and keep her from our enemies, and watch over her
letters, and report on all that she does. She is to be a guest but
she is not to leave until we return her to Scotland. She is to
be a guest but we are to inquire into every letter that she has
in her casket, and discover everything that we can, and then
judge as we see fit.*

You will guess by now who is coming into my keeping, and

why I cannot invite you! The queen is trusting my husband the earl and me to keep Mary Queen of Scots safe in our keeping until such time as the queen is ready to return her to Scotland. We will do this without error, and imagine what honour and profit it will be for us to house the Queen of Scots and to return her to her throne. When she has gone back to Scotland I will ask the queen if you may be freed to live in one of our little houses with great pleasure.

I drop the letter to the floor. I feel as sick as the day that Katherine was taken to the Tower and Elizabeth had me hand her gloves. 'She will never get away,' I predict. 'Mary Queen of Scots will never get away. Elizabeth has her in her web, as she has me. Both of us will die in our prisons.'

GRIMSTHORPE CASTLE, LINCOLNSHIRE, CHRISTMAS 1568

It is a bright cold Christmas at Grimsthorpe and my step-grandmother is with the court so her household and I celebrate the season quietly in her absence. I am allowed to walk in the gardens, down to the stables and all around the courtyard of the beautiful castle, but when the snow falls and the drifts lie thick in the lanes, I cannot go further. I don't mind being imprisoned by snowdrifts, I know that a thaw will come.

My step-grandmother sends me one letter with a Christmas gift of a gold cup and tells me the news. She writes carefully, so that no spy can claim that she is conspiring with me.

I have happy news of Ned Seymour, the Earl of Hertford, she writes, avoiding reiterating any claim that he is my brother-in-law. *He has been released from imprisonment and is able to live freely at his home in Wiltshire, Wulf Hall. His sons, Teddy and Thomas, remain with their grandmother at Hanworth, but they can write to their father, and they may write and receive letters from you. I know this will give you great joy.*

I pause in my reading and think of my little nephews, Katherine's sons, and of their father still parted from them, but able at least to write to each other. Truly, Elizabeth has become a monstrously powerful queen. We are all placed only where she will allow us to be.

My step-grandmother makes it clear that the inquiry that was to examine the treason of Mary Queen of Scots' wicked half-brother has been turned around completely. Lord Moray has supplied the inquiry with a casket of letters that are said to prove that the queen was her husband's murderer, and Bothwell's adulterous lover. It is not the treasonous half-brother but the queen herself who is on trial – as Elizabeth swore she would never be.

The letters do not all appear to be in her true handwriting, my step-grandmother tactfully explains. *So some people doubt they are hers.*

I am very sure of this. I imagine that William Cecil's spies are cutting and copying letters like good children bent over their school books in a frenzy of forgery. But in any case, Elizabeth lacks the courage to come to a definite conclusion and we enter the new year with the Scots queen and me in confinement in our separate prisons, me at Grimsthorpe, she at Bolton Castle, dressed in her royal finery, which she insisted was sent on from Lochleven, both of us hoping for our freedom with the spring.

She does more than hope: she writes to Philip II of Spain, claiming that she is being held, without cause, by Elizabeth. This may gain her freedom, but will certainly win her the absolute enmity of William Cecil and all Protestants. Unlike her, I have no-one to write to. My only royal kinswoman is my only enemy: Elizabeth.

GRIMSTHORPE CASTLE,
LINCOLNSHIRE, SPRING 1569

I can hardly believe that the day has come but it is spring, the land is unlocked from winter, the streams are running alongside the lane and both my imprisoned cousin Mary Queen of Scots and I are to be freed. The season that has always called to me in the singing birds is the season that will see me walk free. Queen Mary is to return to Scotland and take up her throne. The inquiry against her has collapsed and Elizabeth knows she cannot keep her royal cousin locked up with no good reason. She is not even going to keep me locked up, and I don't have Philip II and the Catholic kings advocating for me. It is as if Elizabeth has looked into the horror that she was making, seen the road she was walking. If she proved the case against her cousin Mary she would have had to execute her. If she continued to imprison me indefinitely what is it but a death sentence? Changeable, fearful, Elizabeth turns from persecuting her heirs to setting us free in the hope that Mary in Edinburgh and I far away will trouble her less than when she holds us captive.

'You are to go to Sir Thomas Gresham,' my step-grandmother says. 'I shall miss you, my dear, but I shall be glad to know that you are staying in London, and when there is next a vacancy at court, you will become a lady-in-waiting. You will return to your former place.'

'She thinks that I will return to serve her?' I ask incredulously.

My step-grandmother laughs. 'You will. It is the best way to demonstrate that you are no danger to her, you are no rival. Remember her own sister imprisoned her and then called her to court. She thinks she can do the same with you.'

'But I will be free?'

'You will be free.'

I take her hands. 'I will never forget that you took me in,' I tell her.

'That was nothing,' she says wryly. 'Don't forget that I took the damned monkey, too.'

GRESHAM HOUSE, BISHOPSGATE, LONDON, SUMMER 1569

I ride to London through the richest lands of England. On either side of the track the hayfields have been freshly mown, and I can smell the dizzying smell of green hay. On the hills beyond the fields the sheep are flocking with their fat lambs under the careless supervision of the shepherd boys. In the water meadows beside the river the cows are grazing on the lush grass, and when we ride past them in the evening we see the girls going out with their pails on yokes, carrying their milking stools.

I am so happy to be on horseback that I don't want the journey to end, but before long we go through the Bishopsgate and there is the beautiful large house built by Sir Thomas, using the fortune he has earned by advising my family, the Tudors, how to do business. It was Sir Thomas who warned the queen that she must recall the bad currency and issue good, it was Sir Thomas who lived at Antwerp and guarded the interests of the English merchants against our greatest trading partner, and it was Sir Thomas who advised the building of a great hall in London where merchants could meet and exchange news, confirm the licences and monopolies, and buy into each other's companies.

We draw up outside his handsome London house, almost

a palace in size, and his servants in his livery throw open the double doors and I walk in. There is no-one there to greet me but the steward of his household, who bows to me and offers to show me to my rooms.

'Where is Sir Thomas?' I ask, stripping off my riding gloves and handing them to my lady-in-waiting. 'And Lady Gresham?'

'Sir Thomas is ill, he has taken to his chamber, and Lady Gresham has gone out,' he says, clearly embarrassed at their neglect of their duty and their lack of respect to me.

'Then you had better take me to my rooms and tell Lady Gresham that she may attend on me as soon as she returns,' I say sharply.

I follow him up the great staircase and he leads me past several big double doors to a single door, set in the corner of the building. He opens it. I go in. It is not a box as I endured at Chequers, but it is not a great handsome room to match the imposing house. It is a privy chamber without a presence chamber, and it is clear that I am not to live here as a princess with my own little court.

Beyond it is a bedroom with a good-sized bed and an oriel window over the noisy street below so that I can watch like a nosey merchant's wife and see Sir Thomas's tradesmen coming and going, and the clerks going into their counting houses.

'We were told it would not be for long,' the steward says apologetically. 'We were told that you are going to court.'

'I believe so, and this will do for the time being, if you have nothing better,' I say coolly. 'Please show my lady-in-waiting and my maids to their rooms. And you may bring some wine and water and something to eat. You may serve it in the chamber outside, my privy chamber.'

He bows himself out and I look around me. It is pleasant enough – God knows, it is a thousand times better than the Tower – and it is good enough until I get back to court.

◆◆◆

The happiest, best thing that might happen to me has occurred: a great good in itself, and a harbinger of happiness to come. I cannot even think of it without wanting to drop to my knees and thank God for mercy. My husband, my beloved husband Thomas Keyes, has survived the cold and the hunger and the cramped quarters of the worst prison in England, and finally been released. I get the news in a note from him, himself, the first I have received since we were parted with one kiss, with our farewell kiss. This is the first note that he has ever written me. I know that he is no great scholar and it is not easy for him to express himself in writing, so I treasure the scrap of paper and the careful script. This is better than a poem, better than a ballad, these are the true words of an honest man, my honest man.

> *I am to go to Sandgate Castle in my home county of Kent where I was once captain so I know it is a snug billet and I am glad with all my heart to be freed. I pray for you and for your freedom daily and that you will wish to come to me, who loves you as much as I did the day I first saw you when you were a little poppet not ten years old on a horse too big for you. Come when you can – I will be waiting for you. For I am and will always be your loving and constant husband TK*

I cannot bring myself to burn this, though I have burned every other letter I have received. I put it in the French Bible that belonged to Katherine, where Ned Hertford wrote the birthdates of his sons, my nephews, in the flyleaf. I slide it between the pages and I look at it every day.

My first act is to write to my step-grandmother at court and ask her to speak to the queen about when I am to wait on her.

I don't complain of my rooms but I was happier with you.
And besides, Sir Thomas is half blind from studying his profit
and loss ledgers, and lame from an old injury, and his wife is
quite hateful. It's not a cheerful household. I don't want to stay
here any longer than I have to. Clearly, they don't want me.
They have no children of their own and the place is as tender-
hearted as the mint where he spends most of his time.

I may not like my lodgings but at least they are a change of scene and a sign that I am on my way back to freedom. In this I am luckier than Mary Queen of Scots, who is not on her way to Scotland after all – her half-brother has reneged on his promise to accept her return and the Protestant lords don't trust her either. She will stay on with my aunt Bess at Wingfield Manor until her return can be agreed. She is in a most beautiful house and she will be richly served, but I don't envy her. Like me, she is in a halfway house, within sight of freedom but, somehow, not quite free. We both have to wait on the rise of Elizabeth's compassion, and that is rarely in full floodtide.

GRESHAM HOUSE, BISHOPSGATE, LONDON, SUMMER 1569

The court is on progress when the most extraordinary news reaches us in London. It seems that our cousin Mary Queen of Scots has outwitted her host my aunt Bess, and offended, just as Katherine offended, just as I offended. Absurdly, though married to the missing Earl of Bothwell she has promised herself in marriage and – if that were not dreadful enough for the spinster queen – her choice has fallen on a great English nobleman. Everyone says that she is betrothed to marry Thomas Howard

Duke of Norfolk – Elizabeth's kinsman from the Boleyn side – and he has fled from Elizabeth's court and nobody knows where he has gone.

Sir Thomas dashes out of his house first thing in the morning and does not come back till midnight. Nothing is more hateful to merchants than uncertainty, and if Elizabeth has to send an army against her mother's own family, the Howards, then she will have to fight most of Norfolk, and it is impossible to predict how it will end. It will be the Cousins' Wars all over again. It will be a war as bad as those in France – a war of religion. It will be two queens fighting over the future of England. It will be a disaster for my country and for my sisters' throne.

Elizabeth abandons her summertime progress and rushes the whole court to Windsor Castle to prepare for a siege. She has spent her life in terror, waiting for this one event; and now she has brought it on herself. She has always feared that her heir would marry a mighty subject and together they would turn on her, and now she thinks that Thomas Howard will raise the whole of the east of the country against the court, and the Northern lords will call out their hardened forces to rescue the Queen of Scots. Both regions are known papist; neither region loves the Tudors.

I can hear the bands of citizens and apprentice boys training to defend London. And I swing my window open to look out and see them parading up and down with broom handles over their shoulders in place of pikes.

They say that the Duke of Norfolk will march on Windsor, they say that the Northern lords will march on my aunt Bess's house and take her guest from her by force. Aunt Bess and her husband, the Earl of Shrewsbury, who were so proud of hosting a queen, have to bundle her from Wingfield Manor to Tutbury Castle and prepare the place for a siege. England is breaking into two camps again – as it did before – and Elizabeth's long game of playing one religion against another, one ally against another, one cousin against another, has collapsed into panic.

The Northern lords are riding under a banner that shows the five wounds of Christ. They are making this a holy war and every papist in England will support them. This is a new Pilgrimage of Grace like the one that nearly overthrew the old king Henry VIII, and the treasonous Northern parishes are ringing the bells backwards in every church to signify that they are rising for the old religion and the young Scots queen.

My poor aunt Bess! I have news of her from my host, Sir Thomas, who speaks to me briefly as he meets me, walking through the great hall to go into the garden. He tells me that she is fleeing south, riding hard with a little force, trying to get away from the advancing Northern army, which is sweeping down through England. Aunt Bess is ordered to get Queen Mary behind the walls of Coventry Castle before the Northern lords capture her and her household and massacre them all. Elizabeth has mustered an army from among the London merchants and apprentice boys, Sir Thomas has sent his own men and they are marching north, but they will be able to do nothing if every village is against them and every church is holding a Mass and declaring itself for the freedom of Mary Queen of Scots. They are almost certain to arrive too late. Elizabeth's Council of the North is pinned down in York, surrounded by the forces of the Northern lords. And still there is no news of the army from Norfolk and Thomas Howard at the head of it who could be marching to Coventry to save his bride or marching on London to claim her throne.

GRESHAM HOUSE, BISHOPSGATE, LONDON, WINTER 1569

Sir Thomas tells me that there is a Spanish armada armed and waiting to sail from the Spanish Netherlands, coming to reinforce the army of the North and release Mary Queen of Scots. He says that it will be possible to make peace with the Spanish – they will probably settle for the return of Queen Mary to her Scots throne, and the declaration of her as Elizabeth's heir – but the northern lords may not settle so easily.

'You think that the Duke of Norfolk and the Spanish and the northern Lords can be made to betray each other?' I ask.

He makes a face, a moneylender's, gold merchant's face of judging one risk against another. 'Betrayal is always possible,' is all he says. 'It's all we've got left.'

Elizabeth is lucky, Elizabeth always was lucky, and now fortune smiles on her again. Thomas Howard Duke of Norfolk is the first to break – he submits to her authority. He does not raise an army but he surrenders to her, and for his reward she arrests him and sends him to the Tower. The Spanish don't sail because they doubt the Northern army will march with them, the Northern army give up and go back to their own cold hills because without the Spanish they dare not challenge Elizabeth, and Elizabeth, who did nothing but hide behind the stout walls of Windsor Castle, comes triumphantly to London and proclaims herself the God-given victor.

GRESHAM HOUSE, BISHOPSGATE, LONDON, SPRING 1570

My poor aunt Bess has lost her fourth husband, everyone says. But not this time to death, leaving her a handsome inheritance: she has lost her earl to love, to scandalous adulterous love, for everyone says that he is in love with my cousin Mary Queen of Scots and that is why he failed to guard her, or warn of the uprising.

There is enough in this to make Elizabeth hate him for admiring Mary, and to hate poor Aunt Bess – blaming her for the irresistible attraction of the beautiful queen. Bess falls from royal favour, which she has worked all her life to win. Even worse for Aunt Bess, she and her unhappy husband cannot live in her lovely house (I remember her writing to me of her *many* houses) because they have to keep the Scots queen under close guard and she is to be locked up in the dismal and damp Tutbury Castle. Mary is miserably imprisoned, and Aunt Bess is imprisoned with her, just as I am imprisoned in the handsome house at Bishopsgate and my unwilling hosts are imprisoned with me.

But there is no predicting anything. My host, Sir Thomas, tells me that changeable times are bad for the value of currency and now he does not know what a shilling is worth against a sou. When I ask him what has happened now he tells me that Lord Moray – the queen's faithless half-brother and Regent of Scotland – has been shot dead and now the Scots lords are calling for the return of the Queen of Scots. Last summer they would not have her when Elizabeth was going to return her, now they want her back but Elizabeth has learned to fear her. Instead of the rightful queen, Elizabeth sends my cousin Margaret Douglas's husband, the Earl of Lennox, to be regent.

Even I can see this is unlikely to be a popular choice; is he really going to bring peace to a divided country? Is he going to greet his hated daughter-in-law when she returns to her kingdom? Is he going to do anything but pursue the Scots lords that he accuses of murdering his son and so start their battles all over again?

GRESHAM HOUSE, BISHOPSGATE, LONDON, SUMMER 1570

I hold in my hands that rare and precious thing, a letter from my husband, Thomas. It has come to me in my clean linen, so someone has bribed a laundress to get this one page to me. It is good paper – he must have gone to the clerks at Sandgate Castle and bought a sheet – and he writes a clear steady hand, not a scholarly style, but one that could be easily read by anyone, good for sending a brief order to a gatekeeper beyond hailing distance.

My love, I am far beyond hailing distance. But I hear you. God knows I will always, always listen for you.

> *Dear Wife,*
> *I have spoken to Archbishop Parker (who I know is a good man) about our business, and asked him if it is not true that in a marriage no man should put us asunder. He is going to be a means to the queen for mercy and ask that I be permitted to live with my wife. I would go anywhere to be with you, I*

*would join you in any captivity and hope to make your prison
a little easier for you as the thought of you did for me. I will be
your faithful and constant husband in deed as in thought, TK*

It has to be good news for me that Thomas Howard, the
queen's kinsman, is released from the Tower without charge,
and stays in London, under house arrest. If he, a second cousin,
guilty of betrothing himself to an enemy queen, can be released,
if she can be returned to Scotland, then there is no sense in
keeping me imprisoned.

'I have asked for your release,' Sir Thomas says to me stiffly
when he comes to the door of my privy chamber to pay a courtesy visit. 'I am assured that you will be released next year.'

I write to Thomas:

*Dear Husband, I have had so many promises of freedom that
I have learned to trust nothing, but if I can come to you, I will
do so. I pray for you every day and I think of you with such
great love. I am so happy that you are free and my only wish
is to be with you and be a good mother to your children. Your
constant and loving wife MK*

I sign myself 'MK' for 'Mary Keyes'. I do not deny my love for
him nor my marriage to him, and I kiss the fold of the paper and
then melt the sealing wax and drip it into the spot and imprint
my family seal. He will know to lift the seal and take the kiss.

GRESHAM HOUSE, BISHOPSGATE, LONDON, SPRING 1571

Sir Thomas is beside himself with excitement and his bad-tempered wife at last has some joy in her life. Elizabeth is coming to visit the merchants' hall and the shops that he has built, and then she will dine in his house. Extraordinarily, they will serve my cousin the queen a banquet in the rooms below mine, but I am not to be present. Though I am in the house at her command, I am not to be seen.

'Not see her?' I ask flatly. For a moment I had thought that I would simply join her train of ladies as they entered and she would use this visit to bring me back into royal service without an apology for my arrest, without comment. Elizabeth is so strange in her ways and so cold of heart that I thought her quite capable of taking me back to court without another word spoken.

'No,' Lady Gresham says crossly. 'I asked my husband to explain to Lord Burghley that it would be better if you were not in our house at all, for fear of embarrassment, but he says that you shall stay in your room and that there is no embarrassment for anyone.'

'Lord Burghley?' I ask.

'Sir William Cecil's new title.'

I nod. I see my old friend is rewarded for his unending enmity to the Scots queen.

'You are to stay in your rooms,' she confirms.

'As you have said.'

'And make no noise.'

I widen my eyes at her rudeness. 'I did not intend to dance,' I say. 'Or sing.'

'You are not to try to attract her attention,' she stipulates.

'My dear Lady Gresham,' I say, speaking down to her, though the top of my hood reaches her armpit, 'I have spent my life trying to avoid the attention of my cousin the queen, I am not likely to bellow out to her when she is attending a banquet in your house. I only hope that you can do everything as she prefers. You have not been much at court, I think? Being a city wife, as you are? And not noble?'

She gives a muted shriek of fury and rushes from the room, leaving me laughing. Tormenting Lady Gresham is my principal entertainment. And a royal visit will give me much scope.

In fact it goes off perfectly well. Elizabeth eats her dinner in the Greshams' banqueting hall and watches a play that praises her majesty and her greatness. Then she walks around Sir Thomas's great folly of his merchants' hall. The merchants do not gather here, as they do at the Bourse in Bruges. The goldsmiths and jewellers and sellers of goods have not moved into his little shops, preferring their traditional stalls or the front rooms of their houses on the busy city streets. Sir Thomas has begged all his tenants to bring all their stock for the queen to see, and he gives her gifts at every shop. Elizabeth laps up the presents and the flattery like a fat ginger cat, and calls for a herald to announce that hereafter the hall will be called the Royal Exchange, and Sir Thomas will finally make money here and his grasshopper emblem can hop all over London.

'And you are to be freed,' Lady Gresham says, poking her disagreeable face through the door of my privy chamber at the end of the day. She is flushed with triumph and wine. 'Sir Thomas asked the queen and she said that you could leave us.'

'I shall be glad to go,' I say, keeping my voice steady before this unattractive bearer of good news, a most unlikely herald angel. 'Am I to join my husband?'

'I don't know,' she says, unable to taunt me with a refusal. 'But you are definitely leaving.'

GRESHAM HOUSE, BISHOPSGATE, LONDON, AUTUMN 1571

I wait for the order to pack my books and put Mr Nozzle into his travelling cage, but none comes. Then I learn that William Cecil has been busy with other matters. He has uncovered a great plot to capture Elizabeth the queen. Thomas Howard is accused of working with Spain to raise an army to put Mary on the throne in her place. The court is in an uproar of fear, and nobody is going to release another heir, another Mary, even if it is only me, and everyone knows I have done nothing. Thomas Howard is returned to the Tower, the guards are reinforced at my aunt Bess's house, and once again Elizabeth has three cousins in captivity.

I write to Thomas:

> *I thought I was to come to you but it is delayed. I pray that it is nothing more than a delay. I am with you every day in my heart and my prayers. Your loving and constant wife, MK*

I have no reply from him, but this does not trouble me for perhaps he has not yet had my letter, or cannot get a secret note to me. I am sitting at the window overlooking the London street when I see the doctor arriving and being admitted in the front door below my window. I have not complained of any ill health and so I wonder who has summoned him and if Lady Gresham has poisoned herself with bile.

Sir Thomas himself opens the door and Doctor Smith comes into the room. So he has come to visit me. I get to my feet, filled with unease. If this is my freedom, why have they sent my physician? Why do they both look so grave?

I don't wait for him to be announced or for him to make his bow. 'Please tell me,' I say quickly. 'Please tell me at once whatever it is you have come to tell me. Please tell me at once.'

The two men exchange a look and, at that, I know that I have lost the love of my life.

'Is it Thomas?' I ask.

'Yes, my lady,' says the doctor quietly. 'I am sorry to tell you that he is dead.'

'My husband?' I say. 'My Thomas, Thomas Keyes? The queen's sergeant porter, the biggest man at court? Who married me?'

I keep thinking, there is bound to be a mistake. My Thomas could not survive the Fleet in winter, get himself back to Kent, write that he will come to me, and then fail and die before we are reunited. It is not possible that our love story, such an odd unlikely story, could end so unhappily. I keep thinking, it is another Thomas, not my Thomas who stands as tall as a tree with his shoulders back and his kind eyes scanning everyone who comes to his gate.

'Yes, my lady,' the doctor says again. 'I am afraid that he is dead.'

OSTERLEY PARK, MIDDLESEX, SPRING 1572

Later, a long time later, they told me that I collapsed at the words, that I went white and they thought that I would never open my eyes. I did not speak and they thought that the news had killed me. When I did wake in my bed, I asked if it was true and when they told me, 'Yes, yes, Thomas Keyes is dead,' I closed my eyes again and turned my back on the room. Facing the wall, I waited for death to come to me. It seemed to me then that I had lost everyone that I had ever loved, and everyone who belonged to me, that my life was pointless, a waste of time, that it served only to anger the queen more, that she has become a monster, the Mouldwarp like her father, a great beast that lives in the bowels of England and devours her brightest children.

That Elizabeth's malice should have broken the heart of the greatest man in England, that great man with that great spirit, does not prove her power but it shows the strength of evil when a woman thinks of nothing but herself. Elizabeth is empowered by her vanity. Anyone who suggests to her that another woman is preferable must die. Any man that prefers another woman to her must be exiled. Even someone like Thomas, who loyally served her and whose preference fell on a little woman who came no higher than his broad leather belt, even Thomas could not be suffered to live happily once he looked away from Elizabeth to someone else – to me.

They move me to Osterley Park, Sir Thomas Gresham's country house, as if they are moving a corpse. They think that I will die on my own in the country and that all the inconvenience will be over. And this is my silent wish. It must be God's will and I am not going to blaspheme Him by killing myself; but I don't eat and I don't speak. I lie with my eyes closed and the pillow beneath my head is always damp as the tears constantly seep from under my closed eyelids as I cry for my husband, Thomas, whether I am awake or asleep.

The days get shorter and my bedroom is dark as night from three in the afternoon, and then slowly, slowly the golden light starts to come back to the white walls and I can hear birdsong outside the window in the morning and the skies lighten earlier and earlier and I think that my husband, my beloved husband, would never advise me to give up. He loved me when I was a little girl on too big a horse. He loved my courage; he loved my unbeatable spirit. Perhaps I can find that courage and that spirit once again, for love of him.

And I think, if nothing else, I can deny Elizabeth the victory of the death of all her cousins. I think of Mary Queen of Scots, awaiting her return to Scotland, determined to get back to her country and her son. I think of Thomas Duke of Norfolk, preparing his own defence in the Tower of London. I think of my cousin Margaret Douglas now widowed since her husband was killed in a brawl in Scotland, never stopping her demand for justice, never ceasing to claim the throne for her Scots grandson, and I think I am damned if I am going to spare Elizabeth the problem of dealing with three surviving heirs. I am damned if I am going to oblige Elizabeth by the silent exit of yet another rival. I am Jane Grey's sister – they are calling her the first Protestant martyr – I am not going to slip away in silence; she did not. 'Learn you to die!' does not mean lie down like Jo the pug with your paw over your nose, and give up. 'Learn you to die!' means consider how your death is meaningful, as your life is meaningful.

So, at the end of the long silent period of mourning I get up because I love my husband and I will live the rest of my life to prove it, and because I despise Elizabeth and I shall live the rest of my life to inconvenience her. When spring comes, I get up. It is as simple as that. I rise up and I do my hair, which is showing silver in the gold as befits a widow, and I order black cloth from Sir Thomas's shops in London, and argue with Lady Gresham as to how much material I need to make a gown of mourning black. I want it richly folded, and beautifully made. Then I hear that her stupid *stupid* husband (for the man is a fool, for all that he knows about business) has gone to William Cecil to ask if I may indeed dress as a widow. As if it matters to him, as if it matters to them! As if it should matter to a queen that a widow should wear black for the love of her life. As if a queen should stoop so low as to worry about the black petticoats of the smallest of her subjects, as if anyone should deny me my black gown when I carry the greatest of loves in my heart.

I win my gown of black and I win my freedom. I am allowed to walk in the gardens at Osterley and even take a horse and ride through the parkland. Mr Nozzle likes Thomas Gresham's orchard and when the early fruits come into season is often to be found browsing on raspberries or early cherries. He takes his pick of the crop and I have to suspect that he takes an especial pleasure in annoying our host. More than once when Sir Thomas has sent from London demanding his hot-house peaches, informing the household that he is giving an important dinner to significant guests, we find that Mr Nozzle has been ahead of him. He knows how to unlock the door to the hothouse, and goes in first and eats the best of the fruit. Sometimes he takes only a little nibble from each. I would think Sir Thomas might admire Mr Nozzle's method of driving up value; but he does not.

I write to William Cecil and say that since it is now recognised that my marriage was valid I should like to live where my husband lived, at Sandgate in Kent, and raise his children from his first marriage as my own. They are now orphans and I am a widow; it would be a service to the parish and a joy to me if I could be given their care.

He takes a long time to reply, but I know he has many other things to trouble him. Thomas Howard Duke of Norfolk has stood trial with a host of accusations against him but only one that rings true – and it is the most damning. He preferred Queen Mary to Queen Elizabeth, he planned to marry the beautiful younger woman, and the queen will see him die for that. He knew there was a plot to free the Scots queen and he may have forwarded some money. He did little else. He did not join the plot, he submitted himself to the queen and begged her pardon. She did not accept the excuse that he is promised to the Scots queen in marriage, that he owes her his support. That is the last defence in the world to proffer to a woman like Elizabeth who cannot tolerate any attention being paid to another woman. So Thomas Howard has stood his trial and been found guilty, and the queen can choose to pardon him, or not. In the meantime he waits in the Tower of London, as my sister Jane waited, as Katherine waited, as I wait here at Osterley, to hear the queen's pleasure.

And it is now, when Thomas Howard is found guilty of treason for proposing to marry her, when Bess's husband is despised for falling in love with her, that suddenly, the reputation of Mary Queen of Scots is destroyed. The Privy Council allows the full release of her letters, the famous letters of the silver gilt casket – forged and fictitious. William Cecil has been busy and the papers, which were once so secret that they could not even be shown to royal advisors, are now published so cheaply that every spit boy and kitchen girl in London can buy a copy and read that Queen Mary is no rightful queen, for she whored with Bothwell and blew up her husband with a bombard.

Shocked by this, and frightened by Cecil's many other warnings, the parliament calls for Mary to be accused and executed. Still the unwanted, ruinous guest of my aunt Bess, the Scots queen has to wait to see what Elizabeth will do. My guess is that Elizabeth will hold all her cousins – all of us – indefinitely, until Mary's beauty is worn out, until Thomas's loyal army forgets him, until they die of heartbreak. But she cannot diminish me:

I am already small. She cannot break my heart: it is buried with Thomas Keyes.

When I finally hear from Cecil, he refuses my request. The queen does not wish for me to return to normal life yet. I am not allowed to care for my stepchildren; I am not allowed to raise Thomas's children as he asked me to do. But she need not think that I will quietly die to oblige her. Not for this, not for anything.

ST BOTOLPH'S-WITHOUT-ALDGATE, LONDON, SPRING 1573

And finally . . . I have won. It is as simple and as beautiful as that. I have outlived Elizabeth's malice, and survived her jealousy.

I saw her leave my beloved sister to die of the plague, and then leave her to die of despair. I saw her put my baby nephews in the way of disease and neglect. I saw her execute her cousin Thomas Howard and imprison her cousin a queen – and who would think that you could imprison a Queen of Scots and a royal kinswoman of France? But I have seen Elizabeth do all this. And finally, I have seen her ill will towards me wear out from overuse. It is not me who tires of it and gives up, it is Elizabeth. Finally she releases me.

First, she allows me to stay with my stepfather, Adrian Stokes, at Beaumanor, so I return to my family home. Then, as if weary of her long years of persecution, she sets me free, and promises to restore my allowance. There is no more sense to freeing me than there was to arresting me. I am no danger to her now, I was no danger before. It is nothing but royal whim.

But I don't care, I don't call for justice, nor do I complain that she could have released me seven years ago, she need never have arrested my beloved husband, she could have released Katherine, she need not have died. I know that we are Elizabeth's fear and her folly. But I don't complain. She pays me an allowance, she sets me free. I can afford to live on my own, and I kiss my step-father and his new wife and her enchanting children, and I buy myself a house and set myself up as a householder of London, as proud and as free as Lady Gresham, but far happier.

The city of London is beautiful in springtime. It is the best of all times. The villages that press against the city walls are bright with white snowdrops and festive with yellow lenten lilies that bob in the wind. Mr Nozzle, ageing now, knows that we have come to our own home at last, and spends his day on a red velvet cushion on a high-backed chair in the hall where he can keep an eye on the comings and goings of my little household, like a little sergeant porter. I give him a thick embroidered leather belt and a coat of Tudor green in memory of the queen's sergeant porter, who I will never forget.

I see my husband's children, as I promised him that I would. His daughter, Jane Merrick, is a frequent visitor and she asks me to be godmother to her daughter that she names Mary for me. I have other visitors. I have friends from my old days at court, the bridesmaids at my wedding, and Blanche Parry, first lady of the bedchamber, comes from time to time to talk of the old days. If I want to return to serve Elizabeth I know that Blanche will speak for me, and I could hug myself with joy at the thought that I will consider this. My proper place is at court, but my dislike of Elizabeth is so strong that I may prefer exile outside it. I don't know yet. I shall decide. I have the freedom to choose.

I have other visitors. My step-grandmother and her children come to me whenever they are in London, and I often dine with them and stay overnight. My brother-in-law, Ned, writes with news of my nephews, and I will visit them at Hanworth in the summer. The youngest, Thomas, is a scholar like my sister Jane, a poet like his father. I send him books that are recommended by the preachers who visit me to study and talk of the new theol-ogy that is demanding that Elizabeth's half-papist Church goes further with reform and purity. I buy the new books and go to hear sermons and keep myself informed of the twist and turn of the debate.

Aunt Bess, that fair-weather friend of our family, visits me when she is in London. She cannot bring herself to speak of the division in her household, but everyone knows that 'my husband the earl' has wasted his huge fortune in entertaining and securing the safety of his royal guest, and still she drains his coffers as Elizabeth neither sends the queen back to Scotland in honour nor dumps her on France in shame. Bess lives apart from her husband as much as possible but she could not save the fortune and that is perhaps her greatest grief.

She speaks fondly of her children and of her great house-building projects. She hopes to rescue her fortune from the earl's debts and keep enough money of her own to build a great new house beside her great old house: Hardwick Hall, and found a dynasty. Her earl may have failed her; but her ambition will never fail. God Himself only knows who she will choose as a husband for her poor daughter.

'What d'you think of Charles Stuart for my Elizabeth?' she asks. 'He is kinsman to the queen herself and brother to the late King of Scotland?'

I look at her, completely aghast. 'You think you would get Elizabeth's permission for such a marriage?'

She makes a little puffing sound, as if she were blowing out a candle and, for some reason, it makes me freeze. 'Oh, no, so maybe nothing,' she says. 'But tell me, how much do you pay your chief steward here? Are London men not terribly expensive?'

I let her move the conversation away and I let myself forget that she spoke of it. My aunt Bess was well represented when she had a rampant lion as her crest. Nobody knows where she and her family will end.

Before she leaves I show her all around my little house, from the servants' bedrooms in the attics to my bedroom and privy chamber below. She admires my library of books, she prods my great four-poster bed. 'Everything very good,' she speaks to me as one woman who has come up from nothing to another who lost everything and has won it back.

I show her my hall and my silverware in the cupboard. Twenty people can dine off silver at my table, and a hundred people can be seated below us in the hall. Sometimes I give grand dinners, I invite whoever I choose. Mr Nozzle watches us quietly as we admire my treasures.

I take her through to the kitchens and show her the spit in the fireplace and the charcoal burning tray for the sauces, the bread ovens and behind them the storerooms, the flesh kitchen, the subtlety room, the dairy, the cellar, the brewhouse and buttery.

'It is a proper house,' she says, as if she thought that a small person would need only a doll-size house.

'It is,' I say. 'It is my house, and I have been a long time coming to it.'

I have a stable behind the house, and I ride out when I please. I go as far and for as long as I like. Nobody will ever tell me again that I may walk only to the gate or only see the sky through a small square of glass. I think of my sister Katherine and her sweetness and her silliness, her faithful constant love for her husband and her courageous defence of him and her sons. I think of my husband, Thomas Keyes, and how they kept him, trapped like the bear at Bradgate, a huge beautiful beast cramped by the cruelty of his keepers. I think of Jane and her determination to speak for God when she could so easily have kept quiet for life, and I think that she chose her destiny, and I have chosen mine.

I am glad I did not choose a martyr's death like Jane, and I am glad that I did not break my heart like Katherine. I am glad that I loved Thomas and that I know that I love him still. I am glad that Elizabeth did not destroy me, that I defied her and never regretted it, and that my little life, as a little person, has been a life of greatness to me.

I smooth down my black gown. I always wear black as an honourable rich widow. I remember people telling me that Mary Queen of Scots wore black, embroidered with silver and gold thread, for her wedding gown and I think – that is how it is to be a stylish widow! That is how it is to be a queen. Underneath my black brocade I wear a petticoat of scarlet, as she always did, that shows in glorious flashes of colour as I walk around my good house, or when I step outside in the street. Red is the colour of defiance, red is the colour of life, red is the colour of love, and so it is my colour. I shall wear my black embroidered gown and my red petticoat till the day that I die – and whenever that is, if that poor loveless thing Elizabeth is still on the throne, then I know at least that she will give me a magnificent funeral, fit for the last Tudor princess.

AUTHOR'S NOTE

This book is called *The Last Tudor* and it may be the last novel about a Tudor woman that I write. I am starting a new series of novels and I do not know when I will return to this wonderful era that has been of such intense interest for me for so many years.

I started my work in the Tudor period with the story of an almost unknown woman, Mary Boleyn, sister to the more famous Anne, and the title posed the question as to which was the most important Boleyn and which was the other – *The Other Boleyn Girl*. This inspired an interrogation of their history, and indeed the history of women, the relatively unknown besides the celebrated and controversial.

This new novel also has a famous sister, one of the most famous Tudor women, Lady Jane Grey – condemned for her father's persistent and unsuccessful treason against Mary I – who chose to die rather than recant her faith. Her sisters are hardly mentioned in the general histories of the period but they were unlucky, in that their elder sister defied the religion of the Catholic Tudor, without earning them the favour of her Protestant heir. Katherine Grey's story is an account of a woman inside the Tudor family but outside Tudor favour. Her younger sister Mary Grey is almost unknown but I think she is of great interest – a Little Person, said to be under four foot high, she does not even appear in the specialist histories of little people. She was a woman of persistent courage, showing a powerful instinct to survive where her sisters did not, and while this novel narrates her life as a fiction, her marriage and the dates and places of her confinement are historically accurate, as is her survival and her defiant red petticoat!

The names given to reformers of religion vary throughout this period, and carry very different meanings now, so I have referred to them all with the later catch-all name of Protestants and Reformers, for the ease of the general reader – I hope theologians will forgive me. Quotations from original letters and poems are shown in italics.

The other element in this book that reminds me of *The Other Boleyn Girl* is the theme of sisters. I seem to have written about sisters in many of my books – the bond is a significant one for women who are born with few natural allies in a hard world, and it is a powerful concept for a feminist: we should all be sisters. So this is the book I dedicate to my own sister, with love.

BIBLIOGRAPHY

Ablon, Joan, *Little People in America: The Social Dimensions of Dwarfism* (New York, Praeger Scientific, 1984)

Amt, Emilie, *Women's Lives in Medieval Europe* (eds, New York, Routledge, 1993)

Baldwin, David, *Henry VIII's Last Love: The Extraordinary Life of Katherine Willoughby, Lady-in-Waiting to the Tudors* (Stroud, Amberley, 2015)

Borman, Tracy, *Elizabeth's Women: The Hidden Story of the Virgin Queen* (London, Jonathan Cape, 2009)

Doran, Susan, *Elizabeth I & Her Circle* (Oxford University Press, 2015)

Goldring, E., Eales, F., Archer, J. E., and Clarke, E., *John Nichols's The Progresses and Public Processions of Queen Elizabeth: Volume 1: 1533 to 1571* (eds, Oxford University Press, 2014; first published London, 1823)

Guy, John, *'My Heart is My Own': The Life of Mary Queen of Scots* (London, Fourth Estate, 2004)

Hill Cole, Mary, *The Portable Queen: Elizabeth I and the Politics of Ceremony* (University of Massachusetts Press, 1999)

Hobgood, Allison P., and Wood, David Houston, *Recovering Disability in Early Modern England* (eds, Ohio State University Press, 2013)

Ives, Eric, *Lady Jane Grey: A Tudor Mystery* (Chichester, Wiley & Sons, 2011)

Lisle, Leanda de, *The Sisters Who Would Be Queen: The Tragedy of Mary, Katherine and Lady Jane Grey* (London, HarperCollins, 2008)

Mackie, J. D., *The Earlier Tudors: 1485–1558* (Oxford, Clarendon, 1952)

Marshall, Rosalind K., *Mary I* (London, H.M. Stationery Office, 1993)

Plowden, Alison, *Lady Jane Grey and the House of Suffolk* (London, Sidgwick & Jackson, 1985)

Plowden, Alison, *Lady Jane Grey: Nine Days Queen* (Stroud, Sutton, 2004)

Somerset, Anne, *Elizabeth I* (London, St Martin's Press, 1992)

Southworth, John, *Fools and Jesters at the English Court* (Stroud, The History Press, 1998)

Streitberger, W. R., *The Masters of the Revels and Elizabeth I's Court Theatre* (Oxford University Press, 2016)

Strickland, Agnes, *Lives of the Tudor and Stuart Princesses* (London, George Bell & Sons, 1888)

Warnicke, Retha M., *Mary Queen of Scots* (Abingdon, Routledge, 2006)

Weir, Alison, *Children of England: The Heirs of King Henry VIII 1547–1558* (London, Jonathan Cape, 1996)

Weir, Alison, *Elizabeth the Queen* (London, Vintage, 2008)

Weir, Alison, *The Lost Tudor Princess: A Life of Margaret Douglas, Countess of Lennox* (London, Vintage, 2015)

Whitelock, Anna, *Elizabeth's Bedfellows: An Intimate History of the Queen's Court* (London, Bloomsbury, 2013)

ONLINE

The Calendar of State Papers Foreign: Elizabeth (vols 1–23). Accessed online at *http://www.british-history.ac.uk/search/series/cal-state-papers--foreign*

Lady Jane Grey Reference Guide. Accessed online at *http://www.ladyjanegrey.info/*

The Oxford Dictionary of National Biography. Accessed online at *http://www.oxforddnb.com*

OTHER

Merton, C. I., *Women who served Queen Mary and Queen Elizabeth: Ladies, Gentlewomen and Maids of the Privy Chamber, 1553–1603* (Unpublished doctoral thesis, 1992)

GARDENS
FOR THE GAMBIA

Philippa Gregory visited The Gambia, one of the driest and poorest countries of sub-Saharan Africa, in 1993 and paid for a well to be hand-dug in a village primary school at Sika. Now – more than 200 wells later – she continues to raise money and commission wells in village schools, community gardens and in The Gambia's only agricultural college. She works with her representative in The Gambia, headmaster Ismaila Sisay, and their charity now funds pottery and batik classes, bee-keeping and adult literacy programmes.

GARDENS FOR THE GAMBIA is a registered charity in the UK and a registered NGO in The Gambia. Every donation, however small, goes to The Gambia without any deductions. If you would like to learn more about the work that Philippa calls 'the best thing that I do', visit her website www.PhilippaGregory.com and click on GARDENS FOR THE GAMBIA where you can make a donation and join with Philippa in this project.

'Every well we dig provides drinking water for a school of about 600 children, and waters the gardens where they grow vegetables for the school dinners. I don't know of a more direct way to feed hungry children and teach them to farm for their future.'

Philippa Gregory